Martina Cole has written eig
which have been outstandingly successful bestsellers. Her most recent novel, *Faceless*, shot straight to No. 1 on the *Sunday Times* bestseller list and total sales of Martina's novels now exceed three million copies. *Dangerous Lady* and *The Jump* have gone on to become hugely popular TV drama series and several of her other novels are in production for TV. Martina Cole has a son and daughter and she lives in Essex.

Praise for Martina Cole's previous bestsellers:

'Right from the start [Cole] has enjoyed unqualified approval for her distinctive and powerfully written fiction' *The Times*

'Intensely readable' *Guardian*

'Gritty novel from an author who knows intimately the world she writes about' *Daily Express*

'The slags and scum of Cole's fictional underworld are becoming the stuff of legend . . . It's vicious, nasty and utterly compelling' *Mirror*

'Set to be another winner' *Woman's Weekly*

'Martina Cole again explores the shady criminal underworld, a setting she is fast making her own' *Sunday Express*

'A powerful novel that pulls no punches' *Guide*

*Also by Martina Cole*

Dangerous Lady
The Ladykiller
Goodnight Lady
The Jump
The Runaway
Two Women
Broken
Faceless
The Know
The Graft

# Maura's Game

Martina Cole

headline

First published in 2002
by HEADLINE BOOK PUBLISHING

First published in paperback in 2003
by HEADLINE BOOK PUBLISHING

8



ISBN 0 7472 6759 6

Typeset in Galliard by
Letterpart Limited, Reigate, Surrey

Printed and bound in Great Britain by
Mackays of Chatham plc, Chatham, Kent

HEADLINE BOOK PUBLISHING
A division of Hodder Headline
338 Euston Road
LONDON NW1 3BH

www.headline.co.uk
www.hodderheadline.com

To James McNamara.
Missing you, a much-loved uncle.

For Mr and Mrs Steven and Christine Snares,
two of my best friends,
from your matron-of-honour.

For Pam and Ricky Dayal.
Thanking you for all your help whilst writing this book.
'You are me dorste.'

# Book One

**'Behind every great fortune is a crime'**

*Honoré de Balzac, 1799–1850*

# Prologue

*1994*

'So you're going into the club then?'

Terry's voice was heavy with annoyance and Maura closed her eyes in distress. She hated it when they argued and she knew that they were about to have an argument of Olympic class. This one had been brewing for days. She sighed, and mentally counted to ten before answering him.

'I have to, Terry. Roy can't cope with this on his own.'

Terry walked from the room and Maura watched him go. Her mind was racing but with thoughts of the club in Dean Street, Soho. It hurt too much to think about Terry, the man who was everything to her. She'd noticed the expression on his face as he left. He had coldly looked her over like she was nothing to him, nobody. All the disgust and disappointment he felt were clear for her to see.

She felt broken by it, frightened, even as it angered

her. But he had known, always he had known, that if push came to shove and there was trouble, she would have to sort out the clubs and other family businesses. And that was exactly what they had now: serious trouble.

Her brother Roy did what he could, but he needed Maura's acumen, needed her backing. All the boys did. Roy could cope with day-to-day things but he had never been able to take the real aggravation. He either went over the top or crumbled without assistance.

She pressed her hand to her mouth at the thought of what she was to do later that day. She had thought the violent days were over, that everything was settled and straight, that lines had been drawn. How wrong she had been. Now on top of everything else she had Terry to contend with and his old woman attitude really stuck in her craw.

She glanced out of the large picture window and watched the workmen outside as they cleared away. Her mind registered the fact that they had tidied up after them, having needed to get on to her drive to raise her drains. Automatically she checked to make sure everything was as it should be. It was.

One of the men looked through the window at her and smiled. Maura ignored him. She stood up and walked from the room, through the wide entrance hall and into the kitchen. Terry was standing by the double doors that looked on to the garden. It was their special place, somewhere they worked together, had planted out together and liked to share in quiet moments. It was a garden made for children, for a family, something Maura would never know about now unless it was as a substitute mother, as she was to Roy's daughter Carla and her son Joey. Maura was everything to them, as they were to her.

Even her surviving brothers – three left now of the eight there had once been – looked to her for guidance and help. Roy especially needed her more than any of them. He was supposed to be in charge of all the Ryan family businesses these days: the above board ones like their property development and construction interests, the loan company, street vending and hostess clubs, and the less public side of things. The Ryans lent money to punters to fund their mortgages, true, but they also financed career criminals for a hefty share of the proceeds and provided goods and services not generally offered by your average high street bank: high-performance escape vehicles, weapons of all kinds, safe houses, new IDs. Though Terry thought Maura was out of it all these days, in fact she was becoming more closely involved than she had been in her 1980s heyday when she and her eldest brother Michael had been the King and Queen of London crime.

Maura Ryan could still put the fear of God into even the bravest of men, the most hardened criminals. Especially since she had walked away scot-free from the biggest bullion robbery in history by cleverly brokering the Ryans' carefully compiled dossier of information on corrupt top-level policemen, bent politicians, and even a royal scandal to ensure the continued safety of herself, Terry, and the Ryan family. But now Roy faced serious trouble and it was frightening even to her. She had a bad feeling on her about it all. This wasn't just another takeover bid by a few scruffs out for the big time, this was serious aggravation, and the last thing she needed was Terry on her back as well. Because as much as she loved him, and Christ Himself knew she did more than anything or anyone else, she could not let this go. Could not leave it in Roy's less than capable hands. It could spell the end for them all.

Maura tried a different tack.

Walking up behind Terry, she slid her arms around his waist and hugged him.

'Let's not argue over this, Terry, eh? You know I can't let this go.'

He shrugged her off, scowling. He always looked like a little boy when he scowled, a spoiled little boy – which in some ways he was. As a policeman he'd wielded power and influence and that changes a man. Going back to civilian status had been a real wrench for Terry and he never let her forget that. Even his voice was like a whining kid's as he answered her.

'I expected you to say that, Maura. It's always been the same, hasn't it? Marvellous Maura Ryan, the villains' friend. One little thing goes wrong and off you run to your real home, the place you truly belong: Soho. With all the waifs and strays, the whores, the gamblers, the pieces of shit you call your friends and family.'

Maura stared at the back of his head. If he had thrown a bucket of iced water over her she could not have felt more shocked than she did hearing those words. They were uncalled for, nasty, petty. Her family was important to her, he had always known that.

'How dare you?' she hissed. 'Who the fuck do you think you are?'

He turned around and she almost flinched, so great was the contempt on his handsome face. He poked his thumb into his own chest as he said loudly: 'I'll tell you who I am, shall I, Maura? I am ex-Detective Inspector Terry Petherick. The man who gave up everything for you.'

Maura stepped back from him and, smiling gently, shook her head.

'You are off your chump if you think you can use that kind of crap against me, boy.' She saw the hurt in his eyes and laughed again, louder this time. 'Just what exactly did you give up, eh, tell me that? You found out that the real criminals, the major arseholes of the world, were actually in your own profession – and even then you were quite happy for them to lock me up for the duration, remember? It wasn't until you found out they intended to shaft you too that you shifted sides and threw your lot in with me.'

Terry looked into her face, saw his own hurt reflected there, and sighed.

'You gave up nothing, darlin',' she continued. 'You were on your way out of the police force from the moment you went to your bosses with the files my brother Geoff had kept. They didn't want people like you in their club. You were too honest for them, my love. They'd rather deal with people like me. At least then they know where they are.'

Terry knew that what she said was true; deep inside he had always known it.

'All this crap about your career, giving up everything . . . well, I seem to remember your marvellous career coming first on another occasion. You chose work over me then, only I was pregnant that time, and it was me who ended up losing everything, wasn't it?'

He turned from her once more, unable to look her in the face.

She laughed sarcastically.

'My brother is in shit so deep you wouldn't even want to know about it, darlin'. You could not even comprehend what he is having to sort out. Now I don't know about you and people like you but I will be there for my brother, as I always have been, and he will always be there for me. If you can't hack that, Terry, then you and me have been wasting our time all these years.'

The phone began to ring then, a shrill insistent noise shattering the dangerous tension between them.

'Better get that, hadn't you? Big Brother needs you,' Terry mocked.

She knew it was Roy, a panicking Roy, wondering why she had not got back to him sooner rather than later. She stared Terry out until the ringing stopped.

Looking at her watch, she said quietly, 'I'd better get a move on.'

But she didn't want to leave him like this.

'So you are going then?'

'I don't really have much choice, Terry, do I?'

'Everyone has a choice, Maura, whatever you might like to think.'

She looked into his handsome face. It still had the power to enthral her, make her want him all over again.

'Then I have made my choice, haven't I?'

She walked away, saying over her shoulder, 'And you'd know all about making choices, wouldn't you, Terry? You've made a few yourself over the years.'

'I've never made a single choice I regretted, Maura.'

She smiled at him now, a genuine smile.

'That's because you can't get pregnant, Terry. That single biological fact makes men immune from real choices, real decisions. Any decision you ever made was wholly for you, never for anyone else.'

She walked out into the hall and heard his footsteps behind her.

'What about Joey?'

She thought hard for a few seconds before remembering she was supposed to pick up Carla's son from school for her today.

Terry grinned.

'Forgot him, didn't you? Back in godmother mode with a vengeance, I see.'

She licked her lips before answering him.

'You're jealous, aren't you, Terry? You're scared out of your wits I might find something to interest me more than you do. I've watched you over the last couple of years – avoiding my brothers, pretending they don't exist – and I've swallowed. Almost understand it. But I've never pretended to be anything other than what I am. What I chose to be. You know what Roy said once? He said I was more man than any real male he had ever met. I think he was right. And now I'm too much of a man for you, Terry. But then, I've always been too much of a woman, haven't I?'

She walked up the stairs, leaving him standing there unable to answer her.

Ten minutes later she was changed from jeans and sweatshirt into a beautiful suede suit and looked like a different person. Terry felt the pull of her as she walked into the lounge and smiled at him.

'I'm sorry, Maura – sorry it had to be like this.'

She shrugged.

'It had to happen sooner or later, Terry. Deep inside, we both knew that. I love you with all my heart, but I have other commitments. Unlike you, I can't drop them on a whim.'

'You don't want to, you mean . . .'

'I mean *can't*, Terry. You never listen to what you're being told, do you? I have to sort this out. If I don't, people could be hurt. Seriously hurt.'

'Hardly unusual in your line of business, is it?'

The phone began to ring again.

'You'd better answer it,' he sighed. 'I think we both know who it is.'

She nodded and picked up the phone.

'Listen, Roy, I'll be on my way soon, OK?'

She replaced the receiver and looked at the man she had loved for half her life.

'So this is it then? Finitosberg? Goodbyesville?'

He didn't answer her. They stared at one another for long moments. No other woman had ever affected him like Maura Ryan and no other woman ever would, he knew that. Had always known it.

'I'll pick up Joey, OK?' he offered.

Maura nodded.

'Thank you for that anyway.'

He smiled.

'I'll take your Merc – Joey prefers the convertible. Loves the impression it creates.'

She grinned.

'He's a Ryan all right. Only the best will do.'

Her words were not lost on Terry but he didn't bother to answer her. If only she could see things from his point of view. See what she was doing to herself and her family by keeping up their seedy clubs and their whores. The lifestyle they lived bred danger and violence. That was the law of the street. Even though he knew that this latest problem was something that couldn't be left unattended, the fact she was still getting involved against all his advice galled him. And the fact that he knew she was enjoying it. That was what really got his back up. She was truly alive again for the first time in years and it showed. He had never really been enough for her and they both knew it.

After a few seconds he said, 'You'd better take my BMW. Mustn't keep Roy waiting, eh?'

He was telling her he wasn't leaving her right this minute. They hadn't broken up yet. She felt her heart lift as she realised it. If only he could see that she needed to be involved with her family's business; it was all she had ever known really and the second big love of her life. It gave them the life they both enjoyed, the opportunity to do whatever they wanted, and he had reaped the benefits as much as she had. Terry reminded her of her mother sometimes. They both enjoyed their affluent lifestyle but hated and despised the way the money for it was obtained. Hypocrites, the pair of them.

But Maura smiled at him, because when they were alone and they touched, everything else was forgotten. It would be all right. They could put this behind them too. At least, she hoped so.

Maura wondered uneasily if this argument might just be the straw that broke the camel's back. But if he was coming home then at least she could try and talk to him again. Explain exactly what was going on. Surely he'd understand then?

'I love you so much, Terry.'

He didn't answer her. Instead he picked up her keys and walked out of the house. She stood at the picture window and watched him get into her car. The workmen were gone and she was glad. They had been there for the best part of the morning and afternoon.

Terry opened her car door – it was never locked – and she watched his tall frame bend as he got inside. As he placed the key in the ignition he smiled at her and she was pleased. She really believed then that they would get over this latest spat.

The explosion sent her hurtling back through the beautiful room she had painstakingly created. Landing heavily on the sofa, her back screaming with pain, the last thing Maura heard was the telephone ringing endlessly.

Then merciful oblivion.

# Chapter One

Roy Ryan was terrified. He snatched up the phone immediately it rang. On hearing his wife Janine's voice he slammed the receiver straight back down.

That was all he needed now, her and her great big galloping gob for the next three hours. If moaning was an Olympic sport, his old woman would get the gold. The phone rang once more and he ignored it, knowing it was going to be her again with her usual whining. Janine was a piss head and he hated her more at this moment than he had ever hated her before.

He put his head into his hands and stifled an urge to sob. Fear was making him sweat. He could smell himself, feel the moisture pooling beneath his arms. Where the fuck was Maura? She should have been here ages ago.

Probably still in bed with that prick Petherick.

Roy felt a moment's shame at the thought. She was entitled to have Terry; had fought hard enough to get him. But no matter how Roy weighed it up, Petherick would always be a filth, not only to his way of thinking but to everyone else who counted. Roy was convinced that this was what lay behind their latest trouble. Someone was grassing big time, passing word of forthcoming blags to Old Bill, and it seemed the Ryans were seen as the likely culprits. Ex-filth in the family did not augur well in their line of work – unless of course the filth in question was known to be one of your own. Which Petherick never had been.

In fact, he was such a stuck-up ponce he barely acknowledged any of them, looked down his nose at them – even at their mother, and *she* thought the sun shone out of his hairy copper's arse.

Roy sighed again. His eyes were hurting from lack of sleep and he had a day's growth of stubble covering his face. He really did need to get some sleep but now wasn't the time.

Nearly ten years of peace in the city and now suddenly all hell was let loose. But why? Who lay behind all the arrests, all the aggravation? Someone was stirring it big time, and his family had to find out who it was before they lost all credibility with the bedrock of their business: the big league criminals of London and the south east. Today, they were starting a round-up of all disgruntled former associates. They were going to be made to come up with some answers. But where the hell was his sister? They couldn't pull this off without Maura.

* * *

Janine was smarting from her husband's rudeness. She was gritting her teeth in anger and it made her face seem even more haggard than usual. She poured herself a large gin and swallowed it neat, feeling the burn of the liquid as it slipped into her sagging belly. She closed her eyes to savour the feeling and as she opened them caught sight of herself in the mirror opposite.

She felt the sting of tears then. She looked older than her years, much older. Looked nearer seventy than sixty if she was honest with herself.

On the sideboard was a photo of her on her wedding day and Janine stared at it for long moments, remembering how she had felt then with her brand-new husband beside her and a baby growing inside her belly. Remembered her long red hair that had attracted so much attention and ultimately attracted Roy.

If only she had listened to her mother and father! They had had him taped from the first glance, him and his family. But like many a bride before her, she had been sure she could control her man. As it turned out no one could control him, not even the Metropolitan Police and God knew they'd tried enough times. But she had wanted him, wanted him like she had wanted no other man in her life before or since. And the big problem was she still wanted him, always had and always would. Yet she knew he despised her.

She poured herself another large gin and swallowed

a couple of Valium. Mother's little helpers. The thought made her smile, something she rarely did though in fact if she'd realised, it made her look less haggard and much more approachable.

If only you knew in advance how your life was going to turn out.

She lay on the sofa and thought about her daughter Carla, the baby she had borne with so much hope and then disliked from her earliest days. Because she was a rival female and commanded a besotted Roy's undivided attention – something she herself had never done if she was honest. Carla was more Maura's daughter than hers now and that suited Janine. The auntie and the cuckoo in the nest were welcome to one another. But Janine's son, her Benny Anthony, named for his dead uncle, he was a different kettle of fish. He was *hers*. Whatever Roy thought, he was hers alone. Even though his father had made him into a version of himself, Benny was her heart. Her son was everything to her and Janine knew that once he saw through his father he would come back to her. Eventually Maura and Roy would show themselves for what they really were and then she would be waiting for her boy with open arms.

It was a fantasy she loved. It kept her going even though deep inside she knew it would never happen. Benny was a Ryan from his thick dark hair to his size twelve feet. He was like a born-again Michael Ryan, his dead uncle's double. And not just his physical appearance. Benny thought like Michael too. This was what really frightened her in her more lucid moments. But whereas Michael had adored his mother Sarah, her own son loathed Janine and wasn't afraid of showing it.

She shook her head to clear it of the horrible thoughts she was having about her only boy. He would learn, and learn the hard way. The same as his mother had. He was cute enough to see eventually what all the other Ryans were: scum.

The thought made Janine smile again. Cheered her up. She poured out another large gin and gulped it down neat. She was asleep within the hour.

*Belmarsh Prison, Special Secure Unit*

Vic Joliff was laughing, the picture of jollity – a big bald bastard with hard little black eyes creased in mirth.

'You're sure? It was definitely Maura Ryan, and she was good and dead?'

Petey Marsh nodded solemnly.

'Whoever was in that motor was dead as a fucking doornail, far as I can gather.'

Vic rubbed his hands together.

'Give the screw that relayed that message a good drink. We'll use him again. So Maura Ryan's out of the picture . . . Piss off, I want to think.'

Petey left the cell in double quick time. He didn't really like Joliff, no one did, but his sort were an occupational hazard when you were on a lump. And better him than the fucking Paddies in here who gave themselves airs because they were so-called 'politicals'. At least Vic Joliff was an old-style villain with the money, the kudos and the sheer lunacy to be the main man. But though Petey had to work for him, it didn't mean he had to like him, did it?

He wondered briefly what Maura Ryan had done to Vic, and if this was payback. Everyone knew he could still call the shots from his prison cell, and word on the street was the Ryans were not the family they had been in Michael's day, but Maura was generally seen as a force to be reckoned with. Still, if she *was* brown bread, and according to the message she was splattered all over Essex, then it left her brother Roy in charge, and as everyone knew he wasn't the sharpest knife in the Ryans' drawer. Stephen Hawking's position as brain of the century was not about to be usurped.

Petey rolled himself a nice joint and tried to relax on his bed. The days were long in here, too long. If Joliff was out for a turf war, one good thing would come of it at least. It would help to relieve the fucking boredom.

Petey smiled to himself. There hadn't been this much excitement on the wing since someone half-inched the video recorder. Even after the third cell search they still tried to say it was a con who'd nicked it. In fact, in the most secure prison in Europe, with such high security, it seemed blindingly obvious to them all it could only have gone walkabout with a PO. Still, such was life.

He sighed and lay back, still trying to relax, but it was hard with the constant noise and the relentless boredom. Prison life could be a living death – though the real finite kind could be arranged there too, whether by your own hand or someone else's.

He heard Joliff's high-pitched laughter and put his hands over his ears, hoping the Ryans took him out for revenge sooner rather than later. What an arsehole!

Petey finished his joint quickly and gave up on relaxing in favour of a good hard stint in the gym.

Benjamin Anthony Ryan was big. Huge, in fact. He trained with weights and consequently had a body like an Olympic champion. Benny was proud of his physique, worked on it constantly. Today he was in Pat's Gym in East London and was sweating profusely, his hard-featured face red from exertion.

He saw his minder Abul Haseem walking towards him, mobile glued to his ear and his handsome face looking pained for once instead of showing his customary smile, and guessed that something had come on top.

'What's up?'

Benny's voice was low. He did not want to attract any kind of audience to what he was about to hear.

Abul shook his head slowly before answering.

'Someone's bombed your aunt's drum, that's all I know.'

He watched the changing expressions on Benny's face which registered stark incredulity and seething anger in under a second.

'Fucking what?'

People turned to stare, hearing the fury in Benjamin Ryan's voice.

Abul turned off the phone and whispered, 'Not in here, Benny. The car's outside and your father is expecting you at the hospital, OK?'

Benny followed him without a word, grateful for the fact he had a mate who could keep so calm in a crisis.

And this was a crisis, of Olympic fucking standards.

He felt the sting of tears, and was unsure if they were for his aunt or from sheer anger. Either way, he could happily cry like a baby.

Abul, a friend since school and more like a brother than a mate these days, squeezed his shoulder.

'Let's find out the score first, eh, mate?'

Benny nodded.

'I will personally kill the cunt who thought they could get away with a stunt like this. And if she is hurt, I swear on oath I will take that cunt apart with my bare hands and an Airfix toolkit.'

Abul closed his eyes momentarily. Benny had a thing about gluing people's eyes shut; said it scared them shitless and Abul agreed with him wholeheartedly there. But the thought still made him feel sick.

* * *

In a waiting room at Oldchurch Hospital Sarah Ryan shrugged off her eldest son's arm and cried, 'For Christ's sake, Roy, I'm not in me dotage yet!'

Even in her eighties she was still hale and hearty. Smaller than ever, she seemed to be shrinking on a daily basis but was mentally as tough as she always had been and this was conveyed by her voice.

'Look, Mum, let me get one of the boys to take you home. This is going to be a long night . . .'

She interrupted him with a wave of her hand.

'I've had a few of those over the years with you lot. Especially with Michael and your toerag of a father. Now tell me what the shag is going on!'

Roy stared at the tiny woman before him and marvelled at her strength of will.

'Where's Terry anyway? He should be here.'

Roy licked his lips before answering her.

'It was a car bomb, Mum. Meant for Maura. Terry copped it.'

Sarah screwed up her eyes as if unable to take this in.

'What? You mean, Terry's dead?'

Roy nodded.

'Holy Mary, Mother of Christ! What has *she* caused this time?'

The blame was immediately placed at her daughter's door and Roy felt the urge to fell his mother with one blow at the unfairness of her reaction.

'Wherever she is there's death. Death and destruction. My poor boys . . .'

Sarah's voice trailed off as Roy walked quickly away from her. She felt sick with apprehension. This could mean only one thing: more skulduggery was afoot and Maura, as usual, was behind it all.

Where had she got her daughter from? Sarah had been plagued by Maura since she was old enough to join in her brothers' nefarious activities. But whereas Sarah could swallow wrongdoing from them, she never could accept having a daughter of the same ilk. It was wrong, all wrong in a woman, and this was the upshot. Another pointless death.

Terry Petherick had been a decent man who had loved that blonde-haired whore she had delivered into the world with a passion. He'd been a policeman once, clean-living and good, and what he had seen in her daughter was beyond Sarah's comprehension.

She walked over to her son and pulled him round to face her.

'Don't you turn away from me, boy, when I'm talking to you.'

Roy shrugged her off none too gently and said in a low voice, 'Aren't you going to ask about your daughter? Your only daughter. Don't you want to know how she is? If she's alive, dead, maimed or what?'

Sarah shook her head.

'I'm not interested . . .'

Roy held up his hand for silence.

'Then piss off home, Mum. I'm sure you'll learn all you need to know from Janine later.'

Sarah watched him walk away from her and felt a moment's sadness. Maura had caused all this trouble in the family. Forcing everyone to take sides. Making them choose. She sat herself down in a scuffed plastic chair and placed her large leather bag on her lap.

She could wait to find out what was going on. She was good at waiting, Christ Himself knew; she had had enough practice over the years.

Five minutes later her grandson Benny walked past her as if she didn't exist. She opened her bag, removed her olive-wood rosary and began to pray.

'Fucking old witch, she is! Her and me mother should be put down.'

Roy agreed with his son but an instinct as old as time took over.

'Don't talk about my mother like that. Or your own, for that matter.'

Benny shrugged, temper getting the better of him.

'Listen, Dad, they're a pair of vindictive old hags, you know it and I know it. All that "respect for your parents no matter what" went out with Noah's fucking Ark! I can't bear either of them and I'm sure me Aunt Maura don't want them here. So let's cut the crap and get to the point, eh? Who is the culprit and how do we retaliate?'

Looking at his son, Roy felt as if Michael were alive and kicking and looking out through Benny's eyes. It was spooky, the similarities were so strong – though his boy was heterosexual as far as he knew. But even the timbre of his voice was like Michael's and this was what made him so appealing to people. He had the same arrogance Michael had had, and the same vindictiveness. Maura adored him and he adored her, much to the chagrin of Janine.

The doctor approached.

'How is she, Doc?'

'She's conscious. Took a bad blow to the head, but nothing major. A few cuts and bruises. I can't see any long-term damage. Not physical anyway.'

Roy felt his whole body relax.

'Thank fuck for that! Can we see her?'

'Five minutes only, I'm afraid.'

Benny hugged his father and Roy was reminded of just how strong and young his son was. He had the same quicksilver temperament as Michael, veering between raging anger and an almost puppylike euphoria in the space of seconds.

'What a touch, eh, Dad! What a fucking touch!'

It occurred to Roy that he wouldn't be able to control this boy of his for much longer, and what would happen then he didn't like to contemplate.

Maura looked terrible and Roy guessed she already knew about Terry's death.

'All right, Maws?'

She closed her eyes and nodded.

Benny pulled up a chair. Taking her hand in his, he gently squeezed it.

'We're here now. You're safe.'

Maura smiled faintly.

'Thanks, Benny. Any idea who it was?'

'Has to be that ponce from Shoreditch, don't it?'

Benny's voice was loud and Maura winced. He lowered his tone. 'No one else it can be, is there?'

He looked from Maura to his father who shook his head.

'It's not Jimmy Milano, he's straight as a die. Maura gave him an in a while ago.'

Benny looked crushed.

'Thanks for telling me.'

The bitterness in his voice was not lost on any of them. Benny had been assigned to lean heavily on Milano when he first surfaced in East London. But as it turned out he'd had a good protector who was also one of the Ryans' best lieutenants. Milano was no threat. Unlike his older relatives he was strictly small-time, in his thinking as well as his criminal tendencies.

'I meant to tell you, Benny, but with everything . . .'

Roy's voice trailed off.

'Is there anything else I don't know about?'

Benny was on the defensive as usual. It was his biggest failing and they all knew it.

'We've had hag from all over the show lately, Benny. What we need now is to eliminate our suspects.'

'Fucking right and all. Eliminate is just the word for what I intend to do to the cunts!'

Maura closed her eyes wearily.

'Will you stop saying that word, Benny? It irritates me.'

'All right, Maura, don't get out of your shopping trolley.'

He was very much on his dignity and Maura, feeling suddenly sorry for him, said gently, 'What are the police saying?'

'I can't gather much yet. Our blokes at the Met are going to call us later this afternoon with the general SP.' Roy looked at his son as he spoke. 'You put blokes out and about, OK? See what they can . . .'

Benny interrupted him.

'Already done, Dad. Abul sorted it on the way here.'

Roy nodded.

'Anything else you want done, Maws?'

She shook her head carefully and lay back on the pillows.

'Just get me moved to a private hospital as soon as possible before the papers descend on us and anyone else decides to have a pop.'

'It's done, Maws. We'll be back later, OK?'

As they walked from the room she called out, 'And

keep me mother away. I can't cope with her at the moment.'

When they shut the door she lay back and remembered the events of the day. The fight. Terry leaving like he did. The last sight of him, smiling at her through the windscreen of her car as he turned the ignition key and was blown apart by the bomb that had been meant for her.

Now he was gone, really gone, and the pain and the guilt would stay with her the rest of her life. No time to grieve, though. Open war had just been declared and she had to sift through all the shit and try and make some sense of it all.

She swallowed down the tears. Time to pick herself up and get on with the job in hand. Let personal feelings wait.

It was what Maura Ryan had done all her life.

Garry Ryan was like a raving lunatic and his girlfriend Anita, a beautiful girl with a weight problem and a nervous twitch, watched warily as he went through his phone book. Writing down names, he muttered under his breath. When he was like this he frightened the life out of her.

He looked up at her with deep blue eyes.

'Make me a cup of tea, Nita, and get me a flight to London. Now.'

She nodded.

'Am I coming, Gal?'

She was nervous as usual when she spoke directly to him.

He sighed.

'Do you want to come?'

It was a fair question and he asked her nicely, which for him was a first. She didn't want to leave Marbella. She loved it here, especially without him. But she answered him promptly. ''Course I do, darlin'.'

Garry chuckled and this scared her even more.

'No, you don't. You don't even like me. You just like the kudos, Anita. Look that word up in the dictionary when I leave, OK?'

She nodded, relieved that she didn't have to go with him.

'Then pack your stuff and fuck off.'

She blinked a few times before she said sadly, 'But where will I go?'

Garry was fed up with the conversation now and said dismissively, 'How the fuck do I know, Nita? You'll find somewhere, your type always do.'

She burst into tears.

'You rotten bastard! Why do you treat me like this!'

He stood up. Standing in front of her, he placed one hand gently under her chin. He tilted her face up and kissed her lightly on the lips.

'Because I can, silly. Now, make me tea and book me flight, there's a good girl.'

He saw the stark confusion in her eyes and felt a moment's sorrow for her. But he despised her too because no matter what he did or said she still hung around.

'I tell you what, if you're really good I'll let you stay on here for a week until you find somewhere else. I can't be any fairer than that, can I?'

She walked away from him, utter dejection in her whole stance. An hour later he was on his way to the airport with not even a passing thought for Anita, his companion of two years. Such was the mindset of Garry Ryan.

On the plane he planned his revenge on whoever was responsible for trying to off his sister Maura and ultimately his whole family, because it wouldn't stop there, he was quite sure. Whoever they were they had better be good runners because when he got back to Blighty and sorted himself out there were going to be murders committed.

Garry Ryan was looking forward to it.

Sandra Joliff was tall, with silicone breasts, a sunbed tan and startling white teeth. Her blonde hair was streaked to within an inch of its life and cut so it hung in a shaggy sexy mess around her face.

She felt like shit. She had been on it all night and her kidneys were aching from too much cocaine and too much vodka. Her skin was grey under the tan and she wanted a shower and a cup of tea as soon as possible.

She had to visit her husband the next day and needed to look good for the visit. She knew he was proud of her and didn't want to let him down. He was all right, old Vic. He knew the score with her and they'd built a life together around their personal foibles.

As she pulled onto her drive a car hooted from behind her and a dark-haired man stuck up his finger. She did the same back.

'Tosser!'

She knew she had cut him up as she pulled across the road but was too tired to care. Stepping out of the car, she surveyed the drive. The gardener had been and the front of the house looked immaculate. She never ceased to be amazed at how she lived, thanks to Vic. Originally from a council flat in Woodford Green, Sandra now lived like a queen. Her two little girls went to private school and she had a BMW 330 and money coming out of her ears. It was her lucky day when Vic took a shine to her, bless him. He had taken her from her old life and transported her to this new one without a second's thought.

She opened the door to her five-bedroomed detached house in Emerson Park and turned off the burglar alarm. As she walked through to the kitchen she saw her Doberman Kelly lying in the middle of the floor.

There was blood coming from the dog's mouth and ears, and its body was twitching. She knelt beside the animal and stroked its head.

'All right, Kelly. What happened to you, love?'

Her voice was low and comforting. The dog placed its nose in Sandra's hand and whined gently. Nearby there was a lump of bloody meat. Instinctively she knew Kelly had been poisoned.

As she stood up she felt a presence and turned to see a man standing behind her. He was big and heavyset, smartly dressed though in designer gear. She automatically clocked him as she did all men and rated him on a one to ten scale. This geezer was a four but she put that down to the ski mask he wore. He smiled widely, displaying perfect white caps through the slit in his mask.

'Who the fucking hell are you, and what the fuck are you doing in my kitchen?'

He could see the bravado in her face and admired her for it. He looked her over appreciatively and she felt a moment's disgust as it occurred to her that he might want to rape her. Well, he could have a good fucking try.

She squared her shoulders and balanced herself on her stiletto heels.

'Sandra?'

His voice was low and pleasant with a slight accent.

She frowned.

'Who wants to fucking know?'

She was still on her dignity and determined he wouldn't see the fear she was feeling inside.

'Do you know who I am? Who my old man is? He finds out about this and there'll be fucking murders, mate.'

He smiled.

'I was counting on that, Sandra. It's why I'm here.'

She screwed up her face in consternation.

'You what? What you on about, you fucking nutter!'

The dog whimpered again and she automatically looked down.

'All right, Kelly. I'll get a vet in a minute, baby, as soon as this dickhead leaves the house.'

She looked at the man again.

'You don't know what you're getting involved in here, mate. I warn you, my old man is heavy duty and this will piss him off big time.'

The man opened his coat and she saw the sawn-off shotgun. Her blue eyes widened as she realised what he was about to do. She made a run for the back door; its glass shattered as the first blast caught her in the lower legs. As she hit the floor the man stood over her and laughed.

She was writhing on the floor; her legs felt like they were on fire.

'What you doing to me! Take what you want, mate, take me watch, anything . . . but, please, I have two little girls . . .'

She was sobbing in pain and shock.

'Sorry, love, nothing personal.'

Then he blasted her in the face. He was still smiling while he did it.

Sandra's mum had had to pick the kids up from school and assumed her daughter was out on one of her marathon lunches again. She took the girls back to her own house, determined to have a word with Sandra about her neglect of the kids. Since Vic had been banged up she had gone mad, out all the time, coked out of her nut. Her mother was getting fed up with it. Consequently Sandra's body wasn't found for twenty-four hours.

Vic Joliff had to be sedated when he was told the news, as did Sandra's mother who was unfortunate enough to find her daughter's mangled body along with the dog's. Chantel and Rochelle were now to live with their granny, who smoked too much and lived for Bingo.

The police were baffled. Everyone was.

Sandra was a wife, a civilian, had had no dealings in Vic's business, though some said she had snorted most of the profits. But that was Vic's problem, no one else's.

This certainly wasn't his doing. He'd adored her, even when she was taking on all comers. He swallowed it because he knew she was young and high-spirited. It was only human nature. She hadn't married him for love.

But then the murder was linked to the bombing at Maura Ryan's house and as one astute old lag said sagely: 'No good will come of this. The pavements will run with blood within the week.'

In fact, his prophecy was to come true within two days.

# Chapter Two

Sheila Ryan smiled as her husband slipped his arm around her waist.

'You never give up, do you?'

Lee, the youngest of the surviving Ryan brothers, laughed.

'Never.'

She heaved again, dry racking heaves, and he rubbed her back once more.

'This baby is a troublesome little thing!'

'It's a boy, Sheila, and takes after his father's side of the family!'

She laughed because no matter how bad she felt now, she was so glad to be pregnant again. Sheila loved being pregnant, loved the feel of the babies growing inside her belly. The movement of them, and the knowledge that she was creating a little person from scratch, still filled her with awe every time.

Her grey-blue eyes were ringed black from lack of sleep and her face was pale. Lee loved her with a vengeance no matter how she looked. When she was heavy with a child, her belly swollen out of proportion, he felt like the luckiest man alive. His brothers ribbed him over it, but he knew they admired him too. Since Sheila he had never really looked at another woman, just the odd one-nighter here and there. He couldn't risk losing what he had.

She sighed heavily.

'I feel so rough, Lee. I never felt like this with any of the others.'

'It'll be worth it when he arrives.'

'It could be a she, you know. Especially as this pregnancy is so different from the others.'

He squeezed her shoulder.

'You can hope, girl. But I only have masculine sperms.'

They were laughing again. Lee looked fondly at his wife and was as always thrilled that she was his. He hoped this baby was a girl. Deep inside he would love a daughter, and after four boys it would be a nice change. He knew Sheila wanted one. His mother wanted a girl as well. She acted like it was entirely his fault that they had had four boys, like he could choose or something.

'I love you, Sheila.'

She looked up into his eyes.

'I know.'

The bedroom door opened and his four young sons piled in. Sheila was still trying to throw up in the en suite when Jason the youngest said seriously, 'Is Mummy's baby coming out?'

They all laughed again.

Lee picked up his three year old and said loudly, 'Who wants a bit of brekker then? Eggs, bacon and fried bread for me boys, eh?'

'Oh, stop it, I feel sick enough as it is, Lee!'

As he heard his wife throw up again he called through, 'Sorry, Sheila. Dry toast for you then, eh!'

All the boys laughed and Lee led them downstairs happily. No matter what the trouble at work he never brought it home with him. It was something that had served him in good stead all his life, and Sheila *was* his life now. Her and his kids. As bad as things were for the Ryans in general, his own little family had no inkling that anything was amiss and he was determined to keep it that way. Sheila knew the score and was of the same opinion. Outside the house was another world and they both protected the children from it as much as they could.

The phone rang as he was serving up the eggs and his eldest son Gabriel answered it. At eight he was already big for his age and like the others a miniature Ryan.

'Yeah, OK, then, Uncle Roy. I'll tell him, he's just cooking the breakfast.'

Lee heard his son laugh at something his uncle had said and felt a stab of pride in all his family. They were close, and they loved each other. Nothing could ever come between them.

'Uncle Roy said he'd meet you at the office.'

'OK, Gabriel, thanks.'

Sheila came into the kitchen, her long blonde hair brushed and her swelling belly hidden underneath a satin dressing gown. She smiled wanly at her husband as he placed a cup of tea and two slices of toast before her.

'A late one again today?'

Lee nodded.

'See you when I see you then.'

He kissed her, to the derision of his four sons.

Garry and Roy were having breakfast at their mother's house. Garry still chose to stay there whenever he was in the smoke.

'Joliff had a message saying that we killed his bird, which we didn't, but I think it was Joliff who done Terry right enough. There's something heavy going down all right.'

'It's definitely a set up, but let's wait and see what we garner from the other boys, eh?'

Sarah listened to them with only half an ear. As she placed a Benny Special in front of them they smiled their appreciation.

'Nothing like a bit of grease, Mum. Clog up the old arteries.'

'Shut up and eat it, you stupid fool.'

She left the kitchen and went into the sitting room. It had hardly changed in years, still jampacked with religious statues and overstuffed furniture. Photographs of her five dead sons had candles burning beneath them and rosaries placed across the frames. Four of them butchered – she blamed Maura for those deaths. In Sarah's eyes even Leslie's car crash was attributable to her daughter and not to the amount of alcohol and drugs he had consumed. Hadn't he been working at *her* club that night? Even though they all knew he had developed a drink problem, she'd still had him working where he could get the whisky he craved, Sarah thought grimly.

In fact, Leslie was actually a coke head and an accident waiting to happen. When it finally did, it not only killed him but the nineteen-year-old hostess with him and an elderly couple in a dark blue Lada.

All Sarah could see was that five of her gorgeous sons were dead as doornails and that bitch was still walking around like she owned the whole world.

She knelt down and crossed herself.

As she prayed her gaze took in the view through the window and she marvelled that now this whole area of Notting Hill was worth a fortune. They even had a pop star living two doors down from them in Lancaster Road. It was amazing to Sarah that anyone would want to spend so much money on any of these places. She remembered the days when they were infested with roaches and the tenants were hard pushed to feed their broods of children. This was once the last refuge for the poor and now it seemed people were killing themselves to live here. She blamed that eejit Tony Blair. A classless society? Whoever heard such rubbish!

Her grandson Benny poked his head around the door.

'All right, Nan. Me dad here already?'

His voice was neutral, as if she was a stranger he had just asked directions from.

'He's in the kitchen. Can I get you something to eat?'

'Nah, Abul's mum done us something earlier.'

He shut the door gently and she smiled to herself. He was getting better was Benny. But like her Michael who he was the head off, as she pointed out on a daily basis, he could be a moody little bugger.

Sarah wouldn't admit to herself that he didn't like her but she felt it off him and knew she wasn't alone in suffering his contempt. His mother bore the brunt of it. Yet if her grandson gave her a civil word it made Sarah's day.

Garry had been to early Mass with her so she was relatively happy, but Terry's death had cast a shadow over the whole family. She wondered idly when Maura would be back on the street. And more to the point, what was her darling daughter going to drag them all into next? *That* was what Sarah would like to be told.

Knowing her, the streets would run with blood. Maura was hard and she was dangerous. The beautiful blonde-haired angel she had given birth to with such happiness all those years ago was now the bane of Sarah's life. She had become a force to be reckoned with, by police and criminals alike.

If only *she* lay dead instead of that good man, how much easier Sarah would feel. Now, though, Maura would cause more mayhem, more death. It was what her daughter did when thwarted or angered.

Sarah kissed the cross of Christ on her rosary and began praying once more, her eyes raised heavenward as if Jesus Himself was communicating with her.

Carla swept back her thick red-brown hair. The action made her look even more like her mother Janine, but that was as far as the similarity went.

Carla was a sweet-faced woman who lived for her son Joey and for her Aunt Maura who had been a surrogate mother to her all her life, even though there were only five years difference in age between them.

It was odd but Maura was like her mother, sister and soulmate all rolled into one. Carla knew she was the child her aunt had never had, and she cherished the fact that even after all these years they loved one another and still held the closeness they'd had from childhood.

As she walked into the hospital she checked over in her mind that she had all Maura needed.

In her private room at the Nuffield in Brentwood,

Maura was watching Sky News and fuming as the presenter referred to her as 'Maura Ryan, East End businesswoman'. She was originally from Notting Hill, and she now lived in Essex. The least they could do was get it right. She switched the TV off and stood up as her niece walked into the room.

'Rubbish! It's all rubbish! They don't know me . . . they don't know anything about me.'

Carla rolled her eyes and said jokily, 'Thank God.'

Maura laughed with her.

'I didn't think I had a laugh in me, to be honest.'

Carla put her arms around her aunt and hugged her tightly.

'I am so sorry, Maws, so very, very sorry. Terry was a good bloke.'

It was the first time she had directly mentioned anything about what had happened. Maura hugged her back as if she was frightened to let her go.

'Are you sure you're OK to come home with me?'

Maura swallowed down the tears.

'You bet. I am back, Carla, and I will hunt the scum who killed Terry into the ground. And when I get my hands on them . . .'

'And I'm right beside you, remember that.'

Maura smiled shakily.

'I appreciate you saying that, Carla. It means a lot to me. But you just concentrate on Joey, OK?'

Suddenly the door burst open and Marge Dawson stomped into the room.

'Bleeding cheek! That black git on the door wasn't going to let me in!'

Tony Dooley's eldest son, Tony Junior, stood behind Marge, a surprised expression on his handsome face. The Dooleys were a well-known family of minders. Tony Senior had looked after Maura for years before handing the job over to one of his boys.

'Sorry, Maura, she was very insistent.'

'Right and all, you cheeky little fucker!'

Marge was incensed and it showed.

'I knew her before you were even born, mate, and you tell your father he should have beaten some manners into you by now, young man.'

Tony Dooley Junior shook his head in disbelief and shut the door gently as he left the room. He was six foot six inches and built like the proverbial brick shithouse. To see her tiny friend Marge shouting at him made Maura really start to laugh. It was just what she needed. The three women all began roaring. Marge's distinctive guffaw made Maura laugh harder. Her eyes were watering and she could feel the snot running from her nose. As she grabbed a tissue she felt the enormity of what had happened to Terry bearing down on her. The simple act of laughing had unleashed every trapped emotion and she started to cry. Tears became heart-wrenching sobs and as she sank down into the chair by the window, both Carla and Marge patted her back, murmuring endearments to her.

It was what she needed, Marge and Carla tacitly agreed.

'You cry it out, girl. Get it off your chest.'

As she cried she saw Terry smiling at her for the last time. It was so wrong, so very wrong. It was she who should have died and then she would not have to face a life lived without him.

Maura cried for what seemed an age and then when she quietened Marge ordered a large pot of strong tea.

'Get that down your throat, girl, and we can get you packed and home, eh?'

Maura nodded.

'Thanks. I don't know what I would do without you both.'

Marge had not aged well; she looked much older than her forty-four years. She was still overweight with a bad perm and a bad home dye job. Her make-up was still startling to the uninitiated and she complained about her feet constantly. But Maura loved her with a passion only thinly disguised by the offhand way they talked to each other. They had been friends since kids and had shared each other's grief and happiness over the years.

With both Carla and Marge beside her, for a few minutes Maura could forget the danger that threatened her and get her thoughts in order.

Terry was dead because of her and that knowledge was hard to bear. If only they had never argued. That last bitter exchange was the hardest thing of all to remember. He had loved her, she knew that, and she had loved him. Always had, always would, it was as simple as that.

But her lifestyle had come between them. In her heart of hearts she'd felt only half-alive during the years spent with Terry, and that was harder than anything to admit to herself. Only when she wore the mantle of Maura Ryan, dangerous lady, did she feel truly herself, tingle with anticipation at the start of each new day. She knew she was not cut out to be a housewife; her only chance at motherhood had been ruined in a dingy flat with the abortion of her child. Her child and Terry's.

She knew deep inside she had never forgiven him for abandoning her then, in favour of his job. His precious police career. But it didn't stop her from loving him, even while she resented him. Now she had to bury him. Or what was left of him anyway.

Marge and Carla packed for her and talked to one another with their eyes. When Maura went to the bathroom to wash her face, Marge whispered to Carla, 'One or other of us needs to stay with her at all times.'

Carla nodded.

'I've never seen her like this before.'

Marge shrugged. 'I have. When Michael died. There's been too much death in her life.'

Carla didn't answer her. She didn't know what to say.

Maura walked from the bathroom with full make-up and a smile plastered on her face. 'Come on then, girls, let's get home, eh?'

Carla watched her aunt acting as if nothing had happened. She was putting it all out of her head as usual and wouldn't allow herself to grieve properly.

But trouble was on the way, Carla was sure of it.

In more ways than one.

Benny, Garry and Roy met Lee at a lock-up in Camden. As they closed the door behind them Benny checked the road to see if anyone outside was watching them.

'Who moved the car out?' Garry said.

Benny answered.

'Abul. He's taken it for a jaunt.'

Garry grinned. He loved his nephew Benny, they were of similar temperament.

'Good boy. Now, there's a few interesting bits under here. A couple of Armalites. A rocket launcher. The spades are in the corner, you'd better get digging!'

Lee laughed.

'What are you going to do then?'

Garry shrugged.

'Get the teas, of course. I'll let you work up a sweat first, naturally.'

'Naturally!'

Benny, always hands on, started to dig with a

vengeance. The others watched him for a while, marvelling at the strength of him.

'How's Maura?' Garry's voice was low.

Roy sighed.

'Not good. Reminds me of how she was after Micky went. She's bottling it all up as usual.'

'Fucking good riddance to bad rubbish if you ask me. That Petherick was a ponce. For a shrewd bird she was blinded there.'

'Ain't we all where lovers are concerned?'

Garry laughed.

'Not me. I never met anyone I cared about. Wanted to fuck, maybe take out now and again, but people who get too close can own you. They make you stupid, make you do stupid things.'

Lee knew Garry meant him and Sheila and he reacted angrily.

'Not everyone is just after what they can get, Gal. Not all women are slags.'

Garry raised his eyebrows in an expression of disbelief.

'They are. Show them a few quid, a big cock and a nice motor, and they're yours. Look at Joliff's old woman, a slag of the first water.'

'Not any more, Uncle Garry.'

'Not so much of the "Uncle" if you don't mind, young Benny. Garry will do.'

'We're blamed for that, and you know what it means, don't you?' Roy sounded worried.

Garry nodded, irritated by his brother's reaction.

'It means we have to strike first, that's what it means. So hurry up and dig, boys. Let battle commence.'

'Maura wants us all to go to her flat over the club at lunchtime.'

Roy still sounded unsure and Benny picked up on that fact.

'Do you think she's up to all this?' He gestured with the spade into the hole.

Garry laughed and Lee joined in.

'Maura would shoot *you* if you annoyed her enough, boy, remember that. She'll bounce back. She is the only woman I know who thinks like a bloke. She also has the ability to suppress her feelings. She'll be all right, I guarantee it.'

Benny nodded, satisfied. But Roy kept his own counsel. He would wait and see. Although they were all pleased Terry was out of the picture, Maura certainly wasn't. She had thought the sun shone out of Petherick's arse and nothing any of them said was going to change that fact. This had started out as Maura giving him a hand to sort out a few bits and pieces. Now it was a full-scale war. Watching Benny acting like an extra in *The Godfather* could have been amusing if it hadn't all been so deadly serious.

Lana Smith was small and plump with melon-shaped breasts that not only defied gravity, they actually made her look fatter – if that was possible. Since her baby had been born a few months previously she had piled on the weight.

As she stepped out of her car to go into her local tanning salon she saw a slightly-built, curly-haired man smiling at her. Never one to be backward at coming forward she noted his brown eyes and cocky smile in a nanosecond. She noticed the knife a few beats later.

It entered her stomach and ripped up through to her breastbone, leaving a gaping hole. As she stumbled off the kerb she felt the wetness of her blood as it pumped out of her body. The man was already driving away and the wing of his car clipped her shoulder, knocking her back on the pavement with a heavy thud.

Her new baby Alicia slept contentedly in her car seat until the wail of the ambulances and police cars woke her and then she screamed endlessly, her little face red with anger and exertion.

Maura listened in amazement as she was told of the deaths of two of the south east's most hardened criminals' women. She screwed up her eyes in disbelief.

'Why would anyone think *we* would kill them? They're wives, birds, civilians. What the fuck would hurting them gain us? They both had kids, for fuck's sake.'

Benny shrugged.

'To gain us aggravation if we're put in the frame.'

Maura rolled her eyes to the ceiling in annoyance.

'Fucking hell, Benny, that never even occurred to me. Give him a fucking paper hat!'

The words stung and Benny as usual was on his dignity.

'No need to be sarcastic, Maura . . .'

She interrupted him.

'Shut the fuck up, Benny. This is not the time or place for you and your fucking stupid little boy act, OK? This is serious grown-up shit. Lana's old man Kenny could pick you up and squeeze you to death in the middle of Romford Market and not one person would admit to seeing a thing. He is heavy, and he is serious, and we have to sort this out soon else all the Armalites in the world won't keep Smithy off our doorstep.'

Maura's words sobered everybody. Even Garry agreed they had a problem.

'That is one heavy duty bastard, and now he has a motherless child to add to his annoyance. We'd better arrange a meet as soon as possible.'

Benny was still sceptical. He blew breath from his mouth noisily in a final act of defiance.

'Fuck him, we ain't done nothing.'

Garry turned on his nephew and said slowly, 'Kenny Smith is one of the only people I am wary of. Now *that* should tell you to treat him with respect. He's a decent bloke until he gets upset – and then he's a fucking maniac. He's the guy everyone uses as a go-between for trouble. That's what he does. He's respected and liked, and he's the man we were going to call on to liaise between us and Joliff. Only now we're on his top ten shit list, at number one, we'll have to find someone else to do the dirty work for us.'

Maura rubbed her eyes with the palms of her hands, a sure sign she was upset.

'We have to find out who's putting our faces in the frame. Maybe Kenny can still help us with that, if I try the softly-softly approach. Garry, Roy and Lee – I want you with me for back-up but let me talk to him on me own.'

Garry nodded. Benny was more than aware he was out of the equation but didn't make a direct protest.

'So what do I do while you lot are gallivanting around tonight then?'

Maura looked at him and said seriously, 'You make yourself busy, of course, Benny. You carry on routing out all our minor personnel and you put the fear of Christ up them. See what you can find out. But don't glue anyone's eyes shut, please. It's very bad for business.'

Benny was clearly thrilled at the opportunity for further violence and Maura watched him with distaste.

He was so like her brother Michael, in looks and temperament. But unlike the eldest Ryan who had had an exemplary business sense, Benny as far as

Maura could see was strictly a bullyboy. Like Michael, he would explode into violent rages and now she wanted to tap into that part of him and use it for her own ends. If anyone knew anything they would be most likely to tell Benny Ryan. She loved him but found his wildness hard to deal with, especially when they had so much else to worry them. She knew he was offended by her reaction to him and didn't care. She had no intention of nursing him through this. He had to learn to deal with life, as they all had. She knew his father agreed with her way of thinking and that was all she cared about.

'I have been in touch with a few faces around town to see if I can get the SP on the latest killing, Maura. I'll let you know what I hear.'

Garry let Lee speak then asked her: 'What about the filth, what have they had to say about Terry?'

Maura had expected the question and had also expected it from Garry. None of the others would have had the front to ask her outright. The tension in the room was almost unbearable as she answered him.

'I've batted them off so far. I'll have a meet with our pal Caldwell obviously before I can even begin to think about talking to anyone else.'

Garry nodded, satisfied.

'Well, he was one of their own so they'll be as interested as we are, won't they?'

Benny's voice was dismissive and Maura felt an urge to throttle her nephew until he passed out. Instead she said coldly, 'Do you know something, Benny? One of these days that trap of yours is going to get you into all kinds of trouble, starting with me. Whatever you thought of Terry Petherick, and frankly I don't give a toss what that was, he was part of this family through me and me only. I am warning you, Benny . . .' she looked slowly around the room '. . . I am warning you all, any personal feelings you may have had about him get left at the door. We have to work together on this and I do not want to have to explain myself to you, the filth or anyone else. Do you understand what I'm saying here?'

Her blue eyes were as cold as flint and her perfectly made-up face was hard. For the first time ever Benny saw his aunt as all her brothers saw her and it unnerved him. He knew that in this mood she would order his disappearance without a second's hesitation if it would make her quest easier. Far from finding this scary he admired her for it. Fear was the key in their business and she was one of the few women who knew how to use it.

That she was under immense pressure never occurred to him. That she was trying to keep them together, show a united front to the criminal fraternity, never occurred to him either. He was still too young and too immature to see what was really going on. It would be his downfall if he wasn't careful. He had never been in the middle of a gang war before and Maura knew he was going to be properly blooded before the week was out. She would watch him and help if necessary, but she had no intention of baby-sitting him today. He had to be put in his place sooner rather than later, that much she knew for sure.

One day her nephew's mouth and attitude were going to get him into trouble big time and he had to be made aware of that fact.

All the men in the room were staring at Benny and he felt uncomfortable. He also realised he was going to have to watch himself. Even his father didn't come to his defence against Marvellous Maura.

He had never before seen her in this mode and now, as far as he was concerned, everything he had heard about her was true. He felt proud to be a part of this family and to know deep inside that he was just like them. It made him feel he belonged. Made him feel good about himself.

Benny smiled, one of his big heart-warming smiles that drew men and women alike to him. And as Maura looked at her nephew she saw her brother Michael, the first man she had loved, smiling back at her.

Benny grinned around the room and said roguishly, 'That put me in me fucking place, didn't it?'

Maura couldn't resist him then. Hugging him tight, she said seriously, 'You are one cocky little fucker.'

Garry yawned noisily and remarked to no one in particular, 'You can say that again, Maws. Now then, let's get this show on the road. We're going to have Smithy seeing sense before it's dark.'

Roy watched his son as he blinded Maura with that smile of his. Inside he was worried. Benny was a loose cannon and Roy knew he was going to have to keep a steely eye on him so he didn't balls everything up with his temper and youthful arrogance.

He didn't want to admit that his own son scared him, but he did. Benny frightened the life out of him. Like his uncle before him he was as mad as a hatter, and like his uncle he would not be controlled for long.

Kenny Smith looked at his baby daughter sleeping in her cot and swallowed down the ball of tears bunched in the back of his throat. His scarred face twisted with grief, making him look even uglier. His mother Eileen, an East End harridan with permed hair and a cigarette permanently dangling from her lip, patted his arm.

'Unbelievable, son. Bloody unbelievable.'

He clutched her hand tightly.

'Fucking Ryans! They're putting themselves about all over the place and now my little Lana's gone.'

'Hardly little, son, she was the size of a house since she had the kid.'

Kenny rolled his eyes.

'Don't start, Mum. Whatever you thought of her she was my old woman and little Alicia's mother.'

'She was an old sort, that's what she was. But whatever. I'll sort out the baby, you get this all done and dusted, son.'

'Oh, don't you worry about that. I intend to cause the Third World fucking War.'

Eileen nodded, not at all fazed by her son's determination.

'Listen, I'll take the baby home with me, OK? You work from here. But get it sorted soon, I'm feeling nervous. If they're after the birds, then life is dangerous for everyone, ain't it?'

Kenny nodded.

'I'm seeing a few faces roundabout. Very soon the Ryans might just find themselves in more shit than Basildon dump. What with Vic's old woman and all, people aren't too happy.'

Eileen lit a Benson & Hedges from the endless supply in her apron pocket.

'Not round the baby, Mum,' he said reprovingly.

She snorted.

'Never done you no harm, did it?'

Kenny sighed and left the room. He had to get all this sorted as soon as possible. First the Ryans, then a nanny for the baby. It did occur to him then to wonder briefly if the Ryans had put his face in the frame for the bombing of Maura's boyfriend the filth, and this was quid pro quo but he dismissed the idea. Whoever had killed his Lana had done it for pure wickedness and he would make sure they paid for it in full.

He poured himself a large brandy and drank it straight back, needing the alcohol. As the tears welled up once again he swallowed them down. There would be plenty of time for grieving after tonight. And he wouldn't be the only one grieving, he was determined on that.

[illegible]

[illegible]

[illegible]

friendly chat and a beer. To be taken to a deserted barn in Ramsden Bellhouse did make him feel a little bit nervous.

When he was dragged from the car by [illegible]

# Chapter Three

Radon Chatmore was a Rastafarian with long dreads and a public school accent. He was actually baptised a Catholic but took on the mantle of Rastaman just after his seventeenth birthday, more as a fashion statement than a religious belief. He had his father's business acumen, though he preferred to see it as inherent cunning. His nickname was 'Coco' on account of the fact that he was the number one coke king of the East London club scene. He had been recruited by Benny Ryan a year earlier and they split the profits sixty-forty and drank together on a regular basis. Consequently when Abul had asked him to a meet with Benny he had assumed it was for the usual friendly chat and a beer. To be taken to a deserted barn in Ramsden Bellhouse did make him feel a little bit nervous.

When he was dragged from the car by Benny, Coco knew for sure he was in deep shit and as he was stoned out of his skull it was even more frightening than if he had been straight.

'What the fuck is eating you, Benny?'

His voice was high and the affected Rasta talk long gone. He sounded pure BBC newsreader and this incensed Benny more than ever. He began kicking and punching his friend on the dirt outside the barn. Abul dragged Benny away.

'Wait till we get him inside, we can be seen from the road.'

Breathing heavily, Benny watched as Abul picked up a protesting Coco and dragged him into the barn.

Inside were two tables. One had a hamper on it. The other had the tools of Benny's trade, including the fabled glue and an electric cattle prod. One glance told Coco all he needed to know. Halogen lights lit the place up like a film set.

'What's wrong, Benny? What on earth is this all about?'

Coco's voice was trembling with fear.

Abul could see the confusion in his eyes but couldn't help him. As Coco looked at him in anguish, he held out his hands in a helpless gesture. He was telling him he was on his own. For all they were mates, Abul was with Benny now and that was permanent. Coco understood that even in his panic and fear.

Benny stood before him, his face closed and eyes hard. The deep blue of them that Coco had always envied looked almost luminous with anger.

'What do you know about Vic Joliff?'

Coco swallowed; his throat had gone dry.

'I don't know anything about him, Benny. I know he's heavy, that's about it.'

Benny walked around the barn, shaking his head as if unable to believe what he was hearing. As if he knew he was being lied to and found it shocking and yet strangely amusing. He gave a little laugh before he spoke, his voice incredulous now.

'Excuse me? Are you trying to fucking mug me off?'

Benny looked at Abul, all innocence and hurt.

'Have I got "Cunt" written on my forehead or what?' He pointed to it dramatically and Abul stifled the urge to laugh. In this mood Benny Ryan was better than a play.

Coco, in contrast, felt the urge to cry. He had heard about Benny's temper, who hadn't? But this was the first time the famous anger had been directed at him personally.

Abul didn't answer, he knew he wasn't expected to say anything. He was straight man to Benny's favourite tactics while interrogating.

'Are you going to answer me?'

Coco was nearly crying now. He could feel the loosening of his bowels as he knelt before his persecutor.

'Please, Benny. I swear to you . . .'

The kick to his face was punishing and thankfully it

knocked him spark out. Abul took the man's pulse.

'He'll be out for a while, Ben. Shall I make a cuppa?'

Benny nodded.

'I'm starving. Open the sandwiches and all, we'll have a picnic, eh?'

Abul opened the hamper. He had made sure that all Benny's requirements were met. Hot sweet tea in a Thermos, and plenty of wholesome food and fresh fruit. While he arranged the food on plates Benny cut them both a large line of cocaine. Abul felt his heart sink. Once that kicked in, Benny would go even more over the top than usual.

'I don't think he knows anything, Ben, do you?'

Benny shrugged his giant shoulders and sipped at his mug of tea. He took a large bite from a Marks and Spencer sandwich before answering, his mouth full of food and his voice muffled.

'This is lovely, what is it?'

'Chicken tikka and salad. Filling but tasty.'

On the floor Coco moaned in pain. Benny kicked out at him again with a booted foot. 'Shut up, you ponce, can't you see we're on a tea break!' He laughed at his own wit. 'Can't beat Marks for a good bit of grub.'

Abul nodded agreement.

'Worth paying that little bit extra, ain't it? What are you going to do with him?'

He nodded towards Coco.

Benny chewed on the last of his sandwich before replying.

'Kill him, I expect.'

'You're joking!'

Benny shook his head.

'Never been more serious, mate. People saw you take him: it's the best way I know to put out the message that I am on the fucking war path. Well, I'm right, aren't I?'

Abul sighed.

'He ain't heavy duty, Benny. He has a nice house, a nice mum and dad, and a nice little bird. He earns you dosh. Give him a fucking break, man.'

Benny put his hands to his chest in mock horror.

'What are you, Abul, stuck up his fucking arse or what?'

Abul laughed despite himself.

'You are one mad cunt, I tell you, Benny.'

'I will do a deal with you, OK?'

Abul nodded.

'I will leave him alive on one condition, right?'

Abul nodded again.

'I get the last of the sandwiches.'

Benny was deadly serious and Abul knew this. He pretended to think before he answered. He knew how to handle Benny better than anyone.

'All right. It's a deal.'

Benny poured the last of the hot tea over the unconscious man's face to wake him.

'Come on, wanker, up and out of it. I got a hot date tonight with a big-chested bird.'

When Coco finally came round, the first thing he saw was Benny Ryan standing over him with a cattle prod, a big smile on his face.

Kenny Smith kissed his little daughter goodbye and left his large rambling house in Laindon. He got into his new Mercedes. As he went to put the key in the ignition a snub-nosed revolver was poked into the side of his neck.

Garry Ryan's voice was low and menacing.

'Drive, Smithy, and don't make any unnecessary moves.'

Kenny closed his eyes in distress.

'You piece of shit, Ryan. What you gonna do now? Make my baby an orphan?'

Garry laughed.

'Only if you push your fucking luck, mate. But think about this. If I wanted you dead, you already would be. No discussion, nothing. Now, drive.'

'Drive where?'

'Just drive. We're meeting some friends in a minute. Be nice for you, won't it, eh? We can have a chat about old times.'

Kenny drove away, his heart in his mouth and his hands itching to get into the glove compartment where he kept a strategically placed firearm.

* * *

Prison Officer Danzig walked through the unit quietly. It was early evening and the maximum-security prisoners were on TV hour. Unlike burglars and car thieves in open prisons, the Max prisoners could only watch one hour of television twice a week. It caused endless trouble when they couldn't keep up with the soaps, and now the video had gone AWOL they couldn't even tape things. Danzig sighed. The powers-that-be sometimes forgot that this was a unit dealing with the higher echelons of crime. Boredom and the men's innate intelligence were a worrying combination.

A man looking at an eighteen stretch was on the edge. He needed to be occupied far more than a youngster doing two or three years. It wasn't a case of making their lives easier, more a case of making life easier for the screws in charge. And how could you really be in charge of a crowd of men when all the time you were shit scared of them?

He blew his nose noisily before going into the rec room so they would be alerted to his arrival. That way any nefarious dealings would cease until he had left. Inside he was amazed to see only two men silently watching *Pet Rescue*.

He walked to his small office and unlocked the door, waving at the other POs on the way. Inside the office he found Vic Joliff. He was hanging from a beam on the ceiling, his mouth stuffed with papers from Danzig's desk. One was his Lottery ticket, which annoyed him no end as it was now evidence.

It was also covered in blood because whoever had hanged the fucker up had also cut his throat. Sighing heavily, Danzig rang the alarm.

It was going to be a long night and he had arranged to go and look at a flat with his eldest daughter. He had the down payment ready and waiting for her because he was willing to pass on messages from the outside. Now that little earner was up the Swanee with Vic Joliff.

Marge listened as Maura made arrangements over the phone from Carla's house. As usual she marvelled at her friend's ability to turn off her emotions and concentrate on what she felt was more important: the family and their business dealings. Marge, the mother of two grown daughters and a son, lived by her emotions and knew it was her biggest weakness. Though her husband adored his fiery little wife, Marge knew deep inside that she controlled him with her tears, her anger and her loud voice. She nagged everyone around her and ordered their lives. She'd happily order her friend's life if it would make everything easier for her, and if Maura would let her. Fat chance of that, though.

Joey came into the room. At thirteen he was a handsome boy who resembled his mother rather than his father, and everyone thanked God for that small mercy every day. Malcolm Spencer had been the stuck-up weedy sort, an architect rather too full of his own cleverness. Heaven only knew what Carla had ever seen in him, but it had worn off fast enough once she discovered what a cheat he was.

Joey had dark auburn hair and piercing blue eyes, the Ryan nose and square jaw. He adored his Auntie Maura with a passion.

'Mum said to ask if you needed anything?'

Maura smiled at him.

'No, thanks, I'm off out in a minute.'

'OK.'

As he left the room Marge said saucily, 'If I was only twenty years younger!'

Maura laughed.

'Thirty years younger, you mean!'

Marge grinned.

'True. Where the fuck did all the time go, Maws?'

She shrugged.

'Who knows, Marge? I'd better get moving.'

'Where you off to?'

Maura could hear the fear in her friend's voice. Her own was short as she answered.

'Who are you, Marge, the police?'

Marge stared at her, still waiting for an answer. But she didn't hear what she wanted. Instead Maura said: 'It is best for all concerned if you know nothing, Marge. What you don't know, you can't repeat.'

Marge was insulted and it showed. Her stocky little body bristled with annoyance. 'I would never repeat anything you said, Maws, you should know that by now.'

'You might, Marge, if someone had a gun in your face or a knife to one of the kids' necks.'

Marge paled.

'Is it that serious?'

'Marge, whoever this is, they're killing civilians. No one is safe, love, especially if they're close to me. Do you understand what I'm telling you?'

Marge stared at her silently.

'This place is like Fort Knox,' Maura added, 'but I'm sending Joey and Carla away. They don't know that yet so keep shtoom.'

'Even you're worried, aren't you?' Marge said incredulously.

Maura nodded. Then, picking up her bag, she kissed her friend gently on the cheek and said, 'Get yourself off home, mate. I will ring you tomorrow, OK?'

As she heard Maura laughing with her minder Tony Dooley Junior, the enormity of what was actually going on hit Marge. She had to sit on the sofa to gather her thoughts.

In all the years they had been friends Marge had overlooked a lot of what Maura had done in the name of her job. Anyway, she'd believed the dangerous days were over. She'd just been given a new understanding of her best friend, a glimpse into the world she really lived in.

Marge shuddered.

It had been like staring into the fiery pit of Hell.

Kenny Smith was inside a Ryan safe house in Orsett, Essex. He was none too pleased and it showed. Garry poured him a large brandy from a cut-glass decanter.

'Nice round here, ain't it?'

Garry's voice was neutral. Kenny didn't even bother to answer, his disgusted expression saying more than words ever could. The place had more minders than a Southend nightclub and Kenny knew he had no chance of escape. He had to sit it out and see what the score was, hard for him when he was used to being the main man at most events and commanding the kudos his specialist work exacted.

As he watched that nutter, as he always thought of Garry Ryan, Kenny's mind tried to come up with some kind of getaway plan. He knew the house was large, in its own grounds, and could see a road which he assumed to be the A13 from the window. It was about a quarter of a mile away across open fields. Not much cover but it was dark and if he could get a good run he might be in with a chance. He clutched the glass tightly, wondering at the odds of slamming it into Garry Ryan's face. The thought made him smile and Garry laughed as he watched him.

'The last thing I need is a full face of Mars Bars, but I wouldn't advise it, Kenny. You are in no danger from me or anyone else, I swear to that. But if you start any antics I will have no qualms about nutting you once and for all, OK?'

Kenny nodded. The futility of his own situation was what smarted with him most. He was used to being the man. How many times had he sat somewhere and watched some other mug who had crossed the line shit himself because he had a capture? It was a very revealing few hours.

When Maura Ryan walked into the room Kenny was so relieved he almost smiled at her.

Maura, though, looked far too serious for his liking and he wondered once more if he would ever see his little daughter again or be around to bury his wife.

Sarah Ryan opened the front door to the young priest with a big smile on her face.

'Hello, Father.'

She was preening herself with satisfaction. A man of God at her front door for all the neighbours to see was her idea of Heaven on earth. She knew that they were all aware of exactly who her children were and it amazed her that so many of them were impressed by their violent reputation. She herself was ashamed and scandalised most of the time.

'I am Father Peter, the new priest at St Bartholomew's. I came to say hello.'

His Irish accent was like music to her ears and what a fine handsome young man he was, his curly hair neatly slicked down and dark eyes smiling. She ushered him into her lounge with as much alacrity as her advanced years would allow. She was pink with pleasure and the young man smiled at her kindly. As he settled himself on the sofa she watched him eyeing her religious statues and said with pride, 'I have always been a good Catholic and a true believer, Father. Now, can I get you a cup of tea and a bit of cake?'

'Thank you, that sounds wonderful.'

As she left the room Sarah was walking on air. This was just what she needed to bump her up a bit. She was so down over young Terry and the new priest showing up when she was at her lowest ebb felt like fate at work. As she made the tea she sifted through stories she could regale the priest with that would make her family look less criminal than they were. She could not think of many and knew that their reputations would have preceded them as usual.

She walked back into the room to see if he wanted sugar and was confronted by a sight she'd never dreamed she would see in a million years. The young priest had gone through her dresser, opening drawers and rifling through letters and other personal effects. He was holding an old photograph of Sarah and her nine children, and as she stood in the doorway watching in amazement he tore it in two.

'What in the name of Jesus do you think you are doing?'

Her voice held a note of command. It was the one

she had used years ago when her nine children were rampaging through the house and she had to make herself heard above the din.

The young man stared at her, and suddenly his dark eyes didn't look very friendly at all.

Dr Jamie Snell shook his head in disbelief.

'How the hell he survived is beyond me. We have had to put over forty stitches in his neck and he took a serious beating beforehand. It seems that when they hung him, they actually stopped the blood flow. Lucky really.'

The Prison Officer shrugged.

'Strong old boy, Vic.'

'Well, he's not out of the woods yet. He's still unconscious and until we see how he goes through the night . . .'

Dr Snell left the sentence unfinished.

PO Boston grinned.

'An easy night for me anyway. At least the bastard can't wake up and give me any aggravation.' He sat himself down by the bed in Intensive Care and opened up the *Sun*. He folded the paper at the crossword and licked his pencil earnestly.

Dr Snell wrote his notes quickly, and after talking to the nurse in charge, left the ward.

Vic Joliff had listened to everything through a haze of pain; he was much stronger than any of them thought.

But Vic being Vic knew how to play the game.

* * *

Benny and Abul dropped Coco off at the local hospital at 8.45. Benny was silent as Abul assured their victim that it was nothing personal. Just business. Coco was heartbroken at what had occurred and also knew he needed medical treatment as soon as possible.

Before getting out of the car he said sadly, 'I would never betray you, Benny, you must believe that.'

He nodded, like a bored benevolent pontiff.

'Just fuck off now, Coco. I heard you the fiftieth time.'

As they drove off Abul glanced at him and they both started laughing.

'Did you hear him squeal when I stuck the cattle prod in his ribs?'

'They will guess what happened by the burns, Ben, but he won't say a word.'

Abul sounded very certain of this. Benny just shrugged.

'Who gives a fuck if he does. Prick, he is.'

Forty minutes later the car pulled up outside a block of purpose-built flats in Southend. Benny left the car and made his way up to the penthouse. The door was opened by a small-boned, dark-haired young woman of seventeen.

'Hello, Benny.'

Her voice told him how pleased she was to see him. He smiled at her, one of his blinding smiles that made people want to like him, want to please him.

'Get your kit off, Carol, I have an appointment in an hour.'

Carol tutted as she put her hands on her hips. Her cross expression made Benny laugh.

'Mr fucking Romantic.'

He laughed harder.

'I told you, girl, you want Mr Romantic then give me back the key and go and find him.'

He took her where she stood, up against the wall. He was rough with her, and she cried out in pain. He slapped her hard across the face and she held her breath, frightened to move or make a sound until he had finished. All the time it went on he spewed filth into her ear and she tried to block out what he was saying to her. He would be back tomorrow or later in the evening with money and sweet words to soothe her. That was the Benny she loved, not this maniac who turned up frequently and just used her.

Fifteen minutes later he was back in the car with Abul on his way to Camden. Carol was sitting on the hall floor, sore and hurt and crying her little heart out. She could see the smears of blood on the wall beside her and it made her cry harder.

She kept repeating one word like a mantra under her breath: 'Bastard, bastard, bastard.'

'Hello, Kenny.'

Maura half-smiled at him and he was made aware of

how powerful her presence actually was. He liked Maura, always had; she was one of the few women he actually respected. But then, she wasn't really like other women. She had the same coldness in her that her brother Michael had had. That unpredictability that all successful people in their line of business shared. She was also still very good-looking even if she would never see forty again.

'Maura.'

His voice was clipped. He had no intention of showing his fear though he had an idea that Maura Ryan could probably smell it coming off him in waves. That was what they said about bitches and she could be a bitch when the fancy took her, he was more than aware of that fact.

'Do you need anything to eat, Ken? A drink?'

He shook his head once more.

'What I want, Maura, is some kind of explanation. No more, no less.'

She poured herself a drink, sat opposite him and looked him straight in the eye before saying innocently, 'That was exactly what I was hoping for from *you*.'

Kenny Smith was struck dumb and as Garry watched the changing expressions on his face he felt an urge to laugh.

'You murdered my old woman!'

It was Maura's turn now to shake her head.

'I don't think so, Kenny. We've kept our head

down and our arses up for a good few years now. We have no argument with anyone that we are aware of. But it seems someone out there is trying to cause us untold aggravation by making it look as though we're on the rampage.'

'I lost my fucking wife, the mother of my child!'

Maura kept silent for a moment as if digesting the information. Finally she told him, 'Kenny, I am sorry for your loss, but you forget that someone tried to nut me. Instead they killed my partner.'

Kenny's tirade started up again.

'He was a filth, and he wasn't even a friendly one. I'm sorry, Maura, but people didn't trust you any more once he was part of the fixtures and fittings. Surely you must have guessed that much, love? Clever girl like you.'

Garry stood up. Towering over the man in the chair, he bellowed, 'Who the fuck do you think you are talking to, eh? My fucking family has made you plenty of wedge over the years and we have never once tucked up a single solitary person. We own judges and filth and have helped out many a fucking old lag in our day – so you keep your fucking opinions to yourself and stick only to what is relevant.'

Maura pulled him away forcibly and Kenny realised again how close he was to death.

'Let me and Benny have him, Maws. Give the cheery fucker to us,' Garry insisted.

The thought of Benny Ryan the Airfix King, as he

was nicknamed, made Kenny feel even worse than he already did. A feat in itself. But he wasn't beaten yet.

'Don't you fucking dare threaten me, Garry Ryan. I was in this game when you was still polishing your brother's fucking shoes for him. You don't scare me. I've dealt with them all, mate, from the old masters to the young punks, and you fucking remember that.'

Kenny stood up, his anger so acute he could almost taste it.

'Fucking Super Glue and threats of violence! Do you lot think you're the first hard nuts ever to walk a fucking pavement? Shall I tell you something I learned many years ago, Garry? There is always someone harder out there, and they want what you've got and will do anything to get it. What goes round comes round, remember that. But nobody ever touched wives or family before. That has always been taboo . . .'

'Until now, that is.'

Maura's voice was still level.

'Just sit down, the pair of you, before I take me ball back and then you'll have nothing to fight over. Listen to you, like a pair of fucking kids.'

Both men sat down shamefaced and she continued in the same level tone.

'Kenny, I swear on Michael's grave I had nothing to do with Lana's death and neither did anyone in this organisation, OK? Now I need to know why people suddenly think we're out to cause hag. I want the name of your grass, whoever told you we were behind it, and I want them now, tonight, so we can go and have a friendly chat with them and get to the bottom of this once and for all.'

Kenny still didn't answer her.

She motioned with her head for Garry to leave them and he did so reluctantly. Then, pouring two more brandies, she handed one to Kenny. As they sipped the drinks she felt the tension gradually leave the room.

'I am truly sorry, Kenny.' Maura's voice was warmer now they were on their own.

He hung his big shaven head so she couldn't see his face past the livid white scar that neatly bisected one of his eyebrows.

'She was all right, my Lana, whatever people thought. She was a good kid.'

Maura could hear the grief in his voice.

'Now the fucking baby . . .'

He couldn't finish the sentence.

Maura grasped his hand and squeezed it.

'I know what you are going through, Kenny, but you must believe we had nothing to do with it. Or with Joliff's old woman either. There is skulduggery afoot, mate, and me and mine are in the firing line. I have to sort this out and I have to sort it out fast. You understand that, don't you? I need your help, Kenny, more than ever before.'

He nodded.

'I believe you, Maura, you was always straight with me.'

And he did. Something told him to trust her and he had always trusted his instincts. It was why he was still alive after all these years on the front line.

Maura topped up his glass.

'So, Kenny. Who gave you the information?'

'Rebekka Kowolski – you'd know her by her maiden name. Goldbaum.'

The name made Maura feel dizzy and sick. Took her back to a time in her life she would rather forget even as it haunted her dreams.

'How would she know that?'

'Her old man, of course. He's a minor cog in a big wheel. Works for Joe the Jew, in a firm that runs out of Silvertown.'

'I know Joe well. Why would he be involved with something like this? It's too heavy for him, he would never take me on.'

Kenny shrugged once more.

'What am I, the fucking Oracle? Joe runs with the pack now. He has dealings with most of the crews around about. He can locate any kind of licence, from pubs to boxing matches. Done well for himself actually.'

'How does Rebekka come into it?'

He finished his drink and held out the glass for more before saying, 'She's the brains of the outfit from what I can gather, and she loves drugs – selling them anyway. She is astute, Maura, I know that much. Has a good business brain. Her husband is a fucking Muppet. She'll hold a grudge against you and all, won't she? If memory serves me correctly, you and Michael wasted her old man.'

Maura refilled the glasses, her mind whirling. Once more she was back in the past, and not in any part of it she wanted to revisit.

The door burst open and Garry walked in, his face red with temper.

'Someone has clumped Mother.'

Both Maura and Kenny stared at him in shock.

'What?'

Maura could not believe what she was hearing.

'She's in hospital, I just had a call from a filth on me mobile. She actually gave him my number, can you believe that!'

'Fuck the mobile, Garry, is she OK?'

He nodded.

'More shaken than anything. I'll get Roy to go and see her. Lee's had a phone call from an old-timer – thought it was worth a punt so he's gone for a meet. Now are we out tonight or what?'

Maura nodded.

'Wait till you find out where we're going, Garry. Talk about a blast from the past.'

Kenny watched them warily. As far as he was concerned whoever had decided to take them on must be mad. And if it wasn't the Ryans, then who *was* behind the death of his wife? That was what he wanted to know more than anything. When he found that out, the Ryans wouldn't be in it.

'I'll come with you,' he offered.

Maura glanced at him and said casually, 'You were coming anyway, Kenny, but thanks for the offer. Until we're sure you have told us the truth we'll stick to you like shit to a blanket.'

It was no more than he'd expected.

# Chapter Four

Roy watched as his mother was bandaged up. She had a black eye and a sprained wrist. To see her sitting on a hospital bed in that state made him feel as if he was about to explode with rage. When she looked vulnerable, as she did now, he remembered all sorts of things from his childhood. How she'd fed them and clothed them with hardly any help from their father, a man who'd wanted his drink and his gamble far more than he'd wanted his family. When Benjamin Ryan Senior finally departed this life on the floor of a bookie's in Kilburn five years back, Roy and his brothers had made no secret of their relief. Only Maura seemed to miss the old sod – and their mum, of course. He wanted to put his arm about her shoulders and comfort her now as she had comforted him while he was growing up.

She looked so small, until she started one of her tirades and then as usual she made him close his eyes with unconcealed irritation.

'Don't you look at me like that! I blame you lot for this. *Her*, that hard-hearted whore of a sister of yours, I bet *she's* behind it.'

The nurse was trying not to laugh and suddenly Roy realised that his domineering mother was the archetypal figure of fun to most people. He only wished she was to him.

A young policewoman pulled back the curtain to the casualty cubicle and raised her eyebrows. She was amazed at what was going on and it showed. The Ryans were notorious, and yet here was one of them being shouted at and abused by his own mother. It was said in the station that her boss was in the pay of this family. That they told him to do the things he did, including blocking the promotions of regular policemen and women and bringing through the ranks only the ones who would kow-tow to the Ryans. Her boss was the joke of the station. When he went on holiday one wag had set a rumour going that he was really in hospital, having his chair removed from his arse. He was notoriously lazy. The fact that the holiday in question had been three weeks in a five-star hotel in Florida had caused a few comments as well.

'Mr Ryan, my superior is outside and would like a word with you.'

Roy stood up. Towering over the three women, he growled, 'About fucking time and all.'

As he left the cubicle the girl smiled at Sarah.

'Can you give me a description of the intruder, please?'

Sarah's wrinkled face took on the look of a contestant in a big-money game show.

'He was neatly built, he was good-looking, and he was dressed as a priest.'

The policewoman smirked.

'A priest? That's a new one.'

'He'll be a dead one when I finish with him.'

Benny's voice made the policewoman jump and he smiled at her coldly. She was young and pretty but Benny didn't notice. All he registered was the uniform and she knew immediately that he saw her as the lowest of the low. For the first time in her life she felt seriously threatened and yet this good-looking young man had done nothing to her. She saw the expression on his face as he observed his battered grandmother and was very glad she would not be on the receiving end of his anger.

Sarah tried to defuse the situation.

'Oh, Benny, would you take me home, please?'

She looked very old and very frail and the young policewoman listened in surprise as he answered her in an offhand way.

'You'll survive, Gran. Me dad's getting you picked up.'

He walked from the cubicle and Sarah's face settled into its habitual frown.

'Little fucker.' The strength was back in her voice

now and the policewoman quickly took the statement required and was glad to leave them all behind her.

It was only back at the station that she fully realised who she had actually been dealing with. The higher echelons of the Ryans were now known to her personally and she was amazed. She was queen of the canteen and enjoyed every second of it. She was just glad she didn't have to deal with them any more.

Rebekka Kowolski's house in Totteridge was a shock to Maura. It was huge with electronically controlled gates and the requisite guard Dobermans roaming the grounds.

'Couple of mil here or what?'

Garry sounded annoyed.

'Good luck to them. As long as they tell me what I want to know, I don't give a toss.'

Maura was deliberately dismissive and this annoyed Garry, as she'd known it would. But all she could think about was Sammy Goldbaum's face when she had come for him with Michael. It was the only actual murder she had ever taken part in and it still preyed on her mind. It was so long ago yet it felt as real to her now as it had then. The sickness was in her stomach again and she swallowed it down.

They were now directly outside the property and Kenny was asking for entry on the intercom but no one was answering them. He turned back to the car.

'No one home.'

'We'll see about that.'

Garry opened the panel and tinkered with it. A minute later the electric gates opened. As they drove towards the house they watched with pleasure as the Dobermans made a hasty exit through the open gates.

The house was even larger close up. From the winding driveway they could see the indoor swimming pool and sauna in a glass-sided extension. It really was some property. It was also lit up like Battersea power station yet there seemed to be no one about.

Garry sighed.

'Not Hide and Seek, surely? He's supposed to be a bit of a face, ain't he?'

Kenny shrugged.

'So are you, Garry, remember?'

They finished the drive in silence. When they got to the front door they all climbed out of the car. It was eerie; the whole place had the feeling of echoing emptiness that large houses always have when unoccupied.

'Break in, Garry,' Maura ordered.

He was already working on it. She saw that Kenny was nervous and smiled nastily.

'Don't worry, he's an expert. No Old Bill will arrive. Garry could get into the Bank of England.'

'Knowing him, he's a frequent visitor.'

Even Maura had to laugh at this quip and the atmosphere calmed down a little.

'That's all we need now, done for fucking breaking

and entering! We could never hold up our heads again.'

Maura and Garry laughed uproariously. Two minutes later the front door was open and they were in the spacious entrance hall.

'Fuck me, this is real money. They must be coining it in.'

The awe in Kenny's voice was not lost on Maura.

'Lot of money in grassing, so I hear.'

He didn't answer her. They walked through to an imposing pair of doors and Maura pushed them open. It was an act she was to regret: the scene of carnage before them was as outrageous as it was sickening. It also brought back memories she had long tried to suppress. Maura assumed the headless corpses on the floor of the drawing room were those of Rebekka and her husband, but none of them stuck around long enough to find out.

All Maura saw was Sammy, Rebekka's father. He had been headless as well by the time her brother Michael had finished exacting his revenge. This was so like the death scene that Maura felt the icy fingers of fear on her neck.

Whoever was causing all this carnage knew far too much about them all, and that was what frightened her the most.

This was someone they all knew. It had to be someone very close.

The question was, who?

★ ★ ★

Lee was with one of the Ryans' long-time associates, an old lag called Denny Thomas. Denny had been a breaker in his day and though now retired he made beer money by keeping his ear to the ground. Everyone knew and liked him, consequently he heard most of what was going on. Occasionally, as now, he was used as the bearer of bad news.

'What do you want, Denny?'

Lee looked round the small council flat and tried unsuccessfully to find a clean place to sit. He finally opted for the arm of a battered leather sofa.

'Come on, spit it out, I ain't got all night.'

Denny looked nervous and this told Lee he really wasn't going to like this.

'Someone just tried to nut Vic Joliff in Belmarsh.'

Lee closed his eyes in consternation.

'Who, Denny? Who tried to nut him?'

Denny shrugged.

'I don't know.'

Lee was struggling to keep a lid on his emotions. This was all they needed. He could see how nervous Denny was and felt a moment's sorrow for the wreck of a man before him.

Denny went to an old-fashioned bar unit, which still held traces of its former glory, and poured them both large Scotches. The whole place had an air of dilapidation and disuse about it; Denny looked like he lived on the streets. Lee wondered how it happened to people; he could remember Denny in sharp suits, and always with a girl on his arm. He had been in the life whole-heartedly. Now he looked like any drunk you could see waiting for their Giro outside the Job Centre.

He passed Lee's drink to him with a shaking hand.

'Some young fellow was waiting for me outside the pub. He was in a brand-new Saab and he had a soot with him – Paki, I reckon. They told me to tell you lot that Vic was on his way out.'

Lee rolled his eyes to the ceiling.

'You having a fucking tin bath, Denny?'

Denny gulped at his drink. His face held some of its long-ago hardness as he snapped back: 'Do you think I want to get involved in all this, Lee? Is that what you really think? Your brother Michael and me went back years, mate. I was part of this firm when you was still putting fucking Brylcreem on your hair. I was dragged into this shit by strangers and I'm passing on the message. That is all.'

He was worried and he looked it. Once more Lee felt sorry for him. Denny wasn't stirring, he didn't have the nous. Which was why he'd never risen higher than common or garden breaker in his day. Lee would pass the message on and see what Maura had to say about it. For now he concentrated on getting descriptions but Denny's eyesight was past it as he was.

Vic Joliff was scary even by Ryan standards. Lee

just hoped he was good and dead; it would make their lives so much easier.

Janine watched her husband as he shaved. It was strange but she actually enjoyed looking at him even while she hated him. Roy still had the power to make her want him, which was almost unbelievable because each of them nursed a burning hatred of the other. Her continuing feelings of attraction to him always amazed her.

'Where you off to then?'

Her voice held the edge it always had when talking to her husband. Roy sighed heavily.

'I'm off out.'

'Will you be home?'

He laughed gently.

'Will the sun come up? Will the grass grow? Till Tony Blair finally become a Catholic . . . and who gives a fuck?'

Janine walked away from him, through the bedroom, and as she walked took in the clothes he had laid out ready and satisfied herself he wasn't going out with a girl. And Roy's birds *were* girls. Young ones, with pert breasts and the brains of a gnat. According to him that was how he liked them.

It still hurt even after all these years. As she walked downstairs her son shoved past her without even a passing glance or word.

'How was Sarah?'

She hated herself for the sound of her own whining voice but she would do anything to get him to talk to her civilly. Benny didn't even bother to answer her, just carried on up the stairs as if she had not spoken one word. Janine felt a lump in her throat and swallowed it down; her histrionics, as he called them, only made him more irritated with her.

Her own son ignored her shamefully, but she would wait and one day he would come to her on his knees and beg her to take him back into the fold. It was this thought that kept her going, that kept her alive. And the lifestyle her husband gave her helped, though like Sarah Ryan she would never admit that out loud.

Five minutes later both men were gone and the house was once more empty and cold. As she poured herself a large vodka there was a ring at the doorbell. Tutting loudly she opened the door, expecting her husband or son, assuming they had forgotten something. Instead a shotgun was shoved in her face and she was walked backwards inside the house by a large man in a ski mask.

After the shocking scene at the Kowolski house Maura told Kenny he could go home; they'd be in touch when they had something to go on. He'd seen for himself their shock and surprise, was reluctantly beginning to accept that they were being set up.

After a stiff drink at the club, Maura and Garry met Roy and Benny at their warehouse in Canning Town.

It was warm in the small office, and as they all sipped coffee they were quiet.

'Why Mother?'

Maura's voice was low. Garry shrugged.

'Why not? I mean, whoever this is they're determined to aggravate us, ain't they?'

'It seems wherever we go they've been there first. They definitely have a working knowledge, don't they?'

'Could be following us, could have been following us for yonks.' Benny sounded as annoyed as he felt. His whole body screamed for violence.

Maura nodded.

'True. I think he has a point, don't you?'

Garry wasn't impressed.

'Someone would have noticed it. Fuck me, we ain't amateurs, are we?' He grinned. 'Except for little Benny, of course.'

'Oh, fuck you.'

Garry laughed loudly but Maura was irritated and so was Roy.

'Why don't you grow up, Garry? This is serious.'

'I know it's serious, but we have to keep things in perspective. Laughing at adversity is the great British way, ain't it? I mean, think about it.'

Maura shook her head in consternation.

'Well, I ain't laughing. Mother, as big a pain in the arse as she is, did not deserve a slap, especially not from some little firm with dreams of the big time.

Because that is all this can be. We just have to get out and about and find the culprits. We start by routing old-time members of the family like I said before. Whoever this is knows far too much of our past history. Someone's telling tales.'

They all nodded, digesting this bit of logic.

'What did Old Bill say?'

Roy shrugged.

'The usual, they'll keep their ears open. Fucking real, ain't it? There we are, paying out hefty fucking wedge to that twat Billings, and he's shitting himself now we want a payback. Anyway, I stuck a flea up his arse that will irritate him till the day he dies. Do you know what he had the cheek to say to me, eh? "Don't threaten me, Ryan." Straight up, he said it to me boat.'

Garry's eyes were slits as he answered his brother.

'I remember Billings when he was a DS – a ponce of the first water, he was. Used to take money from the working girls and that is low.'

'It's also how we got to him, Garry, if you remember.'

'He's had his cock sucked more times than Hugh Grant, I know that. One of the girls told me what he really likes and it's chicken shit – jailbait, the babies. Well, he has three little daughters of his own and I wonder how his old woman would feel if he was found out?'

Maura hated it when they talked like this but she swallowed down her annoyance and said seriously,

'Set him up, Gal. I want photos, the lot. Video even. I want that cunt by the short and curlies because we are going to need him. The money we scammed him is forgotten now. We should have blackmailed him from the off, saved ourselves a fortune.'

'Well, we all know what the filth is like, don't we, Maura?'

Garry's voice was malicious and she felt an urge to slap his face, but resisted it. Instead she bellowed at him: 'Keep your fucking stupid observations to yourself, Gal. I am trying to keep it together here but I tell you now: one more remark like that and I will turn on the lot of you. And as nutty as people think you are, there'll be no one else in it when I get started.'

Picking up her bag, she stared each man in the face before leaving the room, bristling with anger.

'That was out of order, Garry.'

He grinned.

'No, it wasn't. It will keep her on her toes, keep her annoyed enough not to grieve too much for that ponce Petherick.'

'That's twisted logic, Uncle Garry, if ever I heard it.'

They were quiet for a while then Garry said in all seriousness, 'Do people really think I'm a nutter then?'

Even Roy laughed at that.

No one was laughing ten minutes later when Lee arrived and told them about Vic Joliff.

* * *

Maura was still fuming as she wheel-spinned on to Carla's driveway. Switching off the engine and lights, she sat in the car and cried. She cried for Terry, for their baby, and she cried for herself.

As the racking sobs shook her body she was once more transported back in time to her first glimpse of the man who would ruin her life in so many ways. Her mother was right all along, they had been destined to destroy each other. He had destroyed her when he had abandoned her while she was pregnant with his child. With the tearing out of that child from her body her whole life had changed dramatically. The previously carefree young girl had been replaced by a bitter and hard woman. She for her part had first ruined his career and ultimately been the instrument of his destruction.

He was to be laid to rest in a few days. What was left of him would be cremated as he'd requested. She was dreading it. Her life felt finished in so many respects, it was becoming harder and harder to get up in the morning. But she forced herself, though deep inside she didn't know why.

Even this latest business wasn't keeping her mind free from thoughts of Terry Petherick. But like so many things in her past she would bury it deep, hide it away, and eventually block it out altogether. Until a chance word or a photo would bring it all back to her. Then, as now, she would face the consequences of her actions.

She was not that far off fifty though the mirror told her a different story. She knew she still looked good but it didn't make her feel any better. She honestly didn't care what she looked like. Had not really cared for years. It was just habit that made her keep herself nice. A mask to face the world. Even Terry, who had loved her looks or so he said, had not been the incentive that made her buy expensive clothes and shoes. She bought them because in her world what you wore said who you were. That 'clothes maketh not the man' was shite as far as she was concerned. They did, otherwise every designer label would have been out of business years ago.

She placed her head on the steering wheel once more and cried bitter tears. Terry's belongings were still at her bombed-out house and she knew at some point she would have to go back there. But she also knew that if she did, she would crack. If she saw a photo of him or smelt his aftershave she would buckle under and die. She had to keep him out of her mind and life or she knew she wouldn't survive, and the family needed her now more than ever. She wiped her eyes and lit a cigarette. As she smoked she felt herself becoming calmer. She pictured her brother Mickey in her mind's eye and smiled gently as she saw him smiling back at her. She missed him so much.

She heard her big brother's voice as she always did when she needed advice. She imagined what he would advise her and then made it her business to go along with what she thought he would want her to do.

As she sat quietly planning, a tap on the window startled her. It was Carla. Smiling, she opened the window and her niece's words gave her the jolt she needed to forget her own grief.

'Mum is in a seriously bad way, Maws. She was shot earlier this evening.'

Carla's tears came then and instantly brought Maura from the car to comfort her. Despite the closeness of their ages, she had always been a rock for Carla to cling to, more of a mother than Janine had ever been. She was about to go to the hospital with Carla when Garry called with the news about Vic Joliff.

Roy looked down on his wife's unconscious form and felt nothing. She had been shot twice, once in the chest and once in the legs. It was a similar shooting to that of Sandra Joliff. It was unbelievable to him that anyone would have brought such trouble to his home.

He glanced at Benny and saw the amazement on his face and knew he was feeling the same. Who could be behind all this? Who in their right mind would dare to take on the Ryans and make it so personal? Janine was his wife, albeit in name only nowadays, but it was the principle of it.

As he stared down at her he finally felt a stirring inside his breast. He remembered the lively redhead who had captured his heart all those years ago, and a lump formed in his throat. He should never have married her, never should have taken her from the security of her parents and their butcher's shop and pseudo-respectability. She had walked away from them for him and he had never realised just how hard that must have been for her. Then she had gone on to his mother's side, always preaching respectability. The two of them had formed a sanctimonious alliance that had exasperated and irritated him nearly all his married life.

Janine's hatred of Maura had been another bone of contention, and the way she constantly worried about Benny and what would become of him. As Roy stared at her now he knew that where their son was concerned at least she had been right. Benny was a cold-blooded thug. Not a villain, not a face as he liked to think he was, but a violent thug. No better than a football hooligan or a creeper. His whole life revolved around violence for violence's sake. He didn't use it wisely, he used it in his everyday life. Even a parking dispute could send him over the top.

Roy closed his eyes and took his wife's hand in his. She was cold; he had forgotten how soft her hands were. He looked down at the engagement ring he had bought her and the wedding band she had worn for so many years and felt the sting of tears. He would make it up to her, he promised himself. He would pretend if needs be, but he would make her happy once more if it was the last thing he did. It had taken this to make him see that she had been right, that all along their son was going to be like Michael but without his cunning. Benny was just violent whereas Michael had used force as a means to an end. Roy himself had helped break Janine's heart and put her on the drink. Would he ever be able to make amends?

If she died, someone would pay dearly for this night's work. They would pay anyway even if she lived.

He felt the urge to kill once more, felt the adrenaline pumping through his body. This was personal now. This was a piss take and he was not going to let it lie. Someone was going to pay for this affront, and pay dearly. He was determined on that much.

Janine's hand clenched in his. It was just a reaction, but he felt inside that she was telling him to go out and cause mayhem until the perpetrator was found.

He smiled gently down at her.

He would, for once, do exactly as she wanted.

Benny watched his mother and father in a detached way. It was fascinating to him to see his father's face, all the emotions on it. He secretly hoped his mother died. She was a pain as far as he was concerned, did nothing with her life except moan, and she was in league with the other bane of his life, his grandmother.

He sat quietly and willed her death even as his

father willed her to live. Such were the conflicting emotions around Janine's hospital bed.

Billy Mills answered his front door at three o'clock in the morning with a scowl on his face. Then, seeing Maura Ryan and her minder Tony Dooley, his face broke into a radiant smile. He had always liked Maura, always.

'Hello, Maws, all right?'

It was a greeting and a question as ever. He knew about the aggravation she faced but wasn't going to mention it until she did, which was only etiquette. Maura smiled and walked into his flat.

Billy lived in a penthouse at Barrier Point in East London. It was one of his many abodes. He was a fixer, and highly rated. Everyone liked him. Like his counterpart Kenny Smith he liaised with different firms while keeping himself completely neutral. It was a dangerous but lucrative business.

As Billy poured Maura a drink he watched her warily. He knew what had just happened to Vic Joliff and to the Ryan family, it was his job to make sure he knew everything, and it occurred to him that Maura was here either to ask his advice or to accuse him of working behind her back. It was a frightening realisation.

She knew this and sipped her drink silently for a few moments before saying: 'What do you know, Billy?'

She was shrewd enough not to tell him anything. She would first listen to what he had to say and then she would decide for herself.

He liked her, he always had. He hoped she still liked him after what he was about to tell her.

Lee snuggled up to Sheila on the Habitat sofa and said once more imploringly: 'Please, Sheila, take the kids and go to the house in Spain.'

She shook her head.

'Don't be so silly, Lee. They have school . . .'

He interrupted her.

'I ain't asking you, I am telling you. Now I mean it, Sheila. I will send someone out there with you, but you are going.' He stroked her expanding belly. 'Do this, Sheila, please. Do it for me.'

'No!'

She pulled herself up with difficulty.

'What on earth is all this about, Lee? Go to *Spain* with the kids, like we can just up and go on a whim? I have loads to sort out for this one here.' She patted her belly. 'Plus the kids are still at school, no holidays due. I refuse to take them out of their routine because of you. So just forget it, Lee.'

'Someone shot Janine tonight.'

He didn't want to tell her, did not want her to know anything about the business. She was kept in the dark by everyone and that was how he liked it. He watched the stillness on her face sorrowfully. He hadn't even mentioned the attack on his mother, it would be too much.

'What, shot her with a gun?'

He could hear the disbelief in her voice, see it in her stance.

'Why would anyone want to shoot Janine?'

She was getting hysterical and he grabbed her in a bear hug, trying to calm her down.

'Who's next then, the kids? Is this why you want me out of the way, in case I'm next on the list?'

She was white with fear.

'Oh, God. Oh, God. Someone is going to shoot me and my baby, aren't they?'

Her voice was now practically a scream and Lee was terrified.

'Of course not, babe, this is just a safety measure. No one will touch you or the kids, I promise. I just want you out of the way to make me feel better. Because I will be away a lot and I can't take proper care of you.'

He was babbling and he knew it.

Sheila threw him off; he was surprised at the strength of her.

'You bastard! You have brought fear into our home.'

'You're over-reacting . . .'

Her eyes stretched to their widest as she screamed, 'Over-reacting? Janine was *shot*, and you want me to run off to Spain, and I'm *over-reacting*? What fucking planet are you on, Lee?'

He could see the terror in her eyes, and as her

hands went to her belly and she doubled over in pain and fright he wished to God he had never entered the family business. But it was too late for thoughts like that because he *was* in it. In it over his head.

'I'm going, Lee. I'm going to me mum's right now. I ain't staying here to be murdered in me own home.'

He tried to take her into his arms once more but she pushed him away.

'Don't touch me. When you kept us out of your dealings I could live with it. Now you have brought trouble to my door . . .'

He remembered his mother saying the same words many years ago to his brother Michael and they saddened him. He knew his marriage would never recover from this night. Already he could see the revulsion in Sheila's eyes. He knew that she loved their children with a passion she had never felt for him in any way, shape or form. If she had the choice between him and the kids she would pick them any day of the week, and that was why he loved her so much. It was what had attracted him to her in the first place. Her homeliness, her family-mindedness. Now the same qualities were going to be the cause of a rift between them so great it might never be resolved.

He was sick at heart that this was happening. She was everything to him and so were his boys. Never once had they had a cross word, never once had they ever had to argue about anything. He had kept his work outside the home and never, ever mentioned it to her. It was something that had held them together; the fact she knew nothing had always made him feel that she was safe. Everyone knew she was a civilian, a real civilian. He never even took her out to the restaurants that were used by the likes of the Ryans and other criminal families. They went to Harvesters with the kids, for fuck's sake. Lee was the family man, it was his joke name. Other criminals always asked after his kids because they knew it was his only other interest in life. He kept away from the lap dancing and the strip clubs. Everyone knew he had no interest in all that shit. He had thought he was going to keep his kids safe, keep Sheila safe with his actions. But now someone had moved the fucking goalposts and he had put all those he loved in danger. Whoever heard of family being targeted before? It was like a fucking nightmare.

Now he had to contend with Sheila terrified out of her wits and holding it against him for the rest of their days. He knew that was what would happen, he knew her so well, especially with a belly full of arms and legs. She would be frightened for the new baby and the boys more than she would worry about herself.

Sheila's crying had brought four watchful pairs of eyes into the room with them. As he looked at the fear on his sons' faces Lee felt for the first time what his own mother must have done all these years, how she must have felt burying her dead sons, and for the first time ever he understood her.

Understood her hatred of their way of life.

To lose his brothers was bad enough but if he lost any of his children he would never recover. He shrank under their clear-eyed gaze because he knew they had heard all that had been said between him and their mother.

Sheila ran to them and cried, 'Pack! Pack your bags now, we're going to me mother's.'

She disappeared out of the room. As Lee watched her shepherd the kids up the stairs he had never felt so alone in his life.

Billy and Maura stared at one another for long moments before he finally answered her question.

'You won't like this, Maura, I warn you, and as it is just a rumour I need you to promise that you won't let on it came from me? I am telling you this as a favour between friends, no more.'

'Go on.'

'You've heard about Vic, I take it?'

She could feel the fear coming off him in waves. She nodded.

'Look towards Liverpool for the answers you want. Vic had dealings up there for a long time and he wanted what you've got.'

He saw her face blanch.

'You are joking, Billy?'

He smiled gently.

'Never been more serious in all my life. But remember, it never came from me.'

Maura was stunned and Billy poured her another drink. As he placed it in her hand she said quietly, 'Tell me what you know, from the beginning.'

# Chapter Five

'Please, Sheila, come back.'

Lee could hear the desperation in his own voice as he beseeched his wife not to walk away from him. His mobile was ringing and he knew he should answer it. If he didn't then Maura and the boys would think something had happened to him.

Sheila stopped on the way to her Mitsubishi jeep to say sarcastically, 'Answer the phone, Lee. Then you won't feel so bad about us going, will you? Your brothers will want you, and you being you will have to do as you're told.'

It was the first time she had ever said anything like that to him and it hurt.

'My work is my affair and you know that. We have never talked about it, especially not in front of the kids.'

The reprimand in his voice was what angered her to say, 'Your job has never intruded into our home before, has it? Even while I'm packing the car with clothes, I think someone might take a pot shot at us.'

'Don't be so fucking stupid . . .'

They both stopped and stared as they realised that he had actually sworn at her. Even the boys were shocked.

'I'm sorry, Sheila. Please don't leave me like this . . .'

She climbed into the jeep with difficulty and without a word drove away from him.

His phone rang again and he threw it to the ground and stamped on it, crunched it underfoot until it was just a small pile of plastic and microchips.

'Fuck, fuck, fuck, fuck . . .'

He was still saying the word when Garry pulled up on the drive half an hour later.

Tommy Rifkind lived in a large house in Chester, in the same turning as three Liverpool FC players and two well-known drugs barons. He loved it there. Gina, his wife of thirty years, had brought in an interior designer and the house now looked like something from a Space Age magazine. It wasn't to his taste but he knew it had the desired effect when he entertained here.

He also had a girlfriend called Simone, a half-caste girl with relaxed hair and doe eyes who was ready to marry him as and when he said the word. It wouldn't happen, but she didn't know that. His Gina was his best friend and life's partner; she also had breast cancer, though no one else had been told. He adored her, and she adored him. Simone was just one of his diversions and Gina, a sensible woman, realised that a man of Tommy's ilk needed a younger woman now and again and turned a blind eye. She was secure in the knowledge he would never leave her.

Their only child, Tommy Junior, had not spoken to his father for over ten years, since Tommy had been up on an armed robbery and conspiracy charge. Tommy Junior, who had gone to university and become a chemist, had actually believed until then that his father was a businessman. He was now married to a nice girl and had two little boys. Tommy Senior only saw them because of Gina's intervention, he knew that and loved her all the more for it. It was his constant lament that he gave his son a better start in life than he had ever had and the boy had thrown it back in his teeth.

Tommy Senior's illegitimate son by a woman called Lizzie from Toxteth was another kettle of fish; he was his father all over again. Only he didn't have his father's nous. He was a thug and this was something that grieved Tommy immensely. The boy was also called Tommy, but known as Tommy B due to his having his mother's maiden name of Bradshaw. Gina welcomed him into their home, another thing Tommy Senior loved her for.

As he watched his two grandsons splashing around in the indoor pool he was smiling. He shouted to his sidekick Joss Campion, 'Try the little bastard again, will you?'

Joss, a large man who looked like he should be in a Hammer Horror film, shrugged his massive shoulders.

'I just did, still no answer.'

Tommy looked puzzled.

They walked through to one of the spacious lounges and as Tommy poured himself a drink he heard the front door being opened.

He smiled at Joss.

'At fucking last!'

He turned towards the door and was shocked to see Maura Ryan standing there, framed like a painting. For a second he wasn't sure who she was.

'What . . .'

'Hello, Tommy, long time no see.'

Her voice had always had the power to make him falter. He had fancied her for years even if he was nervous of her. It was something about her. That coldness in her attracted him. He knew he was the same in many ways.

Joss, always embarrassed around women, went bright red. Maura looked at him and smiled gently before saying, 'Well, leave something on me, Joss, I might catch cold.'

Tommy laughed, as did Maura.

'What brings you up here then?'

'How about a drink first?'

'Of course.'

Maura studied him. Even in his fifties Tommy was still a good-looking man, dark-haired and light-skinned though his eyes betrayed his heritage. His grandfather was a West Indian docker and it had come out in Tommy Rifkind in his eyes. He had a naturally elegant build, and liked to dress in handmade suits. Maura was sorry for what she had to do here this morning. She liked Tommy, always had. But this was family at stake and Tommy would realise what that meant.

As he handed her a Scotch he said sadly, 'Is this trouble, Maura?'

She took the proffered drink and nodded.

'I'm afraid so, Tommy. Big trouble.'

Janine was still fighting for her life and Roy sat by her bed gently holding her hand. A bruised-looking Sarah was beside him, her rosary beads the only sound in the room other than the beeping of the monitors.

Roy found her presence strangely comforting. It reminded him of when he was a kid and there was a thunderstorm. His mother would cover all the mirrors and close the curtains and the kids would all sit in the dark and say the rosary. It had driven Michael and Garry mad, but he had liked it. It had made him feel safe.

Janine's face was so pale and tired-looking, and deep inside he knew he had put every line on it. He felt such guilt as he watched over her, wishing he could take her place in the hospital bed so she would not have to be in pain. He felt protective of her for the first time in years.

A nurse came into the room and broke the spell. He let go of his wife's hand and stretched in the chair.

'Go and have a coffee, I'll watch over her for you, son. You need a break,' Sarah said.

He stood up gratefully.

'Thanks, Mum. I appreciate all this.'

Sarah shrugged.

'Sure, wasn't I always there for you all if you had only realised it?'

'Shall I get you a cup of tea, Mum?'

She nodded.

'I'm getting too old for all this, you know. I won't be long for the top, Roy, and to be honest I am looking forward to it. Your poor father, God rest him, at least has the comfort of his sons at peace with him.'

Her voice was clogged with tears and Roy put his arms around her. Once more he was reminded of how old she was, how frail.

'Can you imagine for one moment how I've felt over the years, son? Burying child after child, and not through illness, oh, no. My sons were murdered, butchered like animals, and I have to live with that knowledge every day of my life. Now look at Janine, look at the mother of your son, caught up in all this because even at your advanced ages you can't be normal people. Can't live like decent men and women. Benny is going the same way and I hope to Christ you never have to identify your own flesh and blood on a mortuary slab, that's me prayer every day.'

She looked back at Janine, her face closed now, and Roy walked from the room. But her words went with him as he went for the teas, as Sarah had known they would. She prayed as her son walked away from her.

'Holy Mary, Mother of God, make my son see the error of his ways. Let one of my children face Christ humbly and with the love of God in his heart.'

Benny and Abul were pulled up on the A13 as they were driving towards the Canning Town flyover. They were stopped by two young policemen in a panda car. The PCs had plenty of attitude and trouble in mind. They were about to find out what happened when you came up against two like-minded individuals with positively no respect for authority.

Benny pulled over while Abul flicked the joint butt from the window.

'What can we do for you, officers?'

Benny was taunting them with words and attitude and he knew it. More to the point, the two PCs knew it.

'Get out of the motor.'

Benny and Abul looked at one another in disbelief.

'I beg your pardon? On whose authority are you making such a request? We were within the speed limit, we were driving carefully and we have our seat belts on. I want to know, as my democratic right, what you are pulling us over for?'

Abul was already laughing. Benny's accent when he was trying to be posh always cracked him up.

'What are you fucking laughing at?'

Abul stopped laughing immediately and the two PCs thought they had scored an important point. Then, as Benny and Abul undid their seat belts, they realised they had aggravation on their hands. Once out of the car, the two men went straight to the boot, reappearing seconds later with baseball bats covered in duct tape.

'After you,' Benny said, waving one hand.

Abul chuckled again.

'No, after *you*.'

The two men then set about the PCs with the baseball bats, loudly cheered on by passing motorists.

Benny and Abul were doing bows to passing cars when DI Featherstone screeched to a halt next to them and told them in no uncertain terms to piss off out of it and stop showing off; he would take it from here. As one of their 'friendly' filth it was his job to act the ambassador and get the two injured men not to press charges.

'You'd better sit down, Tommy mate.'

Joss picked up the tremor in Maura's voice and brought the whisky bottle over to the side table near them. He knew they would need it. The fact that

Maura Ryan was here in Liverpool in person spoke volumes as far as he was concerned. He also had a good idea what she was here for as well, but he kept his own counsel.

Tommy looked amazed when Maura, sitting beside him, grasped his hand and squeezed it.

'I know exactly how you'll be feeling in the next few minutes, I have been there. But remember, this isn't personal, it's just business. I didn't want this but it has been taken out of my hands.

'Your boy, Tommy B, brought guns and trouble into my family's homes. Their fucking homes, for Christ's sake! And it was for nothing, Tommy. Nothing. He has been the perpetrator of the death of partners, and I mean as in wives not business associates . . .'

Tommy was shaking his head.

'No, you're wrong, Maura. He's a little fucker, I admit that, but he ain't got the fucking nous to take you lot on . . .'

'Not the nous, no, but the heart. He certainly had that. I know how you are feeling, Tommy, but this has to be done. Even you must understand as much.'

She watched the play of emotions on Tommy's face and her heart went out to him.

'I can't let it go. He tried to make it look like we were out for a full-scale war and we couldn't understand it. We routed everyone in an attempt to find out what the fuck was going on. Then Roy's wife was shot twice on her own doorstep . . .'

Tommy's dark eyes widened.

'You are fucking joking?'

'I wish I was. It's been a waking nightmare. I will fill you in on all the details when you feel able to take them in. Now have another drink.'

'Is he dead yet?'

Tommy Rifkind's voice was flat, devoid of emotion.

Maura nodded.

'Good as. Garry and Lee snatched him from his flat. You realise they'll have to make an example of him?'

Tommy Rifkind put his head into his hands and cried like a baby.

'Not Garry, Maura . . .'

She looked at him and felt a flicker of sympathy for a man brought so low that he was crying in front of her. She hardened her heart and her voice.

'He insisted, Tommy. We have to send out an important message to others, don't we? Tommy B's associates need to know who and what they are dealing with. We'll get to them in due course.'

Joss poured them all another drink and Maura was glad of the burn as the alcohol hit the back of her throat.

'There was no negotiating then?'

Maura shook her head once more.

'Don't be silly. Would you negotiate if it was you?'

'This will kill his mother.'

Maura shrugged once more.

'Shit happens. Eh, Joss?'

He nodded dumbly. Fortunately he was known to be a man of few words. If he'd opened his mouth now he'd have started bawling like Tommy.

Gina came into the room and, seeing her husband crying, went to him. She pulled him from the chair and led him out of the room, nodding in a friendly way to Maura as she passed her.

Maura looked at Joss and said, 'I told her the score on the phone. I always got on with Gina. I knew Tommy would need someone once he heard the news.'

'Was the lad in with Vic Joliff then?'

Joss's voice was heavy and harsh from disuse.

Maura nodded.

'Ambitious little bastard he was,' Joss said. 'Born in him, I suppose.'

'Who's that, Joss? Tommy B?'

He nodded. 'A word to the wise, Miss Ryan. Before you finish off Joliff, find out who else was in with him. He wouldn't have done anything this big on his own. He's a heavy, not a mastermind.'

'Thanks, Joss, but I already sussed that out for myself. Vic Joliff's safely in prison hospital at the moment with a slit throat. He's going nowhere till we get to him.'

Tommy B was crying, sobbing in fact, deep racking sobs that shook his whole body.

'Oh, for fuck's sake – I'll ask you again, shall I? Who else is in this? You know a lot of my family's business – how? Want something to prick your memory, do you?'

Garry's voice bounced off the walls of the Portakabin in Tommy Rifkind's breaker's yard. Almost casually he passed an electric saw over the man's trussed legs.

At first Tommy B couldn't speak; his eyes were glazed with shock. Garry kicked him then and his mouth strained in a silent scream.

'I – I told you – all I know,' he moaned. 'It was Joliff who gave me my orders. It had to be him running things. Now, please – finish it!'

His bloodshot eyes met Lee's imploringly. Behind Garry's back he nodded then stepped around his brother holding a heavy torch. He swung back his arm and crashed it into the side of Tommy B's skull. The tortured man slipped thankfully into unconsciousness.

Garry was narked.

'Hold up, Lee. Keep your hair on. You shouldn't have jumped the gun.'

Lee turned on his brother.

'That's fucking rich, that is, coming from the biggest nutter this side of the Atlantic. What's the matter? Want me to keep him *awake* while you cut off his arms and legs? He's told us all he knows. He said it was him who done Sandra Joliff too, though fuck knows why. No one takes that much punishment when they can buy themselves out of it.'

Garry was offended and it showed.

'Telling me my business, are ya? Do you want a smack in the mouth or what? You've had the right hump since we left London. All the way up the M1 it was like sitting with a big kid.' He started doing a childish voice. ' "How long till we get there?" I nearly started singing "Ten Green fucking Bottles" to keep you amused!'

Lee laughed despite himself.

'Piss off.'

'Come on, what's wrong?'

'Sheila left me.'

Garry shrugged. 'Well, you can't blame her. All this must have given her one up. I know it did me. Imagine how she must be feeling, especially in the club and all. 'Course she would be worried. She'll be back by the end of the week.'

Garry saw the hope on his brother's face and hugged him.

'Relax, Lee, everything is going to be OK. You and her are like the fucking Brady Bunch. Now help me get him on the table so we can do what we said and go home.'

'Do we *have* to cut his arms and legs off?'

Garry looked at Lee as if he was mad.

'Of course not, but it will give people something to talk about, won't it? And let's face it, everyone will know it was me and you who done it so we enhance our lunatic rating *and* stop any more fucking part-timers trying to take over our patch. Good business practice.'

Lee grinned, happier now that Garry had put his mind at rest about Sheila.

'Well, if you put it like that!'

'See, Bruv, you know it makes sense. Now pass me that electric saw.'

Maura and Joss had to wait half an hour before Tommy Rifkind came back into the room. It was obvious he was still devastated but he had regained his equilibrium. Maura slowly filled him in on what had happened.

She started with the deaths of Lana Smith and Sandra Joliff, watching the changing expressions on his face as he realised just what his son had been party to.

'Joliff was attacked in Belmarsh, not an easy feat in itself and we still don't know who was behind that, but we are assuming he stepped on a few other toes in the course of his scheming. He's still alive, by all accounts. We will be paying him a visit in the future.'

'My boy was used by Joliff then?'

Maura shrugged.

'Or Joliff was used by someone and brought Tommy B into it with him. I don't know yet. We are gradually piecing things together. It was the car bomb at my home that really caused the hag with me brothers, and of course with me. I will not be threatened by anyone, and whatever Terry was to everyone else he was my partner in more ways than one.'

She finished her drink and waited while Joss poured her another. It would give them time to digest this piece of logic.

'I am sorry about this, Tommy, really. But you understand we had no choice in the matter? Especially after someone slapped me mother as well. I mean, no one is going to swallow that, are they?'

Tommy shook his head and sighed.

'Stupid little fucker he was. Wouldn't be told. Thought he knew it all. It's a different world now, Maura. The youngsters are a law unto themselves. He had his fingers in so many pies . . . lap dancing clubs, prostitution, you name it.'

'How about drugs? That is Joliff's preferred game.'

Tommy nodded.

'We're all into that now, Maura, be honest. It's the biggest money-spinner of them all.'

'But I understand your boy was into crack? That's not a legitimate business as far as I'm concerned.'

Even Joss was amazed at Maura Ryan's double standards.

'It's still cocaine, Maura, whatever way you dress it up.'

'Well, I leave that to the younger members of the family. Personally I hate it all. Never dealt in skag or crack.'

'What about the new one then? This crank or whatever it's called.' Joss seemed genuinely interested in her reply.

Maura smiled.

'A bit of puff is about my mark these days, that's practically respectable now.' Her mobile rang and she answered it. She looked at Tommy Rifkind.

'I am sorry, Tommy, it's over.'

He nodded and Maura was amazed by the way he took the news of his own child's death. Still, if the alternative was the continued ministrations of Garry and his saw she supposed any parent would look relieved.

Sarah and Roy kept vigil together.

At 3.28 on the morning of the second day Janine breathed her last. A blood clot found its way to her heart and she was dead in seconds.

Roy sat holding her hand for hours afterwards; it was only when Carla came in with Joey that he finally stopped. He held his daughter then as if he would never let her go, sobs shaking his whole body.

'She's gone, Carla, and no one else was here with her. Neither of her kids was with her.'

Carla didn't say anything, she just held her father. As she looked at her mother's body she was ashamed to find that she felt nothing for her. Janine had ignored her own daughter nearly all her life and now she was gone. It seemed only her father was weighed down with the burden of her death. He had aged within hours, and the haunted look in his eyes would stay with her all her life.

She was saying a prayer with him when a dapper Benny breezed into the room.

Roy's voice was ravaged with hurt and guilt.

'She's gone, Ben, your mum is gone.'

'Look at your mother, child, and remember all your life that you helped to kill her.' Sarah's voice was cold as she spoke to her grandson.

'You know what they say, don't you, Gran? "What's bred in the blood comes out in the bone". Remember that next time you get the urge to preach to me,' he taunted her.

He looked his mother over briefly and left the room. Carla and Joey followed in his wake.

Sarah looked at Roy sadly.

'You've lost him to Maura like I lost all of you to her years ago. You'll bury him, Roy, you mark my words. You will bury him, and as God is my witness I hope you have to do it sooner rather than later. He is dangerous, my Michael all over again. But whereas Michael had a heart inside his body, that child has nothing but hatred.'

Roy didn't answer her because he knew she spoke the truth.

Meanwhile Tommy B's mother was identifying her son's head in a mortuary at Liverpool General Hospital.

As she screamed at the fates and cursed whoever had done this to her son she was thankfully unaware that the two men responsible were back in the smoke where for them it was business as usual.

As far as Garry and Lee were concerned, Tommy B was forgotten already.

But his father wouldn't forget. And neither would Vic Joliff.

The prison medics had been too quick to write him off. Joliff was stronger and more cunning, even after losing five pints of blood, than anyone had realised. With his head held on by stitches, he still managed to throttle the dozy PO standing guard by his bed and force him to unlock the shackles. He put the unconscious screw under the sheet and hid himself in a hamper of dirty laundry, timing his escape for the early-morning collection. He later overwhelmed the driver, and the van was found abandoned on the Kent coast.

After that he seemed to vanish into thin air. There were no further sightings; no body ever turned up.

The Ryans were beside themselves. There were too many loose ends altogether about this business. One of the most annoying was that Joliff was rumoured to have become close to one of their own police friendlies. It seemed Chief Inspector Billings had been stupid enough to accept sweeteners from the Ryans' rival too. Maura couldn't afford to leave this unexplored – or unpunished. She gave Benny carte blanche to find out what he could.

Chief Inspector Roland Billings was eating dinner with his wife and daughters when there was a resounding knock at the front door. He loved the house, a double-fronted detached in the best part of Brentwood. He assumed the visitor was something to do with him, it usually was in the evening. He was not expecting Benny Ryan and his Indian sidekick, though. He heard Ryan speaking before he saw him.

'Is Roly in, my dear?'

He used a mock-posh accent but the hint of menace in it was not lost on either Roland Billings or his wife Dolores. As he rose from his chair Billings' heart was already halfway into his mouth.

Benny walked into the room as if he owned it. Looking around him at the three young girls sitting there with mouths agape, he said heartily, 'Can't see these three on the bash, can you, Abul? Not with them braces on their teeth anyway. Give them a few years though, eh, Mr Billings? They'll cook up lovely then. Just how you like them, young and impressionable. Those are the ones you like, ain't they?'

Dolores was already shepherding the girls from the room and Abul smiled widely at her as he helped.

'Keep them upstairs and stay there yourself, love. Do not make any phone calls until we are gone or there will be real trouble, OK? We just want to talk for the moment.'

Dolores was forty-six years old and well-preserved. She was aware that her husband kept a lot of cash in the house and like many a woman before her had spent it without much thought as to how it was obtained. Now she had an inkling how he'd arrived by the money and she was scared.

Abul said quietly, 'This ain't a game, love. Your old man is in deep shit, and if his superiors get wind of this visit he will be in even bigger shit. Now take the girls and keep quiet no matter what. OK?'

She nodded and hastened to get them away from the two terrifying intruders.

Roland Billings sat back at his dining table with a feeling of extreme sickness in his gut.

'What the hell do you think you are doing in my home?'

His voice sounded far stronger than he felt.

Benny laughed. 'But I thought we was mates, Roland. Me and you and me Aunt Maura. You remember Maura, the one who gives you all that money regular as clockwork?'

He looked around him admiringly. There were two long-case clocks in the dining room alone. There was a large London clock in the hall and numerous carriage clocks scattered around on tables and the mantelpiece. Billings was obviously a serious collector.

'She would be pleased to see what you spent it on

and all. Likes a bit of the old clock, does Maura. Like yourself, see.'

'Get out of my fucking home and take the monkey with you!'

Even Benny was shocked at the hatred in the other man's voice.

'Don't tell me you're racist, Mr Billings?'

His voice was incredulous. He looked at Abul and they both laughed as his mate said scathingly, 'He is definitely filth, eh, Ben?'

Benny was laughing loudly again and Billings was amazed that his own racism would make a criminal like Benny Ryan look down even further on him than he already did because he was a policeman.

'I want you both out of here now.' His voice was harsh but the nervous edge in it was there for anyone to hear.

'But we're your mates, Roland. Me and old Abul here. We pay your wages, my old son, so your daughters can go to a good school and you can get your cock sucked by little girls round the Cross.'

'You are *not* my friends . . .'

'Oh, hark at him, Abul. Well, Roland, my old granny has a saying: "Show me the company you keep and I'll tell you what you are". So what does that make you then?'

Billings stood up.

'Get out of my home, Ryan.'

Benny's voice was dangerously quiet as he said,

'Don't fucking strong it, Mr Billings, because I am really going to hurt you anyway. We know, you see. We know everything now thanks to a visit we made to Liverpool. Vic Joliff was using the Scallies to stir up trouble for us. Now he's on the lam and we think he's had some official help, if you get my drift.'

They watched the policeman sit back down, the fight drained from him.

'Bad, ain't it, Mr Billings, how people can die in their beds of gunshot wounds and other self-inflicted troubles?'

The threat was far from lost on the man before them and they knew it.

'You was up Joliff's arse, mate. Took his money *and* ours. You two-faced piece of shit cunt! My mother was shot on her own doorstep, did you know that? And the worst of it all was she had nothing to do with the family firm. I didn't even like her as it happens but that ain't the fucking point, is it? How would you like it if I shot your wife and daughters, eh? Fuck you right off, wouldn't it?'

Billings stared up at him without blinking. The threats were mounting with every sentence and the terror inside him was building.

'I mean, imagine anyone thinking they could get one over on the Ryans. You wouldn't ever have thought that yourself, would you, Mr Billings? A sensible man like you.'

Billings was shaking his head so fast he felt faint.

'Good man. But I'm sure you realise that some hands have got to be slapped and we thought we'd put you top of the shit list, seeing as how you and Vic were always so pally.'

Benny turned up his own hands in a 'nothing else I can do' gesture and Abul started to laugh loudly, which made Billings more frightened than ever. He knew that whatever happened to him, they would enjoy doing it.

'Look,' he faltered, 'not here . . . not in my home . . .'

Benny was grinning now, and it was a terrifying expression.

'Oh, it's fucking all right to bring guns and trouble to *my* family's homes but not yours? Is that what you think?'

As he spoke he smashed the dinner plates on the floor. The sound echoed through the house and in the distance Benny could hear the crying of the woman and the girls upstairs.

Picking up a fork from the debris, he stuck it forcibly into the back of the policeman's hand, momentarily pinning him to the table top. Then, yanking the man up by his shirtfront, he dragged him protesting through to the kitchen. There was a big pot of water boiling on the Aga. It had spaghetti inside and was obviously the next course of their dinner.

Benny plunged an unresisting Billings' hand into

the pot and watched with glee as the man screamed in pain.

'I bet that fucking hurts a treat, don't it? You must tell Vic all about it the next time you have a chat.'

He pulled the blistering hand from the pot.

'Where is he, Billings? You helped him, didn't you?'

'A-Across the Ch-Channel, that's all. I don't know where he went then. I swear! He was messed up very badly, could be dead . . .'

He was going into shock. Abul stared at his hand. It was red as a lobster and he knew the pain must be excruciating.

Benny held on to his temper for a few beats before he rammed the hand back into the water once more.

Billings finally lost consciousness. When he slid to the floor Benny kicked him in the head with all the force he could muster and splashed scalding water over his face.

As they walked away Abul slipped on the spaghetti that was strewn everywhere. Benny started to laugh and by the time they were in the car they were both in hysterics. They lit a joint and drove away, Shaggy blaring out of the quadrophonic sound system and shattering the peace of the desirable neighbourhood.

Maura finally buried Terry Petherick, but after all that had happened recently she found she couldn't keep her attention on the simple ceremony. It felt as if her mother's accusing eyes were boring into her body.

None of the boys came and she was glad. It was a poor turnout all round but she was glad about that as well. She felt she had closed a chapter in her life. She wasn't to know that the most daunting part of the story still lay ahead of her.

As she clutched Carla's hand she felt at peace for the first time in years. It wouldn't last, but then as Maura had said herself many times, her life had never been peaceful.

Her old pals Marge and Dennis Dawson were beside her as she cried her last tears for Terry Petherick, the man they had introduced her to in another time, another place, an innocent world she could never hope to inhabit again.

# Book Two

'Be not deceived; God is not mocked: for Whatsoever a man soweth, that shall he also reap'

– *Galatians, 6, vii*

# Chapter Six

*2000*

'Happy birthday, Maws.'

Maura was woken by Joey and Carla jumping on her bed like maniacs.

'The big five-O, Maws. What's it feel like?'

She laughed.

'You'll know soon enough, Carla. In five years to be precise. Now where's me breakfast in bed? I am practically a pensioner now, I'll need help being fed.'

'They say that fifty is the new forty, Aunt Maura.'

Joey giggled. At nearly twenty he was still like a young boy, and though it didn't bother Maura, it bothered his mother. He was big like all the Ryan men, but he was effeminate with it. He was a mummy's boy as Benny was always pointing out, and even though he said it for a joke Carla found it hard to laugh with the others. She watched as Joey slipped into bed with his aunt and had to swallow down her irritation. He was too old for all this skitting about and she was going to tell him as much very soon.

She grabbed his arm and said heartily, 'Up and out, you. Get Maws her breakfast while I give her the presents and cards.'

He got out of the bed and his eyes spoke volumes as he looked his mother over. He walked from the room in a huff.

Maura smiled ruefully.

'You might as well get your head round it, Carla, he's gay or my name ain't Maura Ryan. Let him be, for God's sake. It's no big deal.'

Carla didn't answer. She looked so like her mother when she was cross or upset. She had the same red-brown hair and green eyes. Even at forty-five she was a good-looking woman and her slimness gave her the look of someone much younger.

The doorbell rang and a few minutes later Joey came into the room with a huge bunch of flowers. Maura laughed with pleasure and when she opened the card her eyes were bright.

'They're from Tommy Rifkind, wishing me a happy birthday. At least he didn't write "fiftieth" on them so that's in his favour.'

Joey left the bedroom singing 'Love Is In the Air' and Maura laughed again.

Carla smiled.

'He's mad on you, Maura, and he's a nice bloke. I wish he was after me, I'd give in like a shot.'

'Really?'

At the question Carla started grinning like a Cheshire cat and nodded. 'I wouldn't kick him out of bed.'

Maura gave a dirty chuckle.

'Neither did I!'

They screamed with laughter once more, like two teenagers discussing the merits of their latest beaus.

'Is he any good? Bet he is, he looks the rooty type.'

Maura pursed her mouth.

'My lips are sealed.'

Carla shrugged.

'Your legs ain't apparently!'

'You cheeky mare!'

'Open your presents before Graham Norton gets back with your breakfast.' Carla's voice was sarcastic now.

'Don't say that, Carla, he's a good kid.' The laughter had gone from Maura's voice.

Carla sighed. 'I know. But I don't like it, Maura. It ain't natural.'

'Who are we to say what natural is? Remember me dad with a drink in him? "Jesus must have been gay 'cos he hung around with twelve blokes and a prostitute"!'

'Don't let your mother hear you saying that one!'

Five minutes later Maura had her breakfast and Joey and Carla were gone from the room. As she ate her scrambled eggs and smoked salmon she thought about Tommy Rifkind and their new relationship.

He had taken the death of his son badly, and Maura

had understood that. Then out of the blue he had come to London and from courtesy Maura had wined and dined him. They had been nothing but friends until Tommy's wife had died of cancer two and a half years ago. Maura had travelled to Liverpool with Garry for the funeral; it was good PR though her sympathy was genuine. Everyone knew who had topped Tommy's boy and the fact they were seen together gave them all a measure of protection.

But the friendship had slowly turned from mutual respect to something different. Tommy was suddenly in London nearly every weekend and Maura, naturally, was his companion on some of his jaunts. It had been nearly two years before they bedded one another and that was due more to drink than anything else, but it had set the seal on things and they had started a relationship. Now she wondered where it was to go. Where it could go. As it stood she was the bigger fish of the two, being the front for the Ryan businesses. Though Tommy was a face in Liverpool, in London he was small-time in many respects. She was shrewd enough to know that an alliance between them would be far more beneficial to Tommy than it would be to her, a fact also pointed out by Garry on many occasions.

But Tommy's rough love-making, so different from Terry's, and innate honesty when he spoke of himself and his life, brought him closer to her than all the flowery words or caresses could ever do. She had heard through the grapevine that he had even elbowed his long-term girlfriend for her and she gave him credit for that. He had realised that, unlike a wife, she wouldn't settle for anything on the side. Maura's whole life depended on respect: the respect of her peers and especially the respect of her enemies. She wondered again what was to become of them both.

She put out her arm and stroked the pillow where his head had lain so many times. He helped ease the loneliness inside her. She still missed Terry even as she was making another life without him. Gradually his photos had been relegated to inferior positions around the house; in her bedroom he was now in the dressing-table drawer. It hurt her to see them smiling at one another, it hurt her even to think of him, so she just deleted him from her life and her mind. She was good at that, she had had to be.

From a child when her brother Anthony had been murdered in prison by their business rival Stavros she had learned how to put things on the back burner and leave them there until they dried out and disappeared completely. It was how she had survived, and in truth she didn't know any other way. Michael had taught her well, and how she wished he was here now with her. She still missed him so very much.

The phone rang and disturbed her reverie. It was a working day as usual and she took the call and put everything else from her mind. She still had businesses to run and couldn't afford to lie abed daydreaming, even on such a landmark birthday.

As she stepped under the shower later she said under her breath, 'Fuck fifty.'

Sarah put the finishing touches to her daughter's birthday cake and hoped that Roy and Garry would successfully get her round to try and bury the hatchet. Sarah was eighty-seven now and felt her time was near. She wanted to make her peace with Maura if she could. Since Janine's death Roy was like a different man; he went to Mass more often and had a quietness about him that made her feel more comfortable in his company. It was his idea for them finally to call a truce and try and build some bridges, though privately Sarah thought Isambard Kingdom Brunel would have trouble building a bridge as wide as the one needed now.

But if she made things up with Maura, her grandson might come back into her life as well. So she would try. She would try her hardest. Even though inside she still couldn't stand the vicious bitch she'd given birth to.

Sarah said a Novena to Mary the Mother of God because of her unnatural thoughts. But she knew what was still in her heart even if no one else but God could see that far.

Roy and Benny were finishing breakfast. They shared a closeness that had always been there, but since

Janine's death Roy had found himself the needier of the two. He wanted his son round him now more than ever, wanted to try and calm him down even if he knew in his heart that he was fighting a lost cause.

'All right, Dad, I have to get off for a few hours. I have an announcement to make today at Maura's do.'

'What's that then?'

'It's a surprise. But a nice one.'

Roy closed his eyes before saying quietly, 'You ain't killed anyone, have you?'

Benny laughed.

'For fuck's sake, Dad, of course not. Anyone would think I was a right nutter if they listened to you!'

It was on the tip of his father's tongue to say that he was and they both knew it. Roy looked away first.

Benny grabbed his father's hand and said seriously, 'You know what the doctor said. Take it easy, Dad.'

News of Roy's breakdown after Janine's death had reverberated throughout the criminal underworld and now he was a Ryan in name only. But no one disrespected him because he was still Maura's brother and Benny's father, and now Benny was taking over with Garry as undisputed Kings of the Underworld. Their combined lunacy was enough to set the pulses of the most hardened criminals racing because there was no reason to what they did. They took offence at anything and dealt out instant retribution without a second's thought.

In short everyone was terrified of them, including

their own teams. People in the firm and outside wondered how long Maura was going to be able to control them. Even she wondered it herself at times.

Roy knew only too well that his son was capable of causing trouble of cataclysmic proportions. It was just a matter of time. He would bring them all down then and this was what frightened Roy the most.

'Tell me, son, what have you done now?'

It was the terminology that hurt Benny most. He looked wounded, his deep blue eyes innocent as a child's.

'I ain't done nothing, Dad. Not a thing, as hard as that may be for you to believe.'

He left the house minutes later and Roy took one of his antidepressants as he always did when troubled. All the time his son was speaking, he had seen his dead wife's face as she had implored him not to let Benny anywhere near the family business. The fact she had been right had preyed on his mind for so long he would be lost without all the worry and the fear.

Roy was his mother's son all right. Even he realised that now. He had bred a lunatic, like his brother Michael before him had been a lunatic, and the knowledge was almost too much for him to bear.

Sheila and Lee were getting the children ready for school. Lee was going to drop them all off in his brand-new people carrier. They needed it. Five sons and a daughter were a handful for anyone, and Sheila had only just relented and got herself a mother's help. The girl was young, pretty and willing in more ways than one. As she smiled at Lee over the heads of his two youngest sons he felt the urge to tell her to fuck off, but Sheila liked her and wouldn't have a word said against her.

His wife had been different since Janine's death. Terry's murder had bothered her too but she'd always accepted that Maura might have trouble at her door. It had never occurred to her that they might be in danger too. Now she was harder, more protective of the children, and as much as he loved her Lee found it all very wearing. It had taken the birth of their fifth son Jerome to get her to come back home and even then she had only consented when he had found a house like a fortress.

But he had complied with her wishes because he loved her so very much and adored his children with a passion. Sheila had remained a bundle of nerves for a while but when Roy had finally fallen out of his shopping trolley it had been she who had visited him and helped him get back on his feet.

She had also become very close to Lee's mother, and that bothered him, because he knew Sarah worked behind the scenes to try and make her children into what she wanted, as opposed to what they were.

Sheila really believed that the people-carrier had bullet-proof windows, and instead of this making him smile it made him sad. She was as paranoid as Roy now. She was also letting herself go, something he'd never thought would happen. After all the kids he had to expect a bit of a difference in her body, but she ate like a horse now and it was showing on her.

It was her attitude that bothered him most, though. She talked to him as if he was stupid and it was wearing him down. Twice he had been on the verge of telling her to shut her trap but had stopped himself in time. She had the power, and knew it, and used it. What had happened to his lovely little wife?

He knew his eldest son was starting to rebel under his mother's ministrations and felt for the boy. He also knew that Gabriel wanted him to stick up for him but he couldn't, not if he wanted to keep his wife and children by his side.

He would talk to Maura about it all. He had to get it off his chest and she was the best bet. Garry would just advise him to give Sheila a right-hander – though maybe he had a point. After all, they ran their empire through fear and Lee knew it was a great leveller. For today, though, he just did what was required and kept his mouth shut. What else could he do?

Tommy Rifkind was driving down the M1 at over a hundred miles an hour in his favourite from his fleet of flash cars – a metallic blue Rolls-Royce Corniche. He was looking forward to tonight. He was going to meet Maura's mother for the first time and felt that was a real step forward. He knew he was meeting her because it was a surprise party and not because Maura had arranged it, but the fact Lee had invited him spoke volumes. He was now classed as officially part of her life and that was exactly what he wanted to be.

Joss Campion was sitting in the passenger seat looking nervous. He hated it when his boss wanted to drive himself because he thought Tommy was a crap driver and said so on many occasions.

'Fucking slow down, willya?'

His Liverpool accent was even more pronounced with fear running through his body.

Tommy laughed.

'Now remember, you, best behaviour round her mother's. No drinking and slurping like you usually do – and no fucking swearing! She's really religious by all accounts.'

'You've said this fifty times already.'

Tommy laughed again.

'You need telling, Joss, you know what you're like. Remember how my wife used to carry on about you?'

Joss grinned and his face looked far less frightening.

'I miss Gina, don't you?'

Tommy slowed the car to seventy-five and said sadly, ''Course I do. More than I ever thought possible. But she's gone and I'm still here and life is for the living, mate.'

'If you had the choice, Maura or Gina back, who would you choose?'

Tommy put his foot down again and answered with a shout. 'Don't ask such fucking stupid questions.'

He was annoyed and Joss knew he was. But they both knew the answer and Maura wasn't in it.

Garry kissed his girlfriend Mary lustily and she kissed him back with all the fervour of a seventeen-year-old girl.

Garry was amazed at how much he liked her. From the first time he had seen her lap dancing in his club he had known he would possess her and had set out to do just that. Even her extreme youth had not put him off; in fact, it was a big part of the attraction.

From her blonde hair to her red-painted toenails she was the epitome of all he had hated in women previously, and yet it was this that most attracted him now. She was a slag and he knew she was a slag; she had been round the turf more times than Red Rum. It was the taming of her that appealed to him. Even when he gave her a clump she took it and didn't turn on the tears. She was so desperate for him to love her that she was willing to put up with anything.

And he was obsessed with her: with her little breasts that she was desperate to have surgically enhanced, and with her limited intelligence. He couldn't keep his hands off her yet he still wanted her to work. He knew she wanted him jealous enough to stop her having to dance five nights a week. She hated the pole dancing and she hated the lap dancing. It had been a means to an end and he knew he was the wallet on legs she'd always had in mind. Now it was common knowledge she was Garry's bird no one wanted her to dance for them anyway.

She stamped her little foot when he told her she was working tonight and Garry laughed harder and kissed her again. He sneaked a look at his watch and decided he could squeeze in a quick fuck before he went out for the day.

Once he entered her he was lost. She knew it was the only hold she had over him and used it shamelessly.

'It's good, eh, Gal?'

He groaned his pleasure and then shattered her dreams by whispering in her ear as he pulled himself out of her, 'Like a fucking Dyson down there, girl.' Slapping her rump, he roared, 'Now I *am* bastard late, thanks to you!'

But eventually he finished off what she had started and that made her feel a tiny bit better.

Carol Parsons was really pleased to see the man at her front door. 'Hello, Benny.' The joy in her voice was more than evident. 'Why didn't you use your key?'

He'd moved her into his own place three months ago and Carol still couldn't believe her luck.

'I saw a strange car outside so I thought I'd better knock in case I was interrupting something.'

Carol's face dropped.

'Don't be silly, Benny. It's me brother Trevor's mate, he dropped off a laptop for me.'

Benny raised his eyebrows.

'A laptop? That's a new one.'

Carol was nearly crying.

'Please, Benny, not now.'

A tall blond boy with a handsome face and an athletic build walked out into the hall. Benny disliked him on sight.

'All right, mate?'

Benny shook his head sadly.

' "All right, mate?" Is that all you can say when I come to my house and find you here with my bird?'

The boy went white with fright.

'Hang on a minute . . .'

Carol had had enough.

'Go home, Paul. Just go home, there's no reasoning with him when he's like this.'

Benny thought that his ears were deceiving him at her words and the way she said them.

'*What* did you say?'

Paul walked down the hall. At the front door he turned back and said to Carol, 'You sure you'll be all right here on your own?'

The cattle prod caught him in the side and he dropped to the floor like a sack of potatoes. Then Benny started to give him a kicking and Paul, still stunned, could not defend himself. Carol's screams brought Abul inside the house. He dragged Benny away from the prone young man and forced him into the kitchen.

'Stop it, Benny! Stop it, for fuck's sake, before someone gets the filth.'

All that could be heard was Carol crying, her sobs loud and terrified. Abul was holding his friend to his chest, calming him with his words.

'She's a good girl, Carol. You know she is. You have to stop this jealousy or you'll lose her. Now calm down and try and make some sense of all this.'

Benny was trembling with anger and suppressed rage.

'I will fucking kill him *and* her. If I find out she's been playing me I'll chop her fucking head off . . .'

'What the fuck you on, Ben? How much coke have you snorted this morning, eh? It's making you worse than you are, and you are one paranoid fucker as it is. Now go in there and sort that girl out, she's in a right state.'

Benny knew his friend was talking sense but the thought of Carol alone with another man was more than he could bear.

'Why did she do it? She knows what I'm like . . .'

Abul took a deep breath before answering.

'She's a normal girl, Benny, and you can't hide her from every man in the fucking world. Not even you can do that.'

Her pitiful sobs seemed to become audible to Benny for the first time. Pulling himself free he went out into the hallway. He took Carol into his arms and walked her gently to the bedroom.

'I'm sorry, Cal. Fuck me, I am so sorry. I can't help it . . . I love you so much, darling. You know how I am about you? I'm crazy for you. I will make it all right, I promise, I will make it all right.'

'I can't take any more, Benny. I've known Paul all me life, he's Trevor's best mate and goes out with my sister. What will I tell the family when they find out about all this? You know what me dad's like, he'll go bloody mad.'

It was on the tip of Benny's tongue to say fuck her father and her family up hill and down dale, but he stopped himself. His innate cunning was taking over. Instead he said, 'I'll make sure Paul doesn't say a word, OK? I will apologise to him, give him a drink and make sure he keeps it to himself. I promise it will be sorted.'

She looked into his handsome face and wondered how she could still love him like she did, knowing he was as mad as a hatter. But when they were together, just the two of them, he was different, he was kind and he was loving. Well, most of the time anyway.

'Is he badly hurt, Ben?'

He knew he had won when she asked him that and hugged her to him tightly.

''Course not. He's fine.'

He could hear Abul helping the boy up the hall, and prayed that he hadn't hurt him too much.

'Promise me that this will stop, Benny? Please, promise me that this will stop? Especially now with everything . . .'

'We'll have the best wedding of them all, you'll see.'

'It's not just the wedding, Benny. I'm pregnant.'

She watched the joy suffusing his face and her heart lifted. But she had pictured herself telling him when they were happy together, lying in each other's arms. Not after a bout of violence perpetrated in their own home.

'A baby, Cal? A real one?'

She nodded.

'A crying, screaming, real-life one.'

He hugged her tightly and then immediately loosed his grip on her.

'Sorry, Cal, I didn't mean to squeeze you like that.'

She smiled sadly.

'I'm not going to break, Benny. But I can't have this upset while I'm pregnant, OK? I can't be frightened and upset like this any more . . .'

Her voice was trembling with tears and with one of his lightning changes of mood he swept her up and laid her gently on the king-size bed. Then, going out to the hallway, she heard him humbly apologising to Paul and asking him to keep it quiet. For some unknown reason his hearty voice made her feel worse, and as she looked round the large and beautiful bedroom it occurred to her that this luxury bungalow was nothing but a prison, one from which with the child now inside her she could never, ever escape.

'No good will come of tonight, I'm telling you, Dennis.'

Marge's voice was loud as usual and Dennis, her long-suffering husband, was already on autopilot.

'Her mother is doing this for no other reason than to cause aggro. I know her of old.'

She bustled around her country pine kitchen with her usual determination, her startling make-up already in place at ten in the morning and her large bulk encased in a long flowing kaftan.

'Come to bed, Marge, let's have half an hour while the kids are out, eh?'

She laughed.

'You can't shut me up like that any more, the change has put paid to all that, darlin'. I would rather have a cup of tea. Me and Boy George, mate. About all we have got in common though, eh?'

Dennis laughed. He loved his feisty little wife, she was everything to him. Even her moaning was music to his ears. She was loyal and he adored her, even if she did tip the scales at sixteen and a half stone, and wore eye shadow that wouldn't look out of place on her idol Boy George.

'I love you, Marge.'

He meant it and it showed in his voice. She walked

over to him and hugged him to her.

'And I love you, you bald-headed old tosser.'

They kissed as they always did when together for more than five minutes.

'Fifty, eh? Maura fifty. She don't look it, though.'

'No, she don't, Den, but she feels it. I love her, you know that. But for all her clothes and her money and her big houses, she ain't got what we got: three nice kids and each other. I know her better than anyone and she would swap it all in the morning for what we've got.'

Dennis poured them both another cup of tea.

'She's got that Tommy now, though, he seems all right.'

Marge blew her lips out and made a very unladylike noise.

'I don't like him, Den. Don't know why, I just don't trust him. Funny, ain't it? I should be over the moon she's found someone else, and I would be if it was anyone but him.'

'You and your feelings about people.'

She sipped her tea and sat at the scrubbed pine table that held centre-stage in her new kitchen.

'I still feel guilty about Terry. If we hadn't fixed her up with him things might have been very different . . .'

Her voice trailed off and Dennis grabbed her hand and kissed her fat fingers.

'That was over thirty years ago.'

'Oh, don't remind me. How did this happen to us, Den? When did we get this old?'

He laughed.

'I don't know, girl. It just crept up on us. Have you wrapped Maura's present?'

She nodded.

'Of course. Hope she likes it.'

'So do I, it cost enough.'

Marge flapped her hand at her husband.

'I could hardly get her something from Marks and Spencer, could I?'

'I suppose not. But Maura understands we ain't got the money she's got.'

Marge wasn't listening, she was too busy looking at her eldest daughter and her Sikh husband getting their kids from the car.

Dennis followed his wife's gaze and sighed.

'They've been married over twenty years, Marge. You're going to have to get used to it some time.'

'I am used to it and I love them kids, you know I do. But the shit she takes hurts me and I know it hurts her.'

'She's an adult, Marge, and the kids are all growing up now. Leave her be and let them sort themselves out. You talk about bloody Sarah Ryan, you're no better.'

Marge was saved from answering by her daughter's appearance in her new kitchen.

'Oh, Mum, it's bleeding handsome.'

'Do you like it, love? Sit down and I'll make you a nice cup of tea.'

Dennis was smiling as his wife put on her usual best behaviour for her son-in-law. She was a case was his Marge and he loved her with every ounce of his being.

# Chapter Seven

Sarah looked at the table laden with food and hoped she had not worked all day for nothing. If Maura spurned her, Sarah didn't know what she would do. Inside herself she knew that it was important she made her peace with her daughter before she went to meet her Maker. And she wondered if she could honestly meet up with her husband Benjamin Senior and look him in the eye if she left this earth estranged from his favourite child.

She looked around the kitchen. The house in Lancaster Road, Notting Hill, had been bought by Michael and now her daughter owned it. Maura had never once brought that fact up but Sarah knew that she lived as she did because her daughter decreed it. She had never held a grudge in that way towards her mother so maybe, just maybe, there was a chance for them. If she could only turn Maura from the error of her ways she could die in peace.

Sarah welcomed the thought of death. She wanted

to see her husband and the sons who'd gone before, even Michael who she was convinced would be a good and kind man now he was in the Kingdom of Heaven. She could not believe that Our Gracious Lord would put *her* children anywhere else: hadn't she prayed for the repose of their souls for years and years?

Maura was mellowing. Age did that to a body and Sarah had heard through Roy that she was largely handing the bent business over to Garry and Benny these days. That was what had given her the idea of trying to bring her daughter back to the Church, into the Catholic fold. And if she changed, maybe Benny would too.

This set her thinking about death once more. Her own death. Her grandson was her heart, God love him. He was her Michael all over again and she had to try making peace with Maura, for Benny's sake. If she could do it, make Maura a daughter once more, a real daughter, then maybe she could get her on her side to show Benny the error of his ways. It was all very simple really. If only Sarah had thought of it years ago.

Happy now, she pottered around her kitchen cutting more sandwiches and making more cakes. Tonight would be a triumph for her, she was sure.

In fact, she was depending on it.

Benny got to Maura's at just after twelve. She was thinking about Michael and seeing Benny was like seeing her brother before her. Until he spoke.

'All right, Maws? You look like you seen a ghost.'

'I feel like I have. You're getting more and more like Mickey every day.'

Benny loved hearing this. Uncle Michael was his hero. He would sometimes seek out old lags who had worked with his dead uncle and would pump them for anecdotes about him. He wanted to be Michael so badly he even tried to affect some of his mannerisms.

He smiled at his aunt.

'I aim to please. You look lovely, nothing like fifty.'

Maura closed her blue eyes in annoyance. If one more person mentioned the word fifty again she would do someone a damage.

'Do you think so?'

Benny grinned.

'I want to tell you something in private, Maws. Me and Carol already agreed we're getting married. I'm announcing it tonight. She's just told me she's having a baby an' all.'

Maura's face lit up with pleasure.

'This is wonderful news. Congratulations.'

Benny was embarrassed and it showed. Maura was surprised to see just how excited and shy he was about the news. He put the kettle on to stop himself from crying and as she saw the sheer jubilation in him she wondered if this might just be the making of him. Family loyalty was inherent in him; having a child might make him appreciate the benefits of continuity, help calm him down.

She hoped so.

'It's the best birthday present I could have been given. I am over the moon for you, Ben,' she said encouragingly.

He placed the teapot on the table and Maura was amused once more at how finicky he was about such things. When he had served them both he sat opposite her and said seriously, 'I am so jealous, Maura, that I'm ruining my relationship with Carol. But I can't help it, you know? I feel inside like I'm going to explode with love for her, and if I even see her talk to someone else I want to kill them both – even though I know she wouldn't do anything to hurt me. I'm afraid that she'll like them more than me, see?'

His eyes reflected genuine pain as he tried to explain his innermost feelings and Maura knew what it must have taken for him to come to her with this.

'I worry that she'll realise just how bad I really am. How ignorant and stupid in comparison to other blokes.'

Maura could have cried for her nephew. He was talking from the heart, and knowing how proud he was she marvelled at how hard it must have been for him to say all this to her. But he trusted her, respected her, and she knew it was a real compliment that he felt he could talk this way to her.

She stared into his troubled eyes and suddenly felt the urge to run away: from him and her family, from all of it. They came to her no matter what problems she might have of her own. She knew that because she had no children it was assumed she had no life. It had always been like that. She fought the urge to run.

Instead she said quietly, 'What are you going to do then? Have you thought about this? Thought about how you can stop this behaviour?'

He nodded. After taking a sip of the scalding tea, he said with supreme honesty, 'I was thinking of going on one of them anger management courses, what do you think?'

He sounded so earnest she wanted to cry. But she also wanted to laugh out loud. Benny on an anger management course? The Airfix King of Essex? The man who kept a cattle prod on his person day and night just in case someone upset him?

Yet she knew he was serious. That he wanted to change his life if only so he did not lose his Carol.

She laughed, the humour of it too much for her, and Benny laughed with her. Albeit nervously.

'You don't think it's a good idea then?'

He was still grinning nervously and her heart went out to him.

'It's up to you, Benny. But I think you should say this to Carol, not to me. She is the one you should be talking to. She is the one carrying your child and who you need to reassure.'

He nodded and she knew he regretted telling her his innermost thoughts. It was always the way with deep feelings: people resented you once they'd exposed themselves to you. She supposed it was human nature.

'Silly fucker, ain't I? But I want this to be right, Maws. I lost it again this morning and put the fear of fuck up her. I can't bear the thought of hurting her and I know, even while I'm ranting and raving, that what I am doing is wrong. On one level I know I am out of order but the rage takes over. Seems to obliterate everything else.'

He grabbed her hand tightly.

'Help me, Maws. You're the only person I would listen to, you know that.'

'Michael was the same. Garry's like it and all. You sound just like Mickey when you talk: he used to say the same things to me. All I can advise is that you talk to Carol, explain how you feel. It's a form of self-hatred. You don't feel good enough for her, do you?'

He shook his head, pleased she understood him, that he could unburden himself to her without feeling a fool even while he didn't really want to hear what she was saying.

'Well, you have to find a way to make yourself feel good enough for her. You have to use all your strength and force yourself to stop making scenes about things. Do you understand what I'm saying, Ben? You have to make yourself stop hurting her, and yourself, with your behaviour. You need to respect her and her right to talk to other people. She loves you, Benny, you can see that, surely? I mean, she must, some of the stunts you've pulled over the years and she's still there beside you.'

He nodded.

'Yeah. You're right, Maws.'

He stretched, and it was as if he'd had the weight of the world taken off his shoulders.

'In future I am going to leave the prod in the car. I am going to take a deep breath and tell meself that I love her and therefore I mustn't hurt her in any way.'

'That's it, Benny. You know it makes sense. Now, more tea?'

He shook his head.

'No, Maws, I have to get back. I'm taking her out for a few hours before tonight's jollifications . . .'

'What's happening tonight then?'

He grinned once more.

'You'll find out soon enough.' He rose from his chair and hugged her across the table. 'Thanks, Auntie Maura. I feel so much better now.'

'You'll be all right, Benny, just try and keep that temper of yours in check. Keep it for the business, leave family out of it. And Carol is your family now, remember.'

He nodded.

When he had gone Maura thought about what he had said and felt a terrible sadness fall over her day. Benny was mad, everyone knew that. He swung from extreme laughter to murderous rage within a split second. What was the kink in their family that made so many of them like that? Had to be their mother, she knew it inside herself. If her own child had lived, would it have been the same? Maura shook off the thought; she would never have let it be like that. Janine and her mother had made Benny and Michael what they were with their neediness and obsession with their sons. Neither of them had had any time for their daughters, as she herself knew from experience. Sins of the mothers and all that. She sighed, depressed once more.

Then the thought of Benny on an anger management course made her smile again. She could see the newspaper headline now: 'Man on anger management course glues eyes of course leader together and attacks him with cattle prod'.

It wasn't funny really, and she knew that, but it still made her smile.

As she loaded the dishwasher she wondered what her life would become. She was fifty years old and surrounded by a lunatic family whom she loved, but with no children and no real happiness of her own.

She closed her eyes briefly as loneliness descended on her once more. She had to hand over the businesses properly and get a life before it was too late. It was the only way out for her and she knew it. If she didn't do it now she never would. She had done what she could for her family and now it was time to take care of herself.

In her mind's eye she saw Terry smiling at her and

felt the pain of his loss once more. She pushed the thought away and walked from the house.

As she got into her car she wondered where the hell she was going. It wasn't the first time she had driven herself nowhere. In fact, it was becoming a regular occurrence.

She knew that eventually she would end up at Michael's grave. Even though she was inwardly determined she wasn't going there, she knew it would be her journey's end. She missed him so much and being near him reassured her. She still didn't know why that was; he was dead and buried this long time.

But it did.

Sheila and Sarah watched the children running amok in the garden together. They smiled at the antics of the smallest boy and the only girl, who was treated with kid gloves by her brothers and lorded it over them all.

'The food looks nice, Sarah.'

The old woman shrugged.

'It's all her favourites. I remember how Maura used to help me when she was small. She was a good child.'

'All children are good.'

Sarah smiled.

'Not all. You know, my Garry was a bastard from the first day he drew breath. I've been driven demented by him all his life, him and his shagging inventing! Nearly killed my Benny he did once.'

She was quiet for a few seconds before saying sadly, 'He was killed anyway so maybe it would have been better if he had died then. They tortured him, did you know that? My Benny. My baby boy. He died a painful and terrifying death.'

They both shuddered, remembering the way Benny's head had been found on Hampstead Heath. There were tears on Sarah's face now and Sheila placed an arm gently round her shoulders.

'Don't upset yourself.'

But the fear was in her voice and Sarah heard it.

'It's only me reminiscing, it's just me age. My Michael would have been in his sixties now. I have trouble at times realising just how old I am. My Michael would have been sixty-five to be exact. Can you imagine that?'

'I hope I see my children grow up to be old.'

'I wanted that as well, but it never happened, did it? Not with them all anyway.' Sarah grinned. 'He would have hated being a pensioner anyway, my poor Michael.'

They laughed at her words and the dark mood was broken.

'My Lee was always the good boy. He just follows the pack, always did. Bear that in mind when you're cross with him, Sheila.'

She went to make another of her endless cups of tea.

Sheila watched her children closely. She watched for

any of the bad Ryan traits, determined to stamp them out before they took hold. She would not bury any of her kids, she knew that much.

An hour later the house was full of people and now they all had to wait for the birthday girl to arrive. Carla looked fantastic and Sheila, who normally liked her, felt a bit put out. She had certainly gone to town today. In fact, everyone remarked on how lovely she looked and Carla preened herself at the praise.

Benny and his girlfriend were both telling her what a beauty she was and Sheila, catching sight of herself in the hall mirror, realised how dowdy she herself had become. The reflection in the mirror depressed her. Once she had been attractive and Lee had adored her. She knew he still loved her but there had been a subtle shifting in their relationship since the deaths of Terry and Janine.

She saw Roy kissing his daughter and her heart went out to him. He was like a big cuddly teddy these days. All the life had gone from him somehow; it was as if a part of him had died with his wife.

She waved at Marge and Dennis as they came into the room, Marge still in her heavy camel coat and startling make-up. Then a voice surprised her by saying quietly in her ear, 'Penny for them, Sheila.'

She turned to her husband and spontaneously kissed him. She saw the shock and pleasure on Lee's face and wanted to tell him how much she loved him really. How sorry she was for her coldness. But before she could say anything a man walked into the room. He was well-dressed and he was handsome and Sarah Ryan was making him very welcome. Sheila realised that this was Tommy Rifkind, Maura's partner as they called lovers these days. He was gorgeous and she was amazed at the feelings he engendered in her breast. She suddenly felt like she couldn't breathe, and as she watched Carla simpering across at him felt a real urge to go home and get changed and come back slim and beautiful so this man would notice her.

The knowledge made her blush red to the roots of her hair.

Sarah Ryan looked at the eyecatching man before her and decided that if nothing else her daughter could still pick them. He was gorgeous. She wasn't too sure about the heavy with him, he was like a gorilla dressed up in a suit, but he smiled at her and as she shook his hand did a little curtsey-type of movement that made them all laugh.

Tommy rolled his eyes and said kindly, 'He gets nervous round new people. This is my oldest friend Joss Campion.'

Benny smacked Joss on the back and took him out to the kitchen to get him a drink. Sarah chatted to the handsome newcomer and marvelled once more at what these men saw in her daughter. Was it the coldness Maura seemed to have in abundance? Or was it those huge breasts that seemed to be part of another person? Though Maura had never flaunted them they were there for all the world to see. She realised she was being petty, though. She forced the jealousy down, reminding herself this was a bridge-building exercise, and concentrated on chatting to Tommy Rifkind. Sarah decided she genuinely liked him, she liked him a lot. Would he be the catalyst that would bring her daughter to her senses, though? Somehow she doubted it very much.

The phone rang to herald Maura's arrival and Benny dimmed the lights. They all stood in darkness waiting for Garry to bring her into the house. Tommy could feel the nervous tension in the room and hoped there wouldn't be a scene. He hated scenes of any kind.

His wife Gina had been a quiet woman but his girlfriends all tended to be termagents, loud women with noisy voices and even noisier lives. He was getting too old for that now. He sipped his drink and tried once more not to look at Maura's niece Carla with her sexy clothes and come-hither eyes. If he wasn't careful he was going to get himself in trouble there, he knew it.

Tommy Rifkind liked women, couldn't help himself. It was how he was made.

'What do you mean, Mum's ill? If she is then I'm the last person she'll want to see.'

Garry was getting impatient. He had been arguing with his sister all the way here.

'She wants to see you, all right? Fuck me, Maws, she *is* your mother, and it is your fiftieth birthday, and she is a little old lady who wants to see her only daughter. Just say hello to her that's all, and then we can get on with the dinner party at the Ivy.'

'So it's at the Ivy, is it?'

There was laughter in Maura's voice.

'Now I have let the cat out of the bag. Don't tell the others, will you? Act all surprised like, promise?'

Garry fervently hoped that when she found out there was no Ivy she wouldn't create. He really wasn't in the mood.

'Promise me, Maws!'

She nodded.

They were outside the house in Lancaster Road now and Maura looked at the forbidding façade, the darkness of the rooms, and sighed.

'Come on then, let's get it over with. But if she starts I'm going home, I mean it.'

'Oh, shut the fuck up, you miserable old cow.'

'Not so much of the old, if you don't mind.'

Garry put the key in the lock and they walked inside. Maura had not been in this house for years and the familiar smell of food was instantly overwhelming. Then they were walking into the lounge and the light was going on and she was seeing all her family and friends, and in the middle of them all, smiling and holding out her arms, was her mother.

'Happy birthday, child.'

Sarah's voice was old and cracked but sounded friendly. Maura went into her arms without a second's thought.

Tommy felt the tension leave the room. Plastering a smile on his face, he tried not to look at the delectable Carla too much.

But he was as aware of her as she was of him.

Maura stood in the garden with Tommy and Joey. Joss was inside and the boys were taking bets on when he would stop eating. Sarah loved him, his obvious enjoyment of her food was like balm to her.

Though Maura had hugged her mother she had kept her cool. In her heart of hearts Sarah knew it would take time before they were back on their old footing. That is, if they ever got back to how they had been once, many years ago, before Maura had grown up and turned into someone her mother didn't know any more and could not for the life of her like, let alone love. Sarah still couldn't admit to herself that it was the fact that she couldn't control her daughter any more that had been the chief bugbear between them.

Tommy cuddled Maura to him and for once she let him. Normally in public she would discreetly move away from him, but tonight she was happy for everyone to see them together. She smiled at Carla as she came into the garden with a large plate of food.

'Thanks, Carla. The food is great, isn't it?'

'Well, there's certainly plenty of it. Good job and all with that friend of yours, Tommy. He ain't stopped eating for over two hours!'

Tommy laughed with her and Maura watched them. She was glad they got on together, it was important to her that they did. Carla had liked him from the first time they had met, and she knew he liked her niece. It was vital for them to be friends; if things went as planned they would be seeing a lot of each other. Tonight had given her a taste of what had been missing from her life and Maura hoped there'd be some changes made soon.

They were all in the garden now and Benny was making his announcement. Carol was pink with pleasure and Maura felt a moment's jealousy as she thought of what the girl must be feeling. She had a child growing inside her and she had a man who loved her. Maura had only ever felt that for a few fleeting hours in her own life but she remembered it well. Terry had dumped her even while she was still reeling from the shock of finding herself pregnant by him. She watched her mother's face as she contemplated the arrival of a great-grandchild and her joy as Benny kissed and hugged her. He had ignored his grandma for so long and now Maura wondered if it was just because of the way Sarah had cut her off. But she knew at heart that Benny disliked her mother for the same reason he had disliked his own. They were too suffocating.

She only hoped Sarah didn't start interfering in her own life now they were so-called mates again.

Abul kissed Carol and shook Benny's hand warmly. Maura liked him and he liked her, there was mutual respect between them. She knew that other than herself he was the only person able to control Benny. They had been friends since school and Benny loved him like a brother.

Abul's girlfriend Serena was smiling like a Cheshire cat and Maura wondered what she would do if she heard about his arranged marriage. To him Serena was just another easy lay he had met up the Five Rivers in Ilford. It was a predominantly Asian club, but there were not many Asian girls there. Only white girls or African, some West Indian.

Maura sometimes felt she knew Abul as well as she knew Benny, they had been friends so long. As he came over to her she said, '*Borghal lugardi.*'

Abul roared with laughter. She had just told him in Punjabi that his girlfriend Serena was fit. Serena didn't laugh, she had a sneaking suspicion they were taking the piss.

'She's just a *dorst*, Maura, a mate.'

Maura smiled at the girl.

'You look like more than mates to me.'

The girl, unaware who she was talking to, said in a flat voice, 'And what would you know about it?'

Abul looked at her as if she had gone mad before his eyes.

'Apologise this minute.'

His voice was clipped.

Benny, seeing the commotion, came over. Gripping Serena's arm, he walked her from the garden with Abul following closely. Maura gave it a few beats and then she went after them. The girl was young, she meant no real harm.

Outside the house she heard Abul roaring at the girl, '*Dharvaho*, you bitch!'

Maura walked over to them and said gently, 'He is telling you to fuck off, love. Now why don't you let me get you a cab, eh?'

She pushed Abul and Benny back towards the house.

'Leave her alone. Go back to the party, boys.'

Serena was surprised to see they immediately did what the woman told them. She knew their reps; it was the real attraction of Abul for her. He was a face, a gangster, and she loved it.

Maura waited until they went inside before saying, 'You can get a cab round the corner, do you need any money?'

The girl shook her head. She knew she wouldn't be seeing Abul again.

'I'm sorry.'

Maura smiled at her.

'Don't be. Get off home, and remember that Abul is like all men. They use women. They do it with a smile and a kind word, but they use women. He's getting married to a nice little girl from Rajasthan soon. Thought you'd like to know.'

The girl walked dejectedly away.

'That was nice of you, Maws.'

Roy was at the gate and she had not even noticed him.

'Poor little mare.'

'Good news about the baby, though, eh, Maws? And the wedding, of course.'

He looked so pleased after all he'd been through that it broke her heart.

'It's lovely. You'll be a granddad again, won't you?'

He nodded.

'I just hope this one ain't a poof like Joey.'

Maura was so shocked at his words she didn't answer him.

'Everyone says Benny is like Michael but it's Joey who's really like him.'

Kylie Minogue was now blaring from the house and as they walked in Maura's nephew was dancing on his own in the middle of the front room.

'See what I mean, Maws? Queer as a two-bob fucking clock! Just like Michael, a shit stabber.'

Maura was saved from answering by Benny who was by now dancing with Joey, albeit in a piss-taking kind of way. But Joey didn't care, he was the centre of attention and he loved it.

Then Marge was joining in and so was Carla and suddenly it seemed there was a mass exodus to the small dance space. Maura saw Carla shimmying in front of Tommy and watched him as he watched her niece. It dimly occurred to her that Carla was making a play for him.

Then Tommy saw Maura and was making his way to her side, a smile on his handsome face and another drink in his hand. He was flushed from alcohol and coke. She guessed he had had a small toot with Benny and made allowances. But the expression on Carla's face stayed with her for the rest of the night. She hoped it was only the drink because if Carla wanted Tommy Rifkind, like it seemed she did, then Maura had a dilemma on her hands.

She smiled and carried on outwardly enjoying the party. But she watched as Benny kept a beady eye on the proceedings and knew that he missed nothing. She would talk to him about it if needs be.

He saw her watching him and raised his glass to her. Maura smiled back at him and raised her own.

She was going to get pissed, she decided there and then. She was fifty, for God's sake, and she was going to get as pissed as she could.

And she did.

At three in the morning she was asleep beside Tommy when the phone rang. She answered it sleepily then sat bolt upright in bed. Tommy, sensing something was deeply wrong, sat up with her.

'Who is this? Fucking answer me!'

Maura slammed the phone down and it rang again almost immediately.

'Who is this?'

Tommy could see the utter confusion on her face.

'Who is it, Maura? Give me the fucking phone, woman.'

She slammed it down once more then took it off the hook. Getting out of bed, she dragged on a black silk dressing gown and marched down the stairs, Tommy hot on her heels. She still had not said a word.

He was shitting himself, convinced that the call was something to do with him. As he saw Maura pouring herself a large Scotch and swilling it down in one mouthful, he said sarcastically, 'Ain't you had enough tonight? Now who was on the fucking phone, woman?'

She poked a finger in his face, and he could see anger in her eyes.

'Don't call me woman, Tommy. Don't you ever call me that again. And if you want to know who was on the phone, it was Vic fucking Joliff.'

She saw his face go pale, and laughed.

'I assume you want a drink now as well then?'

'It can't be . . .'

'It was. I'd know that fucking voice anywhere. No one could find him when he went on the trot from the hospital, though it's my belief the filth didn't really look that hard.'

'What does he want now? It's been six years, I thought he'd laid down and died – or got himself a place in Spain. Same difference.'

Maura sighed.

'Oh, Tommy, don't be so fucking stupid. His wife murdered, his throat cut . . . Vic Joliff's looking for payback.'

She poured them both a drink. There would be no more sleep for them tonight.

# Chapter Eight

Garry was like a raving lunatic and Tommy Rifkind was sharply reminded of exactly who he was dealing with here. Even Joss was shocked at the way Garry was carrying on, and he had been known to have his moments. Maura and the others stood and waited until Garry had vented his spleen, as if the way he was carrying on was normal, as if it was nothing out of the ordinary. The veins in his neck were prominent and he was practically foaming at the mouth. His dark hair was a mess; he had been running his fingers through it constantly, his agitation showing in the continuous jerky movements of his hands and legs. Tommy was again reminded of how his son had died and the knowledge made him feel sick.

Finally Garry finished punching the walls and cursing everyone, even God, and his breathing gradually became more regular.

Lee's voice rang out in the silence of the small room.

'Calm down, Garry, think with your head not your heart.'

'Are you taking the piss? How could anyone calm down with that fucking nut-nut running around loose? I said we should have hunted him down from the off. And now this is the upshot.'

'Well, maybe you should have questioned Tommy B properly before he died then we might have found out more.'

Benny's voice was low, and even though Tommy and the others had expected the comment from someone, they were still startled to hear it spoken out loud. Everyone automatically looked at Tommy. He kept his gaze on Benny longer than anyone would have given him credit for.

Garry was still fuming as he cried, 'I fucking told you, it was Lee! He crunched his head open before I had the chance to do anything much, let alone have a fucking friendly chat.'

He realised then that Tommy B's father was present and nodded to him in a respectful way. The anger left him as quickly as it had come on and he sighed heavily. The boy's father was in the room after all. Though as far as Garry was concerned it had just been work, nothing more, nothing less. Tommy B could have been anyone. It was only the fact that his sister was trumping the boy's relative that made him bother to be civil.

'You know what I mean,' he growled.

Lee had the grace to look at the floor.

Joss surprised everyone by saying loudly, 'Well, Vic will come after us all. You know what a mad bastard he is. Gut us like fish if we ain't careful. I remember him from the old days. A grudge-holder is Vic Joliff and, no disrespect to anyone here but he is frightened of no one. I don't know what took him so long but he will have used the wait to gather money and forces. Six years will have given him plenty of time to nurse his anger and work out how best to take revenge.'

All the boys liked and respected Joss because, though he didn't talk much, it seemed that when he did it made a lot of sense. Maura, however, didn't need a lecture about Vic Joliff. She knew him of old and certainly didn't need to be reminded by Joss, but hoped it might settle in the others' minds. Benny especially had never really understood the old workings of their business and he needed to. Now more than ever.

'Let's put this in perspective, shall we?' Her voice was soft. 'Vic lost his old woman the same as we lost Janine and Terry.' She looked at Tommy as she said, 'And you lost your boy, as we all know. From his phone call Vic evidently still believes it was one of us who shot his wife, right, though word is well and truly on the pavement that we had nothing to do with any of it. We never got to the bottom of Rebekka's part in it all. I'm going to see Joe the Jew in Silvertown this afternoon as it happens – I've been keeping my eye on him. I'll have a word with him about Vic. But the fact is, at this moment in time we're still none the wiser as to exactly who did what six years ago. There was far more skulduggery afoot than anyone realised at the time. What we have to do now is try and find out who called the shots, and the first stop has to be the filth. If anyone knows it will be them. I hear Inspector Billings is now on desk duty so another visit to him might not go amiss, Benny.'

He grinned. He liked the thought of going to see that nonce again. It appealed to his sense of the outrageous. He might even go and see him at work this time, just for the sheer aggravation of it.

Everyone was quiet as they wondered what exactly lay behind this latest development. Maura and her brothers had never really believed that Vic was solely responsible for all the mayhem, aided by Tommy B, but until now it had been plain sailing for them and no one had stood against them. Until Vic resurfaced.

Garry would not be appeased. He wanted death and destruction and he wanted it now. Maura could read his mind and spoke again.

'No one does anything without my express say-so, OK? We need to collate everything this time so we can find out for ourselves exactly what the fuck is going on.'

Everyone nodded.

'What about us, Maura? What do you want from us?'

Tommy's voice sounded strange. He *felt* strange, taking orders from a woman, especially one he had bedded not ten hours earlier. Women to Tommy fell into two categories, the ones you married and the ones you didn't. He still wasn't sure how he'd classify Maura Ryan but he had a feeling she wouldn't give a flying one whichever way he decided.

'You do what everyone else does, Tommy. Basically you do what the fuck you are told to do, OK?'

He swallowed the insult from Garry because he had to. But it stayed in his mind for a long time afterwards.

'Leave it out, Garry. We have enough enemies as it is without you causing more hag.'

Maura's voice held a reprimand and even Tommy had to acknowledge that she could control her brothers far better than any man could have done. Except of course the saintly Michael. It was funny but he had always liked Michael alive; dead he got on Tommy's nerves. They all talked about him like he was the Second Coming or something. He'd been a thug, like they were all thugs, himself included. This lot, though, thought that they were better than everyone else. It irritated the life out of Tommy sometimes. They seemed to forget that he had lost a child because of the last turn out. No one thought of the consequences for him, did they? It was all about them as usual. Tommy B had been a little fucker but he was still his own flesh and blood. They talked a lot about family, but what about *his* fucking family?

He glanced at Maura and saw that she had guessed what he was thinking. Her half-smile was kindly and he smiled back at her.

'We all have grievances. Let's make them work for us, not against us.'

Everyone knew what she meant and once more Tommy was amazed at the skilful way she controlled the biggest nutters this side of the Watford Gap.

Vic Joliff had changed. He had always been a mean and vicious man in his business dealings but his overall personality had been saved by a streak of generosity that surfaced every now and then if he heard of someone in trouble, and of course he'd loved Sandra and the kids. Since his wife's death, however, that had all changed. He had no generosity any more; in fact, he was what his own mother termed a vicious bastard of a man. But he hated to be double-crossed, hated to be used, and used he had been. Someone had taken a diabolical fucking liberty and he was not swallowing it. No fucking way, José.

Every time he thought about it he felt as if he could kill someone with his bare hands, and he was more than capable of that as everyone knew.

He had fought his way back to health, left with little money and few connections, and he had taken it on the chin. After his old police pal got him out of the country he had been two years on the trot, getting well, living in shit holes, until he finally felt up to following up on old contacts who had used the money from drugs deals he'd set up without a second's thought and tried to forget all about him. But he had bided his time and gradually clawed it back, what was left of it. It amazed him the number of people, some his so-called best friends, who had not only assumed he was dead but had clearly rejoiced in the fact. It had been a real eye-opener. Now some of them were dead themselves, and the others knew better than to cross him again.

Vic Joliff was back. Back with a vengeance.

Sometimes when he glimpsed the scars on his neck he got so angry that he felt faint with anguish and the need to pay the whole lot of them back in the worst way. It was as if this was all his life could amount to now: tracking down the scum who'd brought him to this and making them pay.

He'd bought himself a villa in Majorca with some of the money he'd managed to retrieve; set his mother and ponce of a brother up there too, on the other side of the island. He barely saw them. He'd been careful not to blow his cover, partly because that was the deal he'd made with Billings, and partly because after Sandra's death and the betrayal he'd suffered he'd turned into a recluse. Couldn't stand human company; didn't want or need it. And in his isolation and physical pain he broke one of his own longest-standing rules: he sampled the merchandise. He'd never been a cocaine user before this, thought it was strictly for the mugs all the time he'd dealt in it, but in his years of exile it became his friend, his salvation, the source of all his most brilliant ideas.

After a line or two things always seemed amazingly clear-cut, Vic's best course of action the simplest thing in the world. The Ryans had killed his wife in some brain-dead piece of tit for tat. Now they were living high on the hog off the proceeds of a major drugs distribution network that should have been his. He'd come *that* close to it, him and his band of merry men. He'd scores to settle there too, of course, but for now they could be useful. He started up a few drugs deals, using his former partners. Nothing too big, just enough to draw them back into his web.

Because Vic Joliff had made himself a promise. Every last living soul who'd ever crossed him would be made to realise in full measure what pain and fear really were. He'd blow them away, one by one, saving the Queen Bitch herself for last.

He laughed to himself, softly at first then louder and louder as he stomped across the echoing wooden floors of a smart Docklands apartment, the first in a constantly changing series of safe houses. He itched to be back on the town, in the life, King Vic holding court before the young guns, taking his pick as he put together a gang that would corner the drugs distribution market for the entire country. Piece of piss. He had the masterplan safe in his head.

He had another line to celebrate his own cunning,

and pulled a face. What were they cutting the stuff with nowadays? It took another two before his temper and his equilibrium were restored and he was jolly Vic Joliff again, smiling at the thought of the mayhem he was about to unleash.

Benny was with Abul and they were on their way to see Billings at work. Maura had told him to keep away from the man's workplace but Benny could be conveniently deaf when the fancy took him. Today he had dressed carefully in a dark blue suit, white shirt and blue tie. He looked every bit the respectable young man, as did Abul. They were having trouble keeping their faces straight as they were announced by a civilian secretary who looked as if she had been dragged through a hedge backwards. Benny could handle ugly birds providing they were tidy. This one was a typical graduate: scruffy, bad teeth and a BO problem. Ideal police material as far as he was concerned.

He wondered if Billings was giving her one. He wasn't averse to the rougher end of the shagging market as they all knew. But no, she was out of school uniform so he wouldn't be interested. It was a pleasure to see his face as they were ushered into the office. Disbelief coupled with pure fear. Just how Benny liked it.

'Are you fucking mad?'

Billings' voice was low, so low Benny and Abul had trouble hearing him, but even without hearing anything they would have guessed the drift of what he was saying.

Benny looked scandalised.

'Aren't you pleased to see us? And we made the journey especially, didn't we, Abul?'

He nodded.

'You are one ungrateful old ponce, Mr Billings.' Benny's voice was still pleasant as were his face and his body language. No one observing through the glass partition wall of the open-plan office would guess what was taking place from Benny's behaviour but Billings' face might let the cat out of the bag. Benny said through gritted teeth, 'I am like a long-lost nephew to you, aren't I? So fucking smile and nod while I tell you what you are going to do.'

Billings was in shock so total he wondered if he might actually need hospital treatment to get over it.

Benny Ryan, one of the most notorious criminals in the country, was standing in his office before him as if he had every right to be there.

Billings' broken boiled hand was a sight to behold and he instinctively held it close to his chest. He had undergone extensive skin grafts and his face was only slightly scarred but his hand was useless except for simple tasks. He had refused early retirement, asking to complete his twenty years so he could collect a full pension. Friends had made sure he got his wish. But they wouldn't stay friends for long if they found out he was even on nodding terms with this young man, the very one who had been responsible for his freak 'accident'.

Billings listened with as much composure as he could.

Benny grinned that menacing grin of his and said in a friendly fashion, 'See, that's easy enough, even for you. You know it makes sense. Now, Mr Billings sir, I want you to think long and hard and then tell me where you think Mr Victor Joliff, otherwise known as Dead Cunt, could be at this moment in time? You do not have to answer me yet. I am willing to give you ten seconds' grace.'

Chief Inspector Billings wished the ground would open up and swallow him whole. Instead he kept up the inane smile and tried desperately to stop himself from crying out as Benny took hold of his injured hand in what looked to his curious secretary like a particularly hearty handshake.

Benny said with concern, 'This looks really nasty. Fancy a cup of tea? I'm parched. Abul, switch the kettle on . . .'

'*All right!* I'll tell you all I know but it might be nothing. A routine surveillance logged a possible sighting of Vic with a face called Stern . . .'

Benny smiled widely.

'See, that wasn't so hard, was it? Always a pleasure doing business with you. And you take care of yourself, won't you, Mr Billings. I don't know where we'd be without men like you in the Force.'

* * *

Joe the Jew was an old man. He had a bald head covered in liver spots, arthritic hands, and a girlfriend of nineteen. She was a sweet little thing called Camilla and he had been nicknamed Charles because of it. The name made him smile every time he heard it.

His sunny nature was part of Joe's rep. He came across as the definitive *mensch* – but anyone who believed that was in for a shock. Joe owned just about every spieler and gambling joint in the East End. He also, because of the times we live in, owned two lap dancing clubs, in one of which he'd met Camilla, and a portfolio of development properties. And then there was the debt-collecting agency and a scrapyard. He had tallymen who worked the council estates for him, and he had been banking the proceeds since the Second World War. Joe was as rich as Croesus and he loved it. He always said Camilla was his third childhood sweetheart to date, but she was the best lay of them all. Sign of the times again. Young girls these days would fuck a corpse if it had a few quid. This always raised a laugh, as he knew it would.

When he saw Maura Ryan he smiled warmly. He had always liked her, ever since she had taken on the Milano brothers, a pair of Italian ponces, ice-cream traders whom he had hated with a vengeance for over half his life. In fact, he liked Maura Ryan more than he liked a lot of people. He had also been close friends with Michael and missed him, just like he missed Joe the Fish and all the old crowd.

'Maura Ryan! You look wonderful. Take a seat. Let me get you a drink. More importantly, what can I do for you?'

He was smiling and Maura smiled back. She was in his scrapyard where he was always to be found during the day. He had started it in the war and it had been a gold mine ever since. Joe loved the scrap, it was his forte, and of course an ideal way of disposing of anyone who dared to stray on to his turf.

'You're looking good, boy.'

He laughed out loud, displaying teeth that were old and yellow but, as he proudly told anyone who asked, still his own.

'What can I say? I have regular sex and can highly recommend it.'

Maura was really laughing now and Joe was pleased.

'You look like you need to smile more, Maura. I see the laughter lines are fading from around your eyes.'

'At least some good has come from all that hag then!'

Her quip made him laugh again.

'You women, always chasing after youth.'

'From what I've heard about Camilla you ain't doing too badly in that direction yourself!'

They laughed together again like old friends before he looked at her and said honestly, 'I would need Arnold Schwarzenegger himself to lift it these days, Maura, to be truthful, but I like everyone thinking

I'm still at it. Men are envious of me, women laugh at me. But I'm old and it's the pleasure on other people's faces that I live for now.'

Maura understood what he meant. He was at an age where all he had left was the respect of other people. How he was perceived was important to him and always had been.

'What can I do for you? Trouble again?'

She nodded, the smile gone from her voice now and from her eyes. Joe the Jew had always thought Maura had the most beautiful eyes he had ever seen on a woman. Deep-set and a glorious blue, they were eyes any woman would crave. Now they were a steely shade, a deep sadness reflected in them. That sadness had been there for years. He wondered if she realised that when she looked at herself?

'Trouble with a capital T, Joe. Vic Joliff is walking around and threatening me.'

Joe the Jew sighed.

'Vic is heavy duty, Maura. But he's old news, surely?'

'He still thinks I know who killed his wife.'

'Don't you?'

Those simple words told Maura all she needed to know. Despite all her family's efforts to broadcast word of Tommy B's murderous spree, the old adage 'no smoke without fire' was clearly still alive and kicking in the criminal underworld.

'Do you really think I would have anything to do

with the killing of a fucking civilian, Joe? Give me some credit after all the years we've been friends.'

He said delicately, 'Maybe not you personally but someone close to you, Maura?'

She frowned.

'Such as?'

The hard edge to her voice reminded him exactly who he was dealing with here and he forced an uneasy smile. He had always thought it a shame the way she had hardened at such an early age. He remembered when her brother Michael would take her round collecting rents, such a beautiful, gentle child. Now she was a villain through and through.

He shrugged.

'How would I know? It was just a rhetorical question.'

'And my brother Garry would give you a rhetorical clump round the earhole if he heard you, wouldn't he?'

He took the threat gratefully. There was nothing else for it. He looked saddened though that he and Maura could be talking like this after all the years they'd known each other.

She smiled coldly.

'What about Rebekka Kowolski? Remember her, Joe? She really gave someone the hump, didn't she?'

He threw up his hands.

'Rebekka, Rebekka . . . always you are asking me about her. I told you before, she was just a greedy woman – wanted to live like a princess when her husband was earning *bubches.* Got in too deep with Russian loan sharks. It was a terrible tragedy. What more can I say? She had nothing to do with that trouble of yours. On my life, I swear it.'

She looked into his eyes and said the words she knew would destroy their friendship forever. Whether he was lying or not, it had to be done. She daren't risk looking like an easy touch or they'd all be finished.

'If I ever find out different I'll come for you, Joe.'

His old face sagged and he had difficulty meeting her eyes.

'That it should come to this . . . I'll bear it in mind, believe me. And Maura . . . watch your back, won't you, my dear?'

Vic Joliff walked into Le Marais with his new best friend and ally Jamie Hicks. There was a furore when people realised who he was, some of them being quicker on the uptake than others since they were in the same line of business. This docklands restaurant was where the City boys met the criminal underworld of Essex and London. Chandlery Wharf was a favoured meeting place for many an armed robber or drugs supplier who did their deals in much the same way as the money brokers and accountants did theirs: over a nice meal and a good bottle of wine. It was a different world these days and life for the ready-cash merchants was sweet. Most would get a lump and a half if caught in the course of their nefarious activities, so they made the proverbial hay while the sun shone.

Vic knew it was the criminal equivalent of being on the Nine O'clock News and savoured the covert looks and ensuing gossip. The Ryans would know within seconds that he was here, but after one drink and a cigarette he and Jamie were gone.

Garry got there twenty minutes after Vic had left. The fact Garry Ryan had come in personally told everyone who was anyone what they needed to know. Vic was playing games, and with him and the Ryans involved it could lead to a very dangerous scenario indeed. Two books were set up that afternoon alone. In both, the Ryans came out ahead. But only just. Vic Joliff was a force to be reckoned with and everyone who knew him kept that in mind.

Jamie was just along for the ride was the general consensus, snatched from the Ryans to get up their noses, though some of the shrewder clientele privately thought he was to be the fall guy. Vic would need one, any fool could see that much.

'Jamie Hicks? Are you sure?'

Maura was astounded at what she was hearing.

Garry was incensed.

'Of course I am fucking sure! The slimy little cunt! All I done for him when he was banged up an' all! I made sure he had a few quid, a cell of his own and a drink regular as clockwork. I weighed out a small fortune getting him an easy sleep – and that ponce has the fucking nerve to be seen with Vic Joliff. Well, Maura, this is it. We have tried the softly-softly approach. Now it's all guns fucking blazing and serious aggravation for anyone who might even know their dates of bastard birth!'

Maura, normally the voice of reason, nodded in acquiescence. For once Garry was right. Vic was out in the open now and they had to make a stand, a public stand. It occurred to her that she was getting too old for all this, and the knowledge depressed her slightly. All she wanted to do was go home and get laid, but the way Tommy was acting she had a feeling that was the last thing on his agenda today. He was miffed and she couldn't blame him.

But what could she do really? Once more she had to watch out for her brothers. They were all too lairy to be left to their own devices.

Garry was shrewd enough, but too short-tempered ever to be the real boss. He didn't have a cool enough head to think things through properly. Benny, well, he was Benny, enough said. Lee, God love him, didn't have the brain capacity of a retarded gnat, Roy was on more pills than a Welsh crack dealer, and the workforce was just that, a workforce. No budding Machiavellis among that lot. So as usual it was all left to her, and it was getting a bit wearing to say the least.

Times like today she wondered why she bothered with any of it.

Carla and Joey were walking down the Portobello Road. It had changed so much since she was young but unlike Maura she liked the changes. Carla liked star fucking and being in the company of famous people. As they walked she drew more than a few admiring glances herself. She ignored them. There was only one man on her mind and even though she knew it was wrong, that it could only lead to trouble, Tommy Rifkind had filled her thoughts now for months. He was Maura's and she knew it. All was fair in love and war, though, surely? But the thought failed to cheer her. Maura would not take kindly to Carla's making a play for her man. It would be war all right.

Maura came across all sweetness and light but inside she was a hard fucker and Carla had always known that. But just to look at Tommy set her pulses racing, and knowing Maura like she did, Carla believed her rival was past all that. Had been since she was seventeen years old. How many times had she heard the story of Maura's abortion and subsequent joining of the family firm? Her granny had regaled her with the story so many times it was practically engraved on Carla's heart.

Maura herself never discussed it. They had talked about everything else over the years, and she acknowledged that Maura had been good to her ever since she had been a baby and Maura and her grandmother had taken her from Janine after a serious beating. Carla knew she should be grateful. But how long could gratitude be expected to *last*, for fuck's sake? She was a grown woman now with a son of her own and she was not getting any younger. She knew Tommy watched her. The sensible part of her told her that any man would watch her, the way she carried on around him, but still she was sure he felt a connection as well.

But even if he did, what could become of it?

She was playing with fire and she knew it, but it was years since a man had affected her like this and she was determined to make the most of it.

Joey, seeing a beautiful white dress in a shop window, drew her attention to it.

'Oh, Mum, look. That is *so* you!'

She looked. It was indeed a beautiful dress and might have been made for her.

'That would knock Tommy's eyes out!'

Her son's voice was effeminate and high-pitched. For once it didn't annoy her. She hugged him.

'Naughty, naughty.'

Joey grinned.

'You, Mother, are the naughty one – and good luck to you, I say. But watch yourself. Marvellous Maura won't like you going after what she sees as hers, you know.'

Carla laughed nervously.

'Shall I try it on?'

'Be a crime not to, woman.'

She followed him into the shop like a schoolgirl. They were giggling and laughing together as she tried on the dress. He was more like a daughter than a son and Carla found herself enjoying the fact.

The dress was perfect for her and she bought it there and then.

Inside, that small warning voice nagged away but she shut it out. Surely she was as entitled to a bit of happiness as Maura was? And, she told herself, it was only a little bit of flirting, nothing more.

She pushed down the voice that screamed against her disloyalty and walked out into the street with her son, the carrier bag clutched safely in her hot little hand. It didn't occur to her that she had paid for the dress with money that Maura had provided. She never thought of her allowance as money *given* to her. To Carla it was money that was hers by right. She was a Ryan as well, after all. She deserved a slice of the family fortune. And if it was up to her she would be getting a much bigger piece of the pie. She felt that what Maura gave her wasn't half enough money to keep up her expensive new lifestyle.

Such were the thoughts of Carla Ryan as she walked to her brand-new Mercedes SLK and made the journey home.

# Chapter Nine

Maura drove into the council estate in Essex where she knew Jamie Hicks's wife lived. It was the first time she had been to the house for months. When Jamie had got a seven for possession of firearms he had been working for the Ryans at the time and she had obviously made sure that Danielle was taken care of. Garry himself had looked after Jamie.

Maura had always got on well with Danielle, and liked her. Married far too young she had shunted out kids at an alarming rate. The once pretty girl with the natural blonde hair and smiling carefree manner had soon been replaced by a screaming harridan who was not only overweight but overworked as well. Consequently Jamie had been on the scene less and less.

It amazed Maura that more of these women didn't realise that children drove a wedge between couples – at least, lots of children did. Most men were still children themselves at heart and wanted to be taken care of. A woman with six kids had no time for herself, let alone her old man. She sighed as she thought of the number of times Danny had been on the receiving end of Jamie's latest affair. Even banged up he was still running women. Once Danielle had turned up for a remand visit at the same time as another of his birds. This one was heavily pregnant and very vocal about the love of her life. Danielle had chinned her as she had chinned countless other girls during her married life. Even Jamie was wary of her when she lost her temper and it was surely a sight to behold. Danielle was a laugh, she was kind and she was funny. But woe betide anyone who upset her. Then she was a force to be reckoned with, a tiny, fat fighting machine who made even Garry quip that she could join the family firm if she liked as he could do with a decent minder – this after she had been up before the beak for ABH on a social worker.

But basically, as Maura knew, Danielle was what Jamie had made her. Every day of her life was a struggle, a fight for existence. Jamie was not free with his money, not to his wife anyway. She still had to get her Social Security because he was off the scene so much. Jamie would travel miles for a good shag, as he often declared when drunk, and then his family would be forgotten about. Until eventually, penniless and disgruntled, he would roll home and Danielle would take him back.

Maura walked into the maisonette – the door was rarely locked – and called out in a friendly manner:

'All right, Danny. It's me, Maura.'

Danielle came rushing down the stairs. She was out of breath as usual and, Maura was sorry to see, heavily pregnant. Also as usual.

'Hello, mate. I was just thinking about you! Come and have a cuppa.'

Maura followed her into the tiny kitchen and sat herself at the small breakfast bar that was more a serving hatch into the lounge. From there she observed the usual clutter of kids' junk. The furniture was old and scruffy, and knowing the hefty wedge that Jamie had made over the years it annoyed her. Instead of this place they should have been in a nicely decorated semi somewhere. God knows he could have bought one five times over for cash, the money he had earned from the Ryans over the years. He was a ponce and when she located him she was going to tell him exactly what she thought of him.

Placing a chipped mug full of strong tea down on the counter, Danny said gaily, 'Where is the bastard then? Sent you round to see how the land lies, has he?'

The pleasure in her voice made Maura feel terrible inside. Danny wanted that piece of shit, as she thought of Jamie, so badly and yet he had brought her this low, had brought her to this place and then abandoned her here without a second's thought for her or for his children.

Maura sipped the scalding liquid before replying.

'I was hoping you could tell me where he is?'

Danny looked troubled.

'Don't Garry know then? He always knows where that tosspot is.'

Danny was smiling; Maura knew she was hoping to hear exactly what she wanted to hear. She could feel panic rising in the smiling girl opposite her and felt so sorry for her she could have cried herself.

Maura shook her head.

'It seems he's batting for the other side these days, Danny.'

Danny's bloated face was all worry and fear now. She was intelligent enough to know that if Maura was looking for Jamie herself then he was in deep shit.

'What do you mean?' she said fearfully.

Maura shrugged.

'What I say. He's in with Vic Joliff. They were seen together at Le Marais yesterday. Seems we ain't good enough for him these days. Garry and me want a word with him as well – need to clarify a few things.'

'Such as?'

'Such as what the fuck Vic wants from him.'

Danielle felt her heart sink at the thought of what Jamie had dragged her into this time. He had brought trouble to her door many times: other birds – some with babies, debt collectors, Old Bill. But never had she felt in actual danger until now. Until Maura Ryan, with whom she had always got on, was sitting in her kitchen and asking where the bastard was. She was also telling Danielle in her own subtle way that the few quid that came in regularly each week was on the out now because Jamie had taken up with another firm. Danielle would launch that ponce into outer space when she got her hands on him. She instinctively put her hands to her swollen belly.

'I ain't seen him, Maura. I thought you was here to tell me he was on his way home.'

She started to cry, a silent tearless crying that was all the more powerful because it was so deathly quiet.

Maura lit her a cigarette. She knew that Danny had smoked Silk Cuts throughout all her pregnancies. The girl took it gratefully. She had almost finished it before she spoke again.

'The cunt. I hate him sometimes, do you know that? He walks in and out of here like it's a hotel. Uses me and the kids, then ups and fucks off again without a thought as to how I'm coping. Now on top of all this I've lost the few quid Garry bungs me every week, and I depend on that money, Maura, fucking depend on it. I'm paying off so much, loans he took out for Christmas, and I had Trevor Tanks round here last night looking for him for gambling debts. Threatened me and all. Said he'd use a blade if I didn't tell him where Jamie was. As luck would have it, me little boy Richie came in then and I think he felt bad for letting a kid see that. Trevor ain't a bad bloke, he just wants his dough. Now you tell me that I ain't even got the protection of you lot any more thanks to fucking Jamie, the slimy two-faced shitbag that he is!'

Maura let her talk it out of her system. She knew the girl needed to let off some steam.

'I had the social worker round again last week. My eldest, Petey, crunched another fucking boy at school and broke his pelvis, nicked a motor and slagged off the filth. I have to go to court with him in two weeks' time and this one is fucking due on the same day! I told him: "Petey," I said, "with the name Hicks you will be a natural target for the filth." But he thinks that fucking Jamie is the dog's bollocks. Well, boys do, don't they?'

She was really crying now, heaving with sobs, and Maura put one arm gently around her.

'The money won't stop, I promise you, OK? But you have to promise me one thing in return. If Jamie shows up you must let me know. It's better he talks to me than to Garry or Benny. They've got the right arse with him. You understand what I'm saying, don't you? Don't tell him you're going to call me, sweetie, you just tip me the nod on the quiet like.'

Danielle looked into Maura's serious face for long tortured moments before saying, 'Is Garry going to kill him?'

Hysteria was rising in her again and Maura hastened to reassure her.

'Of course not. But he might have to be taught a lesson, see. He's tucked us up big time and we can't let that go.'

Danny relaxed.

'Maura, could you do me a favour, please?'

She smiled.

'Of course, Danny, what do you want?'

'Break his fucking legs if you find him. At least that way he won't be walking anywhere for a while.'

She was half-joking, half-serious, and Maura's heart went out to her once more. It was at times like this she was glad she had no children. They got you caught up in situations that would be laughable if they were not so tragic. To see this beautiful girl brought so low over a man broke Maura's heart, and the worst of it all was, she knew that if Jamie walked in the door right now, Danny would get down on her knees and thank God for answering her prayers.

Though if Maura had anything to do with it, Jamie Hicks was never coming home again.

Sarah and Sheila had been to early Mass and now they were back at the house making themselves some lunch.

'Your hair looks gorgeous like that.'

Sheila smiled happily.

'Thanks. It cost the earth but it was worth every penny.'

'You look different altogether lately. If I didn't know you better I'd say there was a man on the horizon!'

Sarah laughed at her own wit, but Sheila didn't. She knew her brand-new image, which pleased Lee no end, was really for the benefit of Tommy Rifkind. She was a foolish woman and she knew it, but it made her feel better to look good and Lee thought she was fabulous. But then, he thought she was fabulous in a donkey jacket and wellingtons. That was a lot of their trouble. It was hard being adored all the time, especially when you could not adore the other person back any more.

Sarah answered a knock on the door and Sheila was stunned to see her usher in a big bald man who came into the kitchen carrying a huge bunch of flowers. He had a nice smile and was kissing and hugging Sarah who was loving every second of it.

'How are you, girl?'

The man's voice was loud and genial and Sarah was over the moon. She loved attention and this man was certainly giving it to her big time.

'You're looking good, Mrs Ryan. I had to come and say hello. I was in the area like and I thought, I have to see how that lovely lady Sarah is getting on. I was sorry to hear about the old man, Mrs Ryan. He was a nice old boy. I was on remand at the time but I said a prayer in the prison chapel for him.'

Sarah was nearly crying with happiness. This man had remembered her and she was gladdened by that fact.

'Look at these flowers! My God, they're absolutely fantastic. Thanks, son. Thank you so much for remembering an old woman like me!'

She was being positively coquettish and Sheila was amazed to see her mother-in-law like this. Sarah placed the flowers in the big butler's sink by the window and cried: 'Sit down and have a cuppa. Or can I get you a beer?'

Sheila was watching them with an amused smile on her face. Some of the types the boys knew were outrageous. Most people would take one look at this obvious hard case and run a mile, and yet here was Sarah treating him like a long-lost son. The scars on the man's neck alone told you he was trouble.

'I ain't got time, love. Next time, though, I promise. I just couldn't pass the door without saying hello and paying me respects like, to such a lovely lady.'

Sarah was now on the verge of fainting with happiness.

'And who is this other lovely lady?'

He was smiling at Sheila as he spoke, little black eyes fixed on her. He certainly had a way with him, could make you feel you were the only one who mattered to him.

Sarah slapped her forehead with her hand.

'Where's me manners! This is Lee's wife, Sheila.'

The man shook Sheila's hand gently, swallowing it up in his huge callused mitt.

'How do you do, Mr . . .'

'Joliff, Sheila. The name's Vic Joliff. You make sure you remember me to Lee, won't you? Tell him I can't wait to see him and I'll be in touch.'

He hugged and kissed Sarah once more and then he was gone. The kitchen seemed empty without his huge, oddly benevolent presence, and almost too quiet.

'He was a case!'

Sarah flapped her hand.

'Vic's all right. A bit of a tearaway when he was younger, but then weren't they all?'

She was thrilled to have been remembered like that. And the flowers! She could still see him and Michael as teenagers in her mind's eye, along with Gerry Jackson, Michael's best pal. They had all been friends years ago.

She only wished it was those days still and she knew what she knew now. How different it would all have been! Sighing with happiness, she set about putting the flowers into vases. Vic Joliff had made her day. It wasn't often that old people were remembered like this and when it did happen it made you feel special and wanted once more, something Sarah rarely felt these days.

Tommy and Maura were at her new house. She had purchased the property five years earlier and rented it out. Now she had moved back in for the interim. It was a good base and though she'd never said it out loud she'd been relieved to stop living with Carla and Joey. Tommy had been glad of the change as well, which pleased her.

As they ate she watched him. He was a fine specimen of a man and she knew on one level how lucky she was to have him. On another she didn't really know whether she wanted a man in her life at such a tricky time.

It was always like this with her. Michael always said she was too like a man for most blokes, and she wondered not for the first time if he was right.

'What do you think about Joliff, Maura?'

She closed her eyes in distress.

'If I could only see Vic, on me own, I honestly think I could talk sense into him. He always liked me and I always liked him. We're similar in many respects. Vic's a natural-born villain but he's been knocked off kilter by Sandra's death. Needs to blame someone and exact retribution. I understand that, as do my brothers. We would need to do the same if one of the family died.

'To make it worse, Vic's been on the missing list for six years, and knowing him like I do this will have been festering inside him like a cancer all that time. I assumed he was dead, most people did, but he ain't, is he? He is very much alive and off his trolley, as Garry would say. He feels he is righting a wrong. We need to make him see the error of his ways.'

'Kill him, you mean?'

Tommy's voice was low.

Maura shrugged.

'If necessary.'

She looked into Tommy's eyes.

'I would see anyone dead who threatened me or mine, wouldn't you?'

She realised her mistake the second she saw pain cloud his eyes.

'I know what you're saying, Maura,' Tommy said gruffly.

She was sorry for her clumsiness then, and grabbing his hand said sadly, 'I am sorry about young Tommy B. I wish it was different. Because it will always be there, won't it? He's there between us like a silent ghost.'

It was the first time either of them had mentioned what had happened to his son while they were alone together. Maura wondered what the upshot would be, but she knew that all this had to be said and the sooner the better before they got involved any further.

'I don't blame you, Maura, if that is what you want to know.'

'Then who do you blame, Tommy?'

It was a fair question but a hard one for him to answer. They both knew the reply would set the tone of their future relationship.

He was silent for a while before saying quietly, 'I suppose I blame him, Maura. I blame him for being young and stupid and arrogant. I blame him for throwing his life away and giving his mother a heartache she didn't deserve. That is who I blame. But I would be a liar if I didn't say I hated Lee and Garry at times for what they did, even though I would do the same thing myself if I had to.'

She was glad he had voiced his thoughts out loud, but deep inside she wondered if this would be enough. He had still buried a child, and even if that child was a two-faced little fucker who had asked for all he got, he was Tommy's boy and nothing could ever change that.

'Will it come between us, do you think?'

He shook his head sadly.

'I hope not, Maura. This has all been so good for me. After Gina I wondered if I would ever find anyone to really care about again. I admit I have trouble at times when I see you running the boys and the businesses. But I know that is what you have always done and I respect that.'

His gaze took in the beautiful limed oak kitchen where they were sitting. He had money, but not by her standards. This house was as big as his show-piece home in Liverpool and until he had come down south to see this woman he had been more or less happy with what he had. Now, he often felt disgruntled. He would have trouble keeping up with her lifestyle here and he knew it. This house was only one of her investment properties. Her main home in Essex was a huge place that could practic-ally solve the housing crisis in London. She hadn't lived in it since the bomb. But he knew she had worked hard all her life to attain her style of living, and respected that. Still, it rankled sometimes. Nothing went on in the south east without this woman's express permission. Even he had had to ask nicely before knocking over a bank or post office, and pay her a small percentage for the privilege. It made a man feel diminished somehow and he didn't like the feeling.

She grasped his hand.

'I do care about you, Tommy, very much.'

'Same here, Maura. You know that.'

'Terry had a problem with my family . . . with the work side of things.'

Tommy laughed nastily.

'Well, he fucking would. I mean, once a filth . . .'

He saw her expression and sighed.

'I'm sorry.'

Maura smiled wanly.

'It's OK. The boys were the same about him.'

He put a finger under her chin and brought her face to his. Kissing her gently, he caressed her silky hair with his free hand. He loved her when she was like this. Vulnerable. Feminine. Everything he felt a woman should be. He felt the stirring inside himself that her touch always brought and knew then that he would sit this one out for the duration.

She pulled away first, as always.

'What did you see in him, Maura?'

She heard the genuine puzzlement in his voice and

thought deeply before she answered him. She was as honest as she could be.

'I knew him from when I was a girl. We met on a blind date. Marge, me mate, set us up. I didn't know he was Old Bill, and by the time I found out it was too late. I was head over heels in love with him.'

She said the words so simply that Tommy felt sad for the girl she once was with her broken dreams.

'I got pregnant and by the time I told him, he had already found out about Michael, who was a face by then. In reality I'm amazed we carried on so long before anyone sussed us. Michael went fucking ballistic. Nearly killed him. Terry had already dumped me by then. He never knew about the baby . . .'

Her voice trailed off as she remembered old hurts.

'What happened to the baby then?'

Tommy was interested in what she was saying. It was the closest she had ever come to talking intimately before and he was intrigued as well as pleased that she was confiding in him.

'Me mum took me to an abortionist in East London. This was the sixties and it was still all backstreet and don't let the neighbours find out then. It went wrong and I was left unable to have a child again.'

Her voice faltered and she took a sip of wine before resuming her story.

'So Michael brought me into the family firm and here I still am. But Terry and me, we got back together when there was the usual aggravation from plod and found we still felt the same about each other. So that was it really. I loved him, I always will, but I'm not in love with him any more if that makes sense.'

She had deliberately skimmed over the precise circumstances that had brought them together again. Family matters were none of Tommy's business. No need to fill him in on the way her own mother had shopped her to the police using incriminating files that Geoffrey, the bad apple among the Ryan brothers, had secretly kept on her before he met his own well-deserved end at the hands of the IRA. But not before they had killed her beloved Michael in the mistaken belief that he had betrayed one of their high-ranking officers to the Brits when in fact it was Geoffrey all along. Maura had refused to attend his funeral out of loyalty to Michael's memory. Loyalty was everything to her. It was what being a Ryan was all about.

'That's a sad story, Maura.'

Sadder than you know, she thought.

'No sadder than yours or anyone else's for that matter. Shit happens all the time. It was hard knowing I'd thrown away my only chance of motherhood. That was the worst part of it, I think. I had murdered my own child.'

Tommy was studying her face. Even in the harsh sunlight she didn't look fifty. She was still a stunning-looking woman in every way.

He could feel her pain and her anguish at something that had happened over thirty years ago and wondered if any one of us has no regrets. He doubted it somehow. He wished he had not let his son get caught up in the dealing game, but he had and Tommy B had paid with his life. Tommy knew he was responsible for that and sometimes the guilt and regret were unbearable.

'Come on, Maws, let's go to bed for an hour.'

She smiled and followed him up the stairs. This is one place, Tommy thought, where I am the master. In the kip she was all his and they both knew it. Twenty minutes later she was coming like a freight train and as he watched her face he savoured every second of it.

Carol and Benny walked into Sarah's house happily. He loved having a pregnant girlfriend, loved the way his gran fussed over them. Carol and Sarah got on like a house on fire. As he watched his grandmother making them coffee and cold drinks his eyes alighted on the flowers.

'Got a secret admirer, Gran?'

He was laughing as he said it and Sarah flapped her hand at him in a jolly way.

'I have. An old friend came by today, one of Michael's old pals. He brought the flowers with him. Aren't they gorgeous!'

'Who was it, Gran? Gerry Jackson?'

Benny wasn't really that interested; he was being polite. He was the dutiful grandson today. Just one of his many personas.

'Oh, no. God love him, he rings me every week does Gerry. No, I don't think you'd know this man. Before your time, son. Vic Joliff . . .'

The name sent Benny rapidly out of his chair.

'Did you say Vic Joliff, Gran?'

He had to have heard her wrong; it had to be a mistake. Vic Joliff in this house!

'That's what I said. Came in here as large as life he did . . .'

Sarah was ecstatic, telling the story once more. She had already regaled her old friend Pat Johnston with the whole thing on the phone earlier. She was suddenly aware that her grandson was getting himself into one of his monumental tempers.

'Vic fucking Joliff was in this house? Is that what you are telling me, Gran? You actually fucking let him in here?'

Benny's voice was coming out in staccato bursts.

Sarah, realising that something was badly amiss, was suddenly afraid. All her natural antagonism coming to the fore, she cried, 'And why not, Benjamin Ryan? I knew him before you were even shagging born!'

He put his head in his hands in despair. The thought of what Joliff might have done made his blood run cold. He was taking the piss now, taking the piss big time.

Benny tried to level his voice and act normally.

'Listen, Gran, if he ever comes here again you *do not* let him in, right? You ring me or . . .' He was running his hands frenziedly through his thick black hair, making it stand up. Carol knew the signs and was visibly frightened.

'Better still, Gran, I am going to leave someone outside in future. We should have done it earlier but that's beside the fucking point. Vic Joliff is one mad cunt, Gran, and you *do not* talk to him or see him without my express say so, OK?'

'You can't tell me who I can and can't talk to. Even my Michael couldn't do that . . .'

Sarah's hectoring voice seemed to send him mad. She was provoking him with her show of resistance and she knew it. Benny was so upset he forgot himself and the softly-softly approach went out of the window as he screamed at the top of his voice, 'Oh, shut up, you silly old cow! We've got hag with Vic. He didn't come to see you, he used you to wind us up. Can't you see that, woman? Vic would walk straight past you if you had a heart attack on his doorstep. He wouldn't give a shit!'

Sarah was humiliated and it showed. She seemed to deflate before his eyes and he immediately felt sorry for what he had said.

'Stop it, Benny. Can't you see she's upset enough as it is?'

Carol's voice was low. She was trying to comfort

Sarah who shrugged her off with surprising strength.

'Look, Gran . . .'

His voice was calmer now, kinder. She waved him away as she said wearily, 'I understand, Benny. He was using me. I was used. It wouldn't be the first time that has happened, would it?'

She walked from the kitchen and he saw how fragile and diminished by age she had become. He followed her out. In the hall she turned to face him, very much on her dignity.

'Why don't you go now. And shut the door behind you, Benny. I wouldn't want any more of your enemies coming in here with flowers, now would I?'

It occurred to him then that no one else had brought her flowers in years. He was ashamed, he was angry, and he was going to take Vic Joliff and break his fucking neck for the embarrassment he'd caused if it was the last thing he did in his life.

Sarah sat in her bedroom, alone and upset. It was hard for her to be dismissed like this by her own flesh and blood, her beloved grandson. Benny acted as if she was worth nothing. That Vic Joliff had only come to her home to score points in a game they were all playing.

It hurt. She knew there was some sort of panic afoot, she wasn't stupid: hadn't she reared Michael and his sister? Hadn't she had guns in her outhouse and villains at her breakfast table? It was the way

Benny treated her, like she was a silly old woman, that really rankled. It was this reminder that she *was* old and she *was* useless that was hurting her. In her day she had stood shoulder to shoulder with the best of them, her sons had been the terror of Notting Hill, and yet Benny treated her like she was a fool.

She deliberately put out of her mind the fact that she was supposed to be against their way of life. She was cross and wanted him to remember that she was the matriarch of the foremost criminal family in the south east. Suddenly the respect that afforded her was important to her. She remembered with nostalgia walking down the market and getting her due from the traders and her neighbours. Michael had seen to that, she was his mother and he had adored her. If he was still alive that little snipe Benny would have thought twice before he treated her like a fool!

Sometimes she wished for the old days so badly. The days when Michael was head of the house, and young and strong. When he had been just a bit of a lad, not the mad murdering bastard he had become later. She had fallen out with him over Maura because she could accept her sons being villains but never her daughter, and Michael had called her over that. She had buried her boys in turn, fine handsome young men, her Geoffrey set up by his own family. Maura had arranged his death by talking to her IRA contacts, though Sarah had never let on she knew that. In her heart she knew he deserved it for having betrayed

Michael and framed him as an informant.

Secretly she still craved the notoriety of being the Ryans' mother, especially at times like this when even her own grandson shouted at her as if she was nothing and nobody. He who wouldn't even be here if it weren't for her.

Years ago when she had tried to get Maura arrested, after her Geoffrey's death, she had been sure that all she wanted was for her boys to be out of the criminal way of life. Now she wanted to be shown the respect that the mother of successful criminals should get. In fact, did get. Strangers treated her well enough. Even the young fuckers roundabouts, black and white, gave her her due. Her purse would be safe if she walked about with it on her head. She was Old Mother Ryan, and people knew that. The new and famous neighbours spoke to her about her children, whose exploits sometimes occupied the centre pages of the tabloids though nothing was ever proved, her daughter made sure of that.

Sarah sighed, and felt the urge to cry once more. For Benny to treat her like that! He had finally started talking to her again, coming round with that lovely girl, and then he had attacked her once more.

Silly old cow, indeed! Her husband would have skelped his arse for him.

She missed Janine, missed her so much. They had understood each other. She heard the front door open and footsteps thunder up the stairs. For a split second she was scared, and when her bedroom door flew open nearly cried out in fear.

It was Lee. He bundled her into his arms, fear evident in the close hug he gave her. Sarah finally succumbed to tears.

'All right, Mum. I'm here, mate.'

Glancing out of the window she saw that Benny had sat outside with Carol until Lee arrived and that pleased her too. He wasn't a bad boy really. Just hot-headed. Hadn't he waited until she had someone with her? He must care deep down, he *must.*

That thought was a balm to her hurt feelings.

# Chapter Ten

Trevor Tanks was being dragged up a flight of stairs by his hair. He felt the fear mounting inside him and wondered if he was going to defecate in his trousers. He hoped not, he depended on his own fearsome reputation for his debt collecting. But this lot was heavy duty and he was not about to attempt anything that would give Benny Ryan an excuse to glue his eyelids together and use that cattle prod. It was such an embarrassing way of being taught a lesson, which of course was half the psychology behind it. Instead he just relaxed his body as best he could and hoped against hope that he could tell this lot of fucking Loony Tunes what they wanted to hear.

Maura was at the top of the flight of stairs in her office in Dean Street. They had brought him here because he was a frequent visitor to Le Buxom, the hostess club downstairs, and if he told them what they wanted to hear he'd be getting a free night for his trouble.

Trevor, dishevelled and with a worried frown on his ugly face, looked at Maura and relaxed. If she was here then it wouldn't get too out of hand. At least he hoped that was the case, because on reflection she did not look a happy bunny.

'Hello, Trevor.'

Her voice was soft, friendly. Trevor found himself sweating with fear.

'Have a seat.'

Benny smashed him down into the proffered chair so hard he nearly cracked his coccyx with the force of it.

'Can I get you a drink?'

Maura's voice was still calm, neutral. She was acting like this was quite normal, like it was a tea party or something.

'That depends on whether I will be drinking it or wearing it, Maura.'

Even Benny smiled. You couldn't help laughing at Trevor, he was so funny. He talked like Jeremy Paxman on an *EastEnders* trip. He also had perfect comedy timing.

Maura laughed as she said, 'That's up to Benny really. Eh, Ben?'

He grinned.

'You can drink it, Trev. What do you want, the usual?'

Trevor nodded, relaxing a bit now.

A Bacardi and Coke was delivered to him within

seconds and he took it gratefully.

'So what have I done then?'

His voice was strong but still wary.

Maura smiled once more.

'Who said you had done anything, Trevor?' She stayed pleasant, she knew how to play the game. Thankfully so did Trevor Tanks.

He gulped at his drink.

'Well, let me see.' He made a big show of thinking, his usually open face a picture of concentration.

'I think the fact I was dragged out of me house in front of all me neighbours by an irate and, if I may say so, Benny, horribly strong young bastard then forcibly put into the boot of a rather nice but uncomfortable motor first aroused my suspicions. Now I don't know about you, Maura, but in my book that kind of treatment heralds trouble of some kind. On due reflection – and this is only speculation, you understand – I came to the conclusion I had pissed off someone quite badly, namely your good self. I don't know what I'm supposed to have done but I am sure I will be enlightened at some point in the near future. Whereupon I shall beg and plead and try my best to 'fess up, and hopefully be allowed to go on my merry way.'

Benny was laughing so hard he was ready to bust a gut.

'You should be on the stage, Trevor, you're a fucking scream. Ain't he, Maws?'

Even she laughed.

The constant thud of the stripper's music was clearly audible below and every now and then a loud screech of laughter would waft up the stairs. The place smelled as always of cheap perfume and sweaty bodies. Trevor loved it here and wished he were downstairs now with a nice cold drink and every chance of an experienced blowjob at some point in the evening, instead of up here talking to these two nutters.

'So I ask again, what am I supposed to have done?'

'Where is Jamie Hicks?'

The question threw him and it showed. He was all righteous indignation; this was his livelihood they were touching on, for fuck's sake.

'Is that what this is about? He owes me the national fucking debt, Maura. I know you are a force, and I respect that, but I am only going about me lawful business. If everyone who owed me poke hid behind your skirts I'd go out of business in no fucking time.'

He was properly upset now. He couldn't afford to write off debts. Even Benny was sorry for him. Understanding his dilemma, they both hastened to assure him his business was all right.

'No, it's not that, mate. This has nothing to do with the debts. We just want to know if you located him, that's all.'

'Don't take this the wrong way, Benny, but a phone call really would have sufficed. Of *course* I have seen him. He came to me yard and paid me up yesterday afternoon. I must admit I was shocked – he is a cunt for not paying, is Jamie. I normally have to give him a slap before I even get a down payment. That poor wife of his, how she stands it I don't know. He owes everyone, and it's big amounts, not little pockets if you see what I mean. He's into Jonny Ortega for over twenty grand, but you never heard that from me. He owes the coons in Brixton and the front wheels in East London. To put it mildly he owes more money than a banana republic, and you know Jamie as well as I do. He'll carry on borrowing until he wins back what he owes.'

'Was he on his own yesterday?'

Trevor thought again.

'Yeah. Had a nice motor, though. A white Jag, brand new and still smelling of the showroom. I assumed he'd had a touch, a nice little earner, and was paying up his debts. Unbelievable, I know, but that was what it seemed like. He paid up with a smile and was friendlier than usual, if you see what I mean. Normally the fucking Queen comes to the opening of his wallet, but he was free and easy with the cash. Looked like he'd snorted enough coke to get the whole of a Basildon nightclub off their fucking boats too. But then that's Jamie, ain't it? Mr Sniff, the girls call him.'

'Did he mention Vic Joliff?'

'Did he fuck! Me and Vic ain't spoken for over ten

years on account of him shagging my ex-wife. Though it's academic now. Let's face it, everyone shagged my ex-wife. I was the only one who wasn't getting a fucking portion!'

Maura and Benny were laughing once more. This was old news. Trevor's wife had been a byword. She would shag anyone, anywhere, at any time. The crunch had finally come when she had given birth to a child of indeterminate race. As Trevor had said at the time, he could swallow a lot but no one was going to believe that the boy was his. He was as black as the Ace of Spades. The strange thing was, after the divorce Trevor got custody and openly adored the boy, and the boy adored him. As Trevor said, he couldn't leave the poor little fucker with her, she had no interest in the kid at all. She left him down the shops twice! She was on the game now but everyone knew he still kept in contact with her and bunged her a few quid when she was down on her luck. Trevor Tanks was a good sort in many respects, though his rep said different.

'If you do hear anything about Jamie or Vic, will you tip us the wink? There's a good drink in it for you.'

Trevor smiled, sensing the danger had passed.

'I'll deliver them on a plate, girl, if that's what you want and waive the drink. That ponce Joliff needs a good slap and you are just the people to give it to him. I'll even supply the fucking Super Glue, Benny. I hate the cunt.'

Maura was satisfied and said in a friendly way, 'Go down to the club, it's on the house tonight.'

Trevor smiled.

'Nice one, Maura. And can you do me a favour in future?'

She nodded.

'Send a fucking cab next time, girl. My days of travelling in the boot of motors are long gone.'

He was friendly, but he was also saying it was unnecessary what Benny had done to him. He was a friendly face, not an enemy. Maura was inclined to agree with him. She would talk to her nephew about it later on.

Kenny Smith was going on a meet with an old mate. It was a lovely morning and he was looking forward to seeing Jack Stern. It had been a while since they had talked about old times, and since the demise of his beloved Lana, Kenny had been in a deep depression.

As he pulled into Jack's driveway he glanced at the array of prestige motors and grinned. Jack was one flash bastard.

He parked at the side of the wide in-out driveway and strolled up to the house. It was a lovely place, an old red-brick mansion that Jack had taken in lieu of his usual fee for a contract killing. Jack would kill anyone for a price, but other than that he was a nice bloke. He had buried more bodies than the Flying Squad and that was going some. But he was a good mate and that was all that Kenny cared about.

The front door was ajar and he walked straight in as he always did. He was always a welcome visitor to this house. But as he strode into the large morning room he was nonplussed for a moment.

Vic Joliff was sitting on a Louis XV chair by the French windows, smoking a rather large joint.

'All right, Kenny? Long time no see.'

He didn't answer. Vic was being looked for all over the smoke. Kenny himself had had a call that morning from Maura Ryan asking if he had seen him, and now here he was standing in the same room.

He recovered himself quickly.

'Hello, Vic me old china. Where's Jack?'

'He'll be here in a minute, he's sorting out a bit of business for me. Sit down, Ken, why don't you? I'm sure Jack won't mind.'

He was being treated like a stranger in his best mate's house. But he did as he was asked. Kenny was a fixer and as such took the Swiss stance in any inter-firm disputes. He was a neutral observer. He wondered if his visit was why Vic was here today. Either that or he wanted someone dead. Then again, he could want both a fixer and a death. You never knew with him.

'What brings you here then, Vic?'

Vic Joliff observed him dispassionately for a few moments with dead eyes before saying quietly, 'Who are you? The fucking police?'

Kenny fronted him up and it took all his guts to do so.

'Don't you fucking talk to me like that! I had a casualty as well, you know. I lost me fucking wife. I have a kid at home with no fucking mother now. So listen to me, Vic, I have a few scores to settle and all but they ain't with Maura Ryan.'

Vic sneered at him, lip curling in utter contempt.

'Well, that is your fucking prerogative. Personally I will wrench her fucking head from her shoulders and laugh while I do it.'

Kenny had had enough. He said sarcastically, 'Listen to yourself, Vic. You sound like one of the old Moustache Petes from the black-and-white films! It's the twenty-first century, for fuck's sake. Times have changed. You can't tear around causing this kind of hag nowadays. You're a fucking laughing stock with the youngsters. The Ryans had nothing to do with any of it, and you *know* it. Whoever you was in league with back then is behind it only you are too fucking stupid to accept that.'

'Are you insinuating I am a cunt, Kenny?'

Kenny sighed heavily, his anger leaving him as quickly as it had arrived.

'Of course not. But Vic, tell me this much. *Who* were you in league with when you were in Belmarsh? It had to be you behind that car bomb – or else you know who did it. Whatever you think of Maura, she is one shrewd fucking bird. She'll have worked that out by now. She could give us lessons in skulduggery, I can tell you.'

Vic digested what had been said to him and answered in what for him was a sane and normal fashion.

'I can't tell you who I was driving with in nick, but I can tell you this much: they're close to her. Closer than you would think. And I know she's hiding behind her fucking good-girl façade as usual. She *knows* who killed my Sandra. She knows, and she couldn't care less. I mean, that ponce Rifkind still runs with her pack and they wasted his boy! That should tell you all you need to know about the murdering scum.'

He was poking his finger into Kenny's face now, standing over him like an avenging angel, and Kenny knew that the other man had lost it completely. He was high and half-drunk. Nothing he said made sense. Vic Joliff was not to be trusted in any way, shape or form.

'You might have swallowed your knob over your Lana but I *can't let it go.* It was a fucking liberty. *Her and her fucking Scally shagbag of a ponce!* From filth to Scally, her. Fucks the scum of the earth and then acts like her shit don't fucking stink . . . Well, I've had it. I've had it with the whole bleeding lot of them. Time to clear the decks and do it my way.'

Kenny was saved from any further harangue by Jack coming into the room.

'All right, Vic. Calm down, mate. I just had a phone call from Glasgow complaining about the noise!'

Vic stared at him. He had little flecks of spittle at the corners of his mouth and his hollow eyes were completely devoid of expression.

'Is that supposed to be amusing, Jack?'

Jack Stern walked over to him purposefully. He was a small man with short legs and a powerful torso from years of weight training. Jack was scared of no one and Vic remembered that fact just in time. He needed Jack at the moment and they both knew it.

'Personally, I thought it was fucking hilarious, but then my sense of humour was never one of my strong points as we all know. Now sit down and remember you're a guest in my house and this man here is me best mate.'

Vic stalked from the room and when they heard the sound of his tyres screeching down the drive they both breathed a sigh of relief.

Jack shook his head sadly.

'Fucking Radio Rental or what!'

Kenny sat back down once more.

'Does he want a contract . . .'

Jack was roaring with laughter now as he interrupted his friend.

'A contract? He wants me to take out half the fucking south east and most of Liverpool! The only person not on his list of things to do is fucking Gary

Glitter and I would kill that nonce for free!'

Kenny shook his head once more.

'What are you going to do then?'

'What can I do, Kenny? I'll have to talk to the Ryans, won't I? Try and set up some kind of meet. But I am telling you now, Vic is gone. I don't mean just a bit touched, I mean he is off his fucking loaf of bread completely.'

Jack was quiet for a few seconds before saying, 'I fucking need this, don't I, like a hole in the head. I'm supposed to be working on a deal for the Newcastle boys and now I have Vic on me back all the time.'

'As you say, Jack, we'd better go and see Maura Ryan, find out what she makes of it all.'

'Consider it done, Kenny boy. Consider it done. Now how about a Scotch? Wash the taste of that nutter out of our mouths.'

Roy watched as Carla made him some soup and sandwiches. She was so like her mother that at times it pained him to look at her.

'You look lovely, Carla, really beautiful.'

She smiled, and her green eyes lit up with the compliment.

'How are you feeling, Dad? Better?'

He nodded.

'I think so. The tablets make me feel a bit spaced out but I think I'm getting back to me old self. Gradually, like.'

'Well, that's good, ain't it?'

He nodded once more and Carla was amazed at the change in him. It was as if her father had been replaced by a hollow replica of the man she had known all her life. Even his clothes seemed to hang differently on his large frame.

Roy looked defeated, yet when her mother had been alive he had despised her. Carla had despised her too. Janine, as she thought of her mother, was one selfish bitch. Her only interest had been in her son, her Benny Anthony.

Yet Benny had hated her with a vengeance. Had hated the way she had tried to tie him to her apron strings. He still held a grudge against his granny too over her part in his childhood, though in fairness he was trying to build bridges there because of the new baby arriving. Carla supposed the baby would be a focal point for them all once it arrived, the great-grandchild, the new generation of the Ryans.

They all made her sick at times. Anyone could have a fucking baby. Except for Maura, that was. But maybe that was a good thing. Imagine a child born from her!

Carla was being a bitch and she knew it, but it made her feel better. She was so jealous of her aunt, at times it made her ill. Carla watched her getting everything she wanted, even a good man, and she was fucking fifty, for crying out loud! According to all the women's magazines, most women of forty had statistically more chance of getting blown up by a terrorist than of finding a man! Yet there was Maura, fifty and shagging away like a fucking nineteen year old.

It pissed her off, it really did.

If it had been anyone but Tommy Rifkind, Carla knew she could have coped, but her feelings for her aunt had changed over the years and the resentment was getting harder and harder to deal with.

She was kept by her, a woman who was only five years older than Carla herself. Yet Maura treated her like she was still a child. She was *over forty years old* and they all talked to her as if she was a fucking retard!

Sometimes when they were together she felt an urge to tell Maura what a prat she looked in her outdated suits and her stupid bloody court shoes. Who did she think she was? Big benevolent Maura, looking after everyone. But she didn't look after her own child, did she? That poor little fucker had been ripped from her belly without a second's thought. Only it was Maura doing it so everyone was supposed to feel sorry for her. Even Benny, Carla's own brother, treated Maura like she was something special. They all did and it galled Carla more and more every day she experienced it.

*What about her*? That was what she would like to know. *What about her*? Didn't she deserve some respect instead of everyone just asking how she was, telling her she was good-looking and then ignoring her. And what about poor Joey? She knew what they said about him, but she would see her day with them all. She was going to take Tommy Rifkind from under Maura's nose and then laugh at the lot of them.

These feelings had been building up in her for years but Tommy had been the catalyst that had allowed her to voice them to herself at last. Fuck Maura Ryan, and fuck her uncles and her father. He was Maura's golden boy, and she was his blue-eyed girl. They were right, the people who whispered that the Ryans were a bit too close to one another. It was sick the way they all carried on.

Well, sick was the word all right. Maura would be as sick as a parrot when Carla walked away with Tommy Rifkind, *and she would walk away with him*. She was determined on that. She would show them all that she was a person in her own right, a person to be looked up to, admired even.

These thoughts made her smile once more, her charming smile that hid the viper she really was.

Roy, watching his daughter, said loudly, 'Are you all right, love? You look funny.'

She smiled once more.

'Just thinking, Dad, you know how it is.'

Yes, unfortunately, Roy mused. He did know what she meant. He knew exactly what she meant. And it was this that was bothering him.

* * *

Carol and Abul were on another shopping trip and Abul had had about enough of it. Carol smiled at him sympathetically.

'Getting fed up?'

He nodded.

'Yeah. Not my line, shopping.'

'Especially for baby things, eh?'

He nodded again.

'Let's go in here and have some lunch then.'

He followed her into the Bluebell Restaurant in Chigwell. When they were seated and comfortable Abul rang Benny and told him where they were. He knew that was what Benny expected of him and he was happy to do it. Carol waved and greeted friends as she sat at the table like a queen. She knew that her friendships were mostly based on the fact she was Benny Ryan's exclusive bird. She believed him when he said that he didn't do the dirty on her. She still gave Benny what he wanted when he wanted it. The rough sex had stopped now that she was pregnant and for that she was grateful.

But he worried her at times. He changed with the weather and you never knew when he was joking and when he was serious. Like this morning when she had caught him watching her. It unnerved her when he sat and just stared at her like that. He looked weird, and he frightened her.

As if reading her mind Abul said, 'Benny loves you, Carol. I have never seen him like this with anyone else.'

She smiled, her sweet face wistful.

'Sometimes I wonder about him, Abul, I really do. I worry something will happen to him.'

He was dismissive of her worries.

'What could happen to him, love? Nothing will happen to Benny.'

She sighed.

'You're right. But I feel so bad at times. I get scared . . . He's involved in so much stuff and I know nothing about any of it.'

Abul shifted uneasily in his seat.

'You don't need to know anything, Carol, do you?'

She shook her head.

'I suppose not.'

She knew the conversation was closed and they chatted about nothing until the meal was over. As they walked back to their car Abul was pleased the shopping ordeal was over. It was a routine they had been in for a while now. Benny never let Carol do anything alone, including shopping. Now, as well as food and clothes shopping, he had to traipse around baby shops and maternity boutiques as well. Not exactly his idea of a hot day out. Still, he didn't really mind. It kept Benny appeased, and that was the main thing.

As they drove into the driveway of the bungalow thirty minutes later Abul was surprised to see Benny's car already parked, but inside the house there was no sign of him. So he put on a pot of coffee while Carol changed out of her creased clothes. She changed about twenty times a day, and as much as he liked her he personally thought she was a little insipid. But it was horses for courses, he supposed.

Abul punched in Benny's mobile number and waited for it to ring. A voice informed him the mobile phone he was calling was turned off. He was getting worried now but fought to keep the panic from rising. Suddenly he heard a loud terrified scream. Bolting from the kitchen, he burst into the bedroom and was amazed to see a naked Benny lying on the bed, laughing his head off, and a distraught Carol crying her eyes out.

'You rotten bastard, Benny, you scared me!'

He was unable to talk for mirth. Carol was shaking with fear but Abul knew better than to offer anything by way of consolation.

'He jumped out of the fucking wardrobe at me, Abul. The bloody mad bastard!'

Benny was still busting up with manic laughter. Abul, seeing him naked like that, wanted to laugh as well but didn't. He even looked mad today. His eyes were too bright, and Abul knew that the coke he snorted far too often was not helping these spells of his one bit.

Benny was having one of his mad half-hours. That was how Abul always described them to himself. They occurred now and again, and when they did he was dangerous not only to himself but to everyone around him. He was manic, and he was vicious.

But he was also unable to help what he was doing. Abul remembered the first time he had seen him like this. They had been at school, only young, and the first time he had seen that vacant look come over Benny's face it had terrified him.

He had gone on to attack the school bully, Jimmy Bond, with a machete. The damage had been limited in reality but he had still ended up in a Detention Centre for three months. It had made Benny's rep because Jimmy had been a good three years older than him at the time and it had outraged everyone in the school. It had outraged the judge as well, and it was only thanks to Maura Ryan and her contacts that Benny had not gone away for much longer.

It had scared Abul then. Now he was growing bored with it. As Carol ran crying into the en-suite bathroom it occurred to him that no matter what she thought, she certainly didn't get the best end of the bargain as far as Benny Ryan was concerned.

Benny had stopped laughing and was staring into space. Abul left the room quietly and went back to the kitchen. He sipped a cup of coffee and twenty minutes later Benny was with him, dressed and back to his usual jovial self.

When Carol came into the kitchen, still sniffing, Benny looked at Abul and shrugged his shoulders.

'What the fuck is the matter with her?'

Abul didn't answer. He didn't know what to say.

'Fucking women, eh? Who can understand them?'

Benny carried on drinking his coffee and chatting as if nothing out of the ordinary had taken place. Abul for his part was just glad the episode was over.

Until the next time, of course.

# Chapter Eleven

Tommy and Joss were loading his car up with luggage. Tommy was going back to Liverpool to take care of some business that needed the personal touch. Maura was relieved in a way though she didn't say it. She could cope with Tommy for a week at a time and then he irritated her. She was an independent woman and very set in her ways.

She remembered Michael had been the solitary sort too and wasn't sure if the memory made her feel any better. He had said that living alone became a habit that was hard to break, and now she understood what he'd meant. It was great to do what you wanted to, when you wanted to, without having to discuss it with anyone. Even Terry had been a trial at times as he liked his routine and never wanted it disturbed. She pushed him from her mind and concentrated on Tommy.

Joss kissed her and held her close in a bear hug as he always did, and she hugged him back. He was a really great man and she liked him a lot. She could smell his aftershave, Paco Rabanne. It always reminded her of her brother Geoffrey. He had worn it and a hint of it always hung around him. She immediately shut off that train of thought. Geoff was dead meat. She had seen to that after his betrayal of Michael.

When Tommy playfully dragged Joss away and kissed her passionately Maura was pleased. She stood on the drive and waved them off. She would miss Tommy, but not too much. She had a lot on her mind and needed time alone to sort herself out. Other than Michael, she had never really shared her thoughts with anyone, not even Terry. Not her work thoughts anyway.

Tony Dooley Junior was making her a cup of tea in the kitchen and she thanked him before going into her den to do some work. She checked her voicemail and when it said she had twelve messages, set about listening to them in a bored, distracted way.

Work held no interest for her today. She felt like she just could not settle for some reason and it bothered her. It was probably all the trouble with Vic.

She stared out of the window at the gardens. They were as usual immaculate and this pleased her. When she remembered the patch of weeds that had passed for a garden when she was a kid it made her happy to see the manicured lawns and perfectly tended borders. She'd hated that poverty, and whatever Michael might have been, anything he had done was to get his family out of it. The same with her too, though at times she wondered why she bothered with it all any more. This business with Vic had really taken it out of her in a lot of ways. She was sick of violence; had had her fill of it. She lit a cigarette and inhaled deeply on it, smiling her thanks as Tony brought through the pot of tea.

Alone once more, she poured her tea and smoked her cigarette. But her mind strayed once more to her brother Geoffrey. She fancied he was near her. She did sometimes. She felt he had forgiven her, and wished that even after all these years she could forgive him for what he had done. Betraying Michael, abandoning his own brother to the IRA's tender mercy, was to her the ultimate sin. She still had trouble forgiving her mother for her part in it all: Sarah had found the records Geoff had kept and handed them over to the police, naively believing that if Maura was put in prison the boys would turn away from crime. As if. On some level she could understand her mother's simple reasoning but she could never understand Geoffrey's. Jealousy was such a destructive force.

In some ways Carla reminded her of Geoffrey. She had the same quiet way about her: you never knew what she was thinking. She was one-dimensional and it amazed Maura that it was only lately she had even realised that fact.

Good old Carla with the ready smile and the helping hand had never really been a part of anything.

It had only recently occurred to Maura that her niece was oddly secretive and that she could also be an arrogant little mare if she didn't get her own way. Look at her carry on over Maura's refusal to put up her allowance. Two grand a month and no mortgage, and she reckoned she couldn't live on that! Ranting and raving to her brother and her father about it! But then again, no one had ever told her no before, had they? All her life she had been handed whatever she wanted on a plate. A golden plate at that. Maura asked herself now if they had done her any favours with their constant giving. She lived in a house they provided, spent their money like water.

She pushed the thought away, wondering if she was just miffed at Carla's behaviour towards Tommy. She should be ashamed of herself if so. Carla had always been the mainstay of her life. Was she becoming a bitch in the manger in her old age? Tommy was all hers and if Carla had a crush on him then that was funny and sad, hardly a threat to Maura.

But an inner voice was telling her that the calls she used to get so frequently from her niece had stopped and that even Joey hardly spoke to her any more. He was a mummy's boy and always had been. He rarely saw his father, preferring to hang out with his mother instead of friends his own age. But then, Joey was like Carla; they didn't have friends as such, just acquaintances. Maura wondered why she had not sussed all this out years ago. That same inner voice said to her, 'You didn't want to delve, Maura. With your family you could never be sure what you would find.'

Instinctively, she picked up the phone and punched in Carla's mobile number. Her cheery voice answered and Maura immediately felt ashamed of her thoughts.

'Hello, Maws, I was just on me way over.'

'Oh, lovely. Is Joey with you?'

'Nah.' The line crackled. 'He's gone down East Ham Market. You know what he's like for shopping!'

Maura smiled, forgetting that Carla couldn't see her over the phone.

'Tommy still there?' her niece asked.

Something in the way she put the question bothered Maura and this time she couldn't shrug it off. Carla had questioned her in a peremptory, even disrespectful way. Was she imagining this? She didn't think so.

'No. Why?'

She was shorter with her niece than she'd meant to be and Carla gave it a few beats before she answered.

'I just wondered, that's all. Keep your bleeding hair on!'

There it was again, that arrogance in her tone. It was as if she was trying to goad Maura into some kind of reaction. But why? Maura decided she had best ring off before she said something she would regret.

'See you soon then.'

Maura put the phone down, her heart heavy. She

wasn't imagining anything, and all along she had known that deep inside herself. She waited but Carla didn't turn up as Maura had guessed she wouldn't. There was no reason to come, was there? Tommy was long gone. Maura wondered what she was going to do about the situation.

Maura, in her heart of hearts, couldn't be bothered with any of it today. It was as if she was gradually shutting down, and when the time was right and all of this business was finally over she was definitely handing the reins to Garry.

The decision finally made, she felt better in herself almost immediately. She would give it all over to the boys and if they made another pig's ear of it, then that was tough. She had had enough of the lot of it.

She only hoped this business with Vic wouldn't escalate any more than it already had. He was all over the smoke, yet no one seemed able to pin him down. He was on the run from the filth, but they didn't seem to be looking for him very hard. In fact, it was as if Vic Joliff led a charmed life these days. A lot of influence was being brought to bear and it wasn't hers, so whose was it? Officially there was no one bigger than the Ryans in the whole of the country, so who was the latest contender for their crown? Christ knows there had been enough of them in the past and she had seen them all off. One last battle and she was retiring from the war.

* * *

Jamie Hicks was in a betting shop in Bethnal Green. He had already lost a packet and knew that Vic would have his guts for garters if he found out where he was. But one of his favourite horses was running and Jamie couldn't miss this bet. The trouble was though, that while waiting for the main race he got bored. So he couldn't help betting on a few others.

He had lost nine grand in under an hour.

The manager of the betting office was late in that day and was surprised and not a little pleased to see Jamie when he eventually arrived. He said a friendly hello, offered him tea or coffee, and then nonchalantly strolled into his office and phoned Benny Ryan with the good news. Afterwards he stood with Jamie and engaged him in conversation until such time as Benny arrived to take him away.

As Les Grimes watched Jamie showing off his money and making a spectacle of himself while he played the big man, he wondered if this twat needed psychiatric help or what. What would possess a man wanted by the Ryans actually to go into one of their designated betting shops?

But Les knew what had possessed Jamie Hicks. He was a gambler, a hopelessly addicted one. He would walk over hot coals to put his last twenty pence on a three-legged greyhound if it was phoned through to him as a hot tip. All the shop managers knew Jamie, he was a legend in his own lunchtime. A thieving liar, he bragged about his big wins and laughed off his even bigger losses. Even now, he was making a show of getting out his wallet so everyone could see the stash of cash he had. A stash that was getting smaller by the minute. What made a man want to impress a shower of shite like the clientele in here? There was a BT engineer who never seemed to do any work, a pensioner who spent his whole day planning a fifty-horse accumulator, and a couple of DSS blokes who spunked up their Giros and their children's Family Allowance on a weekly basis. He certainly saw life in this place.

Les Grimes was the best manager a betting shop could have. He not only had a head for numbers, he hated gambling with a vengeance. He also hated bullshitters, which was why the phone call to Benny Ryan had been made so quickly. Everyone on the street was now aware that Jamie and Vic were wanted men. Les would give up Jamie without a second's thought for free such was his disgust at the man, but the hefty drink the Ryans would bung him for his call would not go amiss either.

All in all, it had been quite a profitable morning.

Jamie's mobile rang and it was obvious he knew who it was as he rejected the call. Les laughed to himself. That wouldn't go down too well with Vic Joliff. Vic was not a man with much experience of rejected calls. Now that was a bet even he would lay some money on.

He carried on chatting and watching Jamie so he

didn't try and leave before the designated time. Ten minutes later Benny Ryan and his Indian sidekick burst through the doors like something from a cowboy film.

Poor old Jamie. His former audience had no interest as he was dragged out bodily, protesting loudly, from the shop. The quiet when he left was lovely. Nothing except the sound of the TV commentators and the low drone of the scum of the earth talking horses and dogs among themselves.

As far as Les was concerned, this was bliss.

Vic was fuming. As he pulled up outside Kenny Smith's house he made a mental note to break Jamie Hicks's back at the first available opportunity. Going missing like that. He was a fucking ice cream and the sooner he yelped in pain, the sooner Vic would feel better.

Kenny saw Vic walking up his drive and his heart sank. This was all he needed. His mother was out with the baby, thank God. He quickly took out a small handgun and placed it in the top drawer of a kitchen cabinet. He would have no qualms about shooting Vic, though he knew the Ryans wouldn't appreciate it before they got to him. Well, fuck them, he was not about to get himself clumped by Joliff. Though Garry or Benny Ryan, he admitted, would not be a very good alternative, not in the clumping stakes anyway.

Still, fuck them. He would cross that bridge when he came to it.

As he let Vic in, a big smile on his face, he felt the sense of helplessness that Vic instilled in most people, even tough ones like Kenny. If Vic wanted to see you, he would see you. It was as simple as that. Even a locked and barred prison cell couldn't keep Vic Joliff out if he wanted to come in badly enough. Vic would come in with a Sherman tank if that's what it took, but come in the fucker would. With or without an invitation.

'All right, me old mucker?'

Today Vic's voice was full of forced jollity. He had been a decent enough bloke once, before Sandra's death and his recent descent into paranoia. For a few seconds Kenny felt sorry for him.

'What can I do you for?'

It was an old saying they used to have, years ago when they were young and stupid. Two little gangsters out to make their mark. Well, they had both done that, for all the good it had done them.

'Fell out with Jack already then?' Kenny asked.

In the kitchen of the quiet house Vic looked around him and nodded.

'Jack's always been the tricky sort. Nice drum this, Kenny, must have set you back a few quid?'

'Enough to make me eyes water. Lana wanted it more than I did.'

Vic nodded, understanding. His wife had been the same.

'I miss my Sandra, you know. She was a cunt at times. Her mouth could go like the fucking clappers and I often felt the urge to wring her bastard neck. But there was something about her that got to me like. In here.'

He punched his chest.

'Never thought I would lose me strawberry to a bird, did you?'

'Nah. Now you mention it I can't say I did. Not after me own wife anyway. Now *she* made everyone want to wring her fucking neck. Straight up, even the priest avoided her like the plague.'

Vic laughed, and it was his old laugh. He was relaxed and Kenny was glad. He was perfectly ready to shoot him if he had to, but he would rather not. Vic was old time and they went back many years.

Vic seemed to be reading his mind.

'Don't worry, mate, no aggro today, I promise.'

'Glad to hear it, Vic. Want a cuppa, some coffee, a shot?'

'A cup of tea will suffice, thanks.'

While Kenny made the tea Vic got out a bulging white package and started to cut himself lines of coke on the granite worktop. He snorted two through a small straw, bringing back his head and sniffing loudly until it hit the right spot.

'That's better.'

'You should knock that on the head for a while; it fucks up your thinking.'

Vic shook his bald head.

'Not me. It makes me think better than ever.'

Kenny placed the mug of tea in front of him.

'You just think it does, Vic. It's an illusion. Look at that prick from Baring's Bank. He thought he was invincible but he wasn't. It was just the coke doing its usual dirty work.'

Vic was not listening, he was staring out of the window at the rose garden.

'I like roses. I remember in Parkhurst one time, I joined the art class. Some sort with a face like a tiger but great big Bristols was running it so I thought I'd go and have a shufti, and I drew a rose. She said I was good and all.'

He went quiet again and Kenny wondered when he was going to get to the reason for his visit. He didn't have long to wait.

'I want all the Ryans dead.'

Kenny closed his eyes in distress. He'd had a terrible feeling Vic was going to say something like that.

Jamie was in a state of fear so acute he could almost taste it. Benny Ryan was standing over him, with his trademark Airfix glue and cattle prod, laughing like a fucking drain.

'So, Jamie, how are the kids these days? Remember what they look like, do you? Only we have been keeping them in the manner they're accustomed to.

Or at least me aunt has. Remember me Aunt Maura and me Uncle Garry? You used to work for them once many moons ago, before you decided on a death wish.'

He laughed nastily.

'In fact, if I remember rightly my uncle was very good to you, wasn't he? Got you a nice single cell in prison, got you a drink and a few quid for your bets. Took care of Danielle and the kids you can't remember . . . I think you had a touch actually. Don't you, Abul?'

He looked at his friend who nodded vigorously. Abul hoped Garry or Maura turned up soon; Benny was going on one of his mad half-hours and if that was the case he was capable of killing Jamie before anyone had the chance to speak to him.

'Fancy a beer and a sandwich, Benny?'

It was the only way he knew to keep Benny occupied while they waited for the others. Benny treated this kind of work like a picnic and Abul supposed it was to him. It was an enjoyable way to spend an afternoon or evening as far as he was concerned. At times like this Abul wondered at their continuing friendship. Benny had never once turned his aggression on him. They had been mates since day one and Abul had once loved him like a brother and knew Benny still reciprocated those feelings.

'What have you got then?'

Benny eyed the Marks and Spencer bags hungrily.

'All your favourites!'

Jamie watched warily as they started to unpack the goodies from the bags. He wouldn't put it past them to have vials of acid or brake fluid in them. But it was food and he relaxed when he saw that was all it was.

'Chicken and avocado, me favourite!'

Benny tore the packaging away and took a large bite of the sandwich.

'Fucking handsome. Pour a couple of beers, Abul, and we can have a party.' He looked at Jamie and said in a friendly fashion, 'Hungry?'

Jamie shook his head.

'Your loss, cunt. Could have been your Last Supper and all.'

He laughed at his own wit. Abul joined in but Jamie didn't. Personally, he couldn't find anything even remotely humorous in the words.

As Benny and Abul ate and chatted, Jamie looked around him at the cellar in which he was incarcerated. He was in a house in North London, he knew that much, and as he saw the dilapidated state of it he knew that his screams, and there *would* be screams, he was sure of that, would go unnoticed. He knew he had no chance of escape and decided to do a deal if he could. Not with Benny but with one of the others. He had always got on well with Garry and thought he might be the best one to talk to. Jamie would tell them anything as long as it meant he didn't die.

His heart was pumping and the adrenaline was making him high. He knew the excitement was not good for him; he had a slight heart murmur though he had never advertised that fact. His heart was crashing in his ears now as he waited for them to finish what they were doing and start the fun and games.

The cellar door opened and he saw with relief Lee walking down the steps.

'What's this, the fucking teddy bears' picnic?'

He was smiling as he said it and Benny, high on his own adrenaline, laughed heartily.

'You could say that. Want a sandwich?'

'Go on then, I missed me lunch as usual. Sheila has been a right pain of late and the baby is getting to her. Moan, moan, fucking moan. She always liked being pregnant before. This time, though, all she goes on about is how fat she feels. I can't say, "Well, you would feel fucking fat because you're in the club." Obviously, as you can imagine, she ain't in the mood to hear nothing like that, is she?'

Abul and Benny grinned at his words. They knew how much he loved his wife and his constant bitching about her was just a joke.

'How is she, Lee? All right?'

Jamie's friendly voice could have been a gunshot so quiet did the other three men become. Lee walked over to where Jamie was sitting on the floor and kicked him full force in the face. His head exploded with pain.

'You having a fucking tin bath? Do you think this is some kind of bastard game, you treacherous little ponce?'

Jamie was lying quite still; his brain was on autopilot and telling him not to antagonise them further. This was serious, really serious, and he knew then without a doubt that he was a dead man.

There would be no deals done here today unless it was to make them promise to kill him quickly, so that was what he would do. He would ask them to shoot him or something. Get it over with as fast as possible. In return he'd tell them anything he could. Realising the amount of shit he was in, he began to cry. The other three ignored him and carried on eating and chatting.

Jamie listened with all his might to what they said, trying to gauge what was to be his fate. He hoped Maura decided to come – in fact he prayed that she would; she was the voice of reason among this load of Loony Tunes and he needed her. Christ, how he needed her.

Suddenly Benny stood up. Throwing the crust of his sandwich away, he picked up the cattle prod and walked towards Jamie.

'Strip off.'

'What?'

Jamie was trying to delay the inevitable. Benny, hitting him with the cattle prod in the legs, laughed as his body jumped off the floor.

'Strip him, Abul.'

He did as he was bidden, dragging and ripping the clothes from Jamie's person. Then he hosed him down with freezing cold water. This brought Jamie around enough to realise what was happening to him.

His face was roaring with pain, as was his leg. He could see the two burn marks where the prod had touched and burned through his jeans on to his skin. Lee was standing over him as well. Jamie was trying to hide his crown jewels with his hands.

'Hold him down.'

Benny had the Airfix glue out now.

'Please, not that, Benny! Not that . . .'

He said nonchalantly, 'Oh, shut up, you fucking tart.'

Jamie was pleading now.

'Please, Ben, I am begging you, mate . . .'

Benny bellowed, 'Shut the fuck up! You should have thought of this when you decided that Vic fat cunt Joliff was to be your new best friend. Did you honestly think we wouldn't be a little bit miffed? That we would go, "Oh, all right, Jamie. Fuck all we've done for you . . ." Use your fucking head! You brought this on yourself so take what's coming and take it like a fucking man. Now, will you two hold his fucking head still?'

They did.

The screams as his eyes were glued shut were deafening but Abul and Lee just ignored them. They knew from experience that the noise would be much louder before the day was out. Sightless eyes were always guaranteed to put the fear of Christ up people. It was not knowing what was going to happen and when it was going to happen that was worst. Then Benny stripped off himself and snuck up on them, and the prod touched their skin and they got a double shock.

Jamie felt as if he was already dead. He had no feelings in his arms but a crushing sensation like a slab of ice was lying heavy on his chest.

Suddenly he thought of Danielle and the kids and was sorry for everything he had ever done to them. He saw his old mum, always trying to get him out of trouble when he was a kid. Saw his father, drunk as usual with his wide leather belt clutched in his hand. Saw his sister and her army of boyfriends who all seemed to give her a baby and then fuck off. Saw her bright face and pretty hair before she left school and discovered that if you fucked the boys they stayed around for a while. Then everything went mercifully dark.

'He's passed out, look!'

Benny was laughing once more but he was annoyed. His games had not even started properly yet. They wanted to know all about Joliff and where he was, what he intended. They had another beer and then hosed Jamie down once more. He didn't move. Lee and Abul were getting worried now.

'Is he breathing?'

Lee's voice was low and fear was evident in it. Abul took his pulse then shook his head. He was biting on his lip, unable to say the words out loud.

'Is he dead?'

Benny sounded so affronted, as if Jamie could only have died of fright deliberately to annoy him.

'The fucking little tosser! He died? He had the nerve to die on me, did he?'

'Maura will go fucking apeshit.'

Lee was voicing all their fears.

Benny was hanging his head like an errant schoolboy.

'He must have died of fright.' Abul said the words loudly.

Suddenly the three of them started to laugh.

'Maura will go mad, won't she?'

They all laughed again, and that was how she found them ten minutes later, making up silly jokes about the corpse in front of them. As if it meant nothing to them. Which of course it didn't.

Vic was still snorting coke and trying to explain to Kenny why Maura Ryan and the rest of them should die.

'But she had nothing to do with Sandra's death. How many times have I got to tell you that, Vic? You were the one who had her fucking car blown up. You or your associates, only you won't say who they were. What did you expect her to do, swallow that? I know for a fact it had nothing to do with her about Sandra and my Lana. That was whoever was behind you, stirring things. Why the hell won't you come clean about them?'

Vic stared at him.

'Haven't you guessed yet? Hasn't no one on the street guessed who it was? I have been waiting and wondering how long it was going to take that shower of cunts to find out who pulled that stroke.'

'Who was it, Vic?'

Vic could hear the desperation in Kenny's voice and wondered if he should tell him. The man was entitled, after all. But once he spilled those beans he'd have to make all his moves at once. And to do that, to tie up all the loose ends, he needed reinforcements. Now he had the money to pay for them but for some reason he was having trouble recruiting and wanted Kenny's backing.

'Smithy, I ain't as green as I'm cabbage-looking, but for the moment it suits me if people think I'm on a mission to revenge my Sandra. Not that I'm not, don't get me wrong, but once I start opening my trap I'm in twice the danger. I need to get to these people, and I need a mob with me. Help me out here, Ken. You know everybody.'

Kenny slowly shook his head.

'You got a cheek, Vic, you know that? I'm a go-between, not a fucking recruitment agency. Find your own bodies – I'm strictly impartial.'

Vic winked at him.

'Not when it comes to one lovely lady client, eh? Well, will you do just one little thing for me then? Take a message to Maura Ryan. I want a meeting with her, on her jacksy. Just me and Maura, setting the world to rights.'

Kenny looked at the man before him: the nerve jumping in his cheek, the way his hands shook all the time, slopping tea out of his cup till his saucer was swimming in it and he didn't even seem to notice. Kenny knew that if he put this request to Maura she'd probably agree, and he realised *he* couldn't face the thought. There was bravery, and then there was stupidity. With Vic in this state he could do literally anything.

'I can't do that, Vic. I ain't getting embroiled in something so risky.'

Vic sighed.

'Probably for the best anyway. I could feel myself getting a bit soft for a minute there. Tell you what. If you won't carry a message, will you pass on a threat then?'

Then Kenny knew he'd been right. Vic was so volatile he could turn on a sixpence. There was no way he and Maura could have set things to rights head to head.

'Tell her I've a couple of scores to settle first but she's definitely on me list. I'll be seeing her soon. Pass it on, will you?'

Kenny nodded his head reluctantly. Neutrality be blowed. He would say something. The Ryans were good clients and it was Maura who kept that show on the road so it was in his own best interests to speak up.

'Good boy, Kenny, and it's not as if it's a hardship for you, is it? Speaking to her, I mean.'

He didn't know which was more galling: running a madman's messages for him, or having him look straight through Kenny's calm professionalism to the man beneath. The man who cared rather more than he should about keeping Maura Ryan out of harm's way.

# Chapter Twelve

Maura was so incensed that the three men just stood there like naughty little boys while she screamed at them. And scream she did. When she walked in and saw the body on the floor she felt such a sickening sense of *déjà vu* that it almost made her pass out. It was Sammy Goldbaum all over again. It was Michael's boyfriend Jonny all over again. It brought back memories she would much rather forget.

'I cannot leave you lot to do anything, can I? If I leave you alone for one minute someone is fucking well dead!'

No one answered at first.

'It was an accident, Maura, we didn't *mean* it,' Benny protested.

''*Course* you didn't. You lot couldn't set up a fucking prayer meeting in a monastery.'

Their collective looks of embarrassment made her even angrier.

'Did you glue his eyes shut, Benny Ryan? I

expressly told you not to do that to him, didn't I?'

He didn't answer her.

'I asked you a fucking question!'

Benny looked at her sheepishly and it occurred to her that he was to all intents and purposes a fucking maniac. At this moment in time she could just about control him. But for how long? Even Roy, before he decided to blot out the rest of his life with Prozac, had wondered about that – and he was Benny's father.

Her nephew answered her with more spirit than she liked.

'I didn't do it deliberately, did I? Like I said, it was an accident.'

Maura stared at the three of them; they looked like they were outside the headmaster's office after being caught smoking. Yet they had *killed* someone. Someone was fucking *dead*.

And none of them gave a flying fuck about it.

She knew it was an occupational hazard in their line of work, but needless killing was what this was and that to her was worse than anything. Benny got too much pleasure out of what he did, that had been evident for years. Even as a kid he had shown signs of his true nature. He was smothered by his mother and grandmother when all he had ever wanted was to be a man. From a small boy Benny had wanted to be a man. If only he understood what it took to be a real one, she would be able to walk away from them all. Looking at them now, she despaired of ever being free to do it.

Benny and Lee were smirking and this annoyed her even more.

'It ain't funny.'

Abul and Lee looked at one another and burst out laughing; this in turn caused Benny to crack up and as she stood in the cool of the cellar and watched as they all indulged in high raucous laughter, Maura felt as if she was on some kind of hallucinogenic drug. She felt, like so many times in the past, as if she had accidentally stepped into someone else's nightmare.

Jamie was lying on the floor, his eyes glued shut and his lifeless body twisted at an impossible angle. The pain he'd felt before his death was written all over his face and for some reason he was clutching his balls.

It was a sorry scene, a sad and sorry scene, and she was ashamed that she was a part of it. Somehow when Michael was alive she had not felt the same guilt as she did now, because now the buck stopped with her. Jamie was a prat, had sold himself to the highest bidder. He was a gambler and they were always unreliable. Ponce that he was, though, he did not deserve this. The hardest part was going to be telling his wife and trying to make sure she was provided for in the future. Whatever Jamie was to them, Danny at least had loved him. He was the father of her children. He meant something to somebody, no matter how misguided they might have been about him.

She looked at the men. The laughter was wearing thin now and she knew they thought she was making a mountain out of a molehill, that this was not really that big a deal. She was as usual over-reacting – Benny's favourite expression lately.

Maura tried to calm herself down. Fuck Jamie Hicks, he was history. She needed to know about Vic. That was the object of this exercise. What Jamie had had to say was really the most important thing for the family at this moment in time.

She sighed heavily, her tiredness and anger still evident. But it was futile being angry with them, they didn't give a toss about any of it.

'What did he have to say for himself before he died then?'

Her voice was bored-sounding now. Low. Once again they went all sheepish and quiet on her. They looked like they would all rather be anywhere but in this cellar in North London, and she mentally agreed with them in her head. At this moment in time she would cheerfully be anywhere in the world but here. Looking at a dead Jamie Hicks. Wondering how to break the news to his wife without causing her to drop the kid there and then.

'Well, come on then, out with it. I ain't got all fucking day.'

Benny shook his head.

'Nothing.'

'Nothing?' Her voice was rising again and she tried desperately to lower it. 'What the fuck do you mean, nothing?'

Benny shrugged now; he was getting pissed off with it all.

'What I fucking say. Nothing. Fuck all.'

The insolence was back in his voice.

Lee looked at her as he said, 'He died more or less straight away, Maws. We hardly touched him, did we, lads?'

Maura looked at them all again as if it was the first time she had seen them in her life, so deep was her amazement at what they were telling her.

'I don't believe this. Are you telling me Jamie just upped and died without a word?'

Abul nodded, all business now. 'I think he died of fright meself.' He said it as if he was an authority. For some reason this made her even angrier.

'And who are you, Abul? Dr fucking Bronowski? Any fool can see what he *died* of. One look at his boat should alert even you lot of fucking stiffs as to what he *died* of.'

'What do you want, Maws? A fucking autopsy or what? So he is fucking dead. Big deal. Best thing for him, he was a cunt.'

Benny's voice sent her into a frenzy and seeing her face harden he was once more reminded of what she was. What she was capable of.

'Well, Mr fucking Clever Bollocks, he is a *dead* cunt now, isn't he? And we are *still* none the wiser as to what he fucking knew about Joliff. So what do you recommend we do now then? Hire a fucking medium? Or better still, have you got a direct line to Doris Stokes?'

They were saved from answering by the arrival of Garry. He took one look at the scene before him and said in a loud voice, 'Oh, for fuck's sake . . .'

He was standing on the stairs in utter disbelief, staring at the dead body of Jamie Hicks. Their passport to Vic Joliff. She could see annoyance in every bone of his body. Even his hair looked angry. Someone was going to pay for this fuck up, and she was glad about that. Really pleased.

Maura laughed bitterly as she said, 'You ain't heard the best bit yet, Gal. It gets better. He died before they had found out anything. Benny here, Mr Airfix King, fucking frightened him to death.'

Garry was quiet for what seemed an age before he said gently, 'You *are* joking?'

Lee and Maura knew when Garry was going to go ballistic, they had seen him like it enough times, and both moved back quickly as he descended the steps at a fast pace and launched himself at Benny, knocking Abul flying in his quest to grab his nephew's throat.

It would do Benny good to be on the receiving end of this loony bastard's fury, make him realise that there was someone madder than him walking around pretending to be normal.

'You lairy little fucker! Look what you fucking done now.'

Garry's voice was controlled but the anger was in

his eyes, in his body language.

'You just *won't* listen, will you? Mr fucking Big Shot. He was our way to Joliff and you whacked him without a second's thought. You little bastard!'

As he began giving Benny a kicking Maura walked from the cellar. She had had enough of it all. Tony Dooley held the car door open for her and she sat down inside the Mercedes and lit herself a cigarette.

She didn't need to see Benny getting punished, though in her heart she was glad it was happening. After all, it was not before time. He needed to be reined in and Garry was the right man to do it. Garry frightened *everyone*, he always had, and she had a feeling that even at eighty he would still command fear. He was in his early-sixties now and he still terrified people. It was something about him, something in his make up, that seemed to make itself known to people even when he was being nice and friendly. In fact, he was *scarier* when he was being nice and friendly.

It occurred to her then that she could be doing far more interesting things with her life than mopping up after her brothers. This latest débâcle made her more determined than ever to get out of all this shit as soon as she possibly could.

She might even go and live in Liverpool. Leave them to get on with it. Go and live with Tommy Rifkind. Suddenly that seemed like a really good idea. Tommy was small potatoes really, though she would never say so to him, of course. She, for her part, had had more than enough of the upper echelons of crime.

'Everything all right, Maura?'

Tony Dooley Junior was just being polite and she knew it.

'Oh, yeah, Tony, everything is fucking wonderful, mate. Couldn't be better in fact. Nothing like somebody dying of fright to make my fucking day.'

He decided that he'd best leave her alone with her thoughts. She looked angry and he had no intention of being on the wrong side of Maura Ryan when she had the hump. He had learned *that* very early on.

Maura ended up at her mother's. Sarah had rung her and literally begged her to come by. Inside her childhood home, with a slice of home-made cake and a cup of tea in her hand, she marvelled at how healthy her mother was looking for her age. She also enjoyed the relative tranquillity. The house even smelled the same. The only thing missing was the underlying odour of damp boys, which had always prevailed when she was small. But the smell of baking, her mother's lavender water and the mustiness of the carpets was the same.

'So what can I do for you, Mum?'

Maura's words were stilted. Together they had tried to build a few bridges but it was hard. Too much water had already passed under them.

'It's Carla. I am at me wit's end with her.'

Maura was surprised; Carla was Sarah's blue-eyed girl usually. But she had heard about the big row between them, though she did not mention it.

'What about her?'

She kept her voice as neutral as she could.

'She's not right, and that Joey . . . Do you think he might be . . . a bit . . . you know?'

Maura was smiling at her mother's obvious distress.

'Gay?'

Sarah nodded.

'I think we can safely assume that, Mum. If he ain't I'd be surprised, the way he carries on.'

'That is *so* terrible . . .'

Maura grinned, enjoying her mother's discomfort.

'Won't be the first one in this family if he is, will he?'

Sarah's eyes were slits now at what she saw as an insult, a slur on her children and their offspring. Maura was suddenly sorry for her; she was from another era, another fucking dimension in fact.

'Look, Mum, things like that don't matter any more. And that is how it should be. What people do in the privacy of their own homes is their business. As long as he is happy inside himself, what harm is there in it really?'

Sarah was getting annoyed now and it showed. Her skinny body bristled with annoyance.

'It's a sin against God for a start.'

'Everything is a sin if you want it to be. Look, in the Bible it tells you that soothsayers, meaning mediums and people like that, are wicked, right? That they will tell you nine true things and the tenth thing will be a lie? It will be that one thing that will cause you all the trouble of your life. Remember that? Well, it doesn't stop you and Pat Johnston going to the Spiritualist Church, does it? You still want to contact Michael and Dad and Anthony and Benny – and Uncle Tom Cobbley as well for all I know! Joey is what he is, and neither you nor no one else can change him. The Bible is two thousand years old, Mum. Things are different now and you have to change with the times.'

'I don't.'

The words were said the arrogant Ryan way, meaning that they were different from anyone else. Maura sighed.

'Well, that is all I can say on the subject, Mum. Good luck to him is what I think. I hope he is happy, that's the most important thing in life.'

Sarah heard the underlying sadness in her daughter's words and instinctively hugged her tightly. Maura's perfectly styled hair was crushed against her mother's skinny chest and she loved it. She hugged her back, feeling the prickle of tears.

Sarah pushed her away in a jokey way and said, 'I'll make another cup of tea.'

Maura nodded, not trusting herself to speak.

'I suppose you're right enough about your man, Joey. I am a dinosaur really. I still want it all as it was. I want you all back small to when I was your world and this was your universe.'

Sarah held out her hands to indicate the kitchen. 'When I could walk along the road with you all dressed for Mass and looking gorgeous and hold me head up to the world and say, "Look at my babies, aren't they wonderful?" '

'That was a long time ago, Mum.'

Sarah looked sad.

'I know that, love. But what happened to us? That is what I try and work out every night as I lie in me bed. I say me rosary and then I lie there and think of you all. You and Michael mostly. My lovely son and daughter, my first-born and my last, the two I wanted more than any of my other children. I wonder if it was a punishment because, God forgive me, the others I loved but you and him I adored. I absolutely adored you both.'

Maura knew she was telling the truth.

'I'm still here, Mum, and I can't believe Michael is far away from you. He loved you more than anyone else, you know that. Worshipped the ground you walked on.'

Sarah smiled smugly. Her eyes were sad and her voice strong as she said, 'I know. I feel him at times, beside me. He wants me to be friends with you again. Wants us to be like we were, and I want it too. I miss you, Maura; I miss you like you would never believe. Even when I hated you, I loved you too. My last-born, my only girl.'

Maura could not help wondering cynically if this turnaround had anything to do with the fact her mother had fallen out with Carla big time, and with Janine dead and Sheila a long way away she needed a female to control. Because that was what her mother did. With the best will in the world, she controlled people.

As she watched Sarah bustle around making the tea in her large expensive kitchen Maura felt a spark of the old affection for her nevertheless. She had buried too many of her children, and Maura had to remind herself how terrible that must feel. And she had lost them violently through a job they had all decided to make their own. A job of which Maura was now the prime exponent. The Queen of the London Underworld, the tabloids had called her, until the best lawyer money could buy had put a stop to it.

This sad little old woman had brought up her children and then buried half of them. How hard that must be. That was why she would never move from this house. It still echoed with all their voices and laughter. Maura once more felt the urge to cry. She saw her own baby in the bright orange washing-up bowl and closed her eyes to try and blot out the sight. But it was still there. On some level it was always there. All day, every day. So how must her mother have felt, burying children she had nursed against her breast, had fed, clothed and fought over? She'd taken them to school, helped them with Communion and Confirmation. And then, when her job was done and it was time for her to sit back and enjoy her off-spring's company, they had been violently murdered. Killed like rabid dogs by uncaring people who saw it as nothing personal, just a job that needed to be done.

She smiled wryly to herself. You are getting old, Ryan, old and sentimental. But was that really such a bad thing?

'Gis' another bit of your cake, Muvver. That was handsome.'

It was a childhood saying they'd all used and Sarah, hearing it, turned from the old butler's sink and dissolved into tears. Those words told her that her daughter was finally home.

An hour later Maura left the house, her step lighter than it had been for years. The Mercedes was outside but Tony was nowhere to be seen. She rang his mobile. It was turned off. She felt the first prickle of fear then. Tony was a very trustworthy man; he would never voluntarily have left the car. Never. He knew his job and took pride in it.

She noticed the boot was slightly open and approached it with trepidation. As she pulled it up she saw Tony.

He was definitely dead.

She closed the boot gently and tried to gather her thoughts together. The rock star neighbour smiled and waved as he jogged past with his minder and she absentmindedly waved back. Then she phoned Garry and hastily explained the situation before going back into her mother's house. No way was she driving through London with a dead body in her boot.

All thoughts of getting out were gone. Maura was hell-bent on revenge and that was all she cared about now.

Jack Stern was tired but he was happy tired as it had been a very lucrative day. As he lay down on the bed with his girlfriend of the moment, Leonie, he was a very happy man indeed. A happy and extraordinarily *rich* man.

In fact, he was so happy he was going to relax and let his little Leonie do her famed Hoover act. It was the only reason he was with her. A friend had mentioned her speciality and he had deliberately sought her out. She didn't know that, of course, she thought it was her glittering personality. He didn't like to tell her that she didn't actually have one.

Leonie was only twenty-two but stacked like a porn queen. Every inch was real and every inch was his. As he lay on his seven-foot bed and waited to be transported to Wonderland his mobile rang.

He pushed her head away and picked up the phone. He answered it with a curt 'What?' and then he was jumping off the bed and getting dressed. On his way out of the bedroom he heard Leonie say in her best little girl voice, 'What about me?'

He glanced at her as if he had never seen her before in his life and carried on out of the room.

Leonie, all dark brown curls and almond eyes, shouted: 'Fuck you, Jack,' at his retreating back.

Then it occurred to her that she could watch *EastEnders* and *Bad Girls* in peace. Smiling, she settled back in the bed, remote in hand and tits pointing at the ceiling. She stretched like a tawny cat and decided she was going to send out for pizza and drink herself into oblivion.

Wherever Jack had gone she just hoped it was for the night. She could do with a rest. And at the end of the day he might have the quids but Leonardo DiCaprio he wasn't. He was old, old and wrinkly, and she wanted youth. Most women did. She guessed it was probably something to do with natural selection.

Jack drove three miles down the road and parked outside a derelict barn. Inside he saw his partner in crime and his sidekick. He looked at their miserable faces and said quickly, 'Tell me it's not true, for Jesus' sake.'

'It's true all right, Jack. True as I'm standing here anyway. Maura's minder was topped right under her nose. Has to be Vic, don't it?'

'Has he gone fucking mad? Doesn't he realise he

can jeopardise everything we have worked for?'

'You've got to talk to him, Jack. Make him see sense. This isn't the right time to go steaming in. We've got to build up to it gradually, do a lot more recruiting. I'd tell him myself but he hasn't been in touch. It's you he seems to listen to.'

Jack felt faint at the thought.

'I should never have got back into all this. I knew it would be shit, I fucking knew it. Tony Dooley Senior will be back in action now, you realise that, don't you? Half the macaroons in Brixton will be behind him and all.'

Tommy Rifkind laughed nastily.

'Well, no one ever said it would be easy, did they?'

Jack shook his ugly head and said in a voice that sounded most unlike his own, 'You are one treacherous bastard, do you know that? Going back to your girlfriend, Maura, are you then?'

Tommy grinned that devilish grin of his.

'Might be. Might not.'

Tommy walked nonchalantly out of the barn, Jack's barn to make matters even worse. Nothing like putting him on the spot, was there? Suppose Tommy was seen? The thought made Jack feel ill with fright. He was in over his head this time, there was no doubt about that. What had possessed him to get involved the second time around? It was greed, pure unadulterated greed. Suddenly the money did not seem that important any more.

Joss looked at Jack and shook his head.

'I don't like all this, Mr Stern, I really don't like it. Maura's all right and don't deserve all this, whatever Tommy might think. That boy of his was asking for trouble. Let's face it, someone was going to give it to him.'

Jack was past anger, he was just numb with fear and terror.

'That is one two-faced cunt. What have I got meself involved in here?'

'*You* tell *me*, Mr Stern. You wanted it bad enough, and by Christ you got it.'

Jack looked at Joss and said in a high-pitched voice, 'Oh, fuck off, the lot of you.'

Joss grinned, one of his rare facial movements.

'You should have thought of that. It'll all end in tears, you mark my words.'

Jack had regained his composure and said now, 'I don't doubt that for a second. But the question is, whose?'

He sounded far calmer than he felt.

Joss laughed again as he replied, 'I don't think it would take fucking Einstein long to work that one out, do you? Hope you have all your affairs in order, Mr Stern, because if the Ryans don't get us the filth will. We ain't got a snowflake in hell's chance of getting away scot-free and you and I both know it.'

Still Jack didn't answer him.

As Joss walked from the barn he kicked at the black

plastic-covered tablets piled against the wall. There were well over three hundred of them, each a kilo of pure cocaine.

'Enough coke here to send us down for the rest of our natural. Best get it moved before the Ryans burgle us. I'd lay you evens they know about it by now.'

Tommy was waiting in the car.

'Where to, boss?'

Joss's voice was neutral. The closeness between them was growing more strained by the day.

'You know where.'

'What if you get seen there, what then?'

Tommy laughed.

'What if the fucking bomb drops? What if the Second Coming arrives? What if you just shut your fucking trap and drive?'

So Joss drove.

Tony Dooley Senior was at Maura's house when she got home. She went straight into his arms.

'I am so sorry, Tone, so very sorry.'

'I know, Maws. It was part of the job. He was a good boy.'

He was fighting back the tears. Tony Senior was so like his son it was uncanny and Maura had loved this man like a brother for years. He had minded her first and then groomed his eldest to take over from him. He prided himself on the good job he had done.

'Was it quick, do you think?'

She nodded.

'I reckon so. He was a shrewdie. It had to have been someone he knew. Tony had a *nose* for trouble. Had the same instinct for it as you do.'

He nodded.

'I'll take over until you appoint someone else, OK?'

She nodded.

'Are you sure?'

He hugged her once more.

''Course, girl. I told his mother and his girlfriend he was run over. No need to upset them more than they already are.'

She shook her head.

'Let me get us a couple of brandies, we could do with them.'

'It's Joliff, innit? Him as left me grandchildren without a father?'

She nodded.

'Well, he's got a bigger fight than ever on his hands now, Maws. Me other sons and me relatives are angered.'

She sighed. His 'relatives' actually meant anyone with a black skin in Brixton, Tulse Hill and Norwood. Which was a lot of people.

'Tell them to come to me and I'll stick them on the payroll. Whoever gets Joliff alive gets a cool million in cash.'

Tony nodded, satisfied. His son was worth more

than that to him, but it was a good price all the same. A big incentive.

She gave him the brandy.

'He was a good kid, Tony, a fucking good kid.'

Tony Dooley Senior held her while she cried and in his eyes she was more woman for those tears than any other he had ever met. She was crying for his son, and that meant more to him than anything.

Carla smiled as Tommy slipped into bed beside her. She was thrilled that he was with her once more. Since the first time he had kissed her, or more precisely she had kissed him, he had been like a drug to her. His body was all she craved. His touch. She didn't care about her uncles and certainly didn't care about her aunt. In fact, that was part of the excitement as far as she was concerned. It was so long since she had felt anything even remotely this exciting and Carla was hooked. Well and truly hooked.

It never occurred to her that Tommy might be just using her.

Well, it wouldn't, would it?

# Chapter Thirteen

'Who could have done it? That's what I would like to know. It was a fucking professional job, no doubt about that. Busy street and yet no one saw a thing. In fairness I am more than a little impressed.'

Lee's voice held a note of admiration for whoever had killed Tony Junior that was annoying the rest of them. Maura watched them all carefully. Someone close had to be involved and she was devastated that she was actually suspecting any of the people in this room, her own family. A nagging voice told her to remember Geoffrey. She still felt it couldn't be true, though. She trusted these men with her life. But it had to have been someone he knew, someone he trusted. Tony Dooley Junior was the best, which was why he'd worked for her. He had been headhunted widely over the years, that was how good he was. Which left her back at square one.

Tony knew his killer, and he knew them well. How else could anyone have got close enough to him to do him harm?

'Yeah, I take me hat off to them . . .'

Lee was still openly in awe of whoever had done the dirty deed and even Maura could feel herself getting cross now.

'Oh, why don't you fucking wrap up? When we find them you can be the first to suck their cock, all right, Lee? Before I rip it off and shove it up their arses. Cheeky cunt, whoever it was. It couldn't have been Joliff himself, Tony would have put up a row. So who was it, eh? It had to be someone Tony knew. He was strangled. Who do we know who favours that then?'

Garry had voiced her own thoughts and she knew she should have expected it from him. He was always the analytical thinker if at times madder than a fucking March hare.

She saw the looks of shock as it finally sank in with the others what he was saying. Benny was livid.

'You *are* joking?'

Garry shook his head.

'No. Think about it: Tony was one of the best. There's no fucking way he was going to let Vic Joliff harm him, and no way in this world he would have let him within ten feet of Maura. So it's only logical it had to be someone he knew, ain't it?'

'More to the point, it had to be someone he trusted.'

Maura's voice was quiet as she said the words and that gave them added force.

'Oh, great, now on top of it all we have a fucking traitor in our midst! Just like before, ain't it?'

Benny, battered and sore, was still wholly Ryan and so his little contretemps with Garry had been put on the back burner for a while.

'Who, though? Who the fuck could it be?'

He sounded like a fifteen-year-old boy, so great was his confusion.

'Well, that is what we have to find out, isn't it? From now on meetings are close family only, right?'

They all nodded.

Abul knew he was to be excluded but he could handle that. No one looked directly at him, though. No one spoke either for a while as they all digested what had been said.

Eventually Roy, who had sat in on the meeting, closed his eyes as he said, 'I am feeling a lot better, you know. I can take on some responsibilities for you now. Some of the smaller stuff obviously . . .'

Maura's heart went out to him. He had always been one of her favourite brothers and she managed a smile as she said, 'Thanks, Roy. If you could take over the clubs again it would be a big help.'

'Anything for you, Maws, you know that.'

Lee and Garry smiled at him, and their combined love for him made him want to cry again. He always wanted to cry lately; it was as if all his years of unshed tears had finally caught up with him and now he could not stop them.

'What's this I hear? You are the Chris Tarrant of villainy then, eh?'

Maura screwed up her eyes in consternation.

'What do you mean, Benny?'

'Giving away a million, ain't ya? When we catch the cunt, can they phone a friend?'

'Well, they certainly won't be asking the audience, will they?'

Roy's quip made them all roar with laughter, it was so unexpected. They needed some light relief and they got it. It was business as usual in the Ryan firm.

Sarah faced Carla. They were in her kitchen. As Maura had remarked yesterday, she had probably spent more time in that place than anywhere else in her whole lifetime.

It had made them laugh again, though Maura still looked sad about losing her minder. It was lovely to see her again so soon, though. It showed they were getting back on their old footing.

'You look like a whore, Carla. Do you know that?' Sarah told her.

Carla rolled her eyes to the ceiling.

'So what? I like the way I look.'

'Are you having an early change or something? The way you're behaving lately . . .'

Her words set Carla off once more.

'I'm only forty-four, Nana, for fuck's sake. That's

nothing these days. Look at Madonna, Sharon Stone . . .'

Her words were falling on deaf ears and she knew it.

'Oh, leave me alone, will you? All of you make me sick. It's as if I can't have a life of me own.'

'Don't talk nonsense, child . . .'

'I am *not* a child, I am no one's child, I'm a grown fucking woman!'

'Will you stop shagging swearing! Listen to yourself. Like a bloody tart, the way you dress, the way you talk. I'm ashamed of you. Even Maura said yesterday . . .'

'Oh, I get it.'

Carla's voice was low now, sarcastic.

'You and Maura are best buddies again, are you? Discussing the family like the pair of old crones you are. Well, fuck her, and fuck you too, Nana. I do what I want and you and her had better get used to that fact, OK?'

'Maura said she thought you were unhappy, that was all. She loves you like a daughter.'

Carla rolled her eyes to the ceiling.

'How can I be a daughter to that dried up old witch? She's only five years older than I am. But you all seem to forget that. I just get a pat on the head and treated like a fucking favourite dog. That is my *life*, Nana. I know I deserve better than that. Even me own mother, who we all know didn't want me, treated me with more respect than that.'

Sarah sat down with a bump on the nearest chair. She could not believe what she was hearing. Her lovely Carla effing and blinding. It was unbelievable.

'Are you on drugs, is that it?'

'If I was, Nana, then this family would be the main supplier, wouldn't they?'

'Listen to yourself. What on earth has come over you, Carla? Where has my gorgeous girl gone?'

'She finally grew up, Nana, and smelt the fucking coffee, that is what happened to her.'

Sarah looked at her grand-daughter. She had on a skirt that would pass for a belt and a sheer top that left nothing to the imagination. Her long legs were encased in black leather boots. She was dressed for men or for one in particular, that much was obvious. She looked like one of the girls you saw in the Sunday papers who had slept with a pop star or a famous politician. Not like Sarah's lovely little girl.

And her attitude . . . the willing smile was gone, and what was this in its place? This thing, this mad thing that had cultivated a mouth like a sewer and a clothes sense to match.

The world had gone mad.

Carla felt a moment's sorrow as she looked at her grandmother's sagging shoulders. Hugging her Nana, she said softly, 'Just leave me be, eh? Let me be the person I want to be instead of the person everybody else wants me to be. Good old Carla, the family mascot.' Her voice was earnest now. 'Is that really too much to ask?'

'But look at you, child . . .'

Carla closed her eyes in distress.

'Please, Nana. Let's drop it. I happen to *like* me like this. Let's face it, Nan, all my life I have done what everyone else wanted, expected. I have no identity of my own. Let me find one, please. Leave me be.'

'But I worry about you . . .'

Carla had one of her lightning changes of mood and temperament. She stood up straight and yelled, 'Well, don't! I don't want you worrying. Can't you understand the fucking Queen's English, Nana? Stop trying to live everyone else's life and get one of your own, woman. I can seriously recommend it.'

With that she left the room and the front door slammed a few seconds later. Sarah sat in her huge house and cried the bitter tears of age and loneliness. Get a life, Carla had said, when her life was nearly over. And she was glad about that. The sooner she joined her dead family the better; her work down here was done and a nice long rest would suit her fine. Oh, yes. It would be lovely to sleep the rest of eternity away. She realised then she had lived too long for her own good.

Jack Stern was still trying to track down Vic Joliff when he saw a sight on his drive he'd never thought to see. He rushed from the house, a big welcoming smile on his face as he saw Maura, Garry, Benny and Lee Ryan getting out of a black Mercedes. It was driven by Tony Dooley Senior who, he noticed, did not answer his welcoming smile.

He watched as they all alighted and then Tony drove the car round to the garages. Another ominous sign. Did that mean they didn't want anyone to know they were here? Vic, for instance – were they expecting him to turn up? Jack felt faint once more. What was he involved in? He must have been stark staring mad.

'All right? What brings you here?'

He was determined to act as normally as possible.

Maura shrugged.

'We were in the neighbourhood.'

Jack laughed and ushered them all inside.

'I was just on me way out actually, but I can give you twenty minutes.'

Maura looked into his eyes.

'You, Jack, will give us the rest of your life if we ask you to, OK?'

Her tone told him all he needed to know.

'So, what's the problem?'

He was trying to sound businesslike but his nerves were showing through. He felt sick with apprehension.

'Who said there was a problem?'

Benny's voice was ice cold and Jack was reminded of what a mad bastard he was. He tried to laugh it off.

'Everyone who comes here has a problem.'

'Really?'

Benny's voice was insolent and Jack wondered how far he was willing to go and how far he himself was willing to let him. He devoutly hoped it did not come to that.

'Kenny is meeting us here, we'll wait for him, eh? Then we can start. Stupid to tell the same story twice, ain't it?'

'Can I get you a coffee, some tea, a drink?'

They all shook their heads as one.

Jack was more nervous than ever now. This was definitely not a friendly social call, this was trouble, and he hoped to Christ he could talk his way out of whatever corner he had talked himself into.

Leonie waltzed into the room after a sojourn on the sunbed. All she had on was a small towel and a big smile that encompassed everyone. Only Garry smiled back. She was just his cup of tea even at his advanced age; he had always liked the dark ones. As Jack watched him watching her the atmosphere in the room chilled even further.

'Go and put some fucking clothes on.'

Maura felt sorry for the girl; his words were harsh and spoke of complete ownership. She knew how lucky she had been to be part of her own family. That would *never* have happened to her. But then she would not have pretended to like a man old enough to be her father to make a few quid, whoever her family was.

As Leonie walked from the room, embarrassed and angry, Garry said: 'I don't know, Jack, the kids of today have no idea, have they?'

He didn't answer.

They sat in silence once more. It was twenty minutes before Kenny Smith turned up but to Jack Stern it seemed like a lifetime.

Three miles down the road a big white transit van was sitting outside Jack Stern's derelict barn. Three men, all large and with seriously ugly faces, were loading the blocks of coke on to the van. There was no conversation while they worked. Parked down the road a little way off were two plain-clothes policemen in an unmarked Sierra. They watched the proceedings carefully. One was counting the blocks as they were brought from the barn.

'Fucking few quid there, Sarge.'

He was completely awed by the sight of so much coke.

The other man nodded. He carried on smoking a cigarette and observing the men at work.

'So let's get down to business, shall we?'

Maura was very much in control. Kenny and Jack looked uncomfortable and tried not to glance at one another. She watched them and felt like laughing. Two grown men. Were they all kids in disguise really? Only that was how it seemed to her a lot of the time.

'What do you know about Vic Joliff, and more importantly his current whereabouts?'

Jack sat down on one arm of a distressed leather sofa and shook his head sadly.

'Is this a joke or what? We can't divulge information, no one would ever trust us again. Right, Kenny?'

Kenny was silent. He knew how to play the game.

'This is our fucking livelihood we're talking about.'

'My heart is bleeding for you. What about the other livelihood you have going, Jack? The coke and crack dealing? The puff you pick up from a small airstrip in Kent? Shall I carry on cataloguing your fucking livelihoods, eh?'

Garry was looking straight at Jack now.

'You know, there are people here who might think you are stepping on their toes. I could name a dozen others who would not be pleased to know that you are buying their contacts at Harwich, Gatwick and Heathrow. Customs and Excise are expensive friends, aren't they? I was talking to an old mate of mine, one of the big cheeses, and your name kept coming up in conversation. Funny that, ain't it, Jack?'

Benny started laughing.

'Can I tell him, Gal?'

Garry grinned and nodded.

'You see, the thing is, Jack, we have some friendly filth rummaging around your old barn even as we speak. Now I believe in the old adage "finders fucking keepers", see. And if we just happen to find three hundred kilos of coke then that is a bonus for us, wouldn't you say?'

Jack knew when he was beaten.

'I also heard on the grapevine that you and Vic are now tighter than a nun's arse. So it only seems logical that, being a friend of ours, you should share the information.'

'Who told you that?'

Jack's voice was low and troubled. The Ryans knew they had him.

Garry laughed.

'Funnily enough it was one of your old grasses, Little Sammy. Remember him? You turned him in about fifteen years ago to the filth on robbery and drugs charges. Around the time you were getting done by the VAT and tax people. Anything ever come of that, did it? Anyway, he works in one of my spielers now but still has a few contacts around and about. We put out the word, the way you do, and lo and behold, he couldn't wait to tell us. You are not a liked man, Jack, you do realise that, don't you?'

Maura waited for Jack to digest the information before she said, 'So, enough fucking about; where's Vic Joliff?'

He was quiet. Kenny looked at him in desperation.

'You'd better tell them, Jack.'

He looked at his old pal sadly.

'What have *you* told them then?'

Kenny shrugged.

'All I know. I thought you was going to get in touch with them yourself, Jack.'

He was off the arm of the sofa in an instant.

'You stupid fucking wanker . . .'

Benny laughed uproariously.

'Not a very nice way to treat your guest, is it? Basil Fawlty could do a better job.'

'Listen here, you little punk. Vic came round like you lot have. He wanted me to set you all up for a hit, Maura included. I said *no*. It's not the first time I have been asked to get one of you wasted, especially you, Benny. You are not a liked boy either – a very disliked little boy, as a matter of fact. But I said no. Now I get some right strange requests. One mad bastard even wanted me to arrange a hit on Margaret Thatcher but I didn't do it, see. I have even been asked to waste *Charles* over his treatment of Diana. Do you get my drift? I do not take on every job. It's called business and I will thank you not to fucking well come here and ask me mine. I have never asked you yours. And as for the coke, this is my coke. *Mine*, not fucking yours, and it cost me a hefty wedge and you are thieving it. Burgling it if you like. Each bag is worth fucking twenty-nine grand!'

'Lot of dosh. What's twenty-nine times three hundred?'

Benny was laughing as he asked Lee the question. He pretended to work it out.

'A lot of fucking moolah, that's what!'

They all laughed again. Jack felt as if he was in a nightmare and the worst thing was, he knew he was not going to wake up from this one.

Maura interrupted the merriment to ask seriously, 'So Vic asked you to waste us, you said no and that was that?'

Garry's voice was neutral as he said, 'And if you believe that, folks, you would believe anything!'

But Jack merely nodded, his anger still evident. He was smarting more over the coke than anything.

'That's about the strength of it, yeah.'

Garry looked around the room and his eyes alighted on Kenny Smith.

'Kenny?'

'What, Gal?'

'Have we all got "Cunt" tattooed on our foreheads, by any chance?'

Jack sighed heavily.

'For fuck's sake, Garry . . .'

But he and Benny were out of their chairs now and Jack instinctively held his arms up to his face. Garry had taken a small length of lead piping from his pocket. The crack as it crashed into Jack's face was loud in the room. He dropped to his knees, blood oozing from between his hands which were cupped across his nose and face. Benny was laughing again.

Maura walked from the room, beckoning Kenny to follow her.

He did. Gratefully.

'Leave them to it. Come through to the kitchen and I'll make us some tea.' She smiled wanly. 'He'll talk, and when he does we will at least have a working knowledge of what's going on.'

He followed her into the large state-of-the-art kitchen.

'Thanks for all your help, Kenny.'

'I don't feel happy about it. Jack had a point, you know.'

She nodded wearily.

'We're past playing by the rules now, Kenny. This is all-out war. We have to get that mad bastard Joliff. It's gone beyond a joke now.'

Kenny nodded.

'I worked that much out for meself. No sugar for me, Maws, I'm on a diet.'

Like Maura he knew it was pointless to dwell on something you could not avoid or do anything about. So instead they talked of his little girl and his quest for a nanny to take care of her until Maura's mobile rang and she answered it. Kenny heard the dismissal in her voice as she tried to get whoever it was off the line. She was professional was Maura and he liked her a lot.

'Bring the baby over me mum's one day. She would love it, Kenny,' she said, looking back at him.

He smiled and nodded. He might do that. Mother Ryan was a nice old bird, a good cook and all. He remembered going there with Michael and Geoffrey after a bout of serious skulduggery and getting a large brekker and an alibi all rolled into one.

Leonie sat in the master bedroom and listened to the sounds coming from Jack's front room. It was interfering with her enjoyment of MTV classic grooves. But she knew when to make herself scarce.

Tommy sat in his Roller and waited for Carla to arrive. They were going over to Kent for lunch, as far away from their usual haunts as possible. She was insatiable and he wondered why he wanted her. He could do much better looks wise, and age wise come to that, but he always had liked to shit on his own doorstep. It added to the excitement somehow.

As he waited he watched her son Joey walking down the road. A poof if ever there was one. He didn't like the kid. There was something about him . . . but then most of the Ryans were a few paving slabs short of a fucking patio, and this one would sell his granny if the price was right.

He quickly rang Maura and asked her how she was. She didn't ring him often and by ringing her he made her think he was up in Liverpool. She was curt and he guessed she was in the middle of something. She rang off quickly and that annoyed him, too. She dismissed him at times like he was nobody. Well, she had a shock coming to her and no mistake.

He popped the phone back into his pocket without locking it. Joss was annoyed with him and that grieved him. But his mate had to accept that he would do what he wanted. Always had, always would. Only there was a definite rift between them now and Tommy was sorry about that. His feelings for Joss were the closest he had come to loving another man.

Carla got into the car and Tommy shook his head in amazement. She had no knickers on, that much was evident. He snuck his hand up her dress and she squealed at the coldness of it but he noticed she didn't stop him.

She was fluttering her eyelashes at him like a young girl and he noticed the lines around her eyes. She was pretty enough but she wasn't Maura. Maura at least had a bit of class. She could wear a plain dress that would look like a rag on most women yet on her it looked a million dollars.

When they went out to restaurants even young blokes gave Maura the once-over. It was something about her; she had whatever it was that attracted people. She never wore revealing clothes like this one here. She didn't have to sell anything let alone her body to get attention. She got it anyway.

He knew more than a few old lags who would chance their arm if they had the guts. Carla was the poor man's Maura and she knew it. For all her uplift bras and her Brazilian waxes she would never be her aunt. That was her weakness and that was what Tommy played on.

Carla squeezed against him as he copped a feel. She

kissed him, all tongue and Versace perfume.

Tommy hugged her back, hard.

Maura's phone rang again as she and Kenny looked at the debris that had once been Jack Stern's front room. Sighing, she rejected the call. But it rang again immediately.

'Hello?'

Her voice was short, but she could not hear anything except background noise. Then she heard a car start up and realised that Tommy had accidentally turned his phone on and it had redialled the last number called. As she was going to turn it off she heard a woman's voice. It made her heart stop dead in her chest. Then she heard Tommy replying. The two of them were talking filth as they drove along in the car.

'All right, Maws?'

Benny was looking at her strangely. The others were trying to revive Jack Stern. They noticed nothing.

'Yeah, just come over a bit funny, Ben. I felt rough this morning.'

'Not as rough as this poor bastard.'

Maura could not turn off the phone even though all her instincts told her that was what she should do. She walked unsteadily from the room with it glued to her ear. She listened to them talking together, knowing that at some point she would be brought into the conversation. It was this she wanted to hear and yet she dreaded it.

Then Garry came out and said, 'You better get in here, Maura, he's ready to spill his guts.'

She didn't answer.

'Who's that on the blower? And what's wrong with you, Maws? You look as sick as a fucking parrot, girl. What's up?'

She passed him the phone and he listened. He looked at her with sad eyes then turned the phone off and ground it beneath his foot.

'Fuck him. And fuck her, the little whore. They ain't worth it, Maws. But at least it answers a few questions.'

'What do you mean, Gal?'

'Later, Maws. Let's sort this ponce out first.'

She nodded then walked back into the room and forced away all her hurt and disappointment.

It wasn't the first time she had had to do it and she knew that it wouldn't be the last. Family came first. Michael Ryan had taught his sister well.

# Chapter Fourteen

Vic watched as his latest hideaway was overrun by Ryan scum. It made him laugh to watch them all running about like big tarts. He had been hiding in an old converted barn in Ingatestone. There was nothing in the place to tell them anything. Except the message he had left for them. He had spray painted on the wall: Ha-fucking-ha.

Every time he thought of it he smiled.

He was having everyone watched, and as soon as he knew they had descended on Jack mob-handed had bailed out. Now he studied them through binoculars, busy on their wild-goose chase, and it afforded him a bit of pleasure.

He lay in the long grass and wished he had had the sense to bring a rifle with him. He could have picked them off one by one. He was one step ahead of them all the time and that knowledge pleased him.

He took out his wallet and looked at a photo of his Sandra. She was lovely, and he missed her more and more by the day. There had been something about her; they had connected in a way he had never connected with a woman before. They had understood each other perfectly.

The Ryans would all pay for her death, and he would make himself a few quid into the bargain. Sentiment was no reason to stop work, was it? Life had to go on in some respects. Even if it was an empty life.

He was whistling through his teeth as he watched the commotion below him. His 1000-cc motorbike was well hidden down the hill so he would leave once the coast was clear.

He liked bikes, the helmets gave you anonymity. And that was something he needed these days.

Tommy dropped Carla off at her house and declined her offer of coffee. She had shagged him raw and he had to admit to himself he could not cope with her demands again today.

She pouted like a little girl and he half-laughed as he said, 'Leave it out, Carla. I am knackered.'

'We could just have a coffee and a talk.'

He shook his head. Talking was the last thing on his mind where she was concerned. Her idea of a conversation was about something she'd read in *Hello!*. Hardly the stuff of a stimulating exchange.

'Not today.'

Still she sat in the car staring at him and he

suddenly realised she was not going anywhere. Carla thought they were at the famous impasse. He felt his heart sink to his boots. Her eyes were hard, like pieces of green glass. Why had he never realised that before?

'What's going to happen with us, Tommy?'

She had that little girl voice back again. The voice that did not sit well with her age or obvious experience. He stiffened in his seat. He had been expecting this but not just yet. This was quick, considering he was trumping one of her relatives as well.

'What do you mean?'

His voice was neutral and had the note of dismissal in it that women like her had been hearing for hundreds of years.

'I mean, Tommy, when are you going to tell Maura?'

He smirked.

'Why would I want to tell Maura? I love her.'

The pain was evident on her face as she said, 'Really? So what's going on between us if you love her so much?'

He laughed again.

'We were only having a friendly shag, Carla, remember? Those were your words, love, not mine.'

She lit a cigarette and took a deep pull on it.

'No. Sorry, Tommy, I was under the impression we were together. I know it will be hard telling Maura. I'll do it if you want?'

Her words implied that he was frightened of her

aunt and that was why he wouldn't tell her. He also realised she would *enjoy* telling Maura. Nothing like family loyalty in the Ryan household evidently.

'Listen, Carla, you can tell who the fuck you like but it won't change the fact – I was shagging you, love. I am known for it, can't resist a bit of skirt, and that is all you were. No more and no less. So put away the wedding catalogues and get a fucking grip.'

He could see the tears glistening in her eyes.

'You are a bastard, Tommy Rifkind.'

He smirked again.

'So I have been told by better women than you, love.'

With that she jumped from the car and he copped an eyeful of her knickerless bum. As she let herself into the house he realised he was up shit creek and definitely without a paddle of any kind. He could almost hear Joss saying to him, 'I told you so.'

He sat outside for a few more minutes, tapping his fingers on the steering wheel. If he'd thought he was in trouble before, he was up to his neck in it now.

When he pulled away he didn't even notice Abul tailing him.

Kenny had brought a doctor in for Jack who needed one badly. He had refused hospital, even a friendly private one, and so Kenny had rung an old associate who was now stitching Jack up neatly and quickly.

'You are a cunt to yourself, Jack,' Kenny told him.

He didn't answer, just gulped at his fifty-year-old brandy once more.

'Why didn't you tell them what they wanted to know? No one would have thought any the less of you. Now look at you. You look like you've been hit by a car.'

Jack finally spoke.

'What are you, Kenny, me fucking dad? They are fucking animal scum and they are wankers . . .'

'Yeah, yeah, yeah. And you are a prick if you think you can get one over on them. For crying out loud, Jack, these are the *Ryans.* Do you honestly think anyone is going to take them on lightly? Even Vic ain't got the rep for that. Swallow your knob and let this be a lesson to you. Give it a few weeks and then make your fucking peace, for all our sakes. Every fixer in the smoke will know about this within hours, Garry will make sure of that. He ain't going to let there be a repeat performance, is he? Vic will be stonewalled. That's if they ain't already got him.'

'Vic is having everyone watched.'

'Who by?'

Jack grinned.

'That would be telling, wouldn't it? All I will say to you is the apple don't fall far from the fucking tree.'

Kenny rolled his eyes to the ceiling.

'You must have had a right bang on the head if you're talking in riddles. Get an X-ray, you mad bastard.'

Jack chuckled to himself.

'The Ryans have a big shock coming to them.'

Kenny didn't answer; he had already heard enough. He wasn't sure he wanted to know anything anyway. This was all over his head as it was. The less he knew the better as far as he was concerned. He had his daughter to think about.

They fell quiet. The doctor, who had listened with half an ear, would repeat this back to Benny or Garry, Kenny was sure of that. A few quid was a few quid and he had been struck off for drunkenness and being too friendly with the women patients. He needed all the poke he could get and this conversation would enable him to get drunker than he had been for a long while.

He carried on ministering to Jack with a half-smile on his booze-reddened face.

Maura and Roy were at Le Buxom. It was early evening so it was quiet. The girls were just arriving and their chatter drifted up the stairs. Laughter and camaraderie, it made for a good atmosphere. It was friendly and it was unthreatening. Unless the punters wouldn't pay the wildly inflated bill, of course, then it could get positively terrifying. Maura remembered the first time she had seen the bouncers in action. A bolshy punter was sitting on a chair in the basement and all the doorman would say over and over again between punches was, 'Pay the lady.'

The punter paid and she learned a lesson for life. Everything had to be paid for. No matter what you might think.

Still, Maura liked the atmosphere here, it was friendly and easy-going. No fear of any of the girls trying to kill anyone. Except each other, of course, and that happened only occasionally and almost always over a punter.

It amazed her that the club still did big business; she had thought the lap dancing would have put them away. It did for a while but the punters had soon drifted back. A guaranteed fuck always won hands down with the men who frequented this place. The club was in as much demand as ever.

She watched as Roy tried to work out the takings on a calculator and felt a surge of affection for him. She didn't want him to know about Carla. She wasn't sure yet what she was going to do about it herself.

That Carla could do this to her! It was almost unbelievable – like Marge doing it to her. Maura would never have believed it possible if she had not heard it with her own ears.

It was Roy she worried most about. Carla would be without their protection now, she could hardly expect it. But Roy could not cope with any more hurt, they were all aware of that. She watched him stare at the calculator then cancel his sums and start once more.

'I love you, Roy.'

He looked up at her, surprised and pleased at her words.

'I love you too, darling. What's up, Maws?'

She was surprised at the question.

'Why should anything be up? Can't I tell me favourite brother I love him?'

He linked his fingers together and then leant on the desk.

'Is this anything to do with Carla and Tommy?'

She saw fear combined with sorrow in his eyes and felt her heart go out to him once more.

She nodded.

'She don't mean it, Maura.'

'How do you make that out?'

He sighed.

'I've watched her over the years. Janine blanked her. You took her under your wing. All the boys treated her with the same haphazard affection they gave the old man. She feels lost, I think . . . lost and unsure of herself.'

'Oh, really?'

Maura was annoyed now and in no mood to listen to this.

'So she was unsure of herself, was she? Didn't stop her dropping her drawers, did it?'

The sarcasm in Maura's voice pierced him to the core.

'And you forget, Roy, she lived off me. I gave her everything she needed or wanted, including love and affection. I treated her like me own child, which is more than you or her mother did. Now suddenly she looks like she wouldn't be out of place downstairs. She's sleeping with the same man that I am sleeping with. How do you suggest I sort this one out?'

'Don't hurt her, Maura . . .'

She was really upset now.

'Thanks a lot, Roy.'

He shook his head quickly.

'I mean, don't be horrible to her. She needs you whatever she might think. She needs you like she always did and always will. Her trouble is, she wants to *be* you.'

'You have been watching one too much Oprah Winfrey shows if you don't mind me saying. This is cheap magazine psychology. Carla is a treacherous little whore and she knows it. She knew what she was doing, Roy. She is forty-five years old, for fuck's sake. She ain't a little kid any more, though she acts like one. Even Mother has commented on the change in her.'

He nodded.

'Precisely. Think about it. Forty-five and she's still not mature. Still thinks that if you ain't got a man you've failed. She has never even had a job.'

Maura's eyes widened as she shouted at him, 'And whose fucking fault is that then? Mine, I suppose. Blame me for everything, shall we?'

Roy sighed heavily.

'What I am trying to say is, Maws, put yourself in her place and then you might understand her. She's jealous of you and all you have achieved.'

'Well, I paid the price for all my so-called achievements. They didn't come fucking cheap and you know that as well as I do.'

He looked at her without speaking.

'She was over-protected all her life. Treated like she was some kind of queen. Well, I have had it with her now.'

'What about him?'

Maura laughed bitchily.

'Who? He's already forgotten. It's ancient history now, Roy. They can both get fucked.'

'You stupid-looking git!'

Joss was so angry that Tommy was for the first time ever afraid of him.

'You know what this means, don't you, Tommy? Your wandering cock has finally stuck you in deep shit.'

Joss shook his head in abject disbelief.

'You had a woman most men would have given their right nut for, and you did the dirty on her with her own niece and honestly thought you could get away with it?' He shook his ugly head once more. 'You are a prick and you must know that, Tommy.'

The fact he swallowed what Joss was saying confirmed it. He just sat in the car with his head in his hands.

'What am I going to do?'

Joss laughed.

'You tell me, Mr fucking Big Knob. You're the one who got yourself in this mess, you get yourself out of it.'

He got out of the car.

'Where are you going?'

'To see Maura, of course. Try and make things easier for me, if not for you. I want her to know she's had my loyalty if not yours this past six months.'

'You are joking?'

'Am I?'

Joss walked to his own car without a backward glance and Tommy sat there in utter amazement. He had really fucked up this time.

He had loved Maura, resented her at times admittedly but he had cared for her, and as Joss said, what on earth had made him think he could get away with it? With *any* of it, come to that?

Billy Mills walked into Maura's club like a prince. The girls loved him and once word had gone round that he was inside they all made their way over to him. Billy smiled like a benevolent monarch, and kissed their hands, and called them all 'darlin'' or 'my love'. He treated them with respect, and as always with working girls that went a long way. They lapped it up.

He was good-looking and he was not a scrimper so a good night was guaranteed for whoever nabbed him for the evening.

Two blondes, one with silicone and one without, fought over him in a friendly way. Billy, always going for the natural look, chose the blonde with the nice little tits that wouldn't move about too much when he handled them. There was nothing worse than cheap implants as far as he was concerned, put him right off his stroke.

He ordered himself a large Remy Martin and sipped it while he quietly copped a feel of the favoured blonde, Stella, real name Gloria Stennings. She was twenty-eight and lived with a lazy Rasta called Everton. She was a coke head like most of the girls and her eyes were bright as she told him a complete load of old cobblers about who she was and where she lived.

Billy couldn't give a toss; he knew it was all a load of old fanny but he had always liked a girl with a bit of imagination.

Roy was sent down to ask him to go up and see Maura. He didn't really want to go, but he was not about to refuse. So with one final squeeze of Gloria's tit he said, 'Keep it warm for me!' and was gone.

She basked in the kudos of being Billy's chosen girl for the night. He was a nice man and he paid well. What more could a girl want?

Leonie was back in her small flat in Woodford Green. After Jack's bad afternoon she'd decided that the time had come to make herself scarce for a while. She had been frightened when she saw what those people had done to him but she guessed he had asked for it. Jack had an inflated opinion of himself, in bed and out of it. Though she kept that gem of wisdom to herself. She would wait for a few weeks, see if he contacted her. But he looked bad enough when he wasn't stitched up like Frankenstein's fucking monster.

What she needed now was readies. She spent like water and always needed money. Leonie was high-maintenance and proud of that fact. So she had rung round a few mates and scored herself a bit of whiz and a job dancing at the Spearmint Rhino. Life had to go on, after all.

The knock at her door startled her and she opened it with a frown on her face. She jumped back as something was thrown at her. Then when she saw all the ten-pound notes flying around her little hall she screamed with laughter.

'You nutter! What you doin'?'

Her voice was full of the honey only money could put there.

Garry Ryan took out another stack of notes and started to trickle them over her head. She was practically purring with happiness now. She was wearing a short dressing gown from Victoria's Secrets and remembered her legs needed shaving. But, hey, she wasn't about to look a gift horse in the mouth.

'So are we on then?'

She nodded. He might be getting on a bit but he

was one good-looking old fucker for all that.

'Of course.'

'Search me. Go on, do it.'

He opened his jacket and his pockets were stuffed with money. Down the front of his trousers was a rather large bulge which she half-hoped wasn't just more money. Jack was a cheapskate in comparison and there was nothing like money to get her juices flowing.

She squealed with delight and Garry laughed with her. He hoped she was worth ten grand, but by the look on her boatrace, even if she wasn't she was going to have a damn good try.

He linked his fingers together and cracked his knuckles.

'Lead the way, my little darlin'. You are on for the time of your life.'

Leonie was not about to argue with him. She had always prided herself on knowing *exactly* how to play the game.

Vic was in another safe house. This time it was a flat in Dolphin Square. An Asian girl of about twenty-five was already resident and smiled at him. Vic smiled back and then ignored her. She would be gone by the morning, he would see to that. Never liked the dark birds personally.

Vic preferred what he liked to think of as his English Roses. But then Vic knew he was not only racist, he was also British Bulldog. He hated everyone who wasn't English, including the Irish and Welsh, so he didn't see himself as racist as such, more a man who knew right from wrong.

He looked in the well-stocked fridge, finding smoked salmon and champagne. He sighed. He wanted bacon and eggs and loads of fried bread, none of this poncey fucking stuff. He made himself some toast and then checked out the new mobiles he was using. He changed them daily. Even though they were cloned and impossible to trace he was taking no chances.

The flat was owned by an old associate of his with whom Vic had been banged up many years ago in Durham for an armed robbery.

Georgie Baxter was an old lag, but he had had the sense to sort himself out before he went away for the duration. He had set up a few porn sites with the help of another old lag who'd found out in Wandsworth that he had a penchant for computers and was now coining it in legally. He loved it, they both loved it, and neither of them needed Vic Joliff round their necks like the proverbial albatross.

Vic rang his old mum and chatted to her for a while, blissfully unaware that he was about to be turned over.

Billy listened to Maura with bright eyes and a nervous tic on his face.

'You sure about this, Maura?'

She nodded.

''Course I'm sure. You find Vic and I'll give you a cool three million in cash. What's the matter, you think I ain't good for it?'

As she spoke she opened a leather briefcase and he stared at more money than he had ever seen in his life.

'Get on to all your contacts and find that ponce for me. I have had enough of the runaround. I need to know who is protecting him. I swear I will never, ever divulge who told me, not even to me brothers, OK?'

Billy nodded, weighing up the pros and cons.

'I hear . . . and this is only a rumour, remember, not to be repeated . . . but I hear he is good friends with an old Irish associate of yours. Kelly, I think the name is.'

Maura closed her eyes.

It was Kelly who had killed Michael, believing him to have grassed up some valuable associates in the eighties at the height of the bombing campaign in mainland Britain.

'The IRA? What the fuck would they be involved with Vic for?'

He could hear the incredulity in her voice.

'They're also involved with someone close to you, Maura.'

He was clearly uneasy and suddenly she felt as if she had been punched in the solar plexus.

'Is it Tommy Rifkind by any chance?'

He nodded.

She sat back down in the chair, her face a white mask, just as Roy walked in with the drinks.

Maura sighed.

Vic and the Irish? It made sense. She knew Vic had been in Belmarsh at the same time as Kelly's old associate Patrick O'Loughlin. Maura and Garry had been the ones who'd fixed it for them to get anything they needed there. More fucking fool them! And Tommy had a score to settle over his boy. But the question was, how long had he been working against her? Since the off was he just using her, getting her confidence to set her up? The thought upset her far more than she'd thought possible.

But that was obviously it. All his words of love and all his devotion had been an act, and a good act as well. She had lapped it up. He must be laughing up his fucking sleeve. Well, he would be laughing on the other side of his dead fucking face when she finally tracked him down!

She picked up the phone and dialled a number. Billy saw that her hands were shaking. He wasn't feeling a hundred per cent himself now. He wished he had picked anywhere else in the world to go tonight instead of this fucking place.

Maura's face was hard as flint and he was reminded once more that she wasn't like other women. You upset her and you upset a whole family.

Even the IRA wouldn't faze this little lot.

* * *

Garry lay next to Leonie, smiling. She was worth ten grand of anybody's money as far as he was concerned. He had just spent the best hour of his life, and the funny thing was, so had Leonie. She was amazed to experience her first real orgasm without the aid of her hand or a vibrator. She snuggled into Garry's arms and he hugged her.

Like Vic Joliff before him, he had met the one woman he really connected with and Leonie likewise had met the man of her dreams. It wasn't a phoney fuck and they both knew it and basked in the knowledge.

'I know you won't believe this, Garry, but I have never felt like this before.'

He smiled happily.

'I ain't either, Leonie.'

They didn't talk again for a while, just lay together quietly. Then she said, 'Fancy a cup of tea?'

He nodded happily.

'Just what I wanted, girl.'

She got up and he admired her neat little bod as she skipped happily from the room. He saw her suitcase open on the floor and smiled again. Jack Stern's reaction to her now trumping Garry Ryan would be the icing on the cake as far as he was concerned. Then he noticed a scrap of paper among the underwear and smellies. He got off the bed and picked it up, read it quickly and then shoved it into his trouser pocket. She had inadvertently given him exactly what he wanted in more ways than one.

Leonie came back into the room with two mugs of tea and a plate of hot buttered toast. He decided he would move her into his flat within the week. Fuck his other birds, this was practically love. Or as near as Garry Ryan would ever get to it anyway.

Maura met Joss Campion back at her house. She felt sorry for him. She had always liked Joss.

'He don't mean it, Maura. That's the worst of it. He just can't help himself. Gina understood that, see. She knew he was a born womaniser.'

Maura didn't answer him, just sat and listened and sipped at her glass of Scotch. She knew that Joss felt genuinely bad about what had happened. As they were sitting together she was not surprised to see Patrick O'Loughlin come unannounced into her lounge. But she could tell Joss was.

He shook his head sadly. She knew he was sorry about it all.

'I know, Joss. I know everything now.'

'No, you don't, Maura.' He looked at Patrick and said in a strong voice, 'Are you going to tell her or am I?'

Patrick sighed, a small heavy-set man with a shock of dark hair and fathomless eyes.

He was on the Ten Most Wanted list since he had left his cronies and become part of the Real IRA. He had no time for the Good Friday agreement, he wanted the mayhem to carry on. He also carried out arms deals and other nefarious bits of business, which was what had first brought Vic to his attention.

'I'll tell her, man. But first, isn't that Tommy the fecking eejit?'

Joss nodded.

'Tell me something I don't know.'

Patrick laughed. He liked this funny giant of a man with the rugged countenance.

'You're a good man, Joss.'

Maura sighed heavily.

'Can we skip the mutual backslapping and get down to business?'

'It's a hard woman you are, Maura Ryan.'

She laughed dryly.

'Must be the Irish in me, eh?'

# Chapter Fifteen

Garry was happy, or as happy as Garry Ryan could ever be. He had a new toy and Leonie would sparkle for him now as other women had in the past. He owned people as opposed to went out with them. Leonie for her part was quite happy to be owned and he sensed this about her. As long as she had readies and kudos she was happy; he knew he could supply her with both on a very grand scale. On top of it all, she had given him an insight into Vic's whereabouts and for that he would be forever grateful.

He was whistling through his teeth as he drove into Chigwell High Street. If all went well, Vic could be history by the weekend and he could be winging his way to Marbella with Leonie. The possibilities of her lithe little body and sexual acrobatics in the sun were endless. He liked the overweight sort normally, they were grateful for his attention as far as he could see. He liked to be in charge of them, liked making them dependent on him. Now, suddenly, he was in love and it felt good. Leonie was like him, they were kindred spirits, and he'd never dreamed that it could happen to him. At his time of life he had thought romance and love were for other people, and now he had been proved wrong by a little bird from Romford with dreams of the big time and tits that could stop traffic on the M25.

He was smiling as he drove into Verderers Road a short time later.

Abul and Benny were eating a large evening fry up in the Rosina Café in Essex on the A13. The road was permanently busy and the café was positioned in a prime location that was perfect for lorry drivers. It was also a suitably anonymous place for handovers and pick-ups. Unlike the Granada services at West Thurrock it didn't have a reputation for drugs or handguns. This was the perfect place for a low-profile meal and a chat, especially if you needed to meet with a Northerner, Dutchman or German. The truck stop supplied plenty of cover.

So as they ate and chatted they kept an eye out for numerous friends and acquaintances they had made over the years. They were due a pick-up of guns but this was also a fishing expedition. They both hoped they would get a bite before the day was out.

Maura and Patrick were laughing together and Joss marvelled at her powers of resilience. Most women would have been devastated by the events of the last few months, and Tommy's betrayal on top of it all would have left another woman on the ground. Yet here she was acting as if everything was normal. But then, when you thought of Maura's life, what would she class as normal? Tommy had said she was hard to get really close to and Joss could believe that, but he also understood why she was like that. His own father had been a Scally, a hard man who had lived his life to the full. Joss had half-brothers and sisters his mother had no knowledge of, to whom he talked but had no real feelings for. He knew what it was like to live your life behind a mask. To have to keep secrets that could cause untold damage to too many people. To shoulder the burden of making a living for your family while trying to have a life of your own. Maura had done all that and more because, though they didn't acknowledge it, it was she who kept them out of prison and who controlled their every move. Though how much longer she could control Benny Ryan was the question in everyone's mind.

He hoped that his oldest friend Tommy Rifkind saw the Ryans coming for him, because they would. If only for what had happened with Maura and Carla, they would come for him and for the first time in years Joss would not be there to help him out. For the first time ever he was taking a back seat and leaving Tommy to sort things out on his own. And not before time. Tommy needed a wake-up call. Maybe this would be it. It might teach him a lesson he would never forget. If he lived long enough, of course. Which Joss very much doubted.

Patrick and Maura were finally alone. Sipping Scotch, they watched one another warily.

'Was it Tommy on his own?'

Patrick shook his head.

'Nah, he's working side by side with Vic, Maura. Probably some others but I only met those two. I couldn't say too much in front of Joss, as you'll understand. Tommy doesn't know we've tumbled that as yet. Joss might not know everything that's gone on. Stands to reason Tommy will keep a lot close to his chest. He's at a stage where he can't trust anybody.'

Maura digested this bit of information, feeling her face burn with embarrassment. Patrick ran his hands through his hair.

'It happens, Maura. We all get betrayed in the end. And when it's by people we love it's harder to accept. Didn't my own mother try and turn me in once?'

Maura sighed.

'Been there, done that.'

He smiled.

'I remember. Over the fecking eejit Geoffrey. We never wanted to harm Michael, you know. It was just business.'

She nodded.

'I accepted that a long time ago. I didn't really have much choice, did I?'

'You've lost a lot of people, haven't you? Brothers, Terry Petherick, now your niece.'

She stared into his eyes coldly.

'As you have, Pat.'

He nodded once more and finished his Scotch.

'Me mother died, you know, a few years ago. I went to see her in the hospital; I was on the run at the time. Had everyone after me in them days. But in I went, bold as brass. She opened her eyes and told me that she couldn't wait to die so she would never have to look at me again. Called me a murdering bastard. Always had a nice turn of phrase, my mother.'

The bitterness was evident in his voice and Maura felt a moment's sorrow for him.

'Fucking mothers, who'd have them?'

He laughed loudly.

'Well, none of us would be here without them, girl, that's for sure. We spend our whole life trying to please them and we know that no matter what we do it will never be enough. We all disappoint our parents – it's a genetic thing, I think.'

Maura didn't answer him; she poured herself another drink instead.

'You know all about disappointment, don't you, Maura?'

She lay back on the sofa and held the cold glass to her forehead.

'What am I going to do, Patrick? This will all explode soon and I don't want any more violence.'

He shrugged and sat down on the sofa, putting her feet on to his lap.

'You are going to get it, Maura. Nothing you can do about that. Garry will lose it when he finds out – he never liked Tommy anyway. Everyone knows that.'

Maura smiled.

'Garry doesn't like anyone. He can't. It's not in his make up.'

'He loves you, Maura.'

She shook her head. The Scotch had just kicked in and she knew she should stop drinking; she also knew she wouldn't, couldn't, not just yet. She was still feeling too raw. It wasn't just Carla, it was the Vic/Tommy connection. She should have guessed, should have known, but he had played it so well, she would give him that much. Tommy was a womaniser, she'd accepted that, but she had not known he was also a two-faced, conniving, lying ponce who would betray her whole family. *That* was what really hurt. She had brought this traitor to their door and now she would have to sort it out. She wondered who else knew about it all. Once it was common knowledge her humiliation would be complete. Maura Ryan not only cuckolded by a Scally, but he had tucked the boys up as well.

'Garry doesn't love so much as respect or own. That's his secret, why he gets on like he does. He really doesn't care a fuck what anyone thinks of him.'

Patrick nodded.

'That will always be his strength.'

'How long have you known about Vic and Tommy?'

He sat back and sighed.

'Six years. Rifkind was in with Vic, Maura, when you went to Liverpool to dispose of his boy. Tommy Senior was the missing piece you were looking for all the time. Vic hasn't told you for his own reasons. I assume he was just waiting for Tommy to foul his nest and, be fair, he didn't have to wait long, did he?'

She was speechless for a few moments.

'How come you know so much about it?' she finally asked.

'Vic approached us for help as you know, but between you and me we have no interest. Drugs aren't our forte, even though he had a good deal to offer, I'll say that for him. But we fought for a free Ireland; the last thing we want now is a drugged up Ireland. Drugs are already a big problem in Dublin and Belfast and they're spreading all over the fecking place. Vic picked on the wrong people. He should have known better. We would never let it happen.'

Maura was sobering up rapidly.

'Are you telling me you're out for Vic as well?'

He nodded, a half-smile on his face.

'My old mother used to say something about weaving webs to deceive. Remember that old potato?

Poor old Vic still thinks we're best buddies from our Belmarsh days. We'll let him think it a little while longer.'

Maura nodded.

'Are you going to take him out?'

'No. That little job, Maura, is all yours.'

'Thanks a lot.'

'It's why I'm here. As soon as you knew the score we knew we could leave it in your hands. We can't be implicated in anything like this, not at this delicate time. Let's just say that when it's over, we'll owe you a big favour, eh?'

She laughed heavily.

'A fucking big favour, you mean.'

Patrick shrugged, and squeezing her feet gently, answered, 'Whatever you say.'

'You Irish always like to get someone else to do your dirty work.'

He grinned.

'Of course. The English have been getting others to do theirs for years – it was bound to rub off. You don't have a dog, Maura Ryan, and bark yourself.'

Even she laughed at the droll expression on his face. But he had reminded her of how dangerous his henchmen could be and the thought sobered her. They finished their drinks in silence.

Nellie Joliff was a small woman, under five foot tall and dangerously obese. She looked, as many people had remarked, like Vic in drag. She was an old East Ender and proud of it, used all the old expressions and lived up to the reputation she had garnered as Old Mother Joliff, Mad Vic's mum.

She had visited him all over the country when he was banged up and had helped younger women come to terms with their plight when a long sentence seemed too much for them to cope with. She was a kind person in her way and was known to help out anyone who needed it. She was also a chatterbox and consequently Vic never told her anything he did not want repeated around the streets and the local pubs.

She was now staying at her sister's little house in Chigwell and it was killing her. She wanted to go back to Majorca soon, because Vic was on the run again, and she missed all her old cronies and her own little house there. Life with her hard of hearing Bible-bashing sister was getting her down. So when she saw Garry Ryan on the doorstep she smiled a wide smile and thanked God for the diversion he provided.

'Hello, Mrs Joliff, is Vic around?'

Garry was talking to her with just the right amount of respect and the right tone in his voice. He sounded like a geriatric schoolboy and Nellie Joliff loved it.

'Come on in, love.'

She opened the door wide.

Garry stepped inside, smiling. It was so easy if you knew how to play Vic's little game. Five minutes later he had a mug of tea in his hand and was being told numerous stories of her son's new life in Majorca. He was still smiling when he left an hour later, a very happy man.

See how Vic liked *his* family becoming involved in his shit. It might teach him a valuable lesson.

Benny and Abul brought the heavy package into the house in Lancaster Road. Sarah made them both tea as they unpacked it in the garden. The package contained four Armalites and they had to stop themselves from dragging them out of the box and playing with them like they had when they were boys and the guns had been pretend.

'Fucking look at them, eh, Abul. What a touch.'

Benny had reverence in his voice and Abul, feeling the same, nodded at him.

'Fucking business or what?'

They giggled together and Sarah watched them from the kitchen window. They reminded her of Michael and Geoffrey. Michael had always been the leader and Geoffrey the natural follower. Benny was like his uncle that way, had to be the top dog, the important one in the relationship.

These two had been friends since boyhood and Sarah knew that they would be friends until they died; she forced herself not to wonder when that would be. Benny was her baby, had always been the apple of her eye, but as she watched him now with Abul she was reminded again what a dangerous little fucker he was.

He had had every advantage, unlike her own children, and even the death of his poor mother had not really affected him. Yet Janine had been shot to death on her own doorstep because of her family's activities and so-called businesses.

It had not changed Benny, nor made him re-evaluate his life. He was a Ryan pure and simple, and she was responsible for them all. She saw that now as clear as day and knew she had to accept them all for what they were. Benny looked up at that moment and caught her eye. He winked at her and smiled and she felt as if the sun had come through a dark cloud. He was like her Michael all right. No matter what he did she would forgive him.

'When we going to do it, Benny?'

He grinned once more.

'Soon as Maura gives the word.'

'What's happening with all the coke?'

Benny shrugged.

'Who knows? Maura will sort it, Abul. Stop asking fucking stupid questions. Why do you always question me about everything?'

He was having one of his lightning changes of mood and his best mate knew when to leave well alone.

Justin Joliff was fifty years old and he was big. Like his mother he was heavy-set and enjoyed his food. Like his brother he was a mean enemy and an even meaner businessman. But he was a coward, had hidden behind Vic all his life and lived in his brother's shadow and on his reputation. It was Vic who stopped people smacking Justin one, and the worst thing was that Justin himself knew that. This only added to his absolute hatred of everyone and anyone who came near or by him. He was also a womaniser who had trouble getting one woman let alone a string of them, but it didn't stop him from trying his luck with every sort who walked his way. Even the lap dancers at his favourite club charged him double what they charged anyone else and that was only after they had tried to avoid him, something they did frequently and with as much aplomb as they could considering how they were dressed.

His mum loved him, but not as much as she loved Vic. He knew it, Vic knew it, and their mother Nellie was open about it. All in all Justin was a fucked-up human being with an attitude matched only by Attila the Hun. So when he answered the door to his large villa outside Santa Ponsa he was already scowling. He scowled even harder when a shotgun was shoved into his numerous chins, forcing his head back as far as it would go and straining the muscles.

'Hello, Justin, my old son. Fancy a ride in the boot of the nice man's car?'

He didn't answer the man, he couldn't. He was far too scared.

The two gunmen, brothers who were old mates of

Garry's, were still laughing when they tried to shut the boot, but Justin was too fat.

'What we going to do?'

'Shoot him here?'

'What do you mean, shoot him here? What, on the drive, you mean?'

The men, both dark and feral-looking, were apparently impervious to the fear of the man inside the boot. They talked about him as if he didn't exist, and this frightened Justin more than anything.

'Why don't we just go to the villa next door and ask them if we can shoot him on their drive? Don't be so fucking stupid! What about the noise?'

'Well, what are we going to do then?'

The elder of the two men tapped a finger on his chin as he thought.

'We'll take him back into the villa and shoot him in the bedroom. If we put pillows over his head we can muffle the sound.'

'OK.' The younger man turned to Justin. 'Get out of the boot, please.'

He couldn't move for fear.

'What's with the fucking "please"? Just tell him to get out of the fucking boot.'

'Get out of the fucking boot, fatty, or I'm going to do you here and fuck the neighbours, all right?'

He looked at his brother.

'Menacing enough for you, or shall I burn it into his forehead with a fag?'

Still Justin didn't move.

'Don't be sarcastic, bruv. You want to learn the game, right? So do what I tell you.'

Justin listened in absolute terror, unaware that it was all for his benefit, part of their strategy of fear.

The two men dragged him from the boot, manhandling him roughly and swearing at him as they kicked and punched him back inside the house. They searched the place from top to bottom before they finally forced him on to the back seat of their car and drove away with him.

With him now past caring, the two brothers were still arguing as they made their way to Pollensa.

Maura lay on the sofa long after the Irishman had gone. She couldn't get up the energy to move. Tommy's betrayal was too much for her to bear. On top of everything else she'd been through, the thought that he'd been using her left her stunned and drained of feeling. She had always prided herself on how she was perceived by other people. In her lifestyle that was important. No one could be seen to mug you off. Now she had to face everyone in the knowledge that they knew he had fucked her niece and lain in her bed while secretly working against her with Vic Joliff.

She put her hands over her face. Even in the gathering darkness she could feel the heat of humiliation.

Had she been that desperate for human touch that she had been taken in by a shyster like Tommy? Was that what was wrong with her? Loneliness over Terry had left her so vulnerable she had not seen Tommy Rifkind for what he really was. Garry and Lee had murdered his child. Had she really thought they could be a proper couple with something like that between them? Was she losing her edge?

Now there was all this Irish involvement. She had dealt with them many times in the past and each time it had caused her heartbreak. It had to be the right moment to give it all up, hand over the reins and let herself have a life.

But what kind of life could she have at her age, with no husband, no kids, no nothing? What did she really have at the end of the day?

Nice houses, nice cars and nice clothes.

Nice friends?

She had a few good friends, especially Marge, and her child had been Carla though that was all over now. And Terry had been a husband and lover rolled into one. Since his death she had forced him from her mind, she had had to or the guilt would have driven her mad. Now, like Michael before her, she was finding out that it was all for nothing. That her whole life had been completely meaningless.

She felt the sting of tears and forced them away. Crying solved nothing; she had learned that the hard way. She struggled to sit up but the effort was too much for her. Instead she lay back and cried as she had never cried before.

It was a lonely and unsettling sound, one that came from the depths of her being and was all the more powerful because it wasn't loud. It was a quiet desperate venting of her grief that wore her out with its intensity.

Finally she was spent. Dry-eyed, she lay on the sofa in the dark room and remembered Terry and how they had been together. How he had loved her in the darkness as if she was the only woman in the world. She thought of holidays together, meals shared. Remembered how he would always ask her about herself, her family. He had been there for her, and she had dragged them both back into her old life and in effect killed him.

If she had not answered the call from Roy to sort everything out they would still be together now. In their house, living their quiet life.

Yet she had been willing to turn her back on him for the family. It had always been the family who had been the crux of their problems. But what else could she do? They had needed her, like they needed her now. She was the voice of reason and yet she wanted nothing to do with any of it.

The living-room door opened and she saw a figure in the half-light. It was a woman, and seeing her outline Maura sat up abruptly.

'You've got some nerve coming here, Carla.'

Tony Dooley Senior was standing behind her.

'I tried to stop her coming in, Maura.'

She wiped a hand across her face; aware that once the lights went on the evidence of her tears would be there for them both to see.

'It's all right, Tone. I'll sort this one.'

He walked from the room and Carla said gently, 'I'm sorry, Maws.'

Maura turned on the lamp by her chair.

'You're sorry, are you? Is that supposed to make it all better then?'

'Of course not. I don't know what came over me, Maws . . .'

'Tommy Rifkind *come* over you, didn't he? In more ways than one.'

Carla looked as bad as she did herself and despite her anger Maura felt a flicker of sadness for her. Her niece had never really had the breaks. She shook the thought from her head. This was a conniving little whore who had slept with the same man as she and not thought twice about it. This was the girl who had lived off her for years and who had never once thanked her for it. Never, not even once. She had taken all Maura had had to offer as if she was entitled to it. She was family after all, and family meant everything, didn't it?

Well, not any more.

'Please, Maura, let me try and explain what happened.'

She shook her head.

'Just piss off, Carla.'

Carla looked at her aunt as if she had never seen her before. The words were so heartfelt that she realised in no uncertain terms that Maura was not going to listen to her, no matter what she said.

'Please, Maws . . .' She tried her hurt little girl voice; it had worked in the past.

Maura put her hands up to her face and sighed.

'I said piss off. I meant piss off.'

The words were hard, cold, and Carla turned from her dejectedly. Until now she had thought of Maura as her aunt; now she saw she was dealing with Maura Ryan the head of the family, and it scared her. Everyone knew Maura was behind Geoffrey's death. Suddenly Carla was really frightened. Like her Nana said, Maura was hard and she would never let anyone get the better of her. She went to leave then, her heart heavy and her world destroyed.

'And Carla . . .'

The younger woman turned to her eagerly, hope on her face and in her heart.

'Don't come back. You have a week to vacate your house.'

Carla was stunned.

'But what about Joey . . . my things?'

Maura could hear the shock in her niece's voice and felt an urge to smile. It was always about *her*; everything was always about *her*.

'That, Carla, is your problem, love. You should have thought of that. Or did you see yourself lording it up in Liverpool with Tommy Rifkind?'

The truth of the statement hit her and she felt the sting of tears once more.

'I can't believe you're doing this to me, Maura.'

She looked so like Janine as she stood there, her face bunched up with distress and her gorgeous red-brown hair shining in the light. She was a beautiful woman and Maura still loved her even though she didn't like her.

'Doing what to you, Carla? Was I supposed to let you shit all over me then? Just give Tommy to you like I gave you everything else?'

'I meant taking away my home.'

Maura snorted.

'Your home? *My* home, you mean. I own it and you lived there free. Gratis. I am just taking back what's mine, darlin'.'

'But what am I supposed to do?' The plaintive note in her voice was enough to make Maura laugh.

'Get a job springs to mind. Do you the world of good that would. Working for a living.'

She laughed again.

'Maybe you should sign on. Not exactly the energetic type, are you, workwise that is. I even paid for your fucking cleaner or else the place would have looked like a shithouse. Or how about one of the hostess clubs? You certainly look and act the part. But no, you're a bit long in the tooth for that job these days.'

She poked a finger at her niece.

'You are a lazy little whore and you had better sort yourself out now – I ain't doing it for you any more. Now go on, just piss off, you two-faced little mare.'

'You would really do this to me, Maura?'

'Yep.'

'Over a bloke? You'd split the family over a bloke?'

'Yep. I hope he was worth it, Carla.'

She laughed again and Carla knew she was lost. She tried once more to explain. 'I don't know what came over me, Maura. If I could only turn back the clock . . .'

'Shut the front door on the way out, won't you?'

She walked past her niece and went into the kitchen, where she began to fill the kettle.

Carla stood for a few moments before walking quietly from the house. Whatever she had expected tonight, indifference was not part of it. She would have taken anything; she had half-expected Maura to give her a clump, and in some ways would have preferred that. At least it would have been a normal reaction.

As she got into her car she heard footsteps behind her and, turning, took the full force of a bucket of cold water in her face.

Throwing the empty bucket at her, Maura snatched the car keys.

'Get a cab, sweetie. The car, I think you will find, like everything else belongs to me.'

Tony Dooley Senior watched and shook his head. Give him a man's row any day of the week.

Vic's mobile rang as he was watching *Match of the Day*. He answered it with a grunt.

'Wassup!'

He was laughing as he said it, knowing by the flashing name that it was his brother Justin.

'All right there, Vic?'

He sat up and pushed mute on the remote button.

'Who's that?'

'It's your worst nightmare, Vic. Listen.'

He could hear Justin moaning in the background and then he heard a gunshot and his brother screaming.

'You fucking bastard! I'll fucking . . .'

The man was laughing at the other end of the line.

''Course you will, Vic. Hang on, I do believe his other leg needs a shot as well.'

Vic sat by helplessly as he heard another shot and another scream. He felt as if his heart was about to explode in his chest with shock and anger at what he was hearing. If anything more happened to Justin his mother would kill him stone dead.

'I am warning you, whoever you are, you'd better fucking start running, mate . . .'

The voice was sarcastic now and Vic was gritting his teeth as he listened once more.

'Oh, shut up, Victor, you big tart. Is your old mum still visiting Verderers Road, Chigwell? Or should it be fucking *Murderers* Road, considering you own the gaff, eh? Her sister is getting on her nerves a bit, I hear. You should check on her, mate. See how the poor old cow is getting on.'

The phone clicked off and Vic sat stunned, staring at the mobile as if it was a prehistoric monster that had just crawled out of his own ear.

Then he dialled his mother's number.

No answer.

He was sweating now as he rushed through the flat and began to get dressed. If anything had happened to his mother or brother then there would be a bloodbath in the south east and the Ryans would be top of the list.

On his way to his mother's he phoned his cronies in England and Majorca. But deep inside, for all his bravado, he wondered what else the Ryans had up their sleeves.

# Chapter Sixteen

'What am I gonna do, Nana?'

Sarah rocked her grand-daughter in her arms and whispered softly, 'I don't know, lovey. You'll have to come back here, I suppose.'

In her heart of hearts Carla was the last person Sarah wanted living back at home. She was not an easy person to live with lately and the thought of Joey living here as well made Sarah feel almost depressed. His loud music, his queerness, made her skin crawl. Whatever her Michael might have been, at least he had been a man with manly ways. None of this mincing about. And on top of that there was the high-pitched squealing that seemed to be Joey's only way of communicating.

She wondered if she should talk to Roy, but he had enough on his plate getting through the days without this pair driving him demented.

'I can't believe she would do this to me, Nana.'

Carla's self-pity was all too evident, and even though at times her daughter drove her mad, Sarah was with Maura on this one. What Carla had done to her was beyond bad and she personally thought that the girl had got off lightly.

'Well, you must have guessed she wouldn't be happy, Carla. Surely you must have thought about her reaction if she found out?'

'It was him . . . he came after me, Nana.'

Carla really believed this now; she had a way of rewriting history when it suited her.

'Carla, stop it. Sure I saw the antics of the pair of you meself in this very house. Maura could sniff out something like this with a blindfold and her arms tied together. You were lucky to get away with it as long as you did, and that goes for the pair of you.'

'So you're on her side as well?'

Sarah shook her head in consternation.

'There are no sides in matters like this. You should never have done what you did, full stop.'

'I am entitled to some happiness as well, you know.'

'Well, you shouldn't have tried to get it at someone else's expense, Carla. Maura was good to you, whatever you might think now.'

'That's all I ever hear, how *good* she is. How lucky I am to have her. How kind she is to me.'

Carla sighed heavily. Tears nearly overcame her once more.

'But what about me, Nana? What about *me*?'

Sarah was rapidly losing the bit of patience she had left.

'What about you, Carla? You've been given everything a person could ask for and yet still you aren't happy. I know that your mother was not the best she could be, but in fairness to Maura she was more than a mother to you and there was only a few years between you. She treated you like a little queen all your life. Helped with the boy, gave you everything you wanted. Didn't you feel any kind of shame at the way you carried on with Tommy?'

Carla looked into her grandmother's eyes and said seriously, 'No. He wanted *me*, Nana, not *her*. If it wasn't for all the trouble at the moment he would still *be* with me.'

Sarah looked at the beautiful woman before her and wondered if she was all the ticket. Surely she didn't think that she could do what she wanted, take what she wanted, and never have to pay the price?

'She is acting like I am the bad person here, Nana, when all the time it's her. She is the one everyone is terrified of, not me. She is the one who can't accept that Tommy preferred me to her. She is the one who has left me and my child homeless.'

Sarah had listened to enough. She exploded. This wide-eyed poor old me act of her grand-daughter's was getting on her nerves.

'Would you ever feck off and take responsibility for being a scheming little hoor who should be thankful she's still able to walk, considering it was Maura Ryan you did the dirty on? Was you mad, child, to think you could get away with *that*? She can instil fear into the hardest of men, so what made you think you would walk away unscathed?'

'She's got a point, Carla.'

Benny's voice was soft, but it still made the two women jump.

'You are me own brother and yet you're like all the others. It's always *her* with everybody. She is the only person anyone is interested in.'

Benny smiled.

'That might be because she *is* an interesting person who's achieved something in her life. Maybe if you had done something with yours instead of living off everyone else you might garner a bit of respect. As it is, Carla, you are well past your sell-by date and you still sound like a stupid teenager who can't have her own way. Get a fucking life, woman. I tell you now, if you had done that to me I'd have seen you squirm in agony before I would have swallowed, so think yourself fucking lucky. A bucket of water in the boat is far better than a bottle of acid because that's what you would have got from me, girl, sister or no sister.'

Carla was crying once more. Her eyes, red-rimmed with lack of sleep, were sore as she rested her head on her Nana's shoulder and sobbed her heart out.

Benny laughed before putting on the kettle and making a pot of tea.

'Look at you, Carla. Call yourself a Ryan? Call yourself a fucking woman, come to that?' He was filling the kettle as he said seriously, 'You was out of order and you was used by a man who is at this moment running for his life. But we will find him, Carla, and when we do I can guarantee you he will beg and scream for mercy. And do you know something else? He won't fucking get it, I will see to that personally. Now shut your trap, you're getting on my tits.'

Sarah listened to her grandson and sighed. How many times had she heard conversations like this over the years? Killing, maiming, violence. There had been a time when she could blot it all out. Could forget that it was her flesh and blood talking like this. But though she could accept it from her sons, she had never been able to accept it from her daughter. Yet it was her daughter who had kept them all together, even taking Carla under her wing. She still remembered the day they had gone to Roy's house and found Janine in a terrible state. Little Carla had had a huge bruise on her arm and looked like a gypsy, dirty and unkempt. That whole house had been filthy. Sarah had taken Carla home and Maura had taken care of her from then on, and now look how the girl had repaid her. Maura had been more than a mother to Carla, she had been a sister, mother and best friend all rolled into one. Even now Carla still couldn't see that she had done anything wrong. Sarah was reluctantly coming to the conclusion that, like Benny, Carla was a lost cause and there was nothing any of them could do about it.

* * *

Garry, Lee and Maura were laughing at Vic's dilemma. Apparently he had turned up at his aunt's little house in Chigwell mob-handed to find his mother off having a good night out at Bingo. She had finally turned up safe and sound and berated him in front of everyone. Maura had needed something to make her smile and Garry had provided it.

'We followed after, but it was an impossible task. He's good, old Vic, I will give him that. We lost him in no time. One thing, though – one of his faces was Mickey Ball.'

'Don't surprise me, they was always mates.'

Garry's voice was tight. He had been a good mate of Vic's once and it smarted that they were now at loggerheads. But he understood how the other man was feeling even while he wanted to rip his head off. Especially now he had Leonie. If anything happened to her he would lose it, he was sure. She was like a soulmate, they agreed on everything. At least Leonie agreed with him on everything, but that was another matter.

'What's happening with Rifkind?'

It was Lee who asked the question. Maura, even though she had been expecting it, was still feeling fragile. It was so embarrassing. Everyone knew the score and that was the hardest thing to cope with. She hated pity of any kind when it was directed at her.

She was saved from answering by Garry.

'Leave him to me, Lee. I'll sort him out. We still need to track Vic down and with the help of his brother that shouldn't be too hard. Once we have Vic we'll have Tommy, who incidentally hasn't been near or by his house, Liverpool, or any of his usual haunts. But he will. Tommy ain't got the savvy to take care of himself. He'll make a slip sooner or later. I have put a hefty price on his bonce so we should have a bite soon.'

Lee nodded.

'What's happening with Carla?'

He had to know, he was worried about her.

'Nothing is going to *happen* with her, Lee – what are you trying to insinuate?'

Maura's voice was heavy with sarcasm and Lee felt the full force of her personality then. No wonder he'd been worried. Even he would think twice about tucking her up. He wouldn't want to be Carla for a million quid. She must have been mad to think she could ever get away with it, and as for Tommy . . . well, he had always secretly thought Rifkind was a cunt anyway.

'I heard you'd aimed her out of her house . . .'

'*My* house, Lee. I aimed her out of *my* house. I own it.'

He sighed.

'Whatever, but she's running scared, Maws.'

'And so she should, the two-faced cunt.'

Garry's voice was harsh and even Maura was surprised at the animosity in it.

'She is her mother's daughter all right. Janine was the same, hated the family and the business but lived off the fucking proceeds all her life. As did Muvver, come to that. Fuck Carla, let her go back to Muvver's, let her look after herself. Might make her appreciate her family a bit more.'

'She says Tommy came after her . . .'

'Oh, shut up, Lee, you big tart! It don't matter who come after who, we sound like fucking school kids here. She did it. If it was Old Bill offering her the earth, would she take it? Ask yourself that one. Would she tuck us up if it benefited her? She is nothing but a treacherous whore and I for one will not be giving her any more fucking handouts. Her or that poof of hers either. Leave them to Muvver, the pair of them.'

Lee was hanging his head at the force of Garry's words.

'Mum is upset as well. She thinks that Carla was out of order and all. But I mean, it makes it difficult for us, don't it? If we go round the old woman's and she's there.'

Garry shrugged as if it was all too easy, which it was to him.

'Just fucking blank her, that's what I'm going to do.'

Lee nodded, taking his cue from his brother as always, and Maura, actually feeling sorry for her niece now, swallowed down the words that would have ensured Carla's well-being.

'Benny gave her a piece of his mind this morning.'

Garry laughed.

'He wants to be careful, he ain't got that much he can give some away.'

Maura grinned. Benny would not find that statement in the least amusing. He had too much arrogance to take jokes against himself.

'How's Roy?'

Maura shrugged.

'I haven't spoken to him today.'

'You will.'

Garry's voice was flat now.

'Is he upset then?'

Garry smiled.

'Wouldn't you be if you were Roy? You and Carla are the two most important things in his life.'

'He'll get over it.'

Garry smiled.

'That's the Maura I know and love.'

Lee watched his brother and sister and was aware not for the first time how alike they were in their thinking and attitudes. His wife was right; none of them was even remotely normal. But they were his family and he wanted them in his life. Without them, especially Maura, he would probably be working a nine-to-five somewhere and dying of boredom.

Life was all about choices and they had made theirs many years ago. It was too late for any of them to change now.

Even if they'd wanted to.

* * *

Billy Mills was happy. He had a few quid in his pocket, a dead cert horse, and on top of all that he had a nice bird on his arm. She was one of his real birds, which meant she wasn't a hostess or a lap dancer. She went out with him because she actually liked his company.

He was taking her to Brighton racetrack where a friend's horse was running. He liked Brighton, it was an all-weather track and had a really nice little restaurant that served good wholesome food. Janette was a looker and today she had surpassed herself. All in black leather, he knew she would have more than a few blokes giving her the once over. She had a big arse and unlike most women instead of trying to hide it she flaunted it. He loved a nice arse did Billy and grabbed Janette's at every available opportunity.

As he was helping her into his new Jag he was happy. He copped a feel as she slid into the passenger seat. As he stood up, grinning, his heart sank down into his boots. Jack Stern was standing there with two of his more muscle-bound henchmen, and worst of all he was smiling.

'You do look rough, Jack.'

'I am feeling rough, and also feeling a good few quid lighter, thanks to the Ryans.'

'And you want me to set up a meet, am I correct?'

'Correct. That's what I've always liked about you, Billy. You was always quick off the mark.'

'Well, you can fuck off, Jack, I'm on a day out.'

'Not any more, Billy.'

'Are you having a tin bath or what? I'm going racing and that is that.'

Jack sighed heavily and looked around the quiet road.

'Don't make me kidnap you, Billy. I really can't be arsed and this is too important to wait.'

'I'm sure it can wait twenty-four hours, Jack.'

Janette stuck her head out of the window.

'Are we fucking going or what?'

Jack chuckled.

'Where did you get her? Walthamstow dog track?'

Even Billy smiled at the quip. Jack could be really funny, he had perfect comic delivery.

'Nah, I met her at Henlow. Still dog racing though so you was half there, Jack.'

He grinned.

'It's a gift. Had a few old dogs meself over the years.'

They laughed, two men together.

Jack said seriously, 'I need this meet as soon as possible, Billy. I will make it worth your while, you know that. But this is important. There's big trouble brewing and I need a friendly go-between. You ain't really got a choice, Billy, you must have guessed as much.'

Billy sighed and accepted his fate. Jack was right, the fact he was there personally spoke volumes. Billy looked in the car at a glowering Janette. Taking out a couple of ton from his pocket, he pushed it through the window at her.

'Sorry, Janette, you can see how it is.'

'Up yours, Billy!'

He shrugged and then smiled in his usual happy way.

'It would have been up yours, darlin', but duty calls.'

Jack and his minders laughed. It was a friendly meet, they could afford to be magnanimous. Ten minutes later Janette was standing alone in the street with two hundred quid, a cab number and a murderous expression on her pretty face.

Danielle Hicks was lying on her battered old settee, her hands cradled protectively around her huge bump. The eldest child Petey had let Maura in and she stood uncertainly in the doorway looking at this travesty of a young woman Danny had become, thanks to Jamie.

Danielle stared at her sadly.

'I've been expecting you – the filth have never been off the doorstep.'

Maura nodded.

'I know.'

Danielle forced a smile.

'I guessed you would show up eventually, once it all died down. I got the five hundred bar, by the way.

Told the filth it was a whip round from the neighbours. They swallowed it. Hunted the house out they did, looking for God knows what.'

She heaved herself up from the sofa and shouted, 'Petey, make a cuppa.'

Maura heard the boy putting on the kettle.

'I can do that.'

Danielle shook her head.

'Sit down. Tell me what I need to know and leave it at that.'

Maura sat in an armchair that had lost its springs many years before it was owned by Danielle. She looked around the room, at the faded curtains and carpets. Saw the paper peeling from the damp walls; saw the box of toys that was thrown into a corner. Saw the washing piled on the floor and smelled the sheer futility of a life spent giving birth to too many children, too quickly.

Danielle watched as Maura surveyed her home.

'A dump, ain't it? Jamie had all that poke and yet we got fuck all. It's funny, but since he died I've never been better off.'

She laughed.

'The filth reckons I can get compensation. They came in here mob-handed, all overalls and covered shoes. I said, "What are they for? The place ain't that dirty".'

She laughed at her own wit.

'Did they take anything away?'

Danielle nodded.

'Yeah. Nothing worth having, though. First thing I did was remove whatever would incriminate him, or anyone else come to that. It's all round me mate's. She don't know what it is and she don't wanna know. I'll give it to you when you want it, OK?'

Maura nodded.

'What's the next step?'

'Get this one out and eventually bury that ponce. He's still on ice and they won't give me a date for burial. I saw the autopsy, though, know his eyes were glued shut. They reckon that is what killed him: the fright brought on the heart attack.'

She laughed gently.

'Who'd have thought he would have had a heart attack, eh? I wasn't even aware he had a heart, the way he treated me and the kids.'

Her voice was bitter.

'Now he's dead and do you know the weirdest thing about it all? I'm glad because at last I know where he is. I know he ain't with anyone else.'

Maura could hear the utter desolation in her voice and was glad that she had never let herself be owned by another person like Danielle had been owned by Jamie Hicks. For all her hurt over Tommy, she knew she would survive it. Her pride was hurt more than anything else. Whereas Danielle had lost hers many years ago.

'I used to go round the birds' houses and look for

him, Maura. Even though in my heart I knew that if he wanted to be with me, he would be. He would come out and tell me to piss off and shout and holler. Then a few days later he'd come back with that grin of his and the charm on overdrive and I would swallow me knob, wipe me mouth and have him back.'

Maura took two mugs of tea from the unnaturally silent child and placed them on the small coffee table.

'Now he's gone and this is me. Seven kids, and nothing to show for it. No real home, not even a decent stick of furniture. That selfish cunt wasn't insured.'

''Course he was. I mean, we owe you comp big time. He was a fool to himself and he paid the price. I'll make sure you're provided for, don't worry. There's a nice little semi going begging in Woodford Green. Good catchment area for the kids' schools, all decorated and furnished, big garden, conservatory. It's yours for the asking, Danny. You didn't think I would see you without, did you?'

Danielle shook her head before saying, 'You saw me without *him*, didn't you? You *killed* him, or at least your family did.'

Maura was shocked at the bitterness in the words. Even though she understood that this was a woman alone now, a hurt and frightened young woman, still it annoyed her. She leaned forward in her seat and said quietly, so the kids wouldn't hear, 'Listen here,

Danny, he knew the score same as we all do. If you can't do the time, don't do the crime. Remember that old saying? Well, here is another one, a more up-to-date one. Don't shit on the people paying your wages, it can kill you.'

It was a veiled threat and Danielle was reminded of exactly who she was dealing with here: Maura, with her perfect make-up and hair, with her nice clothes and shoes, who had always been good for a laugh or a few quid, was suddenly Maura Ryan and she was looking out for her family now because this heavily pregnant young woman could put them all away. And then Danielle saw that Jamie had dragged them into shit much deeper than she had first thought.

As long as you played Maura Ryan's game she would look after you, but threaten her or her family and you better watch your step.

'Don't come the poor old fucking moaner with me, Danny. You will get your comp and I won't lose a wink of sleep over Jamie. In fact, everyone thinks I'm a fool for even offering you any comp at all. He tucked us up, love, tucked us up big time. So take my advice and remember another old saying: don't bite the fucking hand that feeds you.'

Danielle was upset and Maura felt a moment's sorrow for her, but she had to play the hard nut, it was the only way to guarantee that this girl kept her trap shut. At the end of the day that was the most important thing of all.

Benny was once more in the frame with his trademark gluing. In her heart of hearts she could murder the little fucker for bringing all this to their door but it was done and all she could do now was try and contain the damage. If that meant terrifying this poor girl before her then so be it.

Danielle knew the score the same as they all did. She was out of order and Maura had to teach her a little lesson before she ran her mouth off without thinking and inadvertently let the cat out of the bag about her husband's demise. And, as Maura consoled herself, the lesson was better coming from her rather than Garry or, God forbid, Benny.

So she played up her hard angle and though she had gained an enemy and lost a friend, could sleep easy in her bed knowing Danielle would be too scared ever to voice her opinions on what had happened to her husband.

'Drink your tea, Danielle, and I'll show you the pictures of the house. It's got four bedrooms so you'll have a lot more space for the kids. It's got a loft room as well that could be a bedroom. It's up to you really.'

Danielle's hand was shaking as she took the proffered photographs and Maura felt a stab of guilt once more. She grasped the girl's hand and said gently, 'I am doing what I can for you, and it's more than most people would be doing in my position.'

Danielle pulled her hand away as quickly as she dared. Plastering a smile on her face, she said bravely,

'I know, Maura, and I really appreciate it. You know that. I'm just a bit upset, that's all.'

Maura closed her eyes in distress. She could see the hatred and fear in Danielle's eyes as if she had spoken about them out loud. When she left a few moments later she sat in her car and watched the goings on around her. Young mums picking kids up from playschool, music blaring out of flats and cars. Kids running around still in nappies, their faces filthy and their eyes already full of cunning and streetwise intelligence. The smell of urine in the lobbies of the flats, the used needles that covered the sparse grassy area outside each block, the rusted cars and the abject poverty were all astounding. She wondered how the new government still let people live like this while preaching about morals and sex education.

Her mother had said many years ago that people make slums, not houses. But that wasn't true. This was the last stop for most of these people, and it was all they had ever known. Yet she knew that as bad as this place was, Danielle would rather be here with Jamie, a philandering ponce and liar, for the rest of her life than ensconced in a nice little place with her kids well provided for with no man beside her.

She drove away a little while later, but she was heavy inside. Even Carla's betrayal had not hurt her as much as the hatred in Danielle Hicks's eyes. Maura had finally seen herself as others saw her and she didn't like the picture she had seen, didn't like it at all.

Sighing, she wondered where it was all going to end. Would Vic kill her? It was the first time she had asked herself that question, but she was not surprised to realise that she didn't really care if he did. She was past caring about anything now except the boys, the family. Though, Heaven knew, that was no way for anyone to live.

Carol was looking through the wardrobes for old clothes to give to her mum for the charity shop she worked in two days a week. She was humming as she opened boxes and studied shoes and bags, trying on clothes to see if they still fitted her expanding waistline. She was so happy with her life now that she was pregnant. It was what Benny had needed, a child to centre him, to make him grow up. Even his scary moods had not been so frequent since she had confirmed it.

So she was a happy and contented girl as she looked through her stuff and decided what she wanted and, more importantly, didn't want.

She could hear the cleaner, Debbie, hoovering away downstairs and a little while later she brought Carol a nice cup of tea and a few biscuits. They gossiped for a while, and then she went back to sorting through the cupboards. She was absolutely content as she enjoyed her day. Never in her life had she been so happy, had so much money and respect.

Finishing her wardrobe, she decided to start on

Benny's. He was pretty good about sending stuff to her mother for the charity shop and would always give money to charities that came begging on the knocker so she had no qualms about sorting through his cupboards. She would make a pile of stuff and anything he wanted to keep he could put back later after he had looked through it.

It was a hot day and the air conditioning made her life so much easier as she pulled open drawers and sorted through the racks of clothes. Grabbing the chair from the dressing table, she climbed up and opened the cupboards at the top of the wardrobes. She began pulling out her own boxes first, and then she started to pull out all of his.

She placed all the boxes on the floor and went to make herself another cup of tea. Debbie was still there, so Carol made her one too and had a laugh before taking her own tea back up to the bedroom to resume her good works. She opened the boxes one by one, and then she noticed a funny smell. She wrinkled up her nose and traced the smell to the top of the wardrobes, in the large cupboard over Benny's suit rail.

It seemed to be coming from a cream-coloured hatbox that he had tucked away at the back of the cupboard. Climbing on the chair once more, she leant in and gradually pulled the box towards her. It was heavier than the others and this intrigued her. A little voice was telling her to leave well alone but she was curious now and also worried that something had got inside the box and died. Perhaps they had mice? She placed the box on the floor and knelt in front of it. It was sealed with duct tape around the edges and she was suddenly unsure if she wanted to know what was in there. The smell was stronger now it was nearer to her.

She started pulling the duct tape off and, holding her breath, opened the box up. Staring up at her was a human head, its milky eyes glazed and its mouth set in a grimace. It was in the advanced stages of decomposition.

Her screams of abject terror and disgust brought her cleaner running, an act she was to regret for the rest of her life. Soon her screams were added to Carol's and the neighbours called the police. It took them twenty minutes to get into the house, and it was a whole day before they finally left it.

Benny didn't visit Carol in hospital or enquire about the threatened miscarriage and that told her all she needed to know.

# Chapter Seventeen

'A what!'

Garry's voice was so full of incredulity that it made Maura want to laugh. She was sensible enough to know this was just nervous laughter, but the urge to shriek and scream with it was hard to suppress. This was so outrageous she wondered if it was really happening. It was, of course, she knew that much. She just *wished* it wasn't true.

'A head, a fucking severed head that he was *keeping* in his wardrobe. Don't ask me what for, Garry, I really have no fucking idea and I don't *want* to know why he was keeping it either.'

Her brother was shaking his head in consternation.

'That is one fucking nutter.'

Maura laughed and said sarcastically, 'No? I never would have worked that one out for meself.'

'So what's the score?'

'Well, apart from poor old Carol's screaming that brought the cleaner, the neighbours and eventually the filth, Benny is still at large. But they will come for him now.'

Garry thought for a few moments before saying seriously, 'Can't we say someone planted the head there?'

'Who shall we say planted it, Gal? Alan fucking Titchmarsh?'

He started to laugh.

'Whose head is it anyway?'

Maura shrugged.

'I dread to think. You know Benny, could be anyone's.'

Garry laughed once more.

'I can't believe we are having this conversation, can you?'

Maura shook her head.

'It's not funny really, Garry, is it?'

'Depends whose head it is, don't it?' He was smiling again, but it was a bemused smile this time. 'Where is he, Maura?'

'Safe enough for the moment.'

'Was it Tommy's head, do you think, Maws? Perhaps he was going to give it to you for Christmas or something. You know what a fucking Loony Tunes he is.'

Maura shook her head and laughed at the absurdity of what he was saying even though with Benny it was completely feasible.

'It was in an advanced state of decomposition, so no, it wasn't Tommy. More's the pity.'

Garry shook his head in wonderment.

'He is fucking Radio Rental that boy. I despair of him, I really do. Does Muvver know about it yet?'

Maura shrugged.

'It hit the early-evening news on the telly so I assume she has an inkling. I ain't heard anything from her, though.'

'I'll drive over and see how she is, eh?'

'Lee's probably there by now, I'll come with you.'

As they were getting in the car Garry started to laugh again. There were two plain-clothes policemen outside and he shouted to them merrily, 'My nephew has given a whole new meaning to the expression giving head, hasn't he?'

He roared at his own wit.

'Leave it out, Garry, for fuck's sake.'

Maura was annoyed now; this was almost too absurd to take seriously though she knew they would have to. The two young coppers were terrified and it showed.

'Leave them alone, Gal, they're hardly out of nappies.' She got in the car and carried on talking. 'They think he's a serial killer apparently, or so they said on the news. He's keeping trophies, a shrink said. You can always rely on ITV to make the most of it, can't you? The house is being torn apart as we speak so let's hope there ain't nothing else there to incriminate him or us. Maybe they'll find a whole herd of heads!'

Garry shrugged.

'Don't matter either way, we own the Old Bill looking into it.'

'Do we, Gal?'

He could hear the surprise in her voice and grinned.

'Put it this way, Maws, we fucking do now. I'll find out who's on it and we'll take it from there. Might do the boy good, though, a sojourn in nick. Might fucking teach him a lesson. Shall I get him put on remand?'

Maura sighed once more; she could follow his logic.

'We'll see, eh?'

He started up the car and waved to the two plain-clothes, one of whom waved back nervously. As they drove away it occurred to Maura that one good thing to come out of all this was that their enemies would realise just what they were dealing with. She wanted to see Vic so badly and end this shit. It was all getting out of hand now, and she was tired of it all.

'Get him on remand, Gal. You're right, it might do the little fucker good.'

Her brother grinned, his face shining with glee.

'My thoughts entirely, Maura. See how he likes grown-up bird.'

'Talking of birds, I'll have to go and see Carol as well.'

Garry yawned, bored now.

'Rather you than me, girl. She is a prat. This is all her fucking fault, she should have left well alone. Typical fucking woman, got to stick her oar in where it ain't wanted.'

'Be fair, Garry, she couldn't have known.'

'That ain't the point, is it? It's her who's put the finger on us all, ain't it? Can you even imagine the shit this is going to cause? I hope he takes *her* fucking head off next.'

Maura didn't answer him and they drove to Notting Hill in silence. She wouldn't want to be Carol at this moment for all the tea in China, she knew that much. Benny was no doubt blaming her as well. He was like her brothers, good at putting the blame elsewhere. It was what they all did to a different degree. She couldn't help wondering why he had kept the head for so long. Did he take it out and admire it? The thought made her feel sick inside but she wouldn't put it past him. She wouldn't put anything past him now.

Sarah and Carla sat together in the kitchen and sipped tea as they tried to come to terms with what Benny had done this time. Lee sat on the stairs and answered the phone, which seemed to be ringing off the hook. They were all in a daze.

When Roy came in Lee smiled at him but his brother ignored him, walking straight into the kitchen.

'All right, Mum. Maura here yet?'

He was warning his daughter and they all knew it.

Sarah shook her head slowly.

'He's as mad as a March hare, isn't he?' she said.

Roy nodded.

'So it would seem, Muvver. I've spoken to him – he seems to think it's hilarious.'

Sarah tutted under her breath.

'How's Carol? The shock must have been terrible.'

'In hospital. They rushed her to the Special Baby Unit at Basildon. It don't sound too good.' He wiped a hand over his face in a gesture of anger and hopelessness. 'I could fucking murder him. Janine always said he wasn't right in the head and she should have known. She was a fucking nut-nut and all.'

Sarah was amazed at his words. Since her death he had seemed to put his wife on a pedestal. Now he was once more acting as if she was the origin of all their ills.

'Roy, son, calm yourself down. Get the brandy from the front room. We could all do with some.'

He rolled his eyes in consternation at his mother.

'Fucking brandy, Muvver? A fucking handful of Es in your tea wouldn't make this lot fucking better. The filth will be all over us like a rash. I've already got them sitting outside my drum, and they're out there now.'

He waved a hand in the general direction of the front door.

Sarah sighed.

'That's nothing new, Roy, they've watched this house for years. I used to make them cups of tea at one time.'

'I don't think cups of tea will appease this lot, Mum. The little fucker he is.'

Sarah nodded and said spiritedly, 'The shame and degradation I feel because of that little bastard! How will I hold me head up with the neighbours? At the church, more importantly?'

Roy was short and to the point.

'The same way you always did, Mum, by giving them a fucking hefty bit of wedge. If anyone can buy their way into Heaven it will be you.'

Never had Roy spoken to his mother like that and her face showed how hurt she was at his words.

Lee was standing in the doorway and said sharply, 'Hold up, Roy, that's enough of that talk. Can't you see how upset she is?'

'Upset? Is that what you call it?'

Roy's voice was incredulous.

'You are over-reacting,' Lee said. 'This will all be sorted by the morning. Leave Mum be now, she's overwrought.'

Roy turned to his brother and, walking towards him, bellowed in his face: '*She* is overwrought? What about me? He's my son. A fucking lunatic I've bred! My God, you all act as if this is fucking normal or something. He is a mad cunt and we all know that but it suits us to have him in the family, don't it? Gives us that extra bit of rep we need. The Ryans. The fucking *mad* Ryans.

'Well, this is too much even for me. A head in a hat box in his wardrobe? Sleeping in that room with that girl having his baby, and all the time he knew there was a head sitting in a fucking box, decomposing and stinking the fucking place out – and you think I am over-reacting? Are you having a fucking laugh or what?'

Carla started crying.

'Stop it, Dad, you're frightening me.'

Roy looked at his daughter.

'I tell you something, Mum, you should have been done like a fucking cat after Michael and Geoffrey. Instead you still churned out little nutters for the old man and now we're turning out some of our own. You are responsible for about fifty per cent of the violent crime in London only you are too stupid to fucking see it. All the people who work for us, the whores, the drug dealers – you inadvertently made all that happen. So you'd better give a big donation this time, love. It's gonna cost you dear for peace of mind and a bed in Heaven after this lot.'

Sarah was white-faced with grief at her son's words. Lee, seeing his mother's hurt, lashed out at Roy without a second's thought and caught him a blinder on the chin. Roy went down like a sack of potatoes and Carla's screaming was all that Garry and Maura could hear as they let themselves into the house.

Garry looked at her and said merrily, 'Not another head, surely?'

Maura sighed once more and said casually, 'I fucking hope not, Gal.'

They walked into the pandemonium of the kitchen and, Maura being Maura, she quickly saw the score. Taking her mother by the arm she walked her from the room. This was one time, she decided, they could sort it out for themselves.

'I'll pack you a bag, Mum. Come home with me for a few days, eh?'

Sarah nodded, unable to speak she was so upset by Roy's words.

Maura hugged her tightly.

'I know how you feel, Mum. I feel the same. It's a wake-up call, ain't it?'

Sarah nodded.

For the first time in years she was genuinely glad to see her daughter in her home. And for the first time in years Maura was genuinely glad that she was there.

Abul and Benny were stoned and at the laughing at anything stage.

'There's another head in the garage.'

'You are joking, Benny!'

Abul's voice was heavy with shock.

'Well, you know what they say, Abul . . . two heads are better than one.'

Abul was cracking up with laughter now.

'Stop it, Benny, me guts hurt.'

'Don't laugh your head off, mate, I'm in enough trouble as it is.'

This started them off once more. They were in absolute stitches as they tried to roll another joint.

'So you don't know who it was then?'

Benny scratched his head in a parody of a cartoon character thinking.

'Nope!'

Abul knew he was lying but didn't say anything.

'You're fucking mad.'

Benny nodded now, seriously.

'I will not dispute that observation. I have been told the very same thing by people with medical qualifications, and who am I to challenge the medical establishment?'

'Shall I get the sandwiches from the car?'

Benny shook his head.

'Nah, we'll go and eat out, shall we?'

Abul shook his head.

'That's not a good idea.'

Benny grinned.

'I know. But if we go Ilford way we can eat at your uncle's place. I fancy a nice curry and rice.'

He could see Abul wasn't happy but didn't care.

'Come on, I'll roll us a nice kinger to smoke in the car. Prime skunk.'

'The family won't be happy.'

Benny shrugged.

'I had a *head* in my wardrobe, a very handsome head actually, so I think going out for a quick meal will be pretty low down on my scale of things not to do, don't you, Abul?'

'You're in charge, Benny.'

He sighed happily.

'If Carol, that nosy stupid twat, loses my baby, I will fucking Muller her and I mean it. If she had left well alone . . .'

He was getting angry and Abul knew that, dope or no dope, Benny could still lose it.

'Come on, Ben, she didn't do it deliberately, did she? I bet she got a fucking fright.'

Benny was laughing again.

'Not half as much as that ponce did when I cut his head off!' He jumped up from the sofa. 'Come on, get a move on, I'm starving.'

Abul followed him from the house. This was freaky even by Benny Ryan standards. But if he wanted a curry, a curry he would have. Benny always got what he wanted, that was half his trouble.

Billy Mills was with Jack when the telephone rang and Jack put on Sky News. The presenter was going through the alleged role the Ryans played in London gangland life, from their control of the ice cream and hot dog vans through to their various clubs, pubs, and other establishments.

The head in the wardrobe had caught the attention

of the nation. There was nothing else in particular going on and it couldn't have been found at a better time in journalistic terms. They were having a field day.

Jack watched with his henchmen and felt a trickle of fear go through his body. Billy shook his head in disbelief.

'The worst of it all is, Jack, knowing Benny, the bloke probably cut him up driving or something. I bet it wasn't over something serious. Benny is a fucking nutter, everyone knows that, but he is a good mate. Me and him go back yonks. I remember a few years ago he was only a kid and he cut up an old lag in Silvertown because he thought he had said something derogatory about him.'

Billy was making a point; *he* had always got on well with Benny. He had drunk with him socially. He was giving Jack a quick warning without having to make it too obvious.

'The sooner someone takes him out the better.'

Billy shrugged.

'You'd have to get past Abul first and then Benny himself – that's without the rest of the Ryans who watch each other like hawks. They give a whole new meaning to the expression "tight-knit family".'

Billy grinned, that easy grin of his.

'Of course, if you still want a meet, I'll arrange it for you.'

'Why don't you shut the fuck up?'

Jack's voice was low and Billy knew he had hit a nerve.

'Well, that's why I gave up a day's racing, a couple of dead certs – one equine and one female – and am having to sit here and watch the fucking news, isn't it?'

'I want my gear back, they robbed me. They fucking *burgled* me, in fact.'

Jack was still smarting from the cocaine loss and it showed.

'Three hundred fucking kilos those cunts stole and at nearly thirty grand a bar you can work that out for yourself.'

Billy wanted to laugh at the absurdity of the situation but had a feeling that right now his humour would go unappreciated.

'That's a lot of dosh. What's my cut if it's returned? Five per cent?'

Jack swallowed down his irritation. He had guessed Billy would need a sweetener but there was no need to take liberties.

'Two and a half and that's a good cut, Billy, so don't start getting too ambitious. I have only so much patience.'

He was pointing his finger in Billy's face and Billy Mills knew when to strong it and when to take a step back.

He nodded.

'I will concede that one, Jack. But I can't offer any guarantees.'

Jack sniffed loudly and nodded.

The deal was struck but it was a deal that Billy knew would never come to fruition. Knowing the Ryans they would offer to sell it back and then negotiations would have to start all over again. They had taken the coke to prove a point, no more and no less. Jack was a prat if he couldn't work that one out for himself.

But then Jack had never been the sharpest knife in the drawer, whatever inflated opinion he might have of himself, and Billy had always had a good nose for a deal. He was also known to be neutral so he could do the negotiating and still live to tell the tale, whoever he ended up dealing with. All in all he was pleased with his new role as Jack Stern's go-between. Either way, he would come out on top.

'Can I have another brandy, Jack? They're going to speculate on who the head could belong to after the break.'

He was rubbing it in and he knew it, but as his old dad had told him many years ago: *use* what you've got. Always find a *use* for what you've got. Never promise what you *can't* deliver, and *always* do a deal with a smile and a friendly word if possible. That advice had served him in good stead all his working life.

Carol was pale and still under sedation when Maura came into the small private room in Basildon Hospital.

She looked awful and Maura was heart sorry for the girl who had just lost her baby, and lost it in the most dreadful circumstances.

'How are you, sweetie?'

Carol shrugged, a helpless little movement that made her seem even younger and more vulnerable than she looked.

'Is Benny doing his nut?'

There was fear in her voice, stark terror deep in her eyes.

''Course not, darlin'. He's worried about you.'

The lie came easy to Maura's lips. Carol had enough to contend with.

'It was such a fright, Maura, seeing that . . . the head . . .'

She was getting upset once more and Maura wished then she had Benny in front of her so she could tear *his* head off with her bare hands.

'Listen, Carol, that was not your fault. It should never have happened.'

Carol nodded, clutching at straws.

'I was silly to go through his stuff, weren't I? I should have kept away from his wardrobe. He was always telling me to keep away from his private stuff, see.'

Her face crumpled.

'He's gonna kill me, Maura, this has caused so much trouble. And the baby . . . my little baby. He'll blame me, won't he? That's why he ain't been to see me, ain't it?'

Her voice was rising and the panic was evident. She wiped her tears away with a trembling hand. Maura stroked her forehead and kissed her gently.

'He won't do nothing to you, Carol. I promise you that, love. But the police, they want to know about the . . . about what you found, see. They think it was something to do with Benny.'

The girl was looking at Maura warily now and she carried on with the lies, trying to make her voice sound as genuine as possible.

'We think someone else put it there, we don't think it was anything to do with Benny. So stop worrying, love.'

Carol, as if desperate to believe her, nodded.

'He wouldn't do *that*. He ain't that mad, Maura, just a bit unstable sometimes. He's got a bad temper, that's all.'

Maura patted her hand.

Carol looked so young with her nose running and her hair plastered to her head with sweat. She was deathly white and her eyes had deep circles around them. She was still crying silently and Maura felt a strong urge once more to bash Benny's head in.

'You'll be all right, I promise.'

Carol turned her face away and buried it in the pillows.

'He'll kill me for this, Maura, I know he will.'

She sat on the bed and cuddled the grieving girl.

'He won't. He's as upset as you are about the

baby but he understands, love. I promise you, he understands.'

Carol sat up.

'Listen, I know him. He's going to go ballistic over all this. But I couldn't help it. When I saw it, when I saw the head . . . I was so shocked, it was so awful . . .'

Maura hugged her once more.

'It was planted in the room, put there to make him look bad . . .' Her words sounded inane even to her ears but Maura persisted.

Carol pushed her away.

'We both know it wasn't. It was put there by that mad bastard.'

'You can't know that, Carol . . .'

Carol cried harder and said in a whisper, 'It was the head of Dean Marks, Maura. It was my ex-boyfriend!'

Maura felt herself pale at the words.

'Have you told anyone else this?'

Carol shook her head.

'Dean went to work in Spain; he left because of Benny hassling him. You know what Benny's like, couldn't stand the thought of me having been with anyone else.'

She wiped her eyes once more and Maura saw that the usually perfectly manicured nails had been bitten down to the quick.

'He wouldn't leave Dean alone. Went to his house, his work. He dragged me over to him once in a club and started slagging us both off. Dean wasn't a fighter, Maura, he was terrified. Especially when he found out who Benny was. He fucked off, went out to Spain to try and escape from it all.'

She was hysterical once more and Maura held her and tried to calm her.

'Dean was such a nice bloke, a really *inoffensive* bloke, Maura. A regular person, you know? Wouldn't hurt a fly.'

'So when did Benny see this Dean then?'

Maura's voice was puzzled.

'I don't know. If Dean ever came back, I never heard about it.' Carol wiped her face with her hands once more and then said, 'But Benny went to Spain a while ago, on a chartered boat with some blokes from Amsterdam, remember?'

Maura nodded and closed her eyes as what the girl was saying sank in.

'He must have done it then, mustn't he? He had it in the cupboard and I never knew that poor Dean was . . .'

Carol was crying again, her voice too choked with emotion for her to continue.

Benny had gone to Spain deliberately to hunt down some poor young fellow, and all because he had been this girl's first serious boyfriend. Maura sat on the bed and put her face in her hands. She felt the anger building up inside her then. It was so strong she wanted to explode with the force of it. He had broken a cardinal rule and taken out a civilian, and all because the other man had once been close to the girl Benny fancied himself in love with. Now because of his stupidity and rank badness the whole family found themselves under the media spotlight, and the Met might just be embarrassed enough to go after them all. Just what they needed with a turf war on their hands.

'Listen, Carol, you must never, ever tell anyone what you just told me, right?' Maura insisted, straight into damage limitation mode.

She nodded.

''Course I wouldn't. I ain't that stupid.'

'Not even your mum, Carol, promise me?'

She nodded her head sadly. It occurred to Maura that even after all this she was still looking out for her nephew. Old habits were hard to break.

'I'll sort this, OK? You just concentrate on getting better.'

Carol looked as though she would never feel better again as long as she lived but Maura didn't say that. Instead she arranged for a private doctor and a secluded nursing home. The policewoman stationed outside the door was helpful and Maura was very polite to her. Inside she was seething.

Benny and Abul were in a restaurant off Ilford High Street. They were stoned and they were rowdy. Abul's uncle was not on the premises and his sons were unsure what to do with their cousin and his drunken friend.

Abul was trying his hardest to calm Benny down but he was nine vodkas up and with all the dope and the Es he had dropped he was not easy to placate. When Maura and Garry walked into the restaurant with four large black men, Abul didn't know whether to applaud with relief or be worried.

When he saw Maura drag Benny, swearing, shouting and protesting, from the restaurant by his hair, he began to worry. Especially when the heavies, at a nod from her, dragged him into the back of a large white transit. Maura followed the van in her Mercedes sports.

Abul stood and watched the scene in consternation. Benny had finally gone too far and, as mad as he was, his family were still a force to be reckoned with.

Benny got away with murder because his last name was Ryan. Well, now it seemed even the Ryans had had enough of him.

# Chapter Eighteen

Tommy Rifkind was sitting in a pub in Toxteth, Black George's, and feeling seriously out of place. He was meeting one of his son's old cronies and realised he had forgotten what this part of Liverpool could be like. He had grown up here, and even though he had made serious money had still come back here from time to time for women. He had long had a penchant for the locals and Tommy B's mother had been Toxteth born and bred.

Now as he sat in the old dilapidated pub in Matthew Street he realised he had finally outgrown his roots. From his handmade suit to his diamond-encrusted watch, he felt overdressed and out of place. He knew he was being stared at by everyone, but he also knew that they were more than aware of who, and more importantly what, he was.

Jonas Crush, a young man with a very unfortunate name and an even more unfortunate heroin habit, walked into the pub twenty minutes late and as always looking as if he had just stepped out of a skip in the middle of Beirut. He walked unsteadily towards Tommy who closed his eyes in distress. Jonas, already whacked out of his box, was smiling widely, his brown teeth and furry tongue horribly in evidence.

'Tommy! Tommy Rifkind! Long time no see!'

Everyone in the pub was staring at them both now and Jonas saw the look levelled at him by Tommy and felt his heart sink.

'Why don't you phone the local filth, Jonas, in case they can't hear your big fucking mouth?'

He spoke quietly but everyone in the pub heard what Tommy had said and looked away accordingly. He knew he had been clocked as soon as he had walked into the place. His clothes were expensive and did not have any logos on them. Instead of tracksuit bottoms and a baggy T-shirt he had on one of his usual Savile Row suits and his ten-grand watch on his wrist. When Tommy B had been alive he had often met him here for a drink. Now he just wanted to get away fast, but first he had to see this disgusting piece of humanity.

Tommy looked at a table full of young men, all clocking him with interest.

'Had your fucking look, sonny?'

The biggest of the men looked away and the others followed suit. Tommy was still heavy duty in Liverpool. For the moment at least.

* * *

Benny was in the back of the transit with Garry, Lee, and Tony Dooley Junior's brother Bing. He was lying on the floor and with Bing's large foot planted on his chest. The van was moving at speed and as he looked up at his uncles and Bing he knew he was in deep trouble.

'Get off me, Bing.'

'No fucking way.'

Bing's voice was disinterested. He was following orders. Benny turned his head so he could see his uncles who stared down at him, looking bored.

'Is this some kind of fucking joke?'

Garry said quietly, 'Shut the fuck up, Benny.'

Benny knew he should shut up. He had a feeling it was the wisest thing to do. But he tried once more.

'Where are we going?'

'You'll find out.'

Garry lit a cigarette and Benny could smell the smoke. The combination of it with vodka, skunk and Es was suddenly too much in this enclosed space and his curry and rice left his stomach without a second's grace. As it pumped out of his mouth all over the floor of the van Bing started laughing.

'Scared, Benny?'

Even Garry and Lee laughed at the expression on their nephew's face.

Tommy looked up into Lizzie Braden's eyes. Even though he had not expected to see her tonight he was glad he had.

'Hello, Tommy boy.'

It was what she had always called him, and it was what she had called his son.

'Hello, Lizzie, you look well, love.'

It was a kindly lie and they both knew it.

'You do, you mean. I look like shit.'

She signalled to the bar for a drink.

'What brings you here, as if I didn't know?'

He was ashamed and it showed.

A young barmaid with green hair and a nose ring brought a large Bacardi and Coke to their table. Lizzie downed the drink in three gulps and immediately signalled for another.

'You want to lay off that, Liz.'

She laughed nastily.

'Like you ever gave a fuck about me . . . or your son, come to that.'

He saw she was already well out of it and swallowed down his annoyance.

'That's not fair, Lizzie, and you know it.'

Her drink arrived with miraculous speed and she downed it once more. Jonas watched them warily. He could feel the antagonism and wished he were back in his flat with a nice hot spoonful of H and a can of Tennent's.

She laughed again. Her teeth, always one of her best features, were yellow now and Tommy watched her with a feeling of sadness. Lizzie had been a beautiful girl in her day and now she looked old before her years. She had been seventeen when she had given birth to Tommy B so she was only just forty now but seemed much older. When he compared her to Maura Ryan, or even his Gina at that age, she was a non-starter. He knew he had ruined her life; she had spent it waiting for him to come back to her though she had known as well as he did that it would never happen.

But every now and then he had sought her out, whispered tender words, then after he had made love to her he would disappear again for months, even years. Consequently he had kept her on the boil, and he knew that had been wrong. He knew now how very wrong it had been. He could have taken her and young Tommy B away from here at any time but he hadn't. He didn't fully know why he had left them to rot but he had. Tommy B had worshipped him when in reality Tommy had never really seen him as his own child even though he undoubtedly was. Maybe it was because he was illegitimate; maybe it was because he had always felt guilty about Gina knowing about the boy, he wasn't sure why. All he knew was he had only pretended love and care, and now the boy was dead he had to deal with that. The fact he had been murdered smarted, though. Tommy B was still his flesh and blood after all.

'He hasn't got a headstone, Tommy. There's nothing to say he was ever ours.'

Lizzie's eyes bored into him as she said the words

and he looked at Jonas, still watching warily, and sighed.

'Not now, Lizzie.'

'I saw Gina's stone by the way – beautiful. "Loving wife and mother . . ." It fair made my heart sing. When we all know it should have read, "Gina Rifkind: turned a fucking blind eye for years and brought up a snob who will get all his father's money even though he hates him".'

She was signalling for more alcohol and Tommy sat there wondering why the fuck he was even listening to this shit. But he knew she needed to get it out of her system and the sooner she cunted him, the sooner she could start feeling better about herself. His legitimate son had not even contacted him since his mother's death; Tommy had not seen the grandchildren he adored in two years.

'Shut up, Lizzie,' he hissed.

She snorted noisily and leant forward in her seat.

'Can you imagine how I am feeling, Tommy? Can you imagine what I go through every day? They cut him up, for fuck's sake. They took my beautiful boy and butchered him.'

She grabbed at her replenished glass and took another deep drink before continuing. 'You didn't see him, Tommy. I couldn't locate you. But that's nothing fucking new, is it? I had to identify him from his body parts. I see his little face every day of my life. Every night as I try to sleep, I see my boy butchered on a mortuary slab. And it was because of you, Tommy. You used him and you didn't care what happened to him.'

She drained her glass again.

'You are a piece of shit and I never realised that until I saw my boy dead. You were everything to me, Tommy, you and my baby. You were the only people I ever wanted in my life.'

He took out his wallet. Removing a wad of fifty-pound notes, he placed them on the table.

'There's nearly a grand there, Lizzie – get him whatever he needs.'

She looked at the money for a few moments before she started to laugh.

'Stick your money up your fucking arse, Tommy Rifkind, it's too late. Twenty years too fucking late. I don't want your money now – I want you to tell me I never wasted my life bringing up our son. I need someone to tell me he was a good kid. That he was loved by someone other than me. But you never cared about him, not really. And he knew that. He tried to be like you so you would love him like you loved your other son. The way he talked about you . . . as if you were a god or something . . .'

He could hear the hurt and desperation in her voice.

'I loved him, Lizzie, you know I did.'

The words sounded feeble even to him.

She wiped her nose with the back of her hand and

he saw the marks on her wrist from where she had attempted suicide. He grabbed her arm and, turning it over, looked at the red scars.

'Oh, Lizzie . . .'

She smiled and once more he caught a glimpse of the girl she once was. Twenty years earlier she had been a stunner, and many men had gone after her. But there had never been anyone else for her but him and they both knew that. He had stopped her having any kind of real life because no one else would touch what was Tommy Rifkind's and she had had to live in that shadow always. Even when they had split up permanently, she had still had to live in that shadow with his child. No one was going to take on his ex-bird and kid; it would be too much like hard work. Once more he wondered why he had never moved them out of here, never given her or the boy a chance of a real life.

At last he recognised his own selfishness. He had always been that way. It was what had got him where he was today. A little voice reminded him then that where he was at the moment was up shit creek without the proverbial paddle, but he forced that thought away. He would sort it, he would sort it all, it was what he was good at.

Lizzie pulled her arm away and another drink appeared as if by magic. She sipped it this time and sighed.

'Keep your money, Tommy. You can't buy peace of mind, mate.'

She stood up unsteadily and, looking at Jonas, said quietly, 'You got me wrap?'

Jonas looked at Tommy and then at the floor. Tommy looked at the two of them for a few moments before saying incredulously, 'Wrap? Did you ask for a fucking wrap?'

His voice was angry and Jonas closed his eyes and sighed. Tommy B's mum was a pain at the best of times and at this moment he could cheerfully strangle her. He had given her a wrap after Tommy's funeral to calm her down and now she was hassling him for it all the time. It was the perfect cop out. He should know that better than anyone. He had been copping out all his young life.

Lizzie looked into Tommy's eyes and suddenly he saw that she wasn't out of it on drink, she was out of it on smack. The full enormity of what had happened to her hit him then and he felt disgust welling up inside. For himself as well as for her. His brain was saying, *Not Lizzie*. Lizzie was strong.

Someone had put the jukebox on and he heard the first strains of Simply Red and 'Holding Back the Years'. Lizzie smiled at him as she swayed to the music. He looked around the pub, at the people and the environment, and wanted to run. He wanted to run as far away as possible. It had just occurred to him that he had wrecked two lives, his son's and the boy's mother's.

He had never been there for any of them, not really. Even Gina had had to wait for him to come to her. All his life he had been loved, and yet he had never really once loved anyone in return.

Maura's family-mindedness had irritated him. Now, seeing Lizzie like this, he had to admit that unlike him Maura was basically a decent person. No matter what they did, she looked out for her brothers, for her family. Even Carla, who had done the dirty on her, Maura had taken care of all her life.

It hit him then that he was not the man he had believed himself to be. Instead he was a destroyer, of people and now, very probably, of himself. He had tucked up one too many and finally tucked up the wrong people. The Ryans would find him, he knew that.

He saw Jonas pass Lizzie the wrap and she walked out of the pub without a backward glance. Somehow knowing that Lizzie was there, in the background, had always felt good. She was his shelter in a storm. Now he knew she was gone from him as absolutely as his son was. Lizzie and Tommy B had always bumped him up, made him feel good about himself. Tommy B had loved his dad with a vengeance, loyal to him to the end.

Tommy closed his eyes and saw Lizzie once more as she had been when he first met her. He wanted to cry. Inside himself he knew he should follow her. That she wanted him to follow her and help her. But money had always come first with Tommy, and Jonas had been running a very profitable distribution business for him. Picking up the money from the table, he looked directly at Jonas as he said, 'So what's the score? Any trouble this end?'

Jonas sighed with relief and explained the situation as best he could. He was glad that Tommy was just back for his cut of the drugs proceeds and not for retribution of any kind. He had had the sense to put Tommy's cut away for him; had always known that he would be back for it sooner or later.

Tommy, for all his big talk, was strictly pennies and half-pennies but Jonas was not about to inform him of that fact. Instead he smiled and told him exactly what he wanted to hear.

Benny was inside the same cellar in North London as Jamie Hicks had been when he died. The irony was not lost on him. He looked around him at his uncles and Bing Dooley and his brothers. Saw his aunt standing silently on the cellar steps. For the first time in his life he felt acute fear.

'What the fuck is all this about?'

Maura nodded and walked up the stairs. When she was out of sight Benny saw the four black men take out rubber coshes. He looked at Garry, shaking his head in disbelief.

'This has got to be a joke. Uncle Lee . . .' He looked appealingly at Lee, knowing he was the most chicken-hearted of his uncles, but Lee was cold-eyed and disinterested.

'You should have thought of that before, son.'

It was his father's voice and Benny saw him walking down the cellar steps.

Garry went towards his brother.

'Go, Roy. You don't need to see this.'

Roy shook him away brusquely.

'I want to see this little fucker of mine get his comeuppance if you don't mind. But first I want to know whose head he had in that fucking wardrobe?'

Benny stared at his father. He looked terrible and Benny was more than aware that he had put those lines and that haggard look on Roy's face.

'Whose head was it, Benny?'

He shrugged.

'I can't remember.'

Bing and his brothers watched him and marvelled at what a nutter he really was. Bing smiled as he said, 'Starting a collection, were you?'

The men all laughed, except Roy and his son.

'Yeah, funny, ain't it, Benny? I am asking you one more time – who was it?'

He stared into his father's face. In the dim light of the cellar he let his gaze roam from Roy to his uncles. Then, taking a breath, he said nonchalantly, 'His name was Dean. He was a ponce who used to go out with Carol.'

'You actually did that to him just because he had once gone out with your bird?'

Lee's voice was incredulous.

Benny nodded. It sounded perfectly fair to him.

Roy took the cosh from Bing and Benny stood, feet apart, his powerful body bracing itself for the blows his father was determined to deliver. But he had not allowed for the strength of Roy, a strength born out of anger, despair and disgust. The first blow caught Benny across the bridge of his nose. He took it without even flinching.

Roy belted him again, faster and heavier.

Still Benny didn't flinch.

Bing and his brothers were impressed despite themselves.

Roy stopped, and throwing the cosh back at Bing, said wearily, 'Do me a favour, lads, kill him. For fuck's sake, someone kill the evil little bastard.'

Benny watched as his father walked away from him and knew instinctively that they were finished. He accepted he was going to be taught a lesson. His father walking away from him he accepted also. Benny didn't really care either way. It was how he was made.

Lee watched proceedings with a wary eye. Benny's stance and innate hardness were mirror images of his own eldest son Gabriel, and this made him take a step back and look around him with wide-open eyes.

Sheila was right: they were a load of nutcases. He walked from the cellar and saw Maura sitting outside in her car smoking. He leaned into the passenger window. Roy sat there, staring straight ahead.

'That is too fucking weird down there.'

They could hear the fright in Lee's voice.

'He is a bastard lunatic and I hope they take him out. Because if they don't do it, I will.' Roy sounded strong and determined.

Maura didn't say anything. She carried on smoking her cigarette, her eyes half-closed and her mind in turmoil. Benny had finally gone too far even for her brothers. If Garry thought he had gone overboard then that spoke volumes. Garry was as annoyed as she was, as Roy was, and Lee. She wondered what Michael would have done faced with this.

But she already knew the answer to that question. He would still have protected his nephew because he was family. In fact, Michael would have adored Benny, seen himself in the boy. She had read once that people liked seeing themselves in other people. You loved yourself so much you couldn't *not* love someone so like you.

But she wasn't sure how to deal with her nephew this time. Roy had told her already that he would take his own son's life if that was what it took to stop him hurting anyone outside the business ever again.

She knew that the police would eventually guess who the victim was. The boy had been reported missing by his family. Carol, safely ensconced in a nice private nursing home, was bound to let the cat out of the bag at some point. It was only human nature. She couldn't be expected to keep something like that inside her for ever, and it was taken for granted that her relationship with Benny was over. He had gone too far with everyone now. Even the girl who loved him. The loss of the child had hit her badly and Maura could sympathise with her on that. The girl's life was in tatters, and she had to try and pick up the pieces as best she could.

Maura was determined to keep Benny away from her. The chances were he was going to want to hurt her over the lost baby and the grief she had caused him. By the same token he might easily decide he wanted her back. Maura wasn't sure which would be worse for the poor girl. Either way she was determined to protect Carol. It was the least she could do.

'Don't worry, Benny's going to get a proper fright in a few hours.'

Lee and Roy nodded. They had guessed as much already.

Justin was lying on a bed in Majorca with his eyes taped shut and his mouth gagged. He was sorry now he had started creating. He had soiled himself and the psychological advantage of that as far as his captors were concerned, coupled with the binding, should sort him out once and for all. He still had not been fed anything and felt sick with hunger. They periodically forced water down his throat and that eased him somewhat. They kept trying to question him and it was getting harder and harder to ignore them. But he knew better than to tuck Vic up.

When they had shot the gun at him he had nearly had a heart attack and his nervousness coupled with his obesity made that a real threat. He could smell them cooking bacon and eggs, and the aroma made him salivate. He didn't know they were doing it deliberately.

He wondered why it was taking Vic so long to pay the ransom. He was assuming he had been kidnapped for money. In his confused state he thought they had scared him to make him more amenable. He wondered how much they were asking and hoped it wasn't too much. Vic was not his biggest fan and Justin knew he had been a pain in the arse once too often in the past. Something he was regretting now. He was also wondering what Vic had told Mum. She must be wondering what the fuck was going on.

The smell of the bacon was making him feel mad with hunger; he had often wondered how Jewish people could stand the smell without wanting a bite. His father had been Jewish, though his mother was Catholic. His father had not been a religious man as such yet he had never touched pork. When his mother cooked breakfast he'd always had everything but the bacon. Justin hoped he wasn't going to be seeing his father soon, even though he often thought about him. Dad had been dead years and Justin wanted to carry on living for a good long while. His dad had been all right as far as he was concerned, though Vic and his mother didn't seem to think so. If he had liked a drink and a gamble, what was the problem? Justin honestly didn't realise that Vic had been keeping them all since he was in his teens. When this was all over he was going to give his brother the bollocking of a lifetime. This capture was going on far too long for Justin's liking.

He felt the bindings being removed and blinked his eyes in the harsh light of the evening sun. The older of the men was holding up a plate of bacon and eggs, with fried bread and toast. There was also a large mug of tea.

'Hungry, Justin?'

He nodded warily.

'What do you fucking think?'

The man smiled in a friendly way.

'All you have to do is answer a few questions for us then this is all yours.'

'What questions?'

'You know what questions. I mean about Vic and his operation over in England.'

Justin had been through this three times already and it was getting harder and harder to refuse.

'Has he paid my ransom yet?'

The man placed the plate of food on the dressing table. Justin felt as if his eyes were glued to it.

'Told us to fuck off basically.'

In his mind Justin didn't believe the man, but the need to eat was stronger and so he decided to believe him anyway. Vic could piss off now as far as he was concerned. He should have had this sorted long ago.

Justin took a deep breath and then said with as much dignity as he could muster, 'What do you want to know?'

Danielle Hicks lay in bed with her baby kicking inside her and her eyes riveted on the photographs of the new house she had been offered by Maura Ryan. On the counterpane was the box of papers she had removed from her home after Jamie's death, just before the police had raided her.

She looked around the bedroom. It was a dump and she knew it was. Her mother had seen the photos and berated her for looking a perfectly good gift horse in the mouth. She had pointed out the benefits for the children as well as Danielle herself. No one would know who they were, she could live in a decent environment and her children could go to decent schools.

Never Jamie's biggest fan, her mum had been relieved at his demise and personally thought the Ryans should get some kind of accolade for getting rid of the man she held personally responsible for ruining her beautiful daughter's life. She constantly pointed out his faults: his infidelities, his obnoxious way of talking to people, his arrogance. The list as far as her mother was concerned was endless. She hated him with a vengeance – all Danielle's family did.

But they didn't know him like she did. They'd

never felt their heart quicken at the sound of his voice or the sight of his smile.

She knew her mum had a point about Jamie. She knew he was a bastard and gambler and liar. She acknowledged he had treated her with contempt and completely ignored her and the kids for weeks, sometimes months, at a time. She knew all that, had always known all that.

But somehow Danny felt that if she took the property offered to her, and the cash compensation, she would be betraying her dead husband.

She looked at the contents of the box. She was going to have to give this stuff to Maura Ryan at some point in the near future. She had always liked her, always, yet now she had no desire ever to talk to or see her again.

But she would have to, not only because of the stuff she had collected but also to tell her whether or not she was going to accept the generous offer of the house and comp. Vic Joliff had offered her nothing, as her mother had pointed out again and again.

Danielle sighed heavily. Her eldest son Petey still wasn't in and she stood up heavily, the weight of the baby making her wince, and glanced out of the bedroom window.

She saw Petey put out a cigarette, at least she hoped it was a cigarette and not a joint, and then stroll across the sparse piece of grass that brought him to his own block of flats. As he walked she saw three boys walking behind him and her heart leapt into her mouth, but they went quickly past, hailing him loudly. She relaxed once more.

She heard him come inside a few minutes later and heard the familiar sound of the fridge being opened as he sought a can of Coke. He walked quietly up the hall and as usual popped his head around her door.

'All right, Mum?'

'Yes, thanks. You?'

He sat on the bed and, opening his jacket, took out a wad of twenty-pound notes. He placed them on the bed ceremoniously, smiling at her as he did so.

'Where did you get that?'

She was whispering because of the littler kids and he smiled as he whispered back. 'I did a drop for a bloke over the other side of the estate. Even if I get caught I'm too young to be charged, see.' He was so thrilled with himself. 'You can get some stuff for the baby now.'

She had her hand tightly across her mouth to stop the scream that had risen to her lips. Swallowing deeply, she said as normally as she could, 'That was wrong, Petey. What you did was wrong.'

He shrugged.

'It's easy money, Mum, and the bloke said I could work for him every night after school if I like.' He sighed again happily. 'He said I had a bit of savvy.'

This would never have happened had Jamie still been alive, but now he was dead her children would all be dragged into the underbelly of the estate. Well, not if she could help it. She picked the money up and kissed him.

'No more, Petey. This is the one and only time, right?'

He didn't answer her. Instead he walked from the bedroom and she heard him cleaning his teeth. She lay back in bed, her mind made up for her. First thing in the morning she was accepting Maura Ryan's offer.

She looked at Jamie's photo and silently said sorry for taking from the people who had in effect ended his life, but she had a feeling he would understand why she was doing it.

# Chapter Nineteen

Tommy was in the Mosquito Bar in Victoria Street waiting for a friend. It was a place he used a lot. He had brought Maura here a few times and they had gone downstairs to the Vampire Bar, with its futons and privacy curtains, and she had loved it.

He had enjoyed it as well. Now, as he sat alone in the nightclub, he wished he was anywhere in the world but here. He felt self-conscious, knew that people were watching him, but this was the only place he could meet Jack Stern safely. He would only meet him in public; Jack was arsed with him over losing the coke and the grief from the Ryans, and Tommy was not going to take any chances.

The music was loud, and the place was rapidly filling up. It was an upmarket club in many respects and screamed of money. It had soap stars, footballers and other Liverpool celebrities in most nights. It also had a liberal sprinkling of the Liverpool underworld and many a deal had been done over a meal in the restaurant or in the secluded Vampire Bar.

Charlie Siega, the local underworld's most colourful character, walked past him and Tommy smiled, bringing up his arm to shake hands. Charlie looked at him coldly and carried on walking. By that one action Tommy knew the Ryans had already put the word out even in his local haunts. He felt physically sick with nerves and humiliation. He could feel Charlie's eyes boring into him, and wanted to leave. But he couldn't, not until he had talked to Jack.

Then Tommy saw Joss and relaxed at once. He had not spoken to him since the night Joss had told him what he thought of him and had gone to see Maura to make his own peace. Tommy had missed his old friend so much and seeing him now when he was at his lowest felt like fate was finally going his way again.

Joss walked towards him, smiling slightly.

Tommy sipped at his drink and waited for Joss to reach him at the long bar. He walked straight past and Tommy watched in disbelief as Joss ordered a drink and then went over to stand with Charlie and his friends. Tommy was burning with humiliation now. Never in all his life had he experienced anything like this. But he should have expected it from Joss; he was a loyal individual unlike Tommy and had had a genuine liking and respect for Maura Ryan.

Tommy pushed her from his mind; he was missing her and that in itself was surprising. He wasn't used to being the underdog in a relationship. He was used to being the main event.

He glanced at his watch surreptitiously. Jack was nearly an hour late, but he knew he had to allow for the traffic on the M1. He ordered another drink and sipped it while he looked around at the gathering crowd. He was admiring the tits on the young women when he heard Joss's familiar voice.

'Jack ain't coming, Tommy.' His old pal was behind him at the bar and talking to him without looking at him. 'Word is all over that the Ryans want you. Jack's meeting with them tonight, trying to get back in with them. Don't go home or to any of your usual haunts.'

He was gone in seconds and Tommy, taking in what he had said, got up a few minutes later and nonchalantly walked from the room. He had never felt so self-conscious in all his life. Or so alone.

So Jack was trying to build fences with the Ryans? Tommy understood that, they had the coke after all. But where the fuck did that leave him now? He had done all the groundwork, and now he was out of the running. Six years back they were to have been a combined force, Tommy in Liverpool, Vic in the south east, with Jack bankrolling the operation from the proceeds of thirty years of murder in return for a cut.

Now Vic hadn't even been in touch with Tommy since his return to England, which was ominous. Word had it he still blamed the Ryans for Sandra's death, but Tommy wouldn't have put money on it.

Looked like he had fucked up all round.

As he unlocked his car he saw a flash of metal beside him. A young man with long hair and goatee beard was standing there holding a long-bladed knife. Joss stepped up behind him and dropped the boy with a heavy blow to the head.

'You'd best fuck off, Tommy. That is the last time I'll be able to help you out, OK?'

He turned swiftly and walked away.

'Joss . . . Joss, for fuck's sake . . .'

Joss could hear the need and the hurt in Tommy Rifkind's voice but he carried on walking. Tommy had made his bed, now he had to lie in it. Joss had no intention of going down with him. Tommy was the nearest he had ever come to loving another human being, but he couldn't forgive what Tommy had done to Maura and the Ryan family. After all their years together Joss was finally seeing Tommy for the treacherous bastard he was.

Tommy watched him walk away and then looked down at the unconscious boy on the ground and kicked him in the head. Finally he got into his car and drove away.

But where to? That was the question.

Maura let herself into her house and was greeted by the smell of beef casserole and fresh cooked vegetables. She plastered a smile on her face before walking into the kitchen and greeting her mother.

'Something smells good.'

Sarah was wearing an apron over a high-necked dress, her wrinkled face set in a scowl.

'How the shag you cook on that shagging Aga I will never know.'

Maura grinned.

'You get used to it, Mum.'

'Sit yourself down, lovey, and I'll make you a nice cup of tea.'

Maura sat at the kitchen table and said nonchalantly, 'I have a few people coming tonight for a business meeting, Mum.'

Sarah scowled.

'A business meeting at this time of night?'

Maura nodded.

'Do I look that fecking stupid, Maura Ryan?'

She smiled at her mother's angry tone.

'I'll do a few sandwiches and a bit of cake, shall I?'

Maura was finding it harder and harder to keep the smile nailed to her face. 'That's all right, Mum . . .'

Sarah interrupted her.

'I used to do that for your brother when he worked from home. Men can eat at any time of the day and night; it gives them something else to concentrate on and makes for a nice friendly atmosphere.'

Maura took the proffered tea and laughed.

'Whatever you say, Mum.'

Sarah served her up a small bowl of casserole and she ate it with relish, not realising until then just how hungry she was. After the trouble she had had with Benny she had not believed she would ever have the stomach for food again.

'What's happened with your man?'

'You mean Benny, Mum?'

Sarah nodded. She couldn't say his name, didn't want to think about him if she was honest, but she had to know what was going to happen to him.

'He went into the police station about half an hour ago, of his own accord and with legal representation. We think someone placed the head in his house and that they were trying to incriminate him.'

It sounded ludicrous even to Maura's own ears and it was costing them a small fortune to have that statement believed by the CPS. But it was worth it, they had all reluctantly decided. Benny was better off under their watchful gaze but would have to spend a while on remand, and perhaps that would teach him in future.

Sarah seized on her explanation.

'Thank God! I knew he wasn't capable of that. As bad as he is, I knew he wouldn't go that far.'

Maura didn't answer her. She just concentrated on eating the delicious food served to her. Benny was battered and torn and she hoped he had learned a very basic lesson. That lesson being they were all sick to death of him.

Tommy Rifkind Junior lived in a nice detached house in Chester. His father had bought it for him many years before when Tommy Junior had first married. It was a large substantial house and now worth three times what Tommy had paid for it. It had the requisite ivy growing all over the front, and long Georgian-style windows that gave the place an upmarket look. It was only about twenty-five years old but it looked as if it had been there a hundred years or more. Tommy always got what he paid for.

As he braked on the drive he saw that both his son and his daughter-in-law were at home. He was nervous as he got out of the car and approached the house. The door was opened by his son before he even got close enough to ring the bell.

Tommy's first-born son was a big handsome man who wore designer glasses and cashmere sweaters. Tommy was proud of him and his academic achievements but didn't like him as a person. He was a hypocrite. Tommy Senior did not like his son's wife Angela either; she was a snob who had moved herself out of a council house and now tried to pretend that she was born upper-middle-class. Gina had got on well with her because Gina could get along with anyone. Tommy had clashed with Angela from day one.

He couldn't understand what the fuck his son had ever seen in this flat-chested woman with the hairy upper lip and the pseudo-refined twang. He conceded she had nice hair and teeth but that was hardly enough to keep a relationship going.

It had never occurred to Tommy that not every man graded a woman on a one to ten scale and put their physical attributes before personality or intelligence. His son had a good solid marriage to a woman who loved him, they had nice kids and took their role as parents very seriously. They travelled and the children went with them. They had a wide circle of friends and gave popular dinner parties. His grandchildren were happy and well-adjusted, but Tommy Senior still couldn't understand what the hell his son saw in that stuck-up mare he called his wife.

They lived in a different world from him, and Tommy being Tommy couldn't understand how they could live as they did and be happy.

He was nervous as he faced his child and hostility was evident on the younger man's face.

'Hello, son.'

Tommy heard the tremor in his voice and tried to control it.

Tommy Junior looked at him for long moments before saying, 'What brings you here?'

He was talking to him as if he was a stranger or a bare acquaintance.

'I wanted to see the kids.'

'At this time of night?'

His son looked pointedly at his watch.

Angela was standing behind her husband and he could see the concern etched on her face.

'My children do not keep nightclub hours and we

have guests. So if you will excuse me . . .'

His son was shutting the door in his face and Tommy, with nowhere to go, was beginning to panic. He put his foot into the door to prevent its closure. He could smell food and hear the low hum of conversation coming from the dining room.

'Who's in there?'

His son sighed heavily; it was uncanny to see him up close, they looked like clones of one another.

'No one you know. No murderers, thieves or liars in this house, I'm afraid.'

He looked desperately into his son's face.

'Please, Tommy. Please don't do this to me. Not tonight.'

Tommy Junior looked at him for a few seconds before saying quietly, 'Leave us alone, would you? Just leave me and mine alone. We don't want you here, I don't want you here, OK?'

'I am your father . . .'

Tommy Junior stepped away from the front door and pulled it closed behind him. His voice was a hiss as he said, 'Do me a favour, Dad. Go back to whatever gutter you crawled out of and don't ever come here again.'

He marched back into the house and closed the door firmly in his father's face. Tommy stood there for a few minutes. He needed his son at this moment, desperately needed his help. He had literally nowhere else to go. He was wanted by everyone, and daren't go home or near or by any of his usual haunts. He had been staying in a hotel just outside Liverpool but had checked out because he had assumed he would be off tonight with Jack on his way to meet Vic. The fact that wasn't happening told him that they were both enemies now, and more enemies he did not need.

Tommy sat in his car and watched as his son pulled the curtains in the lounge. He drove off down the drive and as he did so felt the sting of tears. He swallowed them down, full of self-pity and shame. He had never been there for his son, for either of his sons. He had ignored one and used the other.

It was payback time. Gina had always said, what goes round comes round. How right she was.

Leonie was in Maura's kitchen helping Sarah make the sandwiches and regaling her with stories of her riotous upbringing. Sarah and Maura had both been surprised when Gerry had turned up with the girl, but had made her welcome. It was so out of character for him that Maura and Sarah had looked at each other and raised their brows in wonderment. Leonie, however, had charmed them both and Maura decided she liked her a lot more when she was with Garry than she had when the girl had been at Jack Stern's house. Then it occurred to her that Jack was due to be at tonight's meeting and her heart sank.

Garry, however, thought it would be hilarious.

Sarah had promised to keep the girl in the kitchen

and Maura decided that Leonie probably didn't want to see her ex-beau anyway. She hoped that disaster would be averted.

Tony Dooley and his sons were still at the house and Sarah had fed them all her beef casserole and freshly warmed rolls. She loved feeding people and these huge men with their huge appetites had made her night with their clean plates and heartfelt compliments.

She looked at Maura over Leonie's pretty head and said happily, 'This is like the old days, eh? Michael used to have the house full of his friends and I would cook to me heart's content.'

Maura could see her mother's eyes shining with the pleasure of being useful, wanted, and she loved her again. Sarah grinned at Leonie.

'Mind you, with nine children I spent me fecking life cooking. There was always something simmering on the stove. I loved it, though, I was so proud of me brood . . .'

As Maura listened to her mother she saw again the woman she had been before they hit the big time in the criminal stakes. She'd been content to take care of anyone then even if she didn't know them. That was the Sarah Ryan Maura knew and loved. She hugged the little woman to her and said gaily, 'She is eighty-seven, Leonie! Isn't she marvellous?'

Sarah pushed her off roughly but she was laughing as she said, 'No need to shout it from the rooftops.'

'You are a babe, Mrs Ryan!'

Maura, Sarah and Leonie all laughed, and Garry, hearing them, was pleased. It was important that Leonie got on well with his family, especially Maura and his mother. If it all stayed as it was he was going to marry her. A big fuck-off church do, cake, the lot. He'd decided he was going to have the works.

He looked at the clock. It was nearly time for the meet. Jack was due at the house at two thirty. Garry hoped he told them exactly what they wanted to hear. If he didn't, Garry was going to kill him.

He had had enough of all this piss-balling about.

Benny was sitting in a cell in Basildon police station. He couldn't believe that this was happening to him. He sat on the hard bed and stared around him. He hated it: the smell, the graffiti and the sense of complete isolation he was feeling.

At least the family had made sure he was well treated; he had had a bottle of wine brought to him from a local restaurant and also a shot of Temazepam. The last thing they needed was for him to lose it completely. He was frightened of this happening himself. He knew he had pissed everyone off big time and was going to lie low for a while. He was getting off this charge, it was all practically sorted. He just had to swallow for a few days and that was that.

He settled himself on the narrow bed as best he could and contented himself with thinking of what he was going to do to Carol when he finally saw her. He could smell his own sweat and it made him feel uncomfortable but he forced himself to relax. He wondered how Abul was getting on without him. Benny had only been here a few hours and already he had had enough of it.

He tried the deep breathing techniques he had used as a boy to calm himself. They didn't work but took his mind off his immediate predicament. He knew the meet with Jack Stern was happening tonight and wanted to be there so badly. He also knew that Tommy Rifkind was being hunted down and would have liked to have been the man who took him out.

He was getting more and more wound up.

It didn't help that the drunk in the next cell had woken up and kept singing, 'If You're Happy and You Know It Clap Your Hands'.

All in all Benjamin Ryan was having a seriously shit night.

Tommy dumped his car in a lock-up near Knowsley and exchanged it for a beat-up Fiesta from his scrap-yard. As he looked around the yard he wondered if his dead son had left any impression here. He had seen a programme on Discovery about places being haunted by people who had died violent deaths, and his son's death had been about as violent as it could get.

He tried to visualise Tommy B but couldn't even remember what he'd looked like. He drove to Toxteth and parked in a quiet road. Locking the car, he walked for twenty minutes to his destination.

He crept up the main stairs of the low-rise block of flats and knocked gently on a scuffed front door. The place was filthy. It stank of stale cooking and rubbish bags. There was no answer. He knocked once more, harder this time.

'Fuck off!'

He half-smiled to hear the voice.

Putting his hand through the letterbox, he was amazed to see that a key was still in place there on a piece of string. He put it in the lock but it didn't fit. The sound of him trying to open the door brought the tenant of the property out into the hallway.

'Who is it?'

Lizzie's voice was scared-sounding now.

'It's me, Liz. Let me in, love.'

'Is that you, Tommy?'

'Open the fucking door, will you, Lizzie?'

The door opened and he walked into her flat. It was a long time since he had been inside the place but it felt the same as it always had. He shut the door, looking out first in case he had been followed or spotted.

'So it's true then?'

He looked at her and held his arms wide in denial.

'What you on about?'

She sighed and, turning from him, went back into the little lounge and lay on the sofa. He followed her. The room was warm and cosy as it had always been.

But it was untidy. She had never before had even one thing out of place in her home, it was one of the traits he had always liked about her. Still, he reminded himself, smack heads were not the tidiest of people.

He settled himself on the floor. She was listening to a Pink Floyd album, *Dark Side of the Moon*, and he strained to hear the guitar riff in one of the tracks.

'Turn it up, Lizzie, that's a good track.'

She shook her head.

'I can't.'

He laughed.

'What you on about?'

He was trying to humour her; he wanted to stay until the morning if possible. She sighed and wiped her hands across her sweating face.

'Me head's aching, I jacked up a while ago and I feel like shit. But I like the sound when it's on low, it makes me relax. Reminds me of when my Tommy boy was in his bedroom. He would play his music low and I would hear it through the wall.'

He heard once more the desolation in her voice and didn't know what to say to her. Lizzie, however, didn't seem to expect an answer.

Like most heroin addicts she was happy just to lie there quietly and go into herself.

'Make a cuppa, Tommy. Do something useful seeing as how you're here.'

He went out to the small and cluttered kitchen and put the kettle on. He got the mugs ready as he waited for the kettle to boil and looked around him sadly. It was like a tip. He had to wash up the mugs, they were rotten, and found a scourer under the sink to clean them with. The work surface itself was stained with tea and coffee and God knew what else. But he didn't say anything. He would talk to her in the morning. Try and make her see sense.

He took the teas back into the lounge but she was asleep. He was glad, he didn't know what to say to her anyway. He sat on the floor once more and sipped his tea. The album ended and he kept quiet in the ensuing silence. He could hear music coming from other flats and the sound of a dog barking on one of the balconies. He had forgotten just how noisy these places were, and knew how lucky he had been to be able to buy a nice big detached place with a few acres and a country outlook.

Suddenly she spoke to him and her voice, after the quiet, made him jump.

'What brings you here, Tommy? Aggravation?'

He was startled at her observation but denied it immediately.

'Don't be so silly. It was seeing you tonight at Black George's. I didn't realise how badly you were feeling about Tommy B.'

She opened one eye and looked at him quizzically.

'That's a first, Tommy Rifkind, you even noticing anything about a woman that wasn't to do with nakedness, tits or sex in any other form.'

He closed his dark eyes and stifled the retort that had sprung to his lips; he couldn't afford to fall out with this woman. Not until the morning anyway.

'Don't be silly, Lizzie, I loved you.'

'Yeah, 'course you did, Tommy. Like you loved your wife and your kids. Did you even know you had a new grand-daughter?'

He was surprised and she laughed at the expression on his face.

'Tommy's girlfriend gave birth after he died. Sweet little thing she is – the baby, I mean, not the girlfriend. That child, Leanna, is your worst nightmare, Tommy. You see, she's black.'

He was stunned and through her drug-induced torpor she saw him swallowing deeply.

'Don't worry, Tommy, we don't want anything from you. The mother's family has been great actually. Her mum and dad are really nice people and they're letting her live with them and helping her as best they can. Family, see. Nothing like it, Tommy, and your family is nothing like a family, so hey, there you go.'

He sat on the floor and let her talk. It was easier with Lizzie to let her have her say.

'Did you know Gina came here? After Tommy B's death?'

She had his undivided attention now and smiled to see it.

'Nice woman, Gina. She was too fucking good for

you, I can see that now. Even I was too good for you, Tommy Rifkind. I nearly died when I saw her on the step, but she said she'd come to offer her condolences and meant it. She came a few times more before she died. We talked, resolved a lot of things. I told her how bad I felt about our affair and she just smiled. Said that you were that type of man, needed new people all the time to keep your sense of self-worth. She said once people got close to you they found out what a shallow ponce you really were. Look at what you did to me. Our child was dead and I knew you didn't care either way. Because, you see, I *knew* you let him carry the can even though you were up to your neck in the plot against those southern wankers all along. Tommy B knew as well. He knew what you were and still he worshipped you all his life. That betrayal of your own boy was the worst thing you ever did.'

Tommy had his head in his hands now.

His Gina had actually come here and said those things about him? But that was the type of thing she would do, he knew. Try and make amends. He couldn't even bear to think about what he'd done to Tommy B.

'You've got it all wrong, Lizzie . . .'

She pulled herself up on to her elbows and screwed up her face as she shouted at him.

'Oh, fuck off, Tommy! Your bullshit doesn't wash with me any more. The day our boy died I started to hate you, and I will always hate you. I wasted my whole fucking life on you, can't you understand that? Don't you realise what you did to me and my son?'

She could see utter confusion on the face of the man she had loved once with every ounce of her being. She had never spoken to him like this before, always striving to please him, hoping to lure him back. Well, never again. Her mobile rang and she answered it, saying a curt 'OK' before turning it off.

'Who was that?' Tommy was trying to change the subject and they both knew it. 'Bit late to be getting phone calls, isn't it?'

He was feeling uneasy, and seeing the way she was looking at him understood in nanoseconds what had happened.

'How does it feel, Tommy?' she taunted him.

He was shaking his head in utter disbelief.

'You wouldn't . . .'

She was laughing now.

'Wouldn't I? Fucking try me, boy. There's a price on your head, Tommy Rifkind, and that price is going to take my grand-daughter as far away from this place as she can go.'

He was standing now, unable to look at her and see the triumph on her face. He went to the window and peered out between the curtains. His heart sank as he saw who was standing out there.

'You cunt, Lizzie.'

He stood over her, fists raised, and she put her arms

up to protect herself from the blows she knew were coming. But he didn't have time to punish her. Lizzie was still laughing manically as she heard the flat's front door opening. She'd left it unlocked in readiness. Tommy was frantically trying to open the balcony door, but it had been painted over many years ago and had never worked since.

He turned and saw Abul and two of the Ryans' heavies standing in the room, and almost smiled.

'Here you are, all present and correct.'

Lizzie's voice was stronger than he had ever heard it before, even with the skag rocketing through her veins. Jonas was standing behind the heavies and Tommy saw the half-smile on the boy's cadaverous face.

'Come on, Tommy, we have a plane to catch.' Abul smiled at Lizzie and added pleasantly, 'Someone will bring what you are due in a few days, OK?'

She nodded happily.

Tommy spat in her face as he passed her.

'You treacherous whore!'

Lizzie laughed. 'Takes one to know one, Tommy.' She followed them from the little flat and shouted at the top of her voice, 'Think of me, won't you? Think of me and my boy when you die, you piece of shit!'

Abul smiled at Tommy and said straight-faced, 'Have you upset the nice lady by any chance?'

Tommy looked at him in disdain and didn't answer.

'Upsetting women seems to be your forte, doesn't it, Mr Rifkind?'

'Get fucked, you black bastard.'

Abul grinned.

'Takes one to know one, as the nice lady just pointed out.'

His two henchmen laughed.

Tommy was beyond speech. He didn't say another word all the way to the private airstrip. He didn't know the blokes with Abul and for now it was best to keep his own counsel.

# Chapter Twenty

Sarah and Leonie were still in the kitchen chatting like old friends and Maura smiled at them as she came out to get another bowl of ice for the drinks. They were both tired but determined to make the most of their first meeting. Maura knew that for her mother, having a new member of the family to fuss over and tell stories to was an unexpected bonus.

Jack still had no idea Leonie was in the house and that suited them all, especially Leonie.

'OK, girls? There's a spare room if you feel tired, Leonie.'

She shook her pretty head and grinned.

'I'm fine.'

'You're flying,' Maura nearly answered, but didn't. No wonder Garry liked her; she was the archetypal Garry bird, and Maura was even more surprised to find that *she* also liked her very much.

'Shall I make more sandwiches, Maws?'

Maura shook her head and smiled.

'There's still plenty of grub in there, Mum, and we're getting to the nub of the evening, if you see what I mean. Thanks anyway, they were lovely.'

Sarah thought that Maura looked drawn but didn't say anything. She knew her daughter had a lot on her mind at the moment and once more set her own fears aside. She was back in the heart of her family and enjoying every second of it. In fact, Sarah had not been so happy in years.

This was what she had missed: being with her children, being a part of their lives. If a little voice inside was calling her a hypocrite for this after all she'd said and done she was ignoring it now. She felt needed and she felt wanted and that was all that mattered when you were nearly ninety and ready for the long sleep.

Sarah made another of her famous pots of tea and settled down to have a good gossip with the lovely little girl her Garry had brought to meet his mother. Leonie was young enough to be his daughter, grand-daughter even, but Sarah swallowed that. Leonie was a girl and girls could have babies – and that was what the world was all about, wasn't it?

Jack and Billy sat together in Maura's large dining room. The table was littered with food and bottles, and the French doors open wide to combat the cigarette smoke. Jack had already built himself a few lines to get himself through the night and the atmosphere at the moment was friendly if wary.

Garry was on his best behaviour and for that fact Maura was grateful. Even Roy and Lee seemed relaxed.

Jack Stern watched proceedings with a wary eye and finally asked the big question.

'So what's going to happen with me coke?'

He snorted a line immediately afterwards and Garry said in jocular fashion, 'We only took it to stop you snorting the profits!'

Even Jack had to smile at that one.

'Very funny, Garry, but it don't answer my question, does it?'

Maura heard seriousness in his voice. It sobered up all the other occupants of the room. Billy Mills closed his eyes in disgust. He was supposed to be negotiating about the drugs and Jack had just fucked it all up with his impatience.

'What about Vic Joliff? Shouldn't we deal with the main business first?'

Garry sounded friendly still, but it was obvious he was getting pissed off with the whole thing.

'I honestly have no idea where Vic is. I mean, I hear from him obviously but he don't tell me nothing like that.'

Roy picked up a ham sandwich and bit into it before saying quietly, 'You are one lying cunt, Jack Stern.'

Jack was out of his seat in a second, shouting: 'Oi,

you, hold up there! What the fuck gives you the right to say that to me, Roy?'

Garry picked up a small handgun. Waving it in Jack's general direction, he said merrily, 'Well, this does for a start.'

Maura gestured all the men back into their seats.

'No childish displays if you don't mind, guys. Just sit the fuck down and let's sort this once and for all.' She took a deep breath. 'Roy has a point, Jack. You are dealing with Vic on this shipment, we all know that . . .'

She held her hand up as he tried to interrupt her. Her voice full of barely suppressed irritation, she pointed a finger at him and said: 'Vic got you that coke, don't bother lying about it. Don't ever make the mistake of treating me or mine like cunts, all right? It's a bigger shipment than we allow other outfits to handle. Strictly speaking you should be cutting us in but let's leave that for now. We're trying to get to Vic and other grievances are being put on the back burner for a while.'

She looked around the room before she made her next announcement.

'Tommy Rifkind is as of now on his way here. He's being flown from Liverpool to a nearby farm so we can guarantee we're going to get to the bottom of it all tonight. Abul will bring him straight here.'

They were all watching Jack's reaction closely, even Billy Mills. Jack, as they all remarked later, took the news surprisingly well. That was what let him down if only he'd realised it.

Maura continued in the same clear voice: 'Kenny Smith is on his way over as we speak. He saw Vic again, gave me a message from him. Maybe he's our best way in to the lunatic, but first we have to find Vic and you're going to help us.'

Jack had never felt so exposed in all his life. He knew he had the eyes of everyone in the room on him.

'I can't do it, Maura, you know that.'

She stared at him, her clear-eyed gaze never wavering.

'I ain't a fucking grass. Vic is me mate and me partner . . .'

He was starting to panic, they could hear it in his voice. Still no one said anything and the silence was deafening as he looked around the table.

'You killed my Tony, man.'

Jack was indignant.

'I fucking well did not . . .'

Tony Dooley Senior shook his head sadly.

'You knew about Tommy, and you were in deep with Vic. You are the reason my boy Tony is dead.'

His other sons all nodded at their father's words.

Billy Mills watched in abject terror as he realised what was actually going down in this room.

Jack shook his head in disgust, the coke taking over and disrupting his thinking. He was paranoid and he was upset. He was also loose-lipped and even as he spoke he knew he was burying himself.

'So much for a fucking friendly meet! You can always trust the Ryans to do the fucking dirty on you. Vic was right, you are a load of has-beens. He'll chew you up and spit you out.'

Garry was laughing gently at his words. He looked around the room. 'I told you he was a fucking waste of space, didn't I? He wants to have his cake and eat it. Or should that be coke? Thought he could swan in here, do a deal for it then waltz off without us even suspecting a thing about him. Just how stupid can a man get? This wasn't a one off, Jack. We know you and we know Vic. This was just a toe in the water, wasn't it? Vic Joliff wants what's ours and he won't rest till he gets it.'

Jack stood up, his anger boiling over.

'Bollocks. I ain't sitting here listening to this.'

He signalled to his minder Jerry Sinclair. But Jerry stayed put and Jack shook his head sadly.

'Bought you and all, have they?'

Jerry shrugged nonchalantly. He didn't give a toss what happened to Jack, that much was evident.

'So much for fucking loyalty.'

'You never paid me enough for loyalty, Jack.'

All the men round the table laughed at the words. Jack was gutted and it came through in his voice and the fearful expression that was slowly settling over his face.

'Want another drink while we wait for Tommy to arrive, Jack?'

Roy's voice was sarcastic but he nodded anyway. Jack knew he was finished; inside himself he knew this was the end. He'd already done enough to justify them nutting him. If they spoke to Tommy and found out how far back it went there was no chance of a quick merciful shot to the head. Short of a miracle he was a dead man. He swallowed the drink straight down. He had a feeling he was going to need as much alcohol as he could get. He'd need something to dull the pain once this lot went off.

He snorted another line and pushed the small mirror towards Garry who shook his head.

'Thanks to you, Jack, I've got plenty of me own, mate.'

Everyone laughed again. Except, of course, Jack Stern.

Benny was woken up by the cell door opening. He put up a hand to shield his eyes from the blinding light now flooding into the room. He saw a young man with ultra-fashionable clothes and a buzz cut walk into the cell. The door was immediately closed again and Benny felt anger building inside him. He was *not* sharing a cell. He was most definitely not sharing his space with anyone else.

The young man was obviously drunk and had recently been involved in a fight. Benny decided he had been on the losing end by the state of him.

The boy yawned and said sleepily, 'All right, mate?'

Benny stared at him as if he had never seen another human being before in his life. This type was actually talking to him as if they were friends or something. He swallowed down the retort that had come to his lips.

The boy slid down the wall and lit himself a cigarette, blowing the smoke out noisily. The spy hole closed and Benny heard the grille shut noisily.

'All right, Benny me old son?'

There was laughter in the boy's voice now and Benny opened his eyes wide as he finally realised who was in the cell with him.

'Jonny White?'

He nodded.

'I thought it was you when they put me in here. But in case you was trying to be incognito, I didn't let on I knew you. What a fucking coincidence!'

Benny stopped smiling.

'Coincidence isn't the word.'

Jonny started to laugh nervously.

'Leave it out, Ben, you're always so paranoid.'

'What happened to you then?'

Jonny grimaced.

'Opened me trap once too often as usual. There was a crowd of us went to a nightclub called Raquel's on Micky Harper's stag night. What a shit hole. Anyway I got out of it and pushed me luck with some bird, and her brother was built like a brick shithouse. The rest, as they say, is history.'

Benny started laughing. That was Jonny all over.

'What brought you here? As if I didn't know!' Jonny said. 'Saw it all on the telly. It's the talk of the fucking country, mate.'

Benny preened himself at the words.

'It was all a set up. I had nothing to do with any of it.'

Jonny grinned again.

'What? Someone walked into your house and stuck a fucking human head in your wardrobe, is that what you're saying?'

Benny nodded and just in time Jonny remembered exactly who he was talking to. If Benny Ryan said it was a set up, it was a set up. If Benny Ryan told him his own mum was on the game Jonny would not argue with that fact.

'What a diabolical fucking liberty, Benny, eh?'

'My thoughts entirely, Jonny. Someone wants me out of the frame, that much is for sure.'

He yawned and settled himself on the bed once more. Jonny knew he would not be sleeping there, that much was already plain.

'How's Abul these days? I ain't seen him lately.'

'He's all right, you know Abul.'

Jonny nodded.

'I saw him a while ago, up the Circus Tavern of all places.'

'What – Abul?'

The other man could hear the surprise in Benny's voice and nodded.

'He was up the Circus Tavern? Who with?'

Jonny shrugged.

'I don't know, I only saw him in the car park. They had one of them Sport girls' nights, you know what I mean. A load of old slappers, if you ask me, but well fit and up for the game if you get my drift. I assumed Abul was up there for the crack like.' Jonny burped loudly and carried on. 'Had a fucking barrel load of drink, I'll feel like shit in the morning.'

'Who was he with?'

'Who?'

'Fucking Abul, stupid! Who else?'

Jonny could hear the annoyance that was creeping into Benny's voice and it made him nervous.

'I don't know, some old bloke.'

Benny rolled his eyes to the ceiling.

'*What* old bloke?'

Jonny was non-plussed for a few moments.

'Just a bloke, I don't know who it was. Flash, though. Few grands' worth of tailoring and a brand new sky-blue Roller. What a piece of fucking kit!'

Benny jumped from the bed and, grabbing Jonny by his jacket, dragged him up from the floor with one mighty heave.

'Are you sure it was Abul? Fucking answer me, you stupid cunt!'

Jonny was nodding like mad now.

'Yeah. I spoke to him, said hello like.'

Benny dropped him back down on the floor then

rang the bell by the cell door. As usual no one was interested in answering it. He stood with his finger on the bell without moving it, but ten minutes later they were still being ignored.

'Fuck, fuck, fuck.'

Jonny watched him warily. This was the last thing he needed tonight, Benny Ryan on the rampage. Still, as he consoled himself, it would make a good story one day and life was made up of good stories, wasn't it?

He only hoped he lived long enough to tell this fucking tale in the first place because Benny Ryan did not look like a happy bunny. Then again, he never looked happy period.

Abul sat next to Tommy in the six-seater Cessna. They never spoke once all the way to the airstrip in Rettendon. As they alighted he pushed Tommy out of the plane. He stumbled and landed heavily on his knees.

Abul dragged him up by the scruff of the neck and threw him unceremoniously into a waiting car. He jumped into the back seat with him and ordered, 'Drive!' to a young Indian guy in a turban.

Tommy was seriously narked. Dusting down his suit, he glanced out of the rear window at the two bemused-looking heavies left standing on the tarmac and warned, 'You'd better watch it, boy. Remember, I know all about you.'

Abul grinned and settled back in his seat.

'Relax, Tommy. 'Course you do. Anyway, you didn't think I was really taking you to Maura's, did you? Me and you are off to see Vic, mate.'

Tommy paled, but was instantly on the offensive.

'You know, you are in deep doo-doo,' he said conversationally. 'I mean, your pal Benny will kill you now you've shown your hand like this.'

Abul shrugged.

'He's got to fucking find me first, though.'

'And Vic will tuck you up without a second's thought,' Tommy persisted, trying to get some leverage. 'He's heavily into racial purity and all that – founding member of the Inner City Firm. And besides, he has good reason to hate you, hasn't he?'

Abul half-smiled and answered him in a bored tone of voice.

'In fact, Tommy, it's you he's really pissed off with. I know how to handle psychos like Vic – I've had enough experience, after all.

'His pitiful racist beliefs I can overlook – for as long as it makes business sense. This is a new world, Tommy, and I intend to be a major player. The Ryans and villains like them have had their day. They forgot one very important rule. The key thing with power is knowing when to hand it over. If you don't, someone stronger always comes along and takes it from you anyway.'

Tommy laughed.

'Hark at you! Fucking East Ham's answer to Osama fucking bin Laden.'

Abul laughed with him.

'Amazing, isn't it, how they all took it for granted that I was going to walk in Benny's shadow for the rest of me life? That calming him down and doing his bidding was all I was good for. When the Silvertown mob approached me with their idea I was more than ready to listen. For as long as it suited me. Bunch of lightweights!'

'But taking out Rebekka and her old man like that . . . didn't it turn your stomach?'

'After what I've seen with Mad Benny nothing gets to me, Tommy. Anyway, the woman was a shitter. Couldn't take the heat. I had to shut her up, didn't I? And it was worth it to see the Ryans running scared.'

Tommy remembered Maura waking time and again from a nightmare she refused to describe, and felt a moment's remorse. It was turning out to be quite a night for it.

'Yeah, yeah, very clever,' he said irritably. 'But you went way too far in other directions and where did it get you, eh? Six years on and you're still Mr Step and Fetch It. Now Vic's back and looking for some answers, ain't he? Don't tell me he's forgiven you your sins, 'cos I don't believe it.'

Abul shook his head and slowly drew his hand out of his pocket.

''Course he hasn't. Vic Joliff ain't the forgiving

kind. As you will very soon find out for yourself, I'm afraid.'

Tommy felt a sharp pain in his leg and looked down to see a hypodermic spiking it.

'Here, what you doing to me? What the hell's in that?'

Abul said soothingly, 'It's H, Tommy. The purest form. You'll thank me for it – if you ever come round. Vic's told me what he has in mind, see, and it's not nice, not nice at all. Just pray this gets you first.'

Tommy was struggling to speak.

'But . . . not my idea. *You*, Abul. Said it was too slow . . . didn't need Vic. Not my idea . . .'

His voice failed him. He felt the sides of the car closing in. Abul leaned forward and gave directions to the driver before turning back to prop Tommy up against the door.

'That's right, you go to sleep. Be easier for you that way.'

He prided himself on being one of the new breed of villain – he liked to be as civilised as possible even when he was ridding himself of a dangerous enemy.

When he'd first learned that Vic was back he knew he had to get to him before he spoke to Tommy. The Ryans led him to Jack Stern and his own men, the network of villains and pushers secretly loyal to him and waiting for him to make his move, managed to trace Vic.

Abul had convinced him that the murderous attack

on Sandra and the assault on Vic in jail had been carried out on the direct orders of Tommy Rifkind. But the truth of it was that it was Abul himself who'd decided to cut Vic out of their takeover bid and used the attacks to escalate the trouble for the Ryans. He'd wanted to bring the whole lot of them crashing down, as fast as he could. So he killed Sandra and Janine, and sent word to Belmarsh to top Vic. Tommy B was informed that Abul and his father wanted Lana and Sarah topped – Abul threw them in just to make things truly volatile. Tommy B was a simple soul. Didn't believe in killing old ladies or grassing up his own family. Which was what Abul had relied upon.

He glanced in amusement at the man lolling beside him, a thin trail of spittle dribbling from the corner of his slack mouth on to the shoulder of his handmade suit. Vic would finish him tonight, and after that he was going after the Ryans in his bid to take over their drugs empire. When he'd done the dirty work Abul would step in and finish what he'd started six years before.

Benny was frantic. He had to alert Maura and the others to what Abul was doing. Part of him still couldn't believe it. He had a pain in his heart like a knife was lodged there. Abul . . . the one person in this whole shitty world he'd thought he could rely on. But not any more. The lying scheming toerag was out to get everything the Ryans had. He had to let them know.

Benny looked at his old schoolfriend Jonny and said earnestly, 'I'm going to beat you up so scream as loud as you can, right?'

Jonny shook his head in bemusement.

'This is a joke, right?'

Benny walked towards him, shrugging. As he lifted one meaty fist he said in all seriousness, 'No offence, Jonny.'

He was already screaming before the first blow landed, absolutely terrified of what was about to happen to him.

Tony Dooley Senior took a call on his mobile. He listened for a few moments and then said to the meeting, 'Tommy has gone AWOL with Abul Haseem. We're trying to track them down but they gave our boys the slip at the airfield. Abul's not answering his mobile and he used an unknown driver for the pick-up – not one of ours. I hate to say this but it looks like he's in with Tommy.'

Kenny Smith said quietly to Maura, 'You must have had an inkling, surely?'

She shook her head, her face deathly white.

'Not Abul. No, I don't believe it. I looked after him since he was a kid. Him and Benny have been like brothers.'

Jack Stern snorted.

'What brothers was that then – Cain and Abel? I've never trusted the fucking blacks . . .'

Tony Dooley Senior and his sons all stared at Jack and he remembered where he was and who he was with.

Maura's voice cut like a knife.

'You on a fucking death wish, Jack?'

Tony got up. He had taken all that he could. His sons got up with him, but they were trying to calm him down and Maura was grateful for that much.

'Leave it out, Dad, he's a piece of scum. Not here, Mrs Ryan's in the kitchen. He's not worth it, Dad.'

Maura and her brothers watched as they placated their father. Garry walked around the table and went out to the kitchen. He came back in with Leonie and Jack's face was a picture as he stared at his one-time bedfellow.

'Collect the glasses up, love, and bring in some more of me mother's sandwiches, will you?'

Leonie hardly glanced at Jack as she did what she was bidden. After kissing Garry on the top of his head she waltzed from the room.

Maura knew the girl had enjoyed her little triumph and despite everything felt sorry for Jack.

Everyone helped themselves to more food. Finally a yawning Kenny Smith said, 'Well, personally, I am for the off. Nothing will be resolved tonight now, will it?'

Maura stood up and Jack, looking at her, said seriously, 'Where does this leave me?'

Maura sighed heavily. Was he blind? She was glad she had not chosen to live in the never-neverland that was cocaine.

'It leaves you, Jack, in the capable hands of one of my oldest friends. We don't need you any more, do we? You will tell Tony all we need to know.' She looked at her old friend as she said, 'Won't he, Tone?'

Tony Dooley smiled at Maura and she smiled back. A friendship that spanned many years lay behind that smile, even Jack could see that.

'After all, Jack, you were involved in a lot of the shit that happened, weren't you?'

He knew then he was finished, there'd be no deal made; it was all over and his own greed had led to his downfall.

'So that's me fucked then, is it?'

Garry grinned.

'I couldn't have put it better meself, Jack.'

Jack watched them as they all got ready to leave. He tried to catch Kenny's eye but his old pal wasn't having any of it. He just wanted to go home to the little daughter who was the light of his life. Maura walked him to the front door.

'Fancy a few hours in the park tomorrow with me and Alicia?' he asked.

Maura grinned.

'Why not? Not too early though, Kenny.'

'I'll ring you.'

She nodded.

'What a night, eh? It will all be over soon, I expect, one way or another.'

'I hope so, Maura. For all our fucking sakes.'

* * *

Vic was smiling like a man demented when Abul and his driver walked into Jack Stern's barn carrying Tommy between them, his arms draped over their shoulders.

Vic clapped his hands, eyes twinkling with merriment and Class-A substances.

'So it worked, Abul my son? You're a cool customer, snatching him from under their noses. But what you done to him? He looks dead already.'

Abul knew he could talk his way out of this. Didn't he always?

'He got a bit antsy in the car, tried to make a run for it. I gave him a sedative to make him co-operate.'

Vic lifted one of Tommy's eyelids and shook his own head reproachfully.

'I wish you hadn't taken it upon yourself to do that, I really do. I mean, if I'm working myself up to a killing spree I like to think my audience is still awake. Spoils the fun otherwise.'

He sounded genuinely aggrieved and once again Abul marvelled at his own bad luck. From Benny Ryan to Vic Joliff – why did he only ever seem to work with psychos?

He smiled in a conciliatory way. The sooner he could aim Vic at the Ryans, the sooner he could step in and claim the prize for himself.

'Sorry, but you know how it is. Give a villain like Tommy half a chance . . .'

'Oh, I do.'

Vic took a step back and slid his hand inside his jacket.

'I certainly do. Which is why . . .'

He shot the driver through the eye. The man went down silently, too startled even to cry out. Abul tried to run but Tommy's arm was still around his neck, the man's dead weight bringing him to his knees. He rolled clear and was scrambling for the door when Vic shot him in the thigh. He rolled over on the dirt floor and held up his hands.

'What are you doing, man? We had an agreement . . .'

Vic walked towards him, looking genial.

'We did indeed. You promised I could have the man responsible for my Sandra's death and for this little bit of handiwork.'

He yanked at the collar of his shirt, revealed the livid necklace of scars beneath.

'Did you really think you could pull the wool over my eyes, you jumped-up piece of scum!'

'Vic, please, I can explain . . .'

Abul's voice was at its most persuasive.

'Leave it out!' Vic snarled. 'I ain't your Loony Tunes Ryan kid, still wet behind the ears in villainy. I don't believe the first load of old cod's I'm told. Especially when it's a soot doing the talking.

'Mind, I had to go to a tin lid to get the real version, but Joe's old time. I'd take his word over yours any day.'

Abul closed his eyes momentarily. It was his own fault for leaving that loose end. But the old man had been easily cowed and useful in swearing blind to Maura that Rebekka and her husband had died at the hands of the Russian Mafia. It had covered his tracks. If only his Belmarsh contact hadn't screwed up, none of this would be happening.

He slid his hand down against his leg, surreptitiously feeling to see how bad the damage was. Vic lowered the gun.

'Don't worry, it's only a flesh wound,' he said. 'When my mate Mickey gets here he'll dress it for you. Always carries a First Aid kit, does Mickey. He says he only uses it when I'm around though.'

Abul felt a sense of dread creep over him.

'What are you going to do to me?'

Vic scratched his head.

'I'm still working on that one. First Mickey's going to help me deal with laughing boy here.' He waved the gun at Tommy, slumped on the ground. For a moment Abul almost felt relieved. He'd thought he might be in line for that treatment but it seemed Vic was still going to punish Tommy for going along with the plot even if it didn't start with him.

'You . . . well, I want to take me time over that. Come up with something truly memorable. Look at it this way, Abul. Your name will still go down in the history of villainy – no one will ever forget the way you died.'

He was still squawking like a parakeet at his own wit when Mickey Ball and a few other men arrived later. Abul's leg was roughly bandaged and then they forced him, struggling and protesting, into the boot of a car. The last thing he saw as the door was slammed down was Vic trying to slap Tommy awake. Abul cursed himself for being so soft and giving him the H. He would have given anything now to have an easy way out for himself.

Jonny was in a right state, Benny was beating him and he was screaming his head off. Benny was not letting up at all and when the cell door was finally opened it took three policemen to drag him off and out of the cell.

Then Jonny started to fight the policemen.

It went up like a bushfire.

In the mêlée, Benny walked down the corridor that led from the cells and within seconds was out the back of the police station. Five minutes later he had dragged two young girls from a Peugeot parked outside a kebab van just off the High Street. He went driving off as fast as he could to pick up a decent motor. He couldn't believe he was driving a Peugeot. It seemed to set the seal on what had been after all a really shit day.

Then he saw a mobile and suddenly he felt that things were looking up.

* * *

Maura lay in bed listening to her mother's snores coming from across the landing. She had forgotten that her mother snored. When she had slept with her as a kid, she had liked to hear the sound, it had made her feel safe.

Now she punched the pillow in an attempt to get comfortable. She wondered what was happening to Tommy and tried not to care. Abul's betrayal was going to hit Benny hard. It was a good thing he was out of the way at the moment. This would really send him off at a tangent. She closed her eyes tightly and tried to stop her mind from whirling. It was nearly morning and she needed to get some sleep. Even the brandy she had drunk wasn't making her feel tired.

She wondered what tomorrow at Marsh Farm would be like in an effort to take her mind off other things. She had not seen Kenny's little girl for a while and was looking forward to meeting her in the park.

It didn't work. She couldn't sleep and she couldn't stop picturing what was happening even as she lay in her bed. She had never felt so powerless in her life.

# Chapter Twenty-One

Kenny was shattered. As he let himself into his house he heard his mobile bleeping. He looked at the text and his heart sank into his boots. He knew he had to be careful at this precise moment because the chances were Vic was actually sitting inside his home while texting him.

He used the number on the text and was relieved not to hear a phone ringing nearby. Vic answered immediately.

'Had a nice evening with the Ryans, Kenny?'

'What do you want, Vic?'

He kept his voice level.

'I want to talk to you face to face. I have Tommy here and I think me and you need to discuss a few things.'

'What things?'

'Well, you are a fixer, aren't you, Kenny?'

'So I've been told.'

Vic laughed and Kenny could almost see his bald

head and even white teeth. He could almost smell Vic, he had such a feeling of him. He knew that Vic had something up his sleeve and also knew he wanted no part of it. He didn't have much of a choice, though, and was well aware of that fact. Kenny sighed.

Vic's voice changed as he said in a friendly tone, 'No trouble, I promise you.'

Kenny sighed once more, more heavily this time.

'What does Tommy have to say to you?'

'There's a car outside. Come along and find out.'

'I am knackered, Vic, can't this wait?'

He laughed, a low deep chuckle.

'Just get in the car, Kenny, there's a good boy.'

He rang off and Kenny felt an urge to smash the phone. He was bone weary and had had enough of the lot of it. Once this was all over he was going to retire. He was definitely going to retire.

He picked up his land line and dialled Maura's number. She needed to know the score. After speaking to her he went upstairs and gazed down at his sleeping daughter. She had given new meaning to his life since Lana's death. He knew that if his wife had not died he would not have been as close to this child as he was now. He'd like nothing more than to be her father full-time and was working towards that goal. Once this was all over, he was out of the business for good. He was going to make this child's life as happy as it could be. Give her everything in his power, and that included all his love and all his time.

Something good always came out of tragedy. He had heard that many times and now he knew it was true. God had given him a second chance at life and he was going to grab it with both hands. In Alicia he finally had something more important than money, prestige and respect, and he loved her with all his heart.

He walked from the house as quietly as he had entered it. His day out with Maura and his daughter would have to wait. But there would be other days, God willing.

Benny had driven the crap car to Abul's flat. He let himself in with his key, knowing Abul was still under the impression he was banged up. Inside he stalked around the empty flat looking for his one-time friend, and then he turned on the lights and started to tear the place apart.

He found a mobile in a drawer and turned it on. The first thing he did was look through the text messages and check the numbers. He knew most of them; they belonged to mutual cronies. Next, he sorted through the kitchen until he found a mobile adapter and plugged in the phone he had found in the car. It was dead. He plugged in the phone from the drawer and then picked up the landline. As he was about to dial he stopped himself.

Should he ring Maura or Garry? He decided to ring

neither and phoned his father instead.

Roy picked up the phone sleepily, but his son's voice soon woke him up.

'What the fuck you done now, Benny?'

He was hurt at his father's tone.

'Ain't you heard yet?'

'Heard what?'

'I escaped from the police station.'

'You what? Are you really that fucking stupid?'

Benny closed his eyes in distress.

'You don't understand, Dad. You don't understand what's going on . . .'

He stared at the phone in his hand. It was dead. Roy had hung up on him. He stared at the receiver and felt like crying with temper. No one was willing to listen to a word he said. He knew it was his own fault but still it galled him.

He saw a photo on the television set; it was of him and Abul at Ascot with two girls in big hats and expensive outfits. Abul had his arm around Benny's shoulders and they were smiling into the camera. He closed his eyes to blot out the picture and the memory. He had loved Abul like a brother; had been friends with him for years since they were kids. Benny had trusted him more than he had trusted anyone else outside the family ever.

They went back for such a long time, had done everything together, everything. They had even gone to bed with birds together; shared everything always.

Now to find out that it was Abul who was the double dealer made him feel responsible for everything that had happened to the family. His mother's death; his father's breakdown. Abul knew who had killed Janine, and whether Benny was close to her or not, she was still his flesh and blood. Still one half of his parentage. Abul had even consoled him over his father's breakdown. Had been there with him through the good times and the bad. Benny had trusted him to take care of his own pregnant girlfriend.

It was impossible to believe.

All this time his best friend had been conspiring against him and he, Benny, had never once guessed a thing. Never had even an inkling that everything wasn't as it should be.

He was going to kill Abul, slowly and painfully.

The one thing he should have known was you never, ever tucked up Benny Ryan. Not unless you had a complete and utter disregard for your own life. Which Abul Haseem obviously had. He had to be on a death wish, it stood to reason. No one in their right mind would cross Benny. No one with half a brain anyway.

He carried on systematically searching the flat. If there was anything to find, Benny would find it. And if in the event he didn't find anything it certainly wasn't because he had not looked properly. He'd even dismantled the TV set and stereo.

* * *

Maura was dressed once more and sat sipping coffee with Garry as she waited for Benny to get in touch. He would eventually, she knew that. Garry was waiting for Lee to arrive and she wondered if Roy was going to come too. When she had spoken to him he'd sounded as if he'd had more than enough of his son for one lifetime.

She could understand how he was feeling.

The police had mounted a search for Benny and even the solicitor had told her in no uncertain terms that it would take the National Debt to buy the little fucker out of this one.

Maura had put someone outside Carol's hospital room just in case Benny decided to pay the poor cow a visit.

She had not realised just how much mobile phones had changed their lives until this evening. Years ago you had to wait to contact someone, use a phone box even and get them called to it. Now people could communicate at any time of the day or night without having to leave their homes or cars. Consequently you got used to talking to people as and when you wanted to. If you had a signal, you had a conversation. It was frustrating to sit here and wait for Benny to contact them, which was what they had to do.

'I wonder how Kenny's getting on with Vic? He said Tommy would be there apparently.'

Garry sounded tired and Maura herself felt as if she could put her head on the table and sleep for a month. She saw her own exhaustion mirrored in her brother's face and smiled gently at him.

'If anyone can reason with Vic it will be Kenny. I want to know what Benny is going to do when he finds out about Abul.'

Garry shook his head in despair.

'I can't believe it, can you? But it must be true or Abul would have brought Tommy straight here.'

She nodded.

'I thought it was all Tommy, didn't you?'

'They were probably in it together.'

Maura shook her head. Her voice was stronger as she said, 'At least we know who took young Tony Dooley out, don't we? He would have trusted Abul. Brothers in arms, both helping to guard the Ryans.'

Garry was quiet before saying, 'I saw Abul as the voice of reason. He was the only person who could handle Benny outside the family. I felt better knowing that the boy was with him, didn't you? Felt that he kept Benny out of trouble when he could, talked to him, reasoned with him. Fuck me, I could have done with a mate like Abul meself. You just can't trust anyone these days, can you?'

Maura shook her head.

'So it would seem. I hope Vic doesn't hurt Kenny.'

'Who knows? He hasn't so far. Got that much nous left anyway.'

'I wish this was all over.'

Garry laughed.

'We have the trump card, love, which is why Vic

needs to see Kenny. All the time we have Justin we have Vic by the short and curlies.'

He finished building a large joint.

'Vic is gonna want to do a deal of some sort, and we *will* do a deal with him.' He lit the joint and inhaled deeply before saying, 'Then I am going to kill him, at my leisure of course, him and that piece of shit Abul.'

'What about Tommy?'

Garry shrugged.

'What about him? He's a dead man, Maws. If Vic or Abul ain't turned on him yet we'll have him as soon as he shows his face. You needn't be involved. Just try and forget about him.'

Maura knew she wouldn't be able to but Garry didn't want any girlish confidences.

'This has certainly been a long fucking night, Gal.'

He grinned.

'It ain't over yet, the sun is up and the day is about to begin for everyone but us. It's a waiting game, love, and we will wait. It's all we can do.'

Casha Haseem was woken up by a stinging blow to his face. He opened his eyes to see a fist crashing towards him once more. He tried to evade the blow but it caught him on the cheekbone and collapsed it immediately.

Then he realised who was attacking him. It was Benny Ryan.

Benny grinned down at him and raised his meaty fist once more.

'What the fuck you doing, Benny?'

Casha's voice held equal parts of fear and curiosity. This was his brother's best mate, after all.

'I am smashing your fucking face in. Are you a bit thick or something that you can't work that one out for yourself?'

Casha sat up and put his hands over his face to deflect the further blows he knew were coming. Benny smacked him again and again.

'Where the fuck is Abul? And I am warning you now you'd better tell me, Cash, because if you don't I am gonna kill you and then I am gonna kill your whole family.'

Casha wondered briefly if he was just dreaming. Benny Ryan was the person his brother loved above anyone else.

'How the fuck would I know? He never tells me nothing, Benny, you know that.'

He was nearly crying with fear. Benny saw the boy's face swelling all over and then he hit him again.

'Please, Benny, for crying out loud! What's brought all this on?'

Benny poked a finger in the boy's face.

'Where's your brother? This is the last time I'm asking you.'

Casha felt sick with apprehension.

'I don't know! I swear I don't know, Benny. He could be anywhere.'

Benny knew he was telling the truth, it was obvious

he didn't know what the fuck was going on. Casha was a shitter. If he knew he would talk.

'Who would know? Tell me who he is close to other than me?'

He could see Casha trying to think of an answer to his question.

'Come on, answer me. I ain't got all fucking day.'

'Dezzy . . . ask fucking Dezzy, they're always talking and poncing around together.'

'What, you mean your Cousin Dezzy?'

Casha nodded and Benny was suddenly sorry for the boy.

'It's nothing personal, Casha, OK?'

The boy nodded, relieved it was all over.

'What the fuck is this all about, Benny? What's brought all this on?'

Benny looked on the little night table beside the bed and picked up the alarm clock. It was a heavy affair, all brass and Roman numerals. He brought it down heavily on the boy's head, and then repeated the action over and over again. Each blow was harder than the previous one.

Benny watched the boy in a detached way. Casha knew he was dying and was really struggling to save himself. Benny was impressed. Finally Casha wasn't moving any more and Benny would bet his last pound he wasn't breathing either.

This was meant as a message for Abul. It would bring his ex-friend out of the woodwork once the boy's death became common knowledge.

He sifted through Casha's stuff and found yet another mobile number for Abul. Benny pocketed it and went downstairs. He was buzzing with excitement. He was going to sort this all on his own and then Maura and Garry would see that he was an *asset*, that he could control things, control *himself* when he needed to.

He conveniently forgot about the rapidly cooling body of Casha in the bedroom. He made himself a cup of coffee and some toast in Casha's kitchen. Flipped on the portable TV and watched himself being talked about on the news. It seemed poor old Jonny had been arrested as an accomplice to his escape. Benny would see that he got a drink. He would sort it all out when this was finally over. He turned over to *Trisha* and while he ate his breakfast watched people who had undergone DNA tests to see if they had fathered their own supposed children.

He loved talk shows, marvelled at the predicaments people got themselves into without ever thinking about the life he led by comparison. He honestly thought he was an all right person, thought he was normal. He watched the poor saps on the TV and couldn't understand these people or their complicated lives, but it was compulsive viewing as far as he was concerned.

He thought about his child then and felt sadness sweep over him. If only Carol had not been so fucking nosy, had not looked in the wardrobe, so much could have been avoided.

He was surprised at just how hungry he was. He had to make himself more toast and coffee before he felt even remotely full up. He reminded himself that he had not eaten since the evening before so would be more hungry than usual. He had had, after all, a very demanding night one way and another. He was tired and he was annoyed, not a good combination for Benny Ryan. But he would sort this lot out and then he could have a few hours' kip and be as right as the mail, as his old Nana used to say.

He had a quick shower and then he was once more on his merry way. He used Casha's car this time. It was a nice little BMW and he felt much better driving it than the poxy Peugeot. If anyone he knew had seen him in that he would have died of embarrassment. It would have taken him ages to live that one down. In fact, this little BMW was such a nice motor he thought he might invest in another one for himself.

Benny gave another motorist the fright of his life as he cut him up by hurtling through a red light. He was annoyed with the man and wished he had the time to stop and sort him out. But Benny was a man on a mission and had to swallow this time.

Such was the mindset of Benny Ryan as he set out to track down his oldest friend.

* * *

Jack Stern was silently weeping with pain and all he could hear was Tony Dooley Senior saying over and over again, 'Tell me what I want to hear, Jack, and I promise I will make it quick.'

Jack was nearly going out of his mind. His arm was broken and his face burning from the drops of acid Tony was dripping on to him at regular intervals. But he was buggered if he was going to talk. They had him broken and were going to finish him but he would go to his death with the satisfaction of knowing they had not made him talk. It wasn't a question of loyalty, more his own professional pride. He'd killed dozens of people on contracts and always despised the ones who gabbled and pleaded and tried with their last breath to do a deal. He'd always vowed that he'd never go like that and he wouldn't, whatever they did to him.

'I mean it, Jack. I am starting to lose patience, man.'

Jack was nearly delirious with the agony and the constant burning.

'Please, Tony. No more, mate. Enough!'

He was trying to sit up.

Tony nodded at his second eldest son and Winston Dooley held Jack's good arm while his father cracked the elbow with a baseball bat.

Jack screamed once again but no one cared. As far as they were concerned he could scream all he wanted. No one would hear him in this lock-up in

Brixton, there was too much background noise, and even if they did no one would give a flying fuck anyway. It was that kind of area. There was another lock-up next door that had a sound system playing reggae all day long, and that as far as Jack was concerned was almost worse than the beating. He was throwing up now and as his arms were both useless trying unsuccessfully to roll on to his side. He had never been in so much pain in his entire life.

Tony opened the acid bottle again and held it over Jack's eye.

'I will burn the fuckers out of your head if you don't tell me what I want to hear, Jack. You are not walking away from this, do you hear me?'

He was bellowing now in anger and frustration. Tony had loved his eldest son with a vengeance and Maura Ryan was his greatest friend. Jack was paying double bubble for what Tony saw as his deliberate double dealings. His son was dead and Jack should have thought long and hard before he made an enemy of the Dooleys or for that matter the Ryans.

'You are a dead man, Jack. You can die fast or slow but you are going, man, you are finished. Vic expects you to open your trap, for fuck's sake, anyone would after this lot. No one will think any the less of you.'

Jack couldn't even move his arms now to save his face or more importantly his eyes. Tony dropped some acid on to the eyeball. Jack closed his eyes instinctively but it burned through the lid anyway and now he was screaming. He passed out and Tony poured a bucket of cold water over him.

'Put the water on and hose him down.'

He lit himself a Benson & Hedges and watched as Jack was revived. He was impressed despite himself. Jack had taken far more than he had believed possible. He had always seen the other man as a bully basically.

Just showed you how wrong you could be.

The barn was deserted but for Vic when Kenny reached it.

'What is it this time?' he asked wearily. 'And it'd better be good, Vic, because I need my beauty sleep.'

Vic cuffed him jovially on the arm.

'I'll say you do.' He put his arm round Kenny's shoulders. 'Let's go and get some breakfast, shall we? I'm starving.'

Kenny looked around him.

'Where's Tommy Rifkind?'

Vic shrugged.

'Who knows the answer to that question, mate? Certainly not me.'

True to form then, promising a meeting then not delivering. Vic was losing more marbles by the day.

Kenny said nonchalantly, 'By the way, Benny Ryan went on the trot last night. Just thought you might want to know that.'

Vic was roaring with laughter as they got into the Range Rover.

'Nice one! That Abul is one two-faced little fucker, eh? But he was a much-needed cog in my big wheel of skulduggery.'

Vic was mad, that much was evident. He was also coked out of his head. Kenny was glad he had never really developed a taste for it. Give him a drink any day of the week.

'Where we going, Vic?'

'To Jack's house, of course. Seems a shame to waste such a nice big empty space, don't it? Is he dead yet, by the way?'

His voice was friendly and conversational and Kenny, marvelling at the way Vic seemed to keep tabs on them all, answered him in the same vein.

'Who knows, Vic? *Who* the fuck knows?'

Vic grinned.

'More to the point, Kenny me old son, who the fuck cares, eh?'

Kenny Smith wondered what his daughter was doing. She was expecting him to take her to Marsh Farm to feed the animals. He hoped he would be going home at some point. He just wanted to take her on his lap and love her. Alicia was all that mattered in his life and he had no wish to lose his liberty over this abortion that was taking up too much of his time and energy. It just wasn't worth it. None of it was.

He wished he had learned that lesson years ago. If he had he wouldn't be in the shit he was in now.

He had enough money to live the rest of his life in relative comfort, so what was he still doing fixing when he could be anywhere in the world he wanted, instead of stuck in a Range Rover with a fucking headcase like Vic Joliff?

How much money was enough, for fuck's sake?

It was a good question to ponder, he decided. Anything was better than thinking of the predicament he now found himself in. He was here for Maura Ryan and he knew that. If nannying a coke-snorting psychopath would help keep her safe, Kenny would do it and no complaints. Maura had a way of inspiring loyalty in him, and maybe something more than that.

'Do you ever wonder how we got ourselves into this life, Vic?' he said.

Vic shrugged heavily.

''Course not, Kenny. What else are we going to do, boy?'

He sighed.

'I don't know, Vic. But there has to be more to it all than this, surely?'

Vic pulled over to the side of the road and looked at Kenny as he said earnestly, 'When I met Sandra I felt as if someone had turned on a dirty great big light and it was showing me what I had been missing for years. She was a sort in some respects, I know that, but I felt as if she was the other half of me. The part of me that was missing. If that is love, Kenny, then I loved her. I know this much, I've never felt like it before or since. Did you feel like that about Lana?'

Kenny thought long and hard before he answered the question.

'Yeah. Yeah, I did. She wasn't the brightest bulb on the Christmas tree at times but I thought the world of her, yeah.'

'At least we had that much. Let's hope they both realised it, eh? At the end.'

Vic started up the Range Rover and they drove to Jack's house in silence, each lost in his own thoughts. Vic still hadn't said why he'd wanted to meet and Kenny had a sneaking suspicion it was because he could no longer remember. As he drove he absent-mindedly rubbed his nose and a trickle of blood ran down his chin and splashed on to the steering wheel. Vic didn't seem to notice.

He was on the way out. It was a toss up which got to him first – the coke or the Ryans.

Dezzy Haseem was in his shop in Forest Gate when he saw Benny Ryan walking through the door. He tried to make a run for it but Benny was already all over him like a rash. Grabbing him by his turban, he dragged Abul's cousin bodily from the shop and out to the waiting car.

Dezzy was screaming and hollering and no one was taking any notice. Even his father didn't attempt to stop Benny from taking him away.

He looked at his wife and said sadly, 'I knew this

would happen in the end. It is a criminal that you bred me.'

Dezzy's mum didn't listen to her husband's words, she was too busy running out of the shop in an attempt to help her eldest son. She was swearing and carrying on like a maniac but Benny was already driving away. She sank to the pavement and cried loudly, beseeching passers-by to help her. They ignored her. No one wanted to get involved.

Her husband dragged her inside and shut the shop up. He was fed up with his children; none of them had turned out as he had expected them to do. If they weren't with English girls they were taking drugs or going out with their friends. He was disappointed with the lot of them. Even his daughter was living with a boy.

They all thought he didn't know about any of it, but he knew. He knew everything, whatever his wife might think. She was from Coventry and he decided that was the problem. He should have gone back to India and found himself a wife who would obey him. His mother had said she was too European by half, and she'd been right. He was scandalised and he was angry at the humiliation his children had brought to his door.

He hoped Benny Ryan kicked his son's arse for him: it might teach him a bloody lesson.

Dezzy sat in the stolen BMW, shaking with fear. Benny looked at him and smiled and that made Dezzy feel worse instead of better. He could see the light of lunacy in Benny's eyes.

'How's Abul these days?'

Dezzy was stuttering with fear now.

'I don't know – you see more of him than I do!'

Benny smiled and said in a calm and conversational manner, 'I am going to cut him open and pull his liver out. And if you don't tell me what I want to hear, I am going to make you eat it.'

Dezzy fainted and Benny was still laughing as he cut through yet another red light. He was a cross-patch today, all right. Even Benny found his own anger an annoyance, a first for him and something else to hold against his one-time friend Abul Haseem.

Benny was really looking forward to killing him.

Dezzy was reviving and Benny smiled at him in a friendly manner.

'Do me a favour, Dezzy. You think long and hard about where I could locate Abul and then, me old china, I won't put you away permanently like I did Casha.'

Dezzy passed out once more.

Benny laughed. Never the bravest of souls old Dezzy, but then that would make his own job that much easier. Provided he could keep him conscious, of course.

# Chapter Twenty-Two

Maura listened to her mother as she spoke to the young policemen who were sipping tea and smiling away in her kitchen. One of them looked so comfortable there it was as if he was in his own home.

He was a *friendly*, meaning they owned him. Maura was quite taken with the way he was handling things and was going to tell Garry to give him an extra drink. Her mother was really enamoured of him, anyone could see that.

'I understand what you are saying perfectly, Mrs Ryan, and let's face it, if anyone knows that boy it's *you*.'

Tennant knew who was paying his wages and was determined that they would be paid for a long time to come.

Sarah basked in this unwarranted praise.

'Sure he was always a difficult child, and since his mother's death he has been under a lot of pressure. Stress, I think they call it these days. But he's a lovely boy for all that.'

Tennant's sidekick Tom Kenning was sitting there in utter shock. Benny Ryan was a fucking headcase and everyone knew that, yet the Ryans talked about him as if he was a perfectly normal human being. No accounting for taste, he supposed, and wondered what this lot did of a night for entertainment. Probably set fire to orphanages or tortured kittens. Nothing would surprise him with this crowd. Even the old mother was a joker short of a full deck.

He quietly drank his tea and in the process got himself an education. He had heard the talk about DC Tennant but now he was seeing the proof of it.

Maura Ryan seemed lovely, though, and that surprised him. As he looked at Tennant's designer jacket and thought of how he talked about his frequent holidays and weekends away, Kenning was wondering if he'd be a fool not to take this chance to better himself. After all, if the Ryans owned so many people, and if the rumours were true and they decided who was promoted and who wasn't, then maybe he should think again about his career prospects.

He smiled his most winning smile at the old woman and said in an ingratiating voice, 'Any more of that lovely cake?'

If she was anything like his nan that was the magic sentence. Sarah jumped up and immediately cut him another slice. Tennant nodded at him and then winked at Maura who was smiling despite everything that had happened.

Looked like they had a new recruit. It was best to get them young because then they were into you for a fortune before they knew it and realised exactly what was required for their money.

'If you see him, you will of course contact us, won't you?'

Maura nodded with her mother and smiled.

'Of course. We're as worried about him as you are.'

She was actually worried in case he killed anyone else, in broad daylight this time. He was capable of it, she knew.

Sarah was still smiling as they showed the two young men out. When they had gone she said with a chuckle, 'If you see him, you will contact us, won't you?' She laughed again at Maura's scandalised expression. 'As if! Jasus, that boy will have to leave the shagging country to get out of this one, no matter who's behind him giving him a helping hand. A nervous breakdown indeed! If they believe that they'll believe anything.'

Maura grinned.

'I can buy him whatever medical opinion I want, Mum, you should know that by now.'

'Of course you can, but is it wise? He's as mad as a March hare and twice as demented as that fecking Garry – and that's saying something. God forgive me he's me own child but even I know he's always been a bit loopy.'

The words were said honestly and with spirit.

Maura hugged her little mother to her and said in a jokey voice, 'Mum, we are all a bit fucking loopy in this family.'

Sarah hugged her daughter away and said in all seriousness, 'Well, it comes from your father's side of the family. Sure they were all a bit strange. His mother had delusions of grandeur, you know. The first time my father saw her he said, "Who's the macadamia!" '

She nodded her head to emphasise her words and was very annoyed that her daughter just sat on a chair in the hallway and laughed her head off. It was a desperate sound and Sarah knew that if anyone was under pressure, or stress as the magazines called it, it was this lovely, lost and basically kind daughter of hers.

'Come on, I'll make a cup of tea even though we're floating in the stuff.'

Maura followed her mother meekly and their newly rediscovered closeness was sealed once and for all. As they sat in the kitchen together Sarah was surprised to find that she didn't care whether she went home again or not. Her daughter needed her and she would be there for her as long as Maura wanted her. She had enjoyed herself the last few days, had felt needed and wanted again. Had felt the love her daughter bore her surrounding her like a cloak, and all Sarah Ryan had ever wanted was to feel loved and wanted by her children.

* * *

Carla lay in bed in Sarah's Notting Hill house and thought about her life. Since the to-do with Maura over Tommy she had felt as if she had come out of some kind of trance. How she could have done what she had she couldn't say – though if she was honest she knew she'd been so desperate for a man she was willing to take someone else's. In fact, she had enjoyed it all the more because he was Maura's. She pushed that thought from her mind. Like her aunt she had a selective memory at times. And like her aunt it had served her in good stead.

But all her life she had lived in Maura's shadow and no one had ever thought that she might want to be her own person. She knew she should have worked, should have taken control of her own life in some way. But it was so seductive being looked after, having unearned money and prestige. Knowing that once people knew who your family were they would treat you like a queen. In a way she understood why Benny was like he was. He was so desperate to be like Michael, to be like 'the boys', his uncles, he overcompensated with his violence. He wanted to be known as madder than Michael, as even more frightening. And he was not all the ticket to start with so that made for a dangerous mix.

But it didn't matter how she justified it to herself, what she had done was wrong, so very, very wrong. She had resented Maura for years, ever since she had hit thirty. Maura had got her a new car and Carla could still remember her father's expression as she had proudly showed it off to him. It had suddenly occurred to her then that he, like her mother, thought she was a ponce. Janine had looked at the car and then said grudgingly that she thought it looked very expensive. Her father, though, had said nothing, just walked away, and it had hurt Carla, hurt and annoyed her. Benny, however, who had still been a boy, had loved the car and wanted her to take him out in it to show off to his mates. If she was honest, she had enjoyed showing it off.

But she had finally sussed out then that people actually thought she was a leech, and the worst of it all was she knew on some deep level that they were right. Maura had made it so easy for her. She had given Carla whatever she desired, and had given it with a smile and a good heart. She, for her part, had taken it, had taken all Maura had to give while secretly hating the woman giving it to her.

Now, though, she would do anything to be in her aunt's favour once more. She would love to be able to jump in her car and go over to Maura's house and know that she would get a warm welcome and be treated with kindness and respect. It had finally occurred to Carla that her aunt had always accepted her for what she was. She was only sorry she had not been able to accept it herself. She had blamed Maura for her own feelings of inadequacy, had seen her aunt's success as a yardstick to measure herself against when it had not been necessary. She had made it like that for herself; it had never been a competition, and if it had been, her aunt would have won it hands down.

Maura's personality was such that she would help anyone, try and make other people happy, if it was in her power. Whereas Carla knew her own personality was such that unless she had done something first then she would always denigrate it, put it down.

In fact, at heart she knew that without her family she was basically nothing, a complete nobody. And she was a bully of sorts, making light of other people's problems, especially if they affected her in any way. Even her father's breakdown had got on her nerves in the end, though she had hidden that fact very well. She had done what was expected of her and no one had been any the wiser about how she really felt inside.

She wanted her son to be perfect, and he wasn't. Now, when she needed him more than ever, Joey, being his mother's son, had blanked her as she had grown too needy. He was one selfish little fucker. He was still getting his allowance from Maura but hadn't offered her any of it. She was always overdrawn – it was how she lived, was what she was used to. Maura had taken care of it as she took care of everything. Now Carla was boracic fucking lint and no one seemed to give a toss.

She felt the sting of tears once more. Benny had no time for her, and nor did any of the others. She had friends, but they weren't real friends. They ran each other down and laughed at each other's misfortunes while pretending they were so close they were like family. The big joke had always been how no one wanted to be the first to leave any gathering because they knew they would be in for a hammering as soon as their back was turned. These were the people she had spent a major part of her life with and she knew that she was wasting her time with them. If they heard what had happened with Maura they would drop her like a hot brick. After all, Maura Ryan was what had made them her friends in the first place. They loved hearing all about her and now, when she thought of some of the things she had said about her aunt to her so-called friends, Carla felt hot with shame.

She had been bitchy and nasty and Maura really didn't deserve that; she had done more for Carla than any of her friends would have. In fact, their mindset being what it was they would enjoy hearing about Carla's fall from grace even while they outwardly sympathised with her.

She needed to get back into the fold and not just because of her finances. She also needed a friendly shoulder to cry on and all through her life Maura had been the only person freely to offer her that. Opening the door she was surprised to see her brother standing there. Her face lit up with surprise and then she remembered what he had done.

'What the fuck are you doing here?'

Benny pushed through the door past her, knocking her flying as he went.

'Nice greeting, Sis. Remind me to use it next time I see you, eh?'

He was in the kitchen now and she followed him through it to the garden.

'Make me a cuppa, there's a good girl.'

He shut the shed door in her face and she knew better than to go in there if she wasn't welcome. She went back inside and made him some tea. Two minutes later he was storming back into the kitchen.

'Who's been in the shed?'

Carla shrugged.

'The place was cleared before you was busted. I mean, use your loaf, Benny, they came here and tore the place apart.'

He nodded then as if it had just occurred to him what had happened. He forgot important things sometimes. He was staring into space and Carla watched him uneasily.

'Who was that in the car?' she asked, remembering the slumped figure in an unfamiliar BMW outside. 'Looked like Dezzy to me.' Her words penetrated the fog in his brain and he walked from the house without another word. She chased him out to the car.

'Have you got any money, Ben?'

He put a hand into his back pocket and took out a

wad of notes he'd picked up at Abul's, throwing them at her as he got in the car. By the time she had picked them up he was long gone. Carla strolled back into the house lighter of heart. At least she had a few quid now anyway.

Joey waltzed down the stairs in her dressing gown and said gaily, 'Oooh, money. How much did he give you?'

She saw him then as her grandmother did, and saw herself as everyone else did: a covetous, greedy and unlikeable ponce. It was a startling moment.

'Fuck off, Joey.'

He grinned.

'Get out the wrong side of your bed this morning? Sorry, I forgot, you don't *have* a bed of your own, do you?'

He smiled at the hurt expression on her face. He wasn't smiling, however, when her fist connected with his cheekbone.

He stamped up the stairs crying and she shouted after him, 'And get my bleeding dressing gown off and all!'

Somehow, clumping him had made her feel much better. She went into the kitchen and counted the money Benny had given her. Only then did it occur to her that maybe she should let someone know her brother was on the rampage.

Jack was a bloody mess on the floor. The Dooleys were seriously impressed. He had been burned and tortured over and over again. Now he was delirious with pain and he still wouldn't tell them a thing.

Tony lit himself yet another Benson & Hedges. He phoned Maura on her mobile and explained the situation. She listened grimly to his description of Jack's condition. Feeling sick at the thought of what he had gone through, she asked, 'What are you going to do now?'

Tony smiled.

'Keep at it, Maws. I have an injection of adrenaline and I'm going to administer it in a minute. Hopefully that should keep him alive for a while longer, but I'll be honest, I don't think he'll crack. I never thought I'd say this but he is one strong old fucker, Maws.'

'So it would seem. Keep me informed.'

'What's happening with Benny?'

She laughed but there was no humour in it.

'You tell me, Tone. We can't seem to locate him.'

'You need this, girl, eh?'

'Like a hole in the fucking head. Keep me posted, OK?'

'Will do. But he won't go long.'

Tony turned the phone off and listened with half an ear to Shaggy singing 'Oh, Carolina', tapping his foot to the beat. Jack really looked a mess. His face was nearly gone and most of his bones were broken. He was awake again and mumbling, but incoherently. Tony watched his sons as they drank their McDonald's coffees and smoked a joint. He was so proud of them.

They were good boys. Decent and hardworking, they made sure their women and kids wanted for nothing. They were a family to be looked up to as far as he was concerned. He wondered what would happen with Benny Ryan and voiced his thoughts to his sons.

They discussed the legal ramifications as they finished the coffees and the joint. By then Jack was all but dead. They hosed him down again and administered the injection to his heart.

Jack was awake but he was barely lucid. His eyes were burned clean out of his head. Tony poured petrol all over him and the fumes seemed to penetrate the man's senses. He was making a terrible noise and even Tony's sons looked askance at one another.

'If you can understand me, Jack, you'd better tell me what I want to hear and I'll see you go quick, man. I promise.'

Tony was shouting in Jack's ear now or what was left of it.

'He's talking . . . shut the fuck up! He's trying to talk to me.'

Tony leant forward and listened intently. He heard Jack say clearly, 'Fuck you!'

Tony jumped up. Flipping open his silver Zippo, a present from his dead son, he dropped it on to the wreck of a man at his feet. Jack went up like a bonfire and Tony and his sons watched him writhe about the floor in agony.

'What a fucking waste of time, Dad.'

Tony shrugged and watched the burning body.

'Not entirely. We've paid him out for Tony and that's the important thing, but he was strong and he was determined and as much as I hated him I have to give him respect for that. Not many men could have taken what we gave him and not cracked.'

They all nodded at the wisdom of their father's words.

Tony yawned.

'Dump him on the rubbish tip, but bag him up first. I'm going home to get some kip.'

With that he left the lock-up and went home to his grieving wife. He phoned Maura on the way and told her the score. He had not enjoyed that one bit. He was getting too old for all this gangsta rubbish. Time was he would have enjoyed meting out punishment, but those days had passed and it was definitely time to hand over the reins to his boys. Today had proved that to him.

He threw up twice before he reached his house and had to stop the car in a lay-by to empty his guts, but he knew the smell of burning flesh would haunt him for days to come.

Kenny and Vic were drinking coffee in Jack's state-of-the-art kitchen.

'Wonder who'll get this little lot, eh?'

Vic snorted another line as soon as he had spoken.

'You know something, Vic, you want to lay off that

gear. It's doing your head in, and mine come to that,' Kenny told him.

Vic laughed.

'I bet you're into Maura Ryan's drawers by now, Kenny me old son. Any good, is she?'

He laughed at Kenny's glowering countenance.

'Only a joke, but you used to have the hots for her years ago. I just wondered if now that golden boy has queered his pitch you might be limbering up to take his place, so to speak?'

He pulled a lewd face as he spoke and despite everything Kenny wanted to laugh. Vic was just being Vic.

'How did all this happen? My Sandra, your little Lana. What cunt caused so much mayhem, eh?'

Kenny didn't answer.

'Shall I tell you what it was all about, Ken? So you can run back and tell the Ryans and get me the coke back, not to mention my brother?'

Kenny nodded, hardly daring to breathe.

Vic grinned, his nasty grin, the one that frightened everyone, even his old mum.

'As if! You tell your Maura that I will deal with her and her alone, right?'

Kenny shook his head.

'The Ryans won't swallow that . . .'

Vic interrupted him.

'Fuck off, Kenny! And fuck them all, for that matter. If they want to know then that's what they have to do. I'll give them the time and place at some point in the next twenty-four hours, OK?'

There was not a lot more to say after that. Vic was already snorting another line and Kenny knew he would not listen to a word that was said to him while he was busy with that.

'They took me brother . . . I can swallow me knob over that one, it's business. But you'd better warn them all that if they harm one hair on his ugly bastard head then I will *really* be out for revenge. But you tell them it's the coke I'm after now, or more to the point Jack's coke. Me and him was in partnership and it's a mean few quid there.'

Kenny nodded.

'They understand that. Be fair, they ain't tucked no one up, have they?'

'Not yet, no. Though Tommy would tell you a different story, I suspect.'

'Where *is* Tommy?'

Vic tapped his nose, and winked.

'Keep that out. You'll hear soon enough. I might even push Benny Ryan out of the headlines.'

Kenny had that sinking feeling again.

Radon 'Coco' Chatmore was surprised and not a little intimidated to see Benny on his doorstep. The fright was exacerbated by the fact that Benny was holding up Dezzy Haseem by his turban, a very badly beaten and obviously unconscious Dezzy Haseem. Benny threw the boy on top of Radon who dropped to the floor under the dead weight of his friend and business partner.

'Hello, cunt. Tucked up any more of your mates lately?'

Radon was trying to pull himself up off the floor when Benny caught him with a heavy kick to the stomach.

'Me and you need to have a little chat, Coco, and guess what?' He grinned. 'I ain't got any Super Glue.'

Benny saw the man's relief and taking something out of his coat, said happily: 'But look what I found in Casha's car.'

He was holding up an industrial stapler.

'The only question now is whether I should staple your eyes open or shut. What do you think?'

He was seriously asking for Radon's opinion as if the answer was the most important thing in the world to him. Dezzy was groaning. It was only then that Radon noticed his eyelids had been stapled open and the eyeballs themselves had dried out and were looking horribly sore.

'What are you doing, Benny? We're your friends, yeah?'

Benny grinned once more, his handsome face positively beaming with camaraderie mixed in with a lethal dose of psychotic malice.

'Not any more, Radon. Not any more, you two-faced wanker. You are filth to me, you are the shit on my shoes, and you are going to die in extreme pain with your last sight being me stapling your fucking eyes shut!'

He was laughing again.

Radon saw Dezzy stirring once more. He was moaning and Benny quickly bent down and put a staple into his forehead.

'Handy tool this, eh? Can't wait to get started, can you?'

Benny forced Radon to drag Dezzy through to the lounge. When he saw Radon's girlfriend of the moment, Shamilla, sitting there, he said happily, 'Hello there, Sham, and how are you, love?'

She stared at Radon as he dragged the beaten and stapled Dezzy into the room and then she said, 'I was just going, actually.'

Benny tutted.

'Oh, were you? Got an appointment then?'

She nodded, relief written all over her face.

He leant forward and bellowed into her face, 'You're going nowhere, slag. Now make me a sandwich and a pot of tea. Strong and sweet, just how I like it.'

Shamilla burst into tears and he dragged her through to the kitchen by her little T-shirt with 'Hard Bird' emblazoned across the breasts. He smiled at her once more.

'There now, don't make me a crosspatch, Sham, you'll only regret it. Make the tea and don't even attempt to aggravate me because then I will kick you all over the fucking place, OK?'

She nodded.

'Good girl. You know it makes sense.'

She could hear him whistling as he tied Radon to a chair and made the tea as fast as she could. There was trouble brewing and she wanted no part of it. Absolutely no part of it at all. But she had a feeling she was stuck here for the duration. She opened the fridge and started to make the sandwiches Benny had asked for. If he wanted her to dance naked round the room she would do it, and anyway, she told herself, it wouldn't be the first time she had been required to do something like that.

She walked into the lounge with the tea just in time to see Radon get his left eye stapled shut. His scream of pain and fear made her drop the cup of tea on the floor, scalding her legs in the process. Luckily this made Benny laugh. Taking the kettle of boiling water from the kitchen, he threw the contents into Radon's face.

As she heard his screams and saw him trying to break his bonds Shamilla felt faint. Benny was mad, everyone knew that, but seeing him at work still came as a horrible shock.

Radon had told her stories about Benny and she had listened, laughed, and been impressed at her boyfriend's association with a well-known headfuck. Seeing him in action, though, it didn't seem so funny or clever any more. Especially as she knew he would turn this violence on her without a second's thought to gain whatever it was he wanted.

All *she* wanted was to be back in her mum's house, sitting in the front room watching *Emmerdale*. She hurried out to make him more tea. She couldn't look at her boiled boyfriend one second longer.

Benny stapled Radon's other eye roughly and found it was surprisingly easy to ignore the man's begging and pleading. He finished his work and pulled up a leather footstool. He sat on it and said seriously, 'Now then, tell me all about Abul and you and Vic fucking dead man Joliff.'

Radon's grotesque head and shoulders were shaking with shock. The tremors soon overtook his entire body and Benny sipped his tea and ate his sandwiches while he observed his old friend's dilemma. At length he called Shamilla in and complimented her on the food.

'Lovely grub, Shamilla, but your mum and dad are in catering, ain't they? Still got that nice little café in Islington, have they?'

She nodded, her eyes on poor Radon. This was what Benny loved, this complete power over another human being. He loved to create such fear, an emotion that was so acute it was almost tangible in the room. He could practically touch it in this girl's eyes.

'Seen much of Abul lately?' he queried.

She shook her head.

'He rang, though, last night. Said he was delivering a parcel to Vic at Jack's old barn. I don't know what that meant, I only passed the message on.'

She was racking her brains for more information and Benny was smiling at her as he watched her desperately trying to tell him what he wanted to hear.

'Where does Radon keep his guns, love?'

'In the bedroom, in the back of the wardrobe. He has a false panel at the bottom . . .'

'Shut up, you stupid fucking bitch!'

Radon's voice was high-pitched with pain. Benny slapped him hard, the boiled skin coming away on his hand. Shamilla felt sick at the sight of Benny wiping it off on Radon's wet shirt.

'Let's go up to the bedroom, Shamilla.'

She followed him eagerly. If he wanted a fuck she would give him the best ride of his life. Anything Benny Ryan wanted she was going to give him. This was about saving her own life now, and she was determined to do just that. She had things to do and people to see, and just because she'd been stupid enough to get involved with Coco Chatmore it did not have to mean her life was over.

At least she hoped that was true anyway.

# Chapter Twenty-Three

'He will give you a time and a place. You know Vic, he has to keep everyone on their toes. Be the big fucking I Am.'

Kenny had gone straight round to brief Maura after leaving Vic. She was looking tired and drawn.

'Vic is the least of my problems at the moment, to be honest. Benny has left a trail of destruction all over the smoke as usual and we can't find the bastard anywhere.'

Kenny was not really interested. Benny was Benny as far as he was concerned. A headcase, the local nut-nut.

'Vic wants a meet, Maws. He was holding out for you on your own but I told him that was a non-starter. He's agreed I can be present and says he'll tell you everything you want to know then.'

She nodded, resigned to the prospect.

'In exchange for his brother and the coke, I suppose?'

Ken looked her in the eye as he said, 'His brother is part of it, yeah, but the coke's probably more important. He understands why his brother was taken, though. As long as Justin is being treated OK he will swallow his knob over it. I get the impression his brother is not up on what Vic does so I'm assuming you lot have got fuck all from him?'

'You assume right. He's uncomfortable but in no real danger.'

Kenny sighed.

'He ain't dead then?'

Maura half-smiled.

'Not as far as I know, put it that way.'

He knew she was nearing the end of her tether and asked the question he had wanted to ask her for a while but had never had the guts to do so.

'What will you do if Tommy is dead?'

She shrugged.

'To be honest it'd probably solve a dilemma. He betrayed my family and they want him dead.'

He looked hard at her for any sign of what she was really feeling; as usual she was a closed book.

'And Benny?'

She shrugged again.

'I could iron him out, to be honest. I'm sick and tired of him. But I have to take some of the responsibility. I knew he wasn't all the ticket years ago and should never have let him get to the stage he's at. But I did and now we have to try and limit the damage.'

Kenny wanted to take her in his arms and hug her but he was not that brave. With Maura you waited until she made a move, and he ruefully accepted that he wasn't the most gorgeous bloke on God's earth. Even his own mother conceded he was not exactly the answer to a maiden's prayer.

'How's babes?'

He grinned now and it softened his scarred face.

'Fucking handsome. I just wish this was all over. Once it is, if we're still standing then that's me, Maws. Finished. Out of it. I'm too old for all this shit.'

She stared at him with her clear-eyed gaze and then she lit a cigarette. He watched as she drew the smoke deep into her lungs before blowing it out forcefully.

'That little girl's been the making of you, Kenny. You, unlike me, have someone to care for, someone who needs you. Heady stuff. I wish it was me, Ken. Just normality, that would do me at the moment. Benny banged up, God forgive me for saying that, and me own house and a quiet life.'

He laughed.

'Not too fucking quiet. There's still a bit of life left in us, surely?'

She smiled.

'Do you realise that thanks to Alicia you will stay young for years? You will always know what records are in the charts, know what fashions are in and what's out. Watch TV programmes you would never have dreamt of watching on your own. She will keep you young in mind and heart. You can see her become the person she was meant to be, and you'll be able to sit back and love her and be proud of her. Do you have any idea just how fucking lucky you really are?'

Her voice was desolate in its loneliness, her face open for once, and he could see yearning on it for what he had. For what most women and men took for granted.

'I have wasted my whole life,' Maura admitted painfully. 'I tried to help Carla and she kicked me in the teeth. Benny is mad, there is nothing but a trail of death and destruction wherever he goes. Is this all my efforts will amount to? Everything's wrong, Kenny. It's all gone bad. Even Marge is avoiding me like the plague because she's shit scared of getting involved with Vic and his vendetta. But that's kids again, isn't it? She's frightened for them, not for herself, and that is what is happening to you, and it can only be a good thing if it gets you out of this madness we mistake for a life.'

Kenny was so sorry for her. He knew she was right, that every word she had uttered was not only heartfelt but true. So true. He hugged her then, a gentle friend's hug that she returned.

'This will be over soon, Maura, and then get out of it all, girl. Vic and his kind are like the poor, always with us. Well, let someone else deal with the lunacy they cause.'

Maura hung on to him as if she was drowning, as in truth she felt she was. She was caught up in something over her head and didn't know how she was going to extricate herself and her family from any of it.

'I feel like my brain is going to explode with worry. Benny's on the rampage and going to bring everyone down if we ain't careful. He's over the top, too far gone to reason with. The fact he ain't even been in touch tells me all I need to know. He probably thinks he can make it all right. And that's my fault! I kept on buying him out of trouble, and now I have bought us trouble that even Bill Gates would be hard pushed to pay his way out of.'

Kenny could smell her perfume. She felt so soft against him and he hugged her close once more, enjoying the feel of her and enjoying, if he was honest, seeing her so vulnerable. He wanted to kiss her, taste her. See what she was like when she wasn't being the boss lady. She looked up into his face and he was sure she felt the same about him. But that could just be wishful thinking. Lana had loved him in her own way. His ugly mug had never bothered her, she had seen through it to the man underneath. He hoped Maura Ryan could see that far too.

'What's going on here then? You two secretly at it or what?'

Garry's voice was hearty but puzzled and they jumped apart quickly.

'Don't be so stupid, Garry, and stop creeping up on people.'

He could hear the anger in his sister's voice and knew it was embarrassment that was making her so cross.

'Ooh, touchy. Where's Mother?'

'On one of her marathon shopping expeditions as usual. She feels the urge to feed the five thousand regularly, you know that.'

Garry grinned.

'Handsome grub, though, in fairness to her.'

Maura sighed. Her brothers and their stomachs were of no interest to her at this moment in time. They would have gone to the Last Supper for the food and nothing else. It was all they thought about other than killing, maiming and dealing.

'Stay to dinner then, Gal, be my guest.'

'You are one miserable bitch, Maura, do you know that?'

'So I've been told. By the way, Vic is getting in touch in the next twenty-four hours.'

Garry digested this bit of information before smiling again.

'Are we killing him or what?'

Maura ran her hands through her hair and said testily, 'Let's see what he has to say first. I think you and I both know that there's a story behind this and I for one am interested to hear it.'

'Same here.'

Garry had all but ignored Kenny. Now he looked at him for long seconds before saying, 'Yeah. I expect you would be.'

The words were loaded with menace.

'What's that supposed to mean, Garry?'

Kenny sounded as annoyed as he felt.

'Whatever you want it to fucking mean.'

The atmosphere between them was nasty, and filled with imminent violence. Kenny had had enough.

'Listen here, Garry Ryan, you don't fucking scare me and you never have. You need me far more than I need you at the moment, remember that.'

Garry was instantly on his dignity.

'Who d'you fucking think you're talking to? You think you can barge in here and stick your fucking beak into my family's business, is that it? You think you're something fucking special. Well, let me tell you, you ain't, mate . . .'

Maura crashed her fists down on the table in front of her, shouting, 'Oh, for crying out loud! Have I got to take this shit every time we have some kind of tear up? Well, listen to me hard, boys. You don't fucking frighten *me*, you never have and you never will. I have dealt with the best, and none of them frightened me either.'

The two men looked at her before Kenny said seriously, looking into Garry's face, 'None of them frightened *me* either, as it happens.'

Garry licked his lips and said with a laugh, 'What,

not even your old mate Vic Joliff?'

'Especially not Vic.'

He walked from the room and Maura, watching him go, felt an acute sense of loss. Kenny was the only normal person around her and his departure left her feeling desolate.

'Why do you do it, Gal? Why do you always make everything so fucking difficult?'

She could read the confusion in his eyes, knew that he could not see what he'd done wrong in any way, shape or form. Thought that it was she who was in the wrong, who was rambling.

'He was trying to help us. Kenny is one of the good guys and you just waltz in here and fuck it all up as usual, with your arrogance and your fucking bad attitude. I have never met anyone like you for pissing on their own fireworks.'

'I was trying to help too, Maura. I want this sorted out as much as you do!' He was bellowing now, shouting at her with wild eyes and spittle flying everywhere.

'You call that helping?'

She was screaming back at him. Her own temper was boiling over and she was past trying to reason with him. It just wasn't worth it. Garry listened to no one, never had, never would. But he would listen to her now, she was determined on that much.

'You couldn't help yourself in a fucking grab-a-tit competition if you was the only entrant! You cause more trouble than you fucking prevent. You and Benny are both fucking headbangers, Garry. It's me who keeps everything going. *Me!* I am the one people want to deal with because I am cautious and I am sensible and I don't want to rip everyone's fucking heads off! Except yours, of course, and Benny's. I could do that on a daily basis, you drive me so fucking mad with your carrying on. I am sick of it, you hear me? Sick to fucking death of the lot of it.

'So, I'll tell you what, *you* sort it, Gal. You go and kill everyone and just fucking leave me out of it. I have had enough. Finally, I have had enough.'

He looked at her standing there. She was red-faced with temper and he knew on some deep level that what she was saying was fully justified.

'I don't know why I fucking bother, Maura,' he mumbled, unable to look her in the eye.

'*You* don't know why you bother? Well, join the fucking club.'

Shamilla was crying, and Benny was getting fed up with listening to her.

'Shut the fuck up, Sham. Anyone would think it was you getting tortured the way you're carrying on.'

She could hear the irritation in his voice and tried to stem her tears.

'Go and get the tea towel out of the freezer.'

She ran to do his bidding. When she brought it back he had put another couple of staples into

Dezzy's face. He looked grotesque, but she was happy to see he was still unconscious. Benny used the tea towel to bring down the swelling and tapped his foot impatiently, waiting for his victim to wake up so they could spin the game out a little longer.

'Do you think Dezzy is in a Korma?'

He laughed heartily at his own joke.

Shamilla pulled her little T-shirt down again. It was a crop top and she was very aware of the way it looked over her large breasts.

Benny saw her and grinned.

'I wouldn't touch you with his cock, darling. Fussy what I touch, me. Never had a taste for pig. Funny that, ain't it? Shagged a few old dogs, though. But you're safe enough so stop worrying, I ain't that fucking hard up.'

Even in her distressed state she was dimly aware of the insult to herself. Benny was more aware of it than she was and her hurt expression just made his smile that bit wider.

'You'll be used all your life, Sham, people like you always are. You're a born victim, darling, and you will go to your grave well fucked, well used, and probably with a trail of kids and broken promises behind you, the only things to show you ever existed.'

He watched her cry. He had destroyed her with his words and enjoyed every second of it. He looked around the room at the carnage he had caused, felt his own power once more, loved the feeling of being the instigator of so much fear and desolation.

It was what he was *good* at, what made him the person he was. Benny Ryan, lunatic, headcase. Loony Tune. He loved the different epithets he had garnered for himself over the years. He wondered briefly where Carol might be and then dismissed her from his mind. Plenty of time to sort her out when this little lot was over.

He stared down at the stapler in his hand and grinned once more. He would staple her up once and for all. When he was finished with her no one would touch her with a barge pole. She was the cause of all his problems, he could see that now. Until he'd met her and fallen in love his life had been on course. But she had made him change that course and that was when it had gone wrong. It was what had made everything go so drastically wrong.

When he had sorted things out he would be back on track once more. Then Maura and Garry would see him as he really was, an asset to the business. They would understand that he had fucked up but that he could sort it. Inside he was OK. Inside he was a very astute man who could surmount any problems that came his way. He was as sure of that as he was sure of his own name. He would make Maura and Garry see him in the right light. See him as he saw himself and as others saw him. He would be a fit successor when the time came, take care of them all. His father, the family, even that ponce of a sister of his. He would kick the queerness out of that boy of hers as well, the fucking weirdo. Joey should have been taken in hand years ago. Once Benny was in charge he would sort it all out.

He was humming as he untied Radon and dragged him up to the bathroom. His day's work was just beginning and he was a man with a mission. He was going to get to the truth and when he did he was going to go to Maura and Garry like a conquering hero. The thought cheered him up no end.

When Radon realised what the next step in Benny's mad plan was going to be he tried to fight once more.

Benny sighed.

It occurred to him that being in charge was sometimes a very irritating business and his admiration for his aunt went up tenfold.

There was a lot more to being top dog than he had first realised.

Garry and his mother sat in the kitchen while Maura made them all some tea. As she poured the water into the pot it occurred to her that Sarah must have gone through tens of thousands of tea bags over the years. Now Maura was following in her footsteps as the Tea-drinking Queen of the South East. She was getting old, she knew that, and strangely she accepted it.

'Roy will be here in a minute, put out another cup, Maws.'

She gritted her teeth and put out another cup and all the time she willed the phone to ring so Vic could give them a time and place for the meet. Once they met it would be all over, they could get on with their lives. Providing they were still alive, of course. Vic was not a man to be trusted. On that much at least she and Garry were in agreement.

She heard Roy's voice as she poured out the tea.

'He's killed Casha and gone on the missing list with Dezzy. Kidnapped him in broad daylight, mind. In front of his mother and half of fucking Green Street. I will swing for that cunt, I take oath on it.'

Maura could hear her mother tutting. She had forgotten how irritating that sound could be.

'Sure, Jasus, that fella is off his shagging rocker.'

'Tell us something we don't know, Mum.'

Garry took the laden tray from her and placed it none too gently on the table.

'We can't help him any more, you all realise that, don't you? He will have to go on the missing list now. Spain, wherever.'

'Wherever sounds good to me. Six foot under sounds better – I'm sick of him.'

Roy's voice was low and no one answered him.

'I am getting to the stage where I hate him. Absolutely hate my own son. And the more I hear about him, the more the feeling grows.' He lit a cigarette from Maura's packet and said in a guttural voice, 'I bet he's already killed Dezzy. I fucking bet you a pound to a penny he has already obliterated that poor little fucker.'

As Sarah listened she felt her heart racing. The family was falling apart before her. She could feel the fear in the room, knew that Roy was out of his mind with worry over his son, and that Maura and Garry were worried about Vic Joliff. Vic, who she had always liked and who had come to her home expressly to frighten them. She had been so pleased to see him, so very pleased to be remembered by him. And all the time he was using her.

It still hurt.

She only hoped they got this all out of the way soon so they could get back to normal. She had a bad feeling on her, that dragging feeling in her side she had had when her son Benny was murdered. She had woken up with it today and now felt that it was a warning of something terrible coming to the family she loved and hated equally.

Maura placed an arm round her mother's shoulder and said gently, 'All right there, Mum?'

She nodded and forced a smile.

''Course, child. Would you stop driving me mad with your questions?'

Her words came out sounding more annoyed than she had intended and she saw Roy and Garry staring at her quizzically.

'You ain't grassed us all up again, have you, Mum?'

Garry's voice was jokey but the underlying question

was there. Sarah was devastated at his words and it showed in her tired old face.

'Leave it out, Garry. Haven't you caused enough upset today?'

Maura hugged her mother.

'Don't listen to him, Mum, you know what a stroppy ponce he can be.'

Sarah stood up and left the room.

'I hope you're pleased with yourself, Gal.'

He shrugged and sipped his tea.

'She'll get over it, Maura.'

Roy looked on as his brother and sister faced up to one another.

'Do you realise how old she is? Do you ever think about anyone or anything else other than yourself and your fucking appetite?' Maura railed.

Garry was laughing and she knew it was to antagonise her.

'Hark at you, Mrs Do As You Would Be Done By. Piss off! You don't rule me, you never did. Neither did Michael, but he was too fucking dense to see it and all.'

Maura stared at him steadily.

'Is that right? He was always decent to his mother, though. Pity you ain't more like him really. At least he could see danger before it hit him in the face.'

Garry was still laughing.

'Saw the IRA coming then, did he? How are they, Maws? Heard anything from your mates lately? Still good friends with them, are you, the people who murdered Saint Michael?'

She was shaking her head in disbelief at his words.

'You bastard.'

Roy stood up then and said to Garry, 'My Benny is you all over again. He looks like Michael but he *is* you. Have a fight with his own fingernails, him. And he gets it from *you*. I said it before and I say it again, Mother should never have had any more kids. I mean, what are we? Look at us.'

He glanced around with an expression of utter disgust.

'What are we, eh? Fucking animals, that's what we are. Sitting here at our time of life, waiting to find out about more fucking mayhem.'

He sighed.

'Well, I'm going. I've had enough. You can all do what the fuck you want.' He picked up his cigarettes, and as he walked out of the door looked back at Garry and said: 'I'll tell you something, I never liked you. Even when we were kids I could never stomach you. Poor Geoffrey had more going for him than you did as far as I was concerned. Look at us, take a *good* look at us. We're half the family we were after all the deaths. We're all stuck up each other's arses because we *have* to be, not because we *want* to be. We can't trust anyone, even each other any more. Welcome to the Ryan family. One last word of advice, though. Let Maura sort this lot out – she's the only one of us with even a modicum of brains.'

Garry shook his head and shouted at his brother's retreating back, 'Keep taking the tablets, nutter, keep taking the tablets.'

He looked at Maura, saw the hurt on her face and instantly his expression changed. She knew he was having another of his lightning swings of mood, like Benny did, like Michael used to. Roy was right, they were all a bit touched, the whole family was tainted.

'It's tension, Maws, it's nothing but the tension of all this hag. Now sit down and finish your tea. I'll go up and get back in Muvver's good books.'

Maura sat at the table and lit yet another cigarette. Roy was right, that was the worst of it. He was right and they all knew it, but until the impasse with Vic Joliff was over there was not a thing they could do to sort out their personal lives.

Joe the Jew was as usual in his scrapyard, staring absently at a porn film on the portable flatscreen TV in his office. It was allegedly one of his favourite pastimes, and he knew it enhanced his reputation as an octogenarian cocksman. In fact, the flickering images and cries of fake ecstasy barely registered with him any more, but he'd never acknowledge that before another man.

He was bored with his films, bored with it all if he was honest. He also felt very strongly that time was running out for him. His heart was still strong as an ox's, he knew that from his regular medical check ups. But how much longer could he realistically hope to get away with it?

He had ordered his affairs meticulously and was ready to pass everything on to a young relative of his, a gifted boy currently at business school in the States. He could take the property and loans businesses fully legit, probably not the clubs – or he could choose to follow the same path as his parents and Joe. The decision had to be his.

Joe knew which choice *he* would make, given his time over.

He'd lived all his life on the fringes of the criminal world, his transgressions mostly limited to false accounting, some violence in the pursuit of bad debts, and a lifetime's disregard for the licensing and gaming laws. He'd made himself a handsome living for decades without ever needing to dirty his hands further.

And then, six years ago, he'd made a near-fatal mistake and got in over his head in a scheme to oust the Ryans and take over their drugs empire. Even now he couldn't believe his own stupidity – though of course he'd had his reasons. When it all went tits up he managed to cover his tracks and keep his head down, good old Joe, happy with his dingy clubs and his grubby yard and his little blonde *shiksa*. But always he'd known the fragile peace was built on sand.

True to form Vic Joliff had come back on the scene, an evil genie bursting out of his bottle to wreak havoc all around him, and Joe knew it was the beginning of the end for him.

But he filled Vic in on what he wanted to know, and agreed to do a few favours for him. The latest was getting him down. He lowered the volume with the remote and cocked his head, listening. Everything sounded peaceful . . . But just as his hopes were getting up it started again, a hammering noise, frenzied and insistent, on the ceiling above.

Joe heaved himself to his feet, mumbling curses under his breath as he opened a door in the corner of the room and started on his laborious way up the dusty stairs to a crawl space under the roof.

He knelt on the top step and groped for a flashlight he'd left handy. Shining it into the gloom he could just make out the whites of two frantically staring eyes above a mass of duct tape wound round and round the prisoner's face. He was in chains too but they were the least of his worries at present. There was a slit in the tape apparently but he only got enough air if he kept still and calm.

'I've told you before,' Joe said irritably, 'you're just making it worse for yourself. You need to calm down and . . . what is it Camilla says? . . . chill. Yes, that's it. Chill out, Abul my friend. You're going nowhere until Vic Joliff says so.

'Now shut the fuck up, will you? I'm trying to watch a bluey down here and you're putting me right off my stroke.'

# Chapter Twenty-Four

Radon was dead and Benny was annoyed with himself for losing his temper. In fairness, Radon had taken a lot first and Benny was reluctantly impressed with his old mate; he had stood more than most people and still hadn't told Benny any more than he'd been able to work out for himself – though it never occurred to him that Radon might not know more than this either.

Abul, his best mate, had been planning a takeover since 1994. The Ryans, all of them, were due for the chop, and when the new firm was established all Abul's secret squirrels were due big money and maximum respect.

Benny had spat in his face when Radon had said that, then chucked the electric fire in the bath to finish him off.

He went down to the lounge. Dezzy looked awful and Shamilla was sitting quietly staring at the TV. MTV was showing a video full of black men and scantily clad black girls. Benny watched it with her for a few seconds before he said to her, 'Shamilla, I'm going and I ain't taking Dezzy with me. What are you doing?'

He sounded so normal, as if the day's horrific events had been no more than a picnic to him. She stared back at him in terror. He sighed heavily, bored already now that Radon was dead.

'Come on, Sham, I ain't got all fucking night. Are you going to your mum's or what? I can drop you off, if you like.'

'What . . . what about . . .'

She pointed up towards the ceiling.

'Radon?'

She nodded.

'Oh, he's well brown bread, the cunt.'

'And I can go home?'

Her voice was choked with fear as she asked him the question. Benny, however, was exasperated by now. It came over in some heavier sighing and his usual sarcasm.

'Well, where were you thinking of going then – fucking Harrods for some shopping?'

She shook her head.

'No. I just wanna go home, Benny.'

He smiled then, happy they had finally sorted everything out.

'I'll drop you off, OK?'

She nodded once more.

'Keep shtoom though, Sham. This was private business, OK?'

He held a finger to his lips and she nearly severed the muscles in her neck as she nodded vigorously.

They left Dezzy lying on the floor and walked from the flat.

'Hang on.'

Benny sat her in the car and then got a can of petrol from the boot. Five minutes later they watched as the whole place went up.

'Were they dead, Benny?'

He shrugged.

'I know Radon was, but I ain't sure about Dezzy. Still, he is now.'

She was quiet all the way to her mother's house. Benny dropped her off courteously and even gave her a gentle kiss on the cheek.

'See you around, Sham.'

As she got out of the car, he pulled her back. Smiling at her once more he put a finger to his lips.

'Tell your dad I said hello, won't you?'

It was a threat and they both knew it. She loved her father more than anyone in the world. She nodded, and tried to smile herself into Benny's good books.

As she let herself into the house she could hear the theme music to *Inspector Morse* and cringed as her mother called out in her harsh phlegmy voice, 'That you, Sham?'

She could picture her in the pink Dralon-covered

chair, her face lined and her body old before its time from too many cigarettes and too much cheap booze.

'You fucking come home sometimes then. What's the matter, fell out with Mr Washing Powder?'

Shamilla could smell stale takeaway and cigarette smoke; it was the smell of her childhood, the smell of her whole life. It was what had made her want to be with Coco Chatmore and men of his ilk in the first place. She was determined she was not going to turn into her own mother. She was not going to end up in such a state that a poxy TV programme was talked about as if it was her own life. She hated it here, hated the sameness of her mother's days and the complete desolation of her life. Her father spent all his spare time with his bird, an Italian woman with big tits and very red lips. Shamilla didn't blame him, her mother could bore for England. She loved her father and blamed her mother for his increasing absence from her life.

Though, after what she had just witnessed, her mother's boring life seemed almost seductive to her at this moment in time.

She ran straight up to her bedroom and when her mother finally bothered to come up to see her she assumed she was crying over a man.

'Oh, Shamilla, get a grip, love. None of them are worth it, you know. All wankers, the lot of them.'

She was amazed when her daughter knelt up on her bed, surrounded by her posters of Shaggy and Goldie, and screamed out: 'Oh, Mum, will you just *fuck off*!'

She was still crying the next morning, but her mother being her mother didn't even think to ask her daughter what might be wrong. Which was just as well as she really wouldn't have wanted to hear the answer.

Shamilla was working in a bar in Marbella within the week. The police were slow in looking for her, much to her relief. She didn't see her mother again for nearly six years. So, as she often reflected, some good had come out of it all.

Maura and Garry were still waiting for the call from Vic. Meanwhile Maura had gone into the West End because the clubs needed to be overseen no matter what else was happening. They were all on edge and she was aware that if she didn't get away from her brother she would end up having another row with him.

Inside Le Buxom she walked into hostess bedlam. Two of the girls were fighting, and to make matters worse they were fighting in front of the punters. Hair and nails were flying as Maura walked deliberately between them. The male bouncers were definitely not getting involved; AIDS and hepatitis were foremost in their minds where working girls were concerned.

Maura was already at the end of her patience and when one of the girls, a large African with braided hair and nails like a Hammer Horror vampire, acted like she was still determined to fight, said caustically, 'Go on, Wanda, I fucking dare you.'

Both women realised in seconds that this was not the usual easygoing Maura and stopped their shouting immediately. Her eyes, normally merry, were hard and her face paler than usual. Even her hair looked ruffled not smoothly brushed in its usual immaculate blonde bob. All in all she looked like a woman on the edge and they stood facing one another with all the anger and spite drained out of them for the time being.

'What the fuck is this about?'

The English girl, a dark-eyed blonde from Gillingham, said sheepishly, 'She was after me punter, Miss Ryan.'

The black girl shook her head in consternation.

'Oh, no, I wasn't. He didn't want you. The Germans always like the black birds, everyone knows that.'

Maura rolled her eyes to the ceiling. Her voice was cold as she said, 'You were fighting in my club, in front of paying customers, and you expect me to stand here and listen to this shit?'

The two women stared at the floor, aware that all the other girls were listening intently to what was being said.

'Get your gear and fuck off, the pair of you. Find another club to fight in.'

Even the head girl was shocked at her words. Hostesses had fights, it was par for the course. In fact, it was mandatory if it was a shit night and no one was earning.

If Maura had not come here then this would have been resolved between the interested parties and no one would have been any the wiser. Everyone knew that the Ryans were up shit creek without a paddle, the word had been on the street for a while, and if ever anyone was wired it was Maura Ryan tonight. So there had to be some truth in the rumours.

'Come on, Maura.'

The head girl's voice was placating and friendly but Maura was having none of it.

'Shut the fuck up! I pay you to keep these birds off the gear and on the tables. If you can't manage that, love, I'll replace you and all. It's as simple as that.'

She was not in the mood for any of it and when she walked the two girls off the premises ten minutes later she knew she was causing a sensation.

Next she bawled out the bouncers, her voice so loud it could even be heard above the stripper's music – and as she removed her clothes to 'Wannabe' by the Spice Girls Maura's voice had to be particularly loud.

The two men stood and took it, they had no choice in the matter. But they were not happy about it and it showed. Maura could see the sly looks they gave one another, could feel the lack of respect. This told her that the family's problems were already being talked about on the street. Michael used to say that you knew your standing in the world by the treatment you got from the hired help. This was being proved to her now, and in anger and frustration she slapped one of the men's faces and, though he swallowed it, she knew it would be remembered. Vic was hot news, and it seemed people thought he was already King of the Jungle. Well, she would use all her resources to prove this a lie. It was imperative that they win this stand-off or they might as well write their own suicide note.

'What are you fucking looking at?'

The bouncer stared at her for a few moments before dropping his gaze.

'Well, answer me then! I am paying you fucking serious wedge, boy, and you can't even sort out a couple of brasses. What do you do when a punter kicks off – go to fucking Tenerife for your holidays?'

Still he didn't answer her.

'You'd better get your fucking act together or you can both fuck off and all. I ain't got time for wasters and neither has any of my family. Now piss off and earn your wages. I don't need fucking kindergarten teachers, I need bouncers, and if you can't cut it then you can both get fucked.'

She stared them both down and then bellowed, 'Well, what you waiting for? Your mums to come and pick you up and take you both home? Go and do the job you are being paid for, and getting paid fucking well for if you don't mind me saying.'

It was Maura at her best and they both knew it. She was menacing in her icy coldness and knew that whatever they might have thought before, they would not be writing her off just yet. She knew the benefit of bad language, something she used rarely but to good effect. Even the hostesses curbed their swearing around her because she hated it so much.

The open lack of respect bothered Maura, it bothered her more than she would ever have believed. She was used to the effect her name had on people, used to being given priority over everyone else. She was amazed at just how much the change in her staff upset her. It was at times like this she wished she had someone to lean on, someone to turn to. She had thought she had that in Terry, and then in Tommy Rifkind, but in truth the only person who had ever been fully there for her was Michael. He had been her teacher, her mentor, and also the only man in her life she had respected.

That was a lot of her trouble, she realised now. She didn't respect most men because she was too busy taking care of business. How could you respect someone who was in an inferior position to you? And, with Maura Ryan, that was the case with most men she met. They were nervous of her, wary of saying or doing something wrong. She was, after all, the woman who ran the biggest family in London. No wonder Tommy had had such a hard time trying to stand beside her, lying scheming bastard though he was.

Her head was aching with tension and her mouth

dry with what she suspected was nerves. In her office she swallowed down a large brandy to steady herself. Once it was all over with Vic she could sort herself out. Until then she was trapped and she knew it.

But tonight she had learned a lesson she would not forget in a hurry. Word travelled fast on the street and it seemed that the Ryans were already being written off as has-beens. Well, there was life in this old bitch yet and they would all be shown that in the next few days. Then let them see who was really top dog and challenge her again, if they dared.

Tommy opened his eyes and instantly regretted that fact. He felt as if he had been through a grinder, and knowing Vic that was exactly what had happened to him. He was in the dark in a confined space, that much was evident. He could feel wooden panels close to his body and his legs were slightly bent as if he had been forced into something.

The first prickle of serious unease stirred in his brain.

He closed his eyes once more as the fear spiralled up inside him. He was in a storage container of some kind and suddenly aware that he was buried somewhere which could only mean one thing: he had been buried alive. Vic would see that as a joke. He was only sorry that he couldn't see the humour of it himself.

He felt the bile rising inside his mouth and swallowed it down. It was bad enough in here as it was without the added smell of vomit. He took deep breaths to try and steady his heartbeat but then the panic was rising once more and he wanted to start screaming.

He was remembering the sounds of nails being driven into wood; he remembered Vic talking to him as it was going on but he'd been hovering between consciousness and a heroin haze at the time and oblivion had won. He tried to force the lid up with his knees and arms but even as he expended the precious energy he knew it was never going to work.

Vic and his oinks would have made sure he was in this fucking coffin for eternity.

Garry was sitting with his mother when Carla came into the kitchen followed closely by Tony Dooley Senior.

'She said you had told her to come round, Mrs Ryan.'

Sarah nodded.

Garry stared coldly at his niece and then said, 'What the fuck do you want, Carla?'

Her lip was quivering as she looked reproachfully at her beloved Nana and her uncle, who were both making it plain she was not welcome.

'Benny came round. He came round Nan's.'

Garry shrugged.

'And?'

She sniffed loudly.

'I thought you lot should know. The filth are after him, they've been round twice since.'

She looked at Sarah and smiled ingratiatingly.

'They tore the place apart but I cleaned it all up for you.'

It was hard for Sarah to watch her grandchild struggling to be taken back into the fold. She forced a smile.

'Sit yourself down, child, and I'll get you some tea. You look parched.'

She busied herself with the filling of the kettle, the atmosphere heavy. She wished Garry would leave the room and ease it somewhat. He didn't. He sat back in his chair and stared at his niece, making her feel more uncomfortable than ever.

'Did Tommy ever ask you anything pertaining to the family business?'

His directness startled her and she shook her head.

''Course not. Even if he had, I would never have told him.'

Garry laughed derisively.

Carla leant across the table, her long red-brown hair falling over her face as she hissed at him, 'I can't tell him what I don't know, can I? Think about it, Uncle Garry. What would I tell him? You lot never treated me as an important part of the family, did you?'

He knew she was telling the truth but still baited her.

'You knew enough about Benny and Maura, didn't you?'

She tossed her head.

'Nothing the Sunday red tops didn't know. In fact, that's where I get most of my information about you all. Let's face it, you're hardly unknown quantities, are you?'

Garry shook his head slowly as he watched her stand before him and squirm.

'Maura will be back in a minute, you do realise that, don't you? And I seem to remember an old saying about a woman scorned or some such female fucking nonsense.'

Sarah slapped him none too gently round the back of the head.

'Why don't you stop fuelling the shagging fire and just let her drink her tea in peace? I will sort out Maura, and you as well if needs be. This has all gone on long enough. If this last lot has taught us nothing else it should at least teach us we should all be pulling together, not trying to rip each other apart.'

She sat back at the table and grabbed her son's hand in both of hers. He could feel the papery skin that denotes great age and suddenly felt a huge rush of affection for this old woman he had wanted to kiss and strangle alternately for the best part of his life.

'We all need to stick together for the time being at least, Garry. Her brother is wreaking havoc all over the place and Carla came here to tell us that she's seen him, so give her the benefit of the doubt for once. She is still our blood and that means more than anything.'

Before he could answer her Maura was in the kitchen and he watched as aunt and niece stared each other out. His mother gripped his hand harder and Garry found himself squeezing back.

'Carla came to tell us about Benny, didn't she, Garry?'

He nodded.

'He's been round Muvver's. He was looking for the guns we had there, which can only mean one thing – he's going after Vic and Abul himself.'

Maura watched her niece as she took off her jacket and placed it carefully over the back of one of the kitchen chairs.

'How did he look?'

Carla shrugged, pleased that she had been spoken to directly and without apparent malice.

'Manic would be the word. He had Dezzy in the car with him. I think he'd harmed him . . . well, you know what Benny's like if he's upset.'

Sarah got up and Maura said gently, 'No tea, Mum, not for me. I'm going to have a large brandy.' She looked at Garry and Carla. 'Anyone want to join me?'

It was the hand of peace and they all knew it, especially Carla.

'Please.'

Garry nodded, amazed at the way Maura had

handled the situation. He knew his mother was finding it difficult. He could hear the old woman expel her breath with relief.

'Jasus! I'll have one too – for medicinal purposes, of course.'

They all smiled at her and Sarah felt herself redden with pleasure as their love washed over her. This was what she wanted, needed, more than all the riches in the world. The simple love of her children.

She knew it would take time for Maura and Carla to get back on their old footing, but at least she could die secure in the knowledge that they were not at each other's throats any more.

While they sipped the brandy Maura filled Garry in on events at the club. He didn't seem surprised.

'I heard that one of our betting shops was nearly knocked over at lunchtime. The geezer running it, Sal Bordy, got rid of them with a sawn-off but I guessed we were coming over as on the way out.'

He finished his drink and said, 'Fucking real, eh, Maws? We give these cunts their livelihood and then they turn on us like fucking rats.'

'Who was it then?'

He grinned.

'Two of Joe the Jew's boys.'

Maura digested this bit of information before she sipped once more at her drink. 'Do you think Vic is going to get in touch, Gal?'

He shrugged and lit a cigarette.

'Your guess is as good as mine.'

'We've been sitting here for over twenty-four hours waiting for a call that ain't never going to come, ain't we? He's playing games with us and I tell you something else, Gal, he is going to regret it.'

She slammed her glass down on the table angrily and even her mother felt the force of her daughter's personality when crossed. Maura's hands were shaking as she lit a cigarette, and they all knew the tremor was born of anger not fear.

She drew on the cigarette and blew smoke out noisily. Her eyes were tightly closed as she tried to control herself and Carla wondered what on earth had ever possessed her to cheat this woman who had not only been good to her but was also a fearsome enemy.

'Fucking mug me off? Is that what this is all about?'

She puffed on the cigarette again, and they felt the animosity coming off her in waves.

'Well, this is it. I have finally had enough. Do you know what we are going to do now, Garry?'

He shook his head, a half-smile on his face. She grinned back at him.

'We are going to send Vic a rather grisly and annoying little present. Bring him out of the woodwork.'

'How are we going to do that? We don't know where he is.'

Maura took another deep drag on her cigarette before she said gaily, 'We are going to send his brother's ear to his mother.'

Garry started to laugh with her, and Carla and Sarah felt completely excluded.

'We can pick up a body part from Karen Harper at East London Crematorium – she owes us a favour.'

Garry was laughing uproariously.

'We can also start routing all of Vic's old associates. Fuck him. The gloves are off now and we can do what the fuck we like.'

'What happened to the voice of sweet reason, Maws? This isn't like you, is it?'

She swallowed down her brandy and said gutsily, 'It is now.'

[illegible]

[illegible]

[illegible] She [illegible] down at the [illegible]

[illegible] had [illegible] plan [illegible] to be buried [illegible]

to Harry. A broad [illegible] had said that the [illegible]

[illegible]

# Chapter Twenty-Five

Sandra Joliff's mother and two small daughters were at the cemetery in Romford where she was buried. It was a bright day and the two girls were playing I Spy as they walked the familiar path to where their mother rested. They waited while their granny lit another Benson & Hedges. Her hacking cough could be heard all over the hushed cemetery.

Chantel, the elder of the girls by fifteen months, gripped her little sister's hand as they waited for their granny to catch up with them. Rochelle, a dainty little thing as dark as her sister was blonde, slipped her hand away and ran ahead to her mother's grave.

She looked at the headstone. It was pretty, black marble with gold lettering displaying her mother's full name and date of birth. Then it said 'Beloved Wife and Mother'. She stood staring down at the earth. She knew her mother was underneath there, her granny had explained that you had to be buried to go to Heaven. A boy at school had said that her mother would be eaten by worms and it had made her hysterical. Her teacher, Mrs Harding, had told him off and had also explained that worms haven't got any teeth so that was a relief.

The ground looked as if it had been disturbed. She knelt down and began to tidy the plants they had placed there until the cement cast was laid down. They had picked out lovely pink glass-like stones to be put on the grave. Her mummy would have loved that; she had liked Barbie as much as her daughters and saw to it that they had everything Barbie needed to be a proper girl about town.

Her granny came up behind her with Chantel. The woman stared down at the mound of earth for long moments before saying, 'Looks like it's been dug over, doesn't it?'

Chantel nodded.

'Measuring up for the casing, I expect,' Gran said.

She knelt down by her grand-daughters and stared at Sandra's last resting place.

'I heard Mummy calling me.'

Rochelle's voice was quiet, her little face open and truthful. One thing about Rochelle: she looked like her mother but wasn't a spinner like Sandra had been. Lily Camborn, sixty years old and tired out from too much smoking and too much grief, took her youngest grand-daughter in her arms and whispered, 'Mummy's gone, darlin', she's been gone this long time. But she's watching over you and Chantel.

She always will, she's an angel in Heaven with Jesus.'

'No, Nanny, listen.'

Chantel and Lily strained their ears to hear whatever it was the little girl claimed to have heard.

Nothing.

'Put the flowers and the paintings down and we'll go and get a McDonald's, eh?'

Suddenly the sun went in and it seemed cold. Lily hated cemeteries, always had, and seeing her daughter's grave made her doubly depressed. It was the wrong order; she should have been buried, not her Sandra. Her lively girl, who made everything seem like such fun.

She was seeing her daughter through rose-coloured glasses these days. She had completely forgotten the mouthy, argumentative sort, the one who snorted coke till it sent her reeling and drank herself into oblivion regularly.

Then she heard a faint knocking and felt a chill go over her whole body. She was imagining things, surely? She listened, her heart in her mouth, but there was nothing else. She knew it was her imagination working overtime. She often dreamt of her daughter. Felt that she was close by. Wanted to believe that she was watching over her little daughters, taking care of them – something she was not too good at when she was alive.

A psychic had told her that her Sandra was happy and free and Lily wanted to believe that desperately, and so for the grand sum of fifty-five quid that was exactly what she had been told by an aged woman with tired eyes and a smelly house in Dagenham. She didn't want to think of her daughter unhappy and unsettled in her grave. If she did she would never again sleep at night.

It was important to believe that her daughter was resting in peace, not banging on her coffin lid trying to get out. She had been dead far too long for that, and now that Vic had finally coughed up for the casing the grave would look lovely and the girls and she could visit more often.

Lily forced the silly thoughts from her mind.

'Come on, girls. Race each other to the gates and then we'll get a Mackie D, eh?'

The girls raced off and she walked slowly away from Sandra's grave. That muffled sound had unnerved her. But she knew that there was a perfectly rational explanation. It was just her imagination playing her up. She glanced back over her shoulder at the grave. It looked different somehow, and she couldn't figure out why that was.

Sighing, she put her lined face up towards the sun which had come out from behind a cloud and relished its warmth on her skin. Everything looked better with the sun shining. It cheered you up and made you glad to be alive.

She forced all frightening thoughts from her mind and concentrated on the two young girls running like gazelles across the cemetery. The wind rustled the branches of a yew tree nearby and she heard a faint knocking as the bucket that hung by the stand pipe swayed against it. Breathing a sigh of relief, she hurried from the cemetery, telling herself she was a silly old woman.

Just for a split second there she had actually believed she'd heard a sound from beyond the grave and it had scared her silly.

She hurried away from the graveyard as fast as her arthritic legs could carry her, unaware that she was the last person ever to hear from Tommy Rifkind.

Leonie was singing as she tidied up her Garry's flat. She had not been this happy in her whole life. Garry made her feel good about herself and she appreciated that so much. She was used to men who wanted her for all the wrong reasons.

By the time she was fifteen she had already learned about the power a good body could command if used in the right way. It had been her dream to be a stripper or an exotic dancer of some sort. The lapping had suited her down to the ground, but now she was feeling a little jaded from it all and saw Garry as a fit alternative.

He had money and kudos, two requisites that she was adamant a man should have before she would give them the time of day, but he was also kind to her and treated her with respect. She guessed, rightly, that she was the first person he had ever treated in this way and that also pleased her. It proved to her she was special. Garry had told her she was often enough.

She might even have a baby to cement their relationship and guarantee a few quid if it all fell out of bed at some point. A girl had to look to the future, and Leonie had always prided herself on her business acumen.

She loaded the dishwasher and as she did so heard the front door open. Smiling, she went through to the lounge and saw a large man standing there. She looked past him, expecting to see Garry behind him. The dark-haired man looked vaguely familiar.

'Who are you? Where's my Garry?'

Her voice was strong but there was an underlying tremor in it.

The man carried on staring at her from deep blue eyes.

'Will you answer me, please?'

She was frightened now. This was the downside of being with someone like Garry, and it had been the same with Jack. Their enemies were automatically your enemies.

'Where's Garry?'

Benny's voice was soft, but far from reassuring.

She shook her head.

'I have no idea, he doesn't discuss his movements with me.'

'I bet he's shown you a few movements though, eh, love?'

Leonie was annoyed now. She turned huffily and went back into the kitchen. Benny followed her.

'You got a number for him?'

She shook her head.

Benny, fed up with all the poncing around, grabbed her by the hair and forced her head back on to her shoulders. It was extremely painful.

'Ow! What the fuck do you think you're doing?'

He sighed.

'Have you a mobile number for him?'

She shook her head once more. Benny shoved her away from him none too gently then walked back into the lounge and started to search the place. He finally found a mobile in her bag and scrolled through the address book.

Nothing.

She was far too cute to put actual names in there.

He began ringing the numbers one by one. Leonie watched him from the kitchen. He was trouble all right and she'd just realised this was one of Garry's relatives. Heaven forbid she should ever meet an enemy.

Mickey Ball was watching as Vic listened on his cellphone to his tearful auntie telling him about the severed ear that had arrived at the house minutes before. He saw the veins protruding from Vic's forehead, the way he was pulling his lips back over his teeth like a rabid dog about to pounce on its victim.

'The fucking scumbags! Terrifying old women now, are they?'

He kicked out at a chair that was near him and sent it careering into Mickey's legs. He thought about protesting, then thought better of it. Allies against the Ryans they might be but the last thing he wanted to do was antagonise Vic Joliff when he was in this state.

Sarah sat with Lee while Maura and Garry started on the first stage of their plan. Lee looked haunted and she knew Sheila would be giving him hell over recent events and the possible repercussions.

'You OK, son?'

He shook his head.

'Not really, Mum.'

She could hear the tremor in his voice.

'Is everything all right with Sheila?'

He sighed.

'It isn't, Mum, if you want the truth.'

Sarah watched him smoke his cigarette and decided he looked not only old but deeply troubled. Her daughter-in-law was a handful who led this good son of Sarah's a dance. Sheila didn't know when she was well off. She had six children, another on the way and a husband who adored her as well as working his arse off for all of them. She was too hard on her man, and if she wasn't careful he would find himself an alternative face to look at on the pillow of a morning.

'Is she giving you grief?'

'Since the head incident she's been like a maniac, Mum, and in some ways I don't blame her. It even gave me one up.'

'Jasus, I think about it all the time meself. Sure, that Benny is a fecking case and no mistaking. In a way I'm glad that Janine is dead or this lot would have killed her for sure.'

She saw Lee trying to stifle a laugh and felt a moment's anger at him. That was her children's answer to everything, laugh about it. No matter how bad it was they found a joke in it. And some of the things they did were not funny; Benny decapitating a young man on the threshold of his life was anything but funny in her opinion. Disgusting, violent and depraved certainly, but not funny. Not at all.

'Benny isn't all the ticket, son. Even Sheila must understand that much.'

'She ain't interested, Mum. Wants me out of all this, and if I don't agree then she wants a divorce. Garry and Maura know the score, they've left me out of things for a while, but with all this shit with Vic . . .'

He shrugged.

'How are the boys?'

He smiled now, a genuine smile.

'They're great. And the babes . . . oh, Mum, she is adorable.'

She saw the love in his eyes and heard it in his voice. She grasped his hand in hers.

'Then go home, son. Maura and Garry will understand if I explain.'

He grinned and looked so handsome then with his trademark Ryan black hair and deep-set blue eyes. They were a good-looking family, there was no doubt about that, and in her own way she was proud of each and every one of them. Even Maura made her happy since their reconciliation.

'Go on, get away home. You have a large family to take care of and I have a feeling on me that things are all going to get very difficult before it's resolved.'

'I can't, Mum, I wish I could. I'm as sick of it all as you are but even Roy has been drafted in for this final confrontation. I just hope it's all over soon and with the minimum of fuss, eh?'

She nodded, aware that she was wasting her time. He would do what he had to and wouldn't listen to her, no matter what she said. That was one thing she had learned over the years.

Lee, however, was actually watching over his mother though Sarah was not to know that. When the ear arrived at Vic's auntie's, which it should have done by now, there was going to be murder done. Vic was going to be looking for all the Ryans and he would find them. Vic had a habit of getting what he wanted. But then, so did Maura.

Lee just hoped it would all be over soon so he could go home to his family. Once this was through he was going to get out. Sheila was right, it was all too much now. Their lives were in danger, and their kids'. It was time to break away from it all and get back on the old footing with his beloved wife before it was too late.

Kenny met Maura at Thurrock services and as he climbed into her car he was half-pleased to be in her company once more and half-worried about whatever mayhem she was about to cause. He was gratified she wanted him with her, though. It must show she respected him if nothing else.

She smiled at him and he saw that she was looking far more confident than when he had last spoken to her.

'Where we going?' he asked.

'Vic's auntie's. See if he swings by there to comfort his old mum.'

Kenny's blue eyes looked doubtful. He had nice eyes, Maura found herself thinking. A different shade from the Ryan blue, clearer and paler. Not weak though. There was nothing weak about Kenny Smith. He had a very direct way of looking at you. Kenny inspired trust in people. She supposed it was something he'd had to cultivate in his line of work, but found it reassuring nevertheless.

'I think you should wait for him to get in touch, Maura.'

'I can't, Kenny. I really can't sit around waiting for that ponce any longer. Word is out that we are finished and it's going to cause us a lot more problems if we don't nip this in the bud once and for all. Someone tried having over one of the betting shops, and that in itself speaks volumes.'

He listened attentively. She liked the way he did that instead of always trying to put in his sixpenn'orth like Tommy and her brothers.

'Another thing. It was two of Joe the Jew's boys who tried to rob the shop. Interesting, don't you think? They've got the inside track from someone and it ain't me. I knew that old ponce was hiding something all along. He's in with Vic, I can smell it.'

Kenny closed his eyes momentarily as he realised this was it, what he'd been dreading. It was all about to come down on them and Maura would be right in the firing line.

She glanced sideways at him. Once again his face wore its professional mask of inscrutability. His shaven head, prominent scar and heavy body promoted the impression of a hard man, a bully boy. But Maura knew that inside he was a decent man. She was also shrewd enough to understand that his bad boy looks would attract a certain kind of woman. Kenny looked just like a man in his line of work should look, and that would give some of his admirers a real buzz.

They probably wouldn't have been half so impressed if they knew about his softer side, the one Maura was beginning to appreciate more with every day that passed.

She opened her mouth to speak to him, and her mobile rang. Sighing, she answered the call and recognised Vic Joliff's voice immediately.

Carla and Joey were walking up Lancaster Road. They had a truce at the moment and as they had Benny's money, had been on a marathon shop. Maura was not going to welcome her niece back into the fold with open arms but there was a definite thaw and that pleased Carla. At least she didn't feel that constant sickness any more, wondering what Maura was going to do or say next.

Even Joey seemed happier in himself. He was always out these days and because of what she saw as his aberrant sexuality Carla didn't question him too much about where he went. In truth, she didn't want to know.

She studied him as they strolled along together. He was a good-looking boy and had always had, if not friends exactly, plenty of acquaintances. He was naturally very outgoing and friendly but she knew he had had grief at school because of his effeminate ways. The fact he was related to the Ryans had helped put a stop to all that, of course.

The only people he got on really well with were

Benny and Abul. Benny took the piss mercilessly but Abul had always given him his time. Not that he would any longer, of course.

It was a shame really that she had not kept in closer touch with the boy's father. It was only now that he was older that she realised Joey needed a man in his life. But the decision had been taken all those years ago when Malcolm had betrayed her with that stuck-up bitch of a secretary of his, and that was that. Maura and the boys had seen to it that he had never come near or by them again without express permission.

Joey was squealing now as he waved to Nana's next-door neighbour, an actor who had appeared in many films and always played a gangster or a psychopath. Now, though, he waved and squealed back every bit as loudly and over-exaggeratedly as her son did. If only his legion of female fans could see him – and the pretty boys who seemed to be forever coming and going at all hours of the night. Even his cleaner was a Filipino boy with a tight bod and a rather used-looking mop.

She waved to him half-heartedly and he repaid her with a winning smile that could melt the hardest of female hearts.

'She likes you, Mother.'

'Will you stop referring to men as "she", please, Joey? It irritates me.'

He sniffed loudly.

'Everything irritates you lately.'

Carla knew he was speaking the truth and tried to smile at him. He was glowering at her and she felt sorry because she knew she had hurt him. That she had hurt him many times with her words and her actions.

'Look, Joey, I know me and you don't see eye to eye . . .'

He flounced away from her and she followed him up the steps to the front door.

'Please, Joey.'

He opened the front door with his key and went inside. Carla knew she had hurt him again and was sorry. In the kitchen he put on the kettle and she sat at the table, trying to find the words to make everything better. Why couldn't she be more like Maura, accept everyone as they were instead of pushing them to be how she wanted them to be?

'Look, Joey, things haven't been that easy for me either, you know.'

He faced her then, laughing, and said, 'Oh, really? I would never have noticed if you hadn't mentioned it! Well, Mother dearest, any problems you are experiencing stem from your own bloody actions. You knew that Tommy was with Maura and you were stupid enough to try and hook him when even I know that men like him are just chasing a bit of strange. You're hardly a spring chicken, are you? Now you've been bummed out you want me. Well, it's too fucking late, love. I don't need you, I don't need any of you, and soon you will all find that out.'

He was looking at her strangely as if he was the proud possessor of a great big secret, which of course he was. She realised that by the smug look that had come over his handsome face.

'What on earth are you on about?'

He smiled mysteriously.

'You'll find out soon enough. I have a few tricks up my sleeve, Mother.'

'What kind of tricks, Joey?'

He smiled once more, enjoying her consternation.

'As I say, you'll know soon enough.'

'Life can be very difficult at times, Joey . . .'

Now he did laugh. The thought of her giving him advice about anything made him crack up. She could save the bullshit for someone who believed it.

'Life? What do *you* know about life? At least I *have* a fucking life, which is something you have never had.'

She could see how incensed he was and it actually made her nervous. He had the same quality about him now as Garry had when he was upset. He looked as if he was capable of anything.

He turned towards the kettle and started to make the coffee as he said in a firm voice, 'Just don't try and give me pep talks. Face it, Mother, we are not the close couple you thought we were and as far as I'm concerned it's too late for us to start now. So let's have a coffee and then I'm off out, OK?'

She didn't answer him; she really didn't know what to say.

# Chapter Twenty-Six

Listening to Maura talk to Vic, Kenny felt as if his guts had turned to ice water. She started to laugh and he marvelled at her ability to sound in control even when her heart must have been making its way into her mouth like a rocket. She was good, there was no doubt about that.

'No, you listen to me, Vic. You moved the goal-posts. You should have rung when you said you would. Do you think we ain't got nothing better to do than wait on your calls?'

She listened and laughed.

'I am *soooo* scared, Vic. Can't you hear the way my voice is shaking? Oh, sorry, that's yours.

'Let's cut the crap, shall we? You want a meet. So do we. But we're playing by *our* rules and doing it *our* way. Your mate Jack won't be needing his place any time soon so why don't we say the barn, noon tomorrow, smart casual, guns will be worn. That good for you, Vic?'

She rang off without waiting for his reply and looked at Kenny.

'I wonder where he got my mobile number from?'

Kenny shook his head.

'Is it safe?'

'About as safe as you can get. I only received it yesterday.'

He frowned as he took in the implications.

'Who'd you get it off?'

'Cranky Bob, the BT bloke. He's supplied them to me for the last couple of years.'

'Well, he's sound enough. I use him myself. Wonder if he's working for Vic as well?'

Maura looked grim.

'Must be. I think a visit to Bob is well in order, don't you? Kenny, will you get us there? I need to brief Garry on the arrangements for tomorrow – and then I'm calling in a shedload of favours.'

Sheila always enjoyed some time alone even though she missed her children when they were not around. She was luxuriating in a steaming bath full of lavender oil when she heard the sound of heavy footfalls on the stairs.

She closed her eyes in irritation and waited for Lee to come into the bathroom. The door was eventually thrust open when she called his name. She opened her eyes to see Vic Joliff staring at her.

He smiled appreciatively.

'Mrs Ryan, please excuse me for intruding on your ablutions. But me and you need to talk.'

'What the hell do you think you're doing?'

Sheila was trying to cover her body as best she could.

Vic threw her a towel.

'Get yourself out and downstairs, please. Quick as you can.'

She remembered him from Sarah's the day he had brought the flowers and for some reason she wasn't frightened of him. Why that was she didn't know. She knew she should be scared, very scared, but she wasn't.

She dried herself off as fast as she could and put on a bright blue candlewick dressing gown. She saw that the phone was ripped from the wall but had expected as much. As she walked downstairs to the kitchen she was amazed at just how calm she actually felt.

Vic had made them both some tea and smiled at her in a friendly manner as she entered.

'I must apologise for all this shit, Sheila, but I have no choice in the matter. Your husband's family insists on aggravating the life out of me.'

'What do you want?'

She sat herself down on one of the high-backed stools at the breakfast bar.

'Nice drum, love, very homely.'

She smiled.

'Thank you very much.'

He smiled again and she found that despite everything she quite liked him.

'Why are you here?'

'I want to catch a big fish, and you, my love, are the bait. Now drink your tea and get dressed. We have a little journey to make.'

Cranky Bob was in his forties and had acquired his nickname after having a tear up in a pub in Bristol. He had been there for the weekend and had got into an altercation with two local wide boys, one of whom had glassed him. Forty stitches and a lot of pain later he had been left with no muscles in his face so that even when he smiled he looked miserable. Hence the name Cranky Bob.

As he stood in the betting shop placing his bets he was more than surprised to see Maura Ryan standing in the doorway, motioning for him to follow her outside. Bob being Bob, he finished placing his bets before strolling out of the door and walking over to where she was standing beside a big saloon car.

'You took your fucking time.'

Her voice was hard and he was non-plussed for a second.

'Get in,' the bully boy with her ordered.

Kenny's voice made Bob aware that he could be in danger; all previous friendliness between them was gone now and he got into the car quietly and with the minimum of fuss. Maura sat in the back with him and this made him feel even more nervous for some reason.

'Have you been passing on our numbers to other people, Bob?'

Her voice was low and he knew he was skating on thin ice here.

'What makes you think that, Maura?'

She grinned.

'Don't fuck me about, Bob, I am that far from beating your brains out.' She put her thumb and forefinger together. 'Did you give our numbers to Vic Joliff?'

Even Kenny could see the confusion on the other man's face.

'Why would I give your numbers to him? I don't even know him.'

It was obvious he was telling the truth.

'Well, you have given them to someone.'

'Only your family, love, no one else.'

'Who, for example?'

'Your niece Carla – I gave her a few numbers because she had lost her phone. Oh, and her son, the poofter. I gave him the numbers because he said Benny wanted them.'

'When was this?'

'Well, Carla was weeks ago, but the boy, Joey, he's always on the blower. You know what a dork he is. I said to him yesterday he should get a fucking phone book tattooed on his fucking arse. Gets on my wick he does, always on the phone fucking moaning in that poncey whining voice of his . . .'

'Joey?'

He nodded.

'Yes, wanted your new number again. He also wanted a safe mobile for himself and I dropped it off to him not an hour ago.'

'Where did you drop it off?'

'He was in a wine bar at the top end of Portobello Road. Then I dropped him back at your mother's house.'

'What was his new mobile number?'

Bob opened his black leather Filofax and gave her the number.

'Thanks, Bob.'

He sneered. It was the closest to a smile he would get this side of plastic surgery.

'You are welcome. Can I go now?'

She nodded.

When they were alone in the car Kenny said, 'I had a feeling there was someone close to home but I never dreamt it was him. Vic must have got to him through Tommy or Abul, mustn't he?'

'So it would seem.'

She was nearly in tears at this fresh betrayal.

'I gave that boy everything, you know that. I put him and his mother up when it all fell out of bed with Malcolm, and this is how I am repaid. I bet they laughed up their sleeves at me. I bet they thought it was fucking hilarious. Silly Maura, the prat who paid the bills.'

'Don't be so harsh on yourself.'

'Harsh?' She laughed. 'I tell you what, Kenny, even Benny as mad as he is has more loyalty in his little finger than those two have in their whole bodies. Funny that, ain't it?'

Kenny didn't know what to say to her.

'What is it with me, eh, Kenny? First Tommy and Carla. Now Joey. And fucking Abul thrown in. I mean, the fact he skanked fucking Tommy from under our noses speaks volumes. No one's heard from him since. He must have gone over to Vic. Why don't I see the people I care about for what they are?'

She lit a cigarette.

'I'm supposed to be a shrewdie, right? People respect me for my strength and so-called business head. Yet my niece and her son tucked me up like a fucking kipper and I never saw it coming. Not Tommy, and definitely not Abul. I mean, him and Tommy only ever spoke about two words to one another.'

'You wasn't to know . . .'

'But that's just it! I should have felt this coming. I should have out-thought the fucking lot of them, but I didn't so that tells me something important. I am past all this, mate. I can't trust me own judgement any more and without that I can't lead this family; it makes me a liability.'

'What crap! You have more nous than anyone I know, male or female.'

She shook her head at him.

'No. Listen to me. Tommy Rifkind was a piece of shit and I never saw it, Kenny. I didn't want to see it. Now, through me, the family has been dragged into danger and all because I took a fancy to a smooth-talking Scally.'

She was nearly crying and he said gently, 'You couldn't have known, Maura.'

She shrugged his hand from her arm.

'I *should* have known. If anyone should have sussed that cunt out it should have been me. Yet I was blinded to his faults, the same as I was blinded to Terry's.'

'You loved Terry, whatever he was.'

She sighed heavily.

'I saw him through someone else's eyes, Kenny, never through me own. I mixed up sex and love. I had great sex with Terry and I had great sex with Tommy. That is what caused my downfall.'

'How do you make that out?'

'Terry, believe it or not, was a controlling bastard in a lot of respects, I realise that now, and Tommy was the same. It didn't matter what I might have been doing with my life. Even if I had been director of fucking ICI they would still have wanted me to be the little lady at home. It was always about doing what someone else wanted, not about me and what I wanted.'

Kenny felt that he could have told her as much but decided to keep that piece of wisdom to himself.

'With Terry it was because he was a filth, I think, and wanted to tame me, wanted to be the man Maura Ryan settled down for. There was also guilt for what he had done to me all those years ago when he dumped me. I think he felt that if he could make me into the Housewife of the Year he had finally achieved something. For me he was the love of my life, the father of the only child I would ever carry, and he was finally willing to be with me so I'd got what I wanted. But at what fucking price, eh? As my mum used to say, be careful what you ask for, you just might get it.'

She leaned back in her seat.

'With Tommy it was sex again. But he only wanted me because through me he could get a bigger slice of the pie. He was Maura Ryan's bloke and that gave him kudos with everyone except my brothers and family. Garry hated him and I think Tommy knew that all along. He used me and he used Carla, though I suppose she's worked that much out for herself finally.'

She looked so forlorn that Kenny felt like taking her in his arms and comforting her. He didn't, of course, he wasn't that brave. She flicked her cigarette butt from the window and, climbing out of the back, got into the driving seat of the car.

'I've wasted enough of me time on bastard men. Let's get this poxy show on the road, shall we?'

* * *

Lee and his mother were watching *Countdown* when he took a call on his mobile that was to blow him out of the water. It was his eldest, Gabriel, telling him that they had not been picked up from school and, worse, that their mother was nowhere to be found.

'Mum, in the motor. We have to go and pick up the kids,' Lee ordered.

Sarah was surprised at his tone.

'Where the hell is Sheila then? Why didn't she pick them up?'

Lee was agitated and therefore shorter with his mother than he meant to be.

'If I knew that, Mum, I wouldn't be going to pick the kids up meself, would I?'

She put her coat on and he was maddened by the length of time it took her to do that simple task.

'Please, Mum, get a move on, will you?'

In his mind he wondered if someone was going to go after the kids as well. Surely even Vic Joliff wouldn't go that far? But until Lee had them safe in the car he wasn't going to bank on anything.

Vic and Sheila were sipping cocktails and eating canapés bought from a local delicatessen in Gants Hill. She was very impressed with the house they were in; it had a swimming pool and the largest TV set she had ever seen. They were watching a video of Frank Sinatra and Vic was obviously enjoying it immensely.

'Do you mind if my mother joins us in a little while?' he asked politely.

'I don't have much choice really, do I?'

Vic looked offended.

'With respect, Sheila, if you do not wish for my mother's company, I would not force it on you. I also wanted to reassure you of your safety. I would hardly be introducing you to my mother if I had any ulterior motives, would I?'

He almost wished he did have another agenda. There was something about this woman he liked, probably the fact she mothered six children and mothered them well. He had always admired the way Lee Ryan was a family man. Vic prided himself on giving credit where credit was due.

Sheila might not have it in the looks department any longer but in fairness six kids would even take their toll on Kate Moss. But her decency commanded respect – and the fact she was not even a functioning part of the Ryan family should frighten them into doing exactly what he wanted.

They had his brother and he had one of their wives. It would be a good face-saving trade-off. Even the Ryans would think twice before they pushed it with Sheila on his premises. It was out of order, he knew, she was not part of the family business, but he was past caring about etiquette. He wanted his brother, he wanted his coke and he wanted aggravation – and he wanted it all as quickly as possible. He would take what he could now; it was all he could do. They had made a Grade-A cunt out of him. He couldn't let that go without looking a complete wanker, and Vic Joliff was a lot of things but a wanker wasn't one of them.

He decided he had to make a point to this lot. What had started out as a complete takeover bid was looking suspiciously like a wank job now and that was what he could not stand. The thought of people, even strangers, thinking he was a mug was killing him. A man had his pride and there was no man prouder than Vic Joliff. In fact, he prided himself on his pride.

No one had ever walked over him and lived to tell the tale. That was how you survived in his world. Your reputation, your ability to scare people with your utter ruthlessness, was what set apart the men from the boys. It was a cause for celebration that no one talked about you in a derogatory way, no one treated you like an ice cream, and you never paid for a drink in any pub of note. He was damned if he was going to give all that up because of the poxy Ryans.

He excused himself and went out to the kitchen where he rapidly snorted two lines, one after the other. He had a problem with cocaine and on one level was aware of it. But once the powder went up his nose he forgot his fears and felt invincible. He felt that he could take on fifty Ryan families and still have the strength to take on the Mafia and the CIA in his dinner hour.

He was Victor Joliff and he was man enough to

make the whole world disregard the fact he was the offspring of an ex-prostitute and a drunken thief. He was proving to his peers that he was a man to be admired, a man to respect. And more importantly a man who could take over the south east and ultimately the whole of the UK drugs market. He would be the Escobar of England, and God help anyone who tried to stand in his way.

He heard his mother's nasal twang coming from the lounge and quickly checked his face in the small mirror he had used to cut the coke. Mum hated him on the gear and was very vocal about it.

He poured a large Morgan's rum and after adding some peppermint cordial took it through to the lounge where Nellie Joliff was taking off her duffel coat.

'Only got one bloody number on the Lottery, Vic.'

He smiled in commiseration.

'Never mind. This is a friend of mine. Her name's Sheila, Mum.'

'Pleased to meet you, I'm sure.'

Sheila smiled at the little old lady who had obviously seen better days. She had the worn and haggard look of a woman who had worked hard all her life with fuck all to show for it.

Sheila wondered why she wasn't feeling worried about her children. She should be out of her mind with the fear of never seeing them again. But she wasn't. In fact, she was enjoying being without them and teaching Lee a valuable lesson into the bargain. This might be just the incentive he needed to make him see things her way.

Vic was a decent enough man inside, she was sure of it. Or at least she hoped so anyway. She watched him listen to his mother ramble on as if it was the most fascinating conversation in the world. Funnily enough, she found she really liked this kindly considerate man who had kidnapped her and was holding her to ransom.

Vic nodded to his mother and smiled at their guest and let the whole bloody irritation of it wash over him. He kept his mouth shut and his attention focused on tomorrow. The arrangements with his boys and the Irish were all in place. No matter what that cunt Kenny advised about peaceful negotiation, Vic Joliff was going in with all guns blazing.

Maura was on her phone or paying visits until late that night. She rang or talked personally to every face the Ryans were ever on friendly terms with – and some of their enemies. She was matey, she was cajoling and she was threatening. She was whatever she had to be to get people on the Ryans' side, and to destroy whatever shreds of credibility Vic Joliff had left. Showing people they were better off sticking to the devil they knew was the best way to avoid all-out war, she knew.

She wanted no bloodshed but the bare minimum.

There was no way Vic would ever topple the Ryans now and he had probably guessed as much for himself in his increasingly rare intervals of lucidity, but that wouldn't stop him turning up. He'd had six years of running and hiding and tomorrow he'd have his showdown with them, come hell or high water. She was banking on it.

At eleven o'clock that night, hoarse from her efforts and craving nothing so much as a large brandy and her own bed, Maura asked Kenny to do her a favour. He accompanied Bing and Carlton Dooley and a few handpicked men to Joe the Jew's Silvertown yard.

They found Joe in his office over the scrap heaps. A couple of bodyguards with an Alsatian straining at the leash put up a protest when they rammed open the gates, but melted away when they realised who they were disrespecting.

'Stay out here on the steps,' Kenny told the others. 'I can handle this on my own.'

Joe had obviously seen their arrival. When Kenny strode into the office without knocking he found the old man already in his overcoat, sitting behind his desk with two letters in his hand.

'Oh, it's you, Kenny,' he said, looking surprised. 'I always thought it would be Maura who came for me. She's generally a woman of her word.'

Kenny scowled.

'Yeah, well, she's got a big day tomorrow, thanks to

you and your mates. The Ryans and their allies will be head to head with Vic and his. Maura wants you there, Joe. Meanwhile, she's asked me to put you up for the night in a safe house. I take it you don't mean to fight?'

Joe glanced out over the deserted yard.

'Looks like it. There's no such thing as loyalty these days.'

Kenny's expression hardened.

'Tell that to Maura – you and her were good friends once, I hear. What in God's name got into you, going up against her and her family like that?'

Joe's lined face suddenly looked older than time.

'You just answered your own question there, Kenny, if only you knew it. But I'll explain myself to Maura and no one else. Meanwhile, a favour, please?' He handed the two letters to Kenny. 'Will you see these get to the right people? It's my final request.'

One was to go to Camilla, Joe's girlfriend. Her payoff, no doubt. The other . . . when Kenny saw that name he suddenly had an inkling what lay behind Joe's involvement in this whole sorry mess.

'I'll see they're passed on,' he said. 'OK, let's be having you.'

As he was walking down the steps outside between Bing and Carlton Dooley, Joe suddenly stopped and looked back at his office.

'Oh, I nearly forgot. You're the Dooley brothers, I believe?' he addressed his captors.

Bing nodded without speaking.

'How opportune. You'll be very interested to meet my house guest then. Go and look in the attic – there's a door in the corner of my office.'

Kenny nodded at Bing who went back inside with two of the men. They all heard the shouts of surprise.

'Abul – it's Abul! Bring those cutters up here.'

Kenny and Joe waited in the yard while the others worked to free Abul. He finally appeared at the top of the stairs, barely able to stand, his wounded leg on fire and his face and head smarting where the tape had been ripped away. The other men seemed delighted to see him.

'What happened, man? We thought you'd took off with Tommy Rifkind,' Bing was saying to him.

'Did *he* do this to you? Miss Ryan's put the word out on you. She thought you'd tucked us up,' Carlton warned.

Abul opened his mouth to reply. Joe beat him to it.

'Why don't you ask him who killed your brother?'

In a hoarse voice Abul started to protest.

'No! Not me . . . it was Vic . . .'

Kenny took a step forward.

'*Now* it makes sense. I never believed Vic got that close to Tony without him knowing. He was too good at his job to let that happen. And anyway if he had, why stop there? Why not kill Maura too while he was at it? No, someone else did that for his own reasons and it had to be someone Tony knew . . .

Why did you do it, Abul? On to you, was he?'

There was an electric silence for a moment and then the Dooleys moved as one. They pushed Abul down the iron stairs and laid into him with a ferocity that made even Kenny shudder. He called them off after a couple of minutes.

He knew Maura would want Abul alive for the meeting tomorrow. But his chances of living past that were less than zero.

Garry, Roy and Tony Dooley Senior were at Jack Stern's barn at daylight the next morning. Garry had his men combing the surrounding area to check it was secure and that Vic did not already have the place staked out, lying in wait to give them a nasty surprise. So far he'd proved remarkably elusive.

Roy put into words what they had all been thinking.

'It's like he can fucking appear and disappear by magic, ain't it?'

Garry nodded.

'The lads have routed everyone and not a fucking dicky bird.'

'Well, he can't be far off now. He will show up, won't he?'

Tony shook his head.

'Couldn't say, man. I really couldn't say.'

'And as for fucking Benny . . . when he finally shows his boatrace, Roy, I am going to fucking Muller him. Who the fuck does he think he is? Roy fucking Rogers?' Garry fumed.

Roy took a couple of deep breaths before he said, 'Go for it, Gal. Personally I think it's my fault, though. When he called me I shouldn't have mugged him off. Now, when we need him, he ain't about. I was hard on the boy. Told him none of us wanted anything more to do with him.'

They all heard the desolation and fear in his voice.

'I can't believe he ain't been in touch again . . .'

Garry and Tony didn't comment. Like Roy they privately wondered if Benny was still alive, but no one wanted to say it aloud.

'What about fucking Abul though, eh? I'm still having trouble with it.'

Roy had collected himself again. His voice was hard. The news that Abul had been the one to kill Tony Dooley Junior as well as being in league with the enemy had shocked and depressed them all.

'Still, we got him now,' said Garry, touching Tony Senior on the arm. 'And Maura will see he gets everything that's coming to him.'

Tony forced a smile and they both clapped him on the back.

Cars were pulling up outside as they reached the barn entrance. Every man jack who worked for them was due here for a briefing. Garry was determined that by hook or by crook he was going to have his day with that slippery bastard and take him out.

This was personal now; Vic was taking the piss.

He smiled as he saw Gerry Jackson walk in. Even at his age and wearing one of his repertoire of wigs he still looked menacing, and the scars from the fire at the club all those years ago made him look even more frightening than he actually was. He was a legend among the younger fellows because he had been Michael Ryan's best friend. That in itself made him a one-off in their eyes. He'd also taken a bomb blast and come out fighting.

His rep was such that even Garry gave him his due. He shook Gerry's hand, grabbing his forearm as he did so in a display of friendship and respect.

'I knew you would come, Ger.'

Gerry grinned.

'I wouldn't have missed this lot for the world, Gal. Have a guess who's outside?' He smiled once more as he answered his own question. 'Me four eldest boys.'

Gerry's boys had become the drugs barons and local scallywags of their home turf in Kent. In fact, it was rumoured that nothing came in or out of the docks there without their express permission. The Channel Tunnel was also their property and Garry had dealt with them many times over the last few years. He had found them both trustworthy and civil-tongued. They would be assets to this job and he was pleased at the show of solidarity. Not many people would take on Vic Joliff, he was more than aware of that fact and glad to be able to make a show of force much larger and more diverse than anyone would have guessed at.

The Ryans had a show of support from Asians from East London and Deptford, West Indians from South London, and British Bulldogs from all over the smoke – and just let any of them start getting the arse with each other before this little lot was over. Vic wouldn't know what the fuck had hit him this time. Whatever Maura said, this was all-out war and they were going to win it.

It was years since Garry had felt this alive and he was determined to enjoy every second of the next few hours.

[illegible]
[illegible]

[illegible]
[illegible]
[illegible]
[illegible]
[illegible]
[illegible]
[illegible]

[illegible] on the morning of his [illegible] Benny
[illegible]
[illegible]
[illegible]
[illegible]
[illegible]
[illegible]

Now he was driving to the barn, with anger burning inside him and the four new mates he had called
[illegible]
[illegible]
[illegible]
[illegible]
[illegible]
[illegible]
literally been getting away with murder because of
his association with the powerful Ryan family, and his
friendship with Benny in particular.

Everyone knew they were very close, and as far as

# Chapter Twenty-Seven

At ten o'clock on the morning of the meet Benny finally contacted Maura at home. He'd decided talking to his aunt was the best bet. She was calm and sensible, as he'd expected, but refused to discuss anything with him, explained the meet was on at noon and where so he should get his arse in gear, and put down the phone.

Now he was driving to the barn, with anger seething inside him and the four new mates he had called on rattling round in the back of a white transit van. They were Asian, four brothers from a Bangladeshi family in Forest Gate, young men who were sworn enemies of Abul's because of tear ups that had occurred between them in the past few years. Benny had realised belatedly that his former friend had literally been getting away with murder because of his association with the powerful Ryan family, and his friendship with Benny in particular.

Everyone knew they were very close, and as far as

Benny had been concerned they were. But Abul had had a different agenda all along. Well, when Benny got hold of him he was going to teach the fucker a lesson he'd never forget – and then kill him.

Ricky D, the eldest brother, had always got on with Benny. They had dealt in drugs together over the years through a mutual association with Radon Chatmore – not that Ricky was shedding any tears for the Rastaman. His death left the way clear for Ricky's kin, and that had cemented their new alliance with Benny.

Now he was going to see his family and he was going with a new firm of his own and the deaths of his former friends as proof of his complete loyalty. He was nervous inside, though, hoping he would not be made to look a fool in front of Ricky and his brothers.

He had been on the missing list in the midst of the biggest war his family had had to deal with, and he had also become public enemy number one over the head incident. The head still annoyed him every time he thought about it. He should have dumped it, he saw that now. He was a fool to have kept hold of it but had enjoyed knowing it was there. Yet Carol, who had caused the entire furore, had not only lost their child for them, she had caused all this hag into the bargain. If she had not been such a silly bitch none of this would have happened.

It had taught him a lesson for the future, he knew that much. He would take whatever the family gave him on the chin and prove to them he was a fully functioning member of the Ryans. And then he would allow them to buy him out of this latest spot of bother – but only after he had denied he needed their help for a suitable amount of time. Let them sweat a little. They didn't want him turning Queen's Evidence any more than he did.

He was pleased with himself now as they made their way to Jack's. Maura would pave the way for him, he was sure. At heart they had to know that whatever he might have done, he was loyal to them, would always be loyal to them, no matter what.

He was a Ryan, and proud of that fact. Maura would see him all right, she was family-minded, always had been. After all, their strength lay in the fact they were the Ryan family, the equivalent of Royalty in London's underworld.

To the Ryans, blood was more important than anything.

Sarah made herself yet another pot of tea and a little bit of toast. She had fed the children and settled them down to watch TV. She had that dragging pain again, like the one she'd had when her son Benny had been snatched and when her Michael had been shot down in the street.

She knew that there was serious trouble afoot if that Vic had taken Sheila. She was scandalised a wife would ever be taken hostage but, as Roy said, it was a sign of the times. There was no decency left in the world any more. Little bits of girls were running round the TV screen naked, and that was just the adverts. Was it any wonder the established order had changed and people like Vic involved the women of the family in their dealings?

She nibbled at the toast and sipped the tea. She wasn't really hungry or thirsty but it was something to do.

She had been thinking about her Michael a lot today. The atmosphere was just like it was when he'd died, and when her Benny had been taken. Her own gorgeous boy who had been her last-born son, her baby.

She pushed the thoughts from her mind. Life was hard enough as it was without creating problems before they made themselves known. But the pain was getting more insistent and she felt sick with fear.

She felt in her apron pocket and took out her rosary. It had seen her through many a crisis in its time. It was olive wood and almost worn out now, like herself. She smiled at the thought. Yes, worn away practically to nothing. Once again she blessed herself and kissed the Cross of Christ, praying for the safe return of Sheila and of all her children.

In her mind's eye she saw them as she loved to see them, all small, all clean, and dressed for Mass on a lovely sunny Sunday morning.

The image that had always given her such pride

brought tears to her eyes now and she cried for the wasted lives of her children.

All of them.

Vic already knew that the Ryans and their cronies were all over Jack's place like a rash. It was what he had expected. However he still had a few tricks up his sleeve himself. He shook his head to clear it and pulled his Range Rover over to snort some more coke. His blokes watched him and he sensed they were worried about the forthcoming showdown.

'I have a lot of back up on the payroll – I hope you lot aren't starting to shit now?'

They hastily assured him he was wrong but he wasn't sure of them any more; he wasn't sure of anything. It was paranoia setting in and he knew he should never have snorted so much coke before a confrontation. But he had Sheila and they had Fatty and he had to trade for his mother's sake, though if it was left to him he would let Justin rot. Not forgetting he also wanted his coke back and the Ryans dead. All of them, even Maura for whom he had a grudging respect now he knew the full story. But she needed bringing down a peg and he was just the man to do it.

He had once harboured thoughts of giving her one but she was a bit long in the tooth for him these days. He knew Kenny wouldn't kick her out of bed, though. The thought made him smile. Kenny was another one who was going to get the shock of his fucking life. He was on the off list along with a few other mates who had switched their allegiance to the Ryans.

Oh, Vic had a few more scores to settle and settle them he would. He had the big guns. It didn't matter who the Ryans mustered, he had the *crème de la crème.* He had people beside him far more frightening than a bunch of old lags. In fact, they were the only people who had ever taken on those ponces and won. The thought reassured him.

But first he had to convince this shower that he was in control. That he had the means and the know-how to walk all over the enemy. He could see Mickey, his most loyal associate, staring out of the window as the Range Rover sped along the country lanes. Vic made eye contact with him through the windscreen mirror and Mickey smiled back at him as he lit another cigarette.

'I have the Irish contingent meeting us there so stop your fucking arses quivering and get the weapons primed; we're going to need them.'

The news that the Irish were involved cheered up the men no end and they all breathed a silent collective sigh of relief. No one in their right mind would take on the IRA.

Privately, Mickey Ball acknowledged that his old mate Vic was starting to worry him. He had started out so clever and focused but as time had gone on he had let his behaviour become more and more outrageous. It was not just the coke, Vic had always been a few paving slabs short of a patio. Now Mickey wondered if the patio was ever going to be built at all.

Still, they all had their own agenda today. No need to tell Vic his before he was sure how the land lay.

Vic was singing loudly as he swerved to avoid the oncoming traffic. He'd been driving in the wrong lane for the past few minutes but no one had wanted to tell him. As usual it was the theme tune to *Flipper*, the only song he knew all the way through.

As he sang, the men in the Range Rover looked askance at one another. Suddenly, siding with Vic Joliff didn't seem such a fucking good idea any more, Irish or no Irish. Thank God Mickey had had the commonsense to hedge their bets.

'Vic's on his way. I just got a text from Mickey Ball,' Gerry Jackson announced.

Garry nodded. Now Maura and Kenny had arrived the show could finally get on the road. He had placed people everywhere. The whole of the barn was covered and the filth all duly warned off. Afterwards, they would clear up any mess, and they would clear it up thoroughly. All that would be left for the filth to find would be Vic and his dead fucking cohorts.

Kenny and Maura smoked as they watched the men rushing around the place sorting out last-minute details.

A white transit appeared and screeched to a halt. Maura groaned inwardly as Benny and his mates jumped from it like conquering heroes.

'All right, Maws?'

Benny made a beeline straight for her as they all knew he would.

Out of the corner of his eye he saw Garry running across the dirt road towards him, a high-velocity rifle in his right hand, and felt his bowels loosen as he saw the look on his uncle's face.

'Where you been, you little fucker?'

Benny was terrified but he hid it well. Every man there admired him for his front. He actually looked as if he didn't care, when everyone knew he had to.

'All right, Gal. I brought along a few boys. I have a lot of information for you . . .'

Garry hit him with the butt of the rifle, hard, and Benny sagged to his knees. Maura stepped in and stopped her brother from repeating the action.

'We already know everything, Benny, you daft little twonk. Do you think we are so stupid we need little boys to do our fucking dirty work?'

Garry's voice was so low at first it was indistinguishable to the others but Benny heard him as if he had shouted in his ear. It was his father Roy's expression of disgust that hurt him most.

'Who do you think you are, Benny?' Garry taunted. 'You disappear from a fucking nick while you are on a bought sentence and go on a fucking one-man rampage, and then have the nerve to think you can walk in here and act like fucking Clark Kent come to the rescue. Do you have *any* idea of the shit you are in? That you nearly put us all in?'

His uncle was bellowing now as he asked once more, 'Well, do you? We can't buy you out of this one, boy. You went too far this time. Even we would be hard pushed to explain away a daylight kidnapping, arson and three murders after a fucking severed head in the wardrobe. Are you that fucking dense you can't see that there are some things you just don't do?'

'I wasn't thinking, Garry . . .'

'That's the trouble with you, Benny, you never fucking do, do you? This is the south east, mate, not the fucking Wild West. What frightens me is you seem to think that it's no big fucking deal. You chopped the head off some poor little fucker because he shagged your bird before you. Don't you think that's a mite over the fucking top, even for you?'

Before Benny could answer his uncle, Maura motioned to them all for quiet. Gerry was waving to her and holding up his phone.

'They've been seen.'

Garry nodded then proceeded to kick Benny into the dirt. He covered his head with his arms and took the beating quietly and with dignity. The watching men all admired him even as they wondered how he could be so stupid considering he came from a family that was respected for its nous. Sadly he had not inherited it, was the general consensus.

Benny took the humiliating beating in his stride, but one day he knew he would pay Garry back, and his father too, for standing there and allowing it to happen.

Maura finally stepped in and Benny saw that she was unconcerned by what Garry had done to him, and knew that as she saw it her brother was within his rights.

'They're at the Rettenden turn-off. We need to get into place.'

Garry nodded and Gerry and Tony Dooley helped Benny into the barn. He was in no fit state to help fight a tiny baby, let alone take part in a gang war on this scale. It grieved him, but he knew he had to swallow and get over it. He couldn't help wondering, though, what was going to happen in the next few hours, but knew better than to ask.

As he sat in the barn nursing his wounds he saw that he was with armed men and it occurred to him that they were guarding him, not just sitting with him, and that was when the fear really started to kick in.

Vic saw the three IRA men as he turned into the lane that would take him to Jack's place. He slowed down and smiled as he did so. It was only when he felt the gun pushed at his head through the driver's window that he realised he had been set up.

Michael Murphy grinned down at him.

'Hello there, Vic. Long time no see. Come to call on my friends the Ryans, have you?'

He felt his bowels turn to ice water and hot anger in his head.

'You fucking two-faced . . .'

Murphy grinned.

'Get in the back, Vic.'

He was dragged from the Range Rover, searched thoroughly and pushed unceremoniously into the back. He felt the heat of humiliation as he saw Mickey Ball shaking hands with Bing Dooley, one of Tony's boys, who had been sent to accompany the welcome party.

Vic was cornered and he knew it. But he should have seen this coming and the fact he had not even had an inkling told him all he needed to know about himself and his intake of the coca plant.

He was coming down now, and a feeling of depression after the high would hit him any second. He put his hand into his pocket and squeezed the package that would send him straight back to cloud nine.

'Need a line, Vic?'

Mickey Ball's voice was hard and cold. Vic had to be restrained by Bing's boys and a pair of handcuffs.

'Don't mark him! In no way mark him. No bruises, no nothing, right?'

Bing's voice was rich with authority and the other men did as he said without a second's thought.

Vic stared at the rabble around him with open hatred but there was nothing he could do to help himself now.

Maura watched as Vic's Range Rover was positioned in the narrow lane leading to Jack's barn. There was no danger of any passing traffic because it was a private road and not used by anyone other than Jack and his visitors. Vic was dragged from his car.

Once inside the barn he saw Benny and grinned at him. Benny spat in his general direction as a sign of disrespect.

Lee was on Vic in a second.

'Where's me wife?'

Vic smiled but didn't speak.

Mickey Ball answered the question.

'She's safe, don't worry. Me two best boys are watching her and Vic's mother. She'll be on her way in a few minutes, OK?'

Lee visibly relaxed. He had been so frightened that someone might have hurt her and until he saw Sheila with his own eyes knew he would not feel right inside. He went to attack Vic but he was stopped by Garry and Tony.

'No marks on him, remember.'

Lee nodded but was hustled outside anyway.

Vic's eyes settled on Maura as she walked back into the barn with Kenny discreetly trailing her. Her face was hard and he saw the tightness around her mouth.

'Hello, Vic.'

He grinned at her, face red with anger, his bald head shining with the sweat of cocaine and exertion.

'You must think you've drawn the rollover on the Lottery, eh, Maura?'

She shook her head.

'We never wanted this, Vic, but as you can see, when it came down to it we were the best for everyone concerned. We have every major villain in the country on standby.'

He laughed.

'Well, I hope that makes you feel safer, Maura.'

She shook her head at his stupidity.

'You wanted this, Vic. You tried to kill me, and you fucking killed Roy's wife. You had to know we would never have touched Sandra, never in a million years. You started bringing family into this, we didn't.'

'That, Maura, was never down to me. OK, you had no part in it, either, I realised that a while ago. Bit late in the day but my fucking Sandra dying like that . . . it's hard for me to think straight sometimes, you know?'

Particularly after a hefty toot or two, she thought, noticing the shaking hands which she knew owed nothing to fear. Even now, surrounded by the Ryans' army, Vic was completely unafraid. That suited her. She wanted him calm and cooperative if she was ever to get the full picture.

'I just want to hear your side of it, Vic,' she told

him. 'Things started going pear-shaped for us six years back. The filth started feeling collars all around us, and it looked like we were grassing our mates big time.'

'Well, you were. In a manner of speaking,' he said genially.

Maura stepped back as if he'd slapped her.

'You cheeky bastard! Me and mine tell the police what we want them to do for us. We don't need to go sneaking round doing them favours.'

Vic threw back his head and laughed, the picture of merriment despite the hard faces and drawn weapons all around him.

'I said, in a manner of speaking. Not the Ryans personally but you had a certain Abul "Big Ears" Haseem in on all your meetings, didn't you?'

'That fucking two-faced ponce!' Garry exploded. 'We already knew he was in with Rifkind but . . .'

Vic shook his head sadly.

'You haven't got a clue, have you? It's a miracle really how you've lasted so long.'

Maura shot her brother a warning look. He'd never normally have let this go, but there was nothing normal about today and they had to swallow Vic's insult to get to the bottom of this.

'The link up with Tommy came later. Abul was in on it way before it was even a glimmer in Rifkind's greedy eye. In it up to his neck. And you know who recruited him, dreamed up the entire dirty tricks campaign against you? Rebekka Kowolski. Or Rebekka Goldbaum as was. Now *she* had a legitimate grievance against you, didn't she, Maura?'

She kept her voice as hard as her face.

'I should have worked it out for meself. It takes a woman to come up with a really subtle piece of revenge like that – ruin our reps then step in and take what's ours. But did she really think she could run our businesses?'

'She and Joe were going to confine themselves to drugs wholesaling. Abul was going to take the other businesses, and distribute for them in the south east. He'd been building up his own firm among the soots for years. They're always looking for an in. Only you was too thick to see that.'

Garry hurled himself at Vic, fists flying.

'Let me have him. We've heard enough. I want to—'

'Leave it!' Maura ordered. 'Won't be long now, Gal, but we need to hear this. I mean, I still can't believe a couple of no-hopers like Rebekka and Joe actually thought they could take over our drugs operation.'

'Yeah, well, that's where the rest of us come in. They pretty soon realised they'd need a banker – Jack, building up his pension fund – distributors outside the south east – our Liverpool friends – and a hard man to deal with the suppliers – no prizes for guessing who. We all agreed to come in on it if they could topple you. Then we just sat back and watched you take the heat. It was so fucking sweet! They were taking on the Ryans and winning – with nothing more than some well-chosen tip-offs and a whispering campaign. Beautiful! Tommy said it was like all his Christmases coming at once.'

Maura refused to react to this, and continued listening calmly to Vic's gloating voice.

'Then I got my fucking collar felt for a piece of aggro I'd almost forgot it was so bloody long ago and ended up in Belmarsh. Which wasn't so bad really – I palled up with the Paddies, was getting the screws onside. I could have carried on my end of things from there, just needed a bit of time to set them up. Only bloody Abul couldn't wait, could he? He decided things was moving too slowly, and persuaded Tommy Rifkind that they could pull it off without me. He was gonna set you and me at each other's throats, Maura, or make it look as if we were.

'He had the bomb put in your car – couldn't believe it when he got the ex-filth instead. From what I can make out he done Sandra and Roy's wife, and told Tommy B to go after Lana Smith and your mum. Kenny's a well-liked man and Abul thought it would stir up even more hatred for the Ryans. Since his dad was in with Abul, Tommy Boy did as he was told – only he drew the line at killing the old woman and just gave her a kicking instead.

'Then they got to me in jail. I was more use to

them dead – just another statistic in the Ryans' gang wars. Rebekka got the hard word an' all. She was a clever woman but mouthy with it, and so up her own arse about you, Maura, she really got on Abul's nerves. And by killing her the way he did . . . well, he might as well have left the Ryans' calling card.'

She felt the bile rise in her throat. She was having difficulty taking it all in, the treachery and deceit by friend and lover dating back all those years. Well, one of them at least was in their hands and they'd settle that score very soon. But another was beyond their justice.

'Where's Tommy?' she asked.

'What's the matter, Maura love? Missing him?'

This time it was Kenny who hit him, a hard punch in the mouth that rocked Vic back on his heels. He almost lost his balance for a moment then shrugged nonchalantly.

'Let's just say I'll take that secret to me grave, shall we? He's dealt with, Maura. He was scum. He trumped your niece, got your nephew on my bandwagon . . . worst of all he tucked me up.

'Tommy Rifkind didn't know the meaning of the word loyalty. He could have saved his own boy's arse by speaking up. Me or you would have done that without a second thought, Maura, 'cos to us family matters. That's what Joss had the problem with an' all.'

He shook his head sorrowfully and decided to get his last request in while they were still reeling at the skulduggery of the late Tommy Rifkind.

'Now, cards on the table, I know I haven't got a snowflake's chance in hell of walking away from this lot. All I ask is that you leave me mother and Justin out of it. I mean, fair's fair. I've co-operated, ain't I?'

Maura nodded with grudging respect. Vic was a violent psychopath, off his head on drugs – and he still had a stronger sense of values than Tommy Rifkind. It was a sobering realisation.

He looked relieved.

'Thanks, Maura. You're well off out of it, you know that? Far better off with good old Kenny here. With him, what you see is what you get.'

Kenny reddened and walked out of the barn.

'Any chance of a last line so I can meet me Maker with a smile on me boat?' Vic was saying behind him. They all heard the sound of cars starting up and Vic said nonchalantly, 'The Exodus begins.'

Sheila gathered her children into her arms and hugged them. They thought she had just gone to visit a friend and were back watching TV in an instant. She was going to let them all stay up late tonight and keep them off school the next day. It was time for Lee to make a decision and he had better make it soon. Now that she had been dragged into this twisted world of his he must see it would be better for all of them if he got out. Before he was killed or banged up or she left him forever.

She hugged Sarah to her and her mother-in-law hugged her back.

'Are you all right, love?'

Sheila nodded.

'Vic was all right to me, you know? I didn't feel threatened and that's the truth.'

Sarah nodded.

'Sure, he was always a decent enough lad. He was great friends with my Michael once. In fact, if my Michael was still alive none of this would have happened . . .'

Sheila closed her eyes and let Sarah ramble on. It was the kindest thing to do even if the elderly woman was speaking a load of old cod's.

# Chapter Twenty-Eight

Abul, Joe and Vic were all being held at gunpoint in the barn. They watched the clean-up operation going on around them, wondering when it would be their turn to be dealt with.

The telling of his tale had left Vic quiet and subdued. He didn't even bother to bait his accomplices any more. He was tired and accepting of his fate. He was also coming down faster than the Lockerbie airliner. What he badly needed was a pick-me-up snort, but didn't see any chance of getting one.

Benny sat in one of the Ryans' cars outside and watched as Vic's Range Roger was cleaned and scrubbed so that it was practically sterile. He contemplated the mammoth operation they had undertaken and shook his head in amazement. Maura had real nous, there was no doubt about it.

Garry walked past him and ignored him and Benny

felt the sting of tears as he realised everyone was blanking him, even his father. When Roy appeared a little later Benny called out to him softly, 'Please, Dad.'

Roy stood and stared at his son. He had loved him once with all his being. Now he couldn't bear to look him in the face. He was Michael, all right, but this was a Michael for the new millennium. He was a selfish and dangerous individual; even his poor little girlfriend had not been able to tame him. He had taken his violence out on an innocent boy and it had caused the demise of his own child.

The Ryan family had used violence to gain what they now had, Roy knew that, but it had been controlled violence perpetrated for a clear reason. His family had always treated violence with respect, used it in a respectful way. Yet this boy, his own son, was capable of violence for its own sake, just for a laugh, and Roy found that repugnant even as he pitied his son for the plight he was in.

He saw the pleading expression on Benny's face and was nearly taken in. Then he remembered the boy's head in the wardrobe and reminded himself who he was dealing with.

'Dad, please talk to me. I said I was sorry, didn't I?'

Roy leaned wearily against the car. Looking at him closely, Benny saw the extra years that seemed to have been piled on him overnight. He was greyer than he had been and looked haggard.

'Sorry ain't good enough this time, Benny, you went too far.'

Benny was fed up. As far as he was concerned it had happened so fucking deal with it. But he was shrewd enough to know he should not voice that kind of opinion to his father.

Anyone would think he had killed the fucking Queen or someone the way they were all carrying on. It was a laugh, that was all. He would do it again if he could, and next time he would make sure the fucker disappeared for good.

He had learned his lesson over this last lot. He knew he would have to keep his head down and his arse up for the foreseeable future, so why couldn't they just get over it and let him get on with things?

Roy walked away and Benny saw how his shoulders sagged and how he had lost his spark. He remembered how his dad had been years before, the big man who would come in and pick him up on his shoulders. Who would talk to him and help him with his growing pains. Who had given him the earth on a plate. His dad loved him, Benny knew that. He had caused untold aggravation and was sorry but it would get sorted, it always did. His dad would come round eventually and then the others would follow suit. Benny was family, after all.

Garry was laughing at Maura's plan and even Kenny had to admit it was a blinder. The place was more or less empty now and they were just waiting for the right time to complete the operation. There was one last thing needed to put it all into practice and once that arrived they would be home and dry.

'Do you know something, Maura, you are one shrewd bird.'

It was what Michael had always said about her and it made her feel good, reminded her of what she now saw as the good old days, the time when the final responsibility did not rest with her. She could not relax until this was all over.

Kenny stood by her and watched the cleaning operation with a wary eye.

'No one will ever know what happened here, will they?'

'No one who matters, no.'

'Garry is right, you know. You are shrewder than most of the men I know and that is not a compliment, it is a fact.'

She smiled.

'I just want it over.'

'Don't we all? What do you think Vic did with Tommy? Everyone else has been located but no one seems to want to talk about him, do they?'

She shrugged and took a sip of Scotch.

'He's dead. I feel it inside.'

'Are you sorry?'

It was a loaded question.

Maura thought for a while before she said slowly, 'Not really.'

She saw the relief on Kenny's face and smiled at him.

'You are a very nice man, do you know that?'

He grinned and she saw his merry eyes and friendly smile, not the hardened scar-faced villain everyone else seemed to see.

'Don't tell anyone, it's a secret.'

They laughed together until Maura's face clouded over again.

'We are going to do something terrible tonight.'

Kenny didn't answer her for a few moments.

'It's terrible, I grant you, but it's necessary as well,' he said finally. 'This will be an end to it all, Maura, once and for all. This whole episode will finally be over.'

She nodded and stared into the glass of Scotch in her hand.

'I hope so, Kenny. I really do hope so.'

Sarah was in bed and couldn't get comfortable no matter what she did. The pain was worse now and it wasn't just a dragging pain any more, it had travelled up her arm and into her chest.

She wondered how little Carol was. The loss of her great-grandchild had been hard to bear. Almost as hard as the loss of Maura's poor little baby. That weighed heavily on her these days. For years she had convinced herself that the child was better off never having lived, but now she wasn't so sure. Maura, God love her, was a natural nurturer, a woman who should have had children by the dozen.

Sarah shook the troubling thoughts away.

Whenever she thought about that day she always felt guilty. Guilty and sick. She had taken her daughter there and basically held her down while a dirty backstreet abortionist had ripped the only good thing that had ever happened to her out of her belly. And all because she, Sarah, had not wanted to face the neighbours, had not wanted that kind of disgrace on her child and family.

An illegitimate baby. It was commonplace now and yet then it had been a disgrace that would follow you all your life. Yes, she had been frightened of the disgrace, and of course of Michael's reaction though he would have come round in the end, he would have had to.

It was ironic really. Considering all the other shite she had had to contend with where her family was concerned, poor Maura's baby was nothing by comparison. It would be a grown man or woman now and she would have loved it and Maura would have had someone of her own. Would have had someone to love.

Sarah saw the baby then in her mind's eye, lying in the Day-Glo orange washing-up bowl surrounded by blood, and closed her eyes tightly to block out the shocking image.

But it wouldn't go away.

The pain was back again now and so she moved on to her side to try and ease it. She would make it all up to Maura, she was determined on that. She closed her eyes and started the familiar prayer.

'Sacred Heart of Jesus . . .'

God was good, He would give her peace and rest, she was sure of that. She prayed for that child as she prayed for her own children and the repose of her husband's soul. It was important that she made everything right before she finally left this earth. She prayed then, harder than ever. She didn't know what else she could do. The pain was worse; it was travelling across her chest and she was having trouble breathing.

She made herself breathe deeply and evenly and all the time she prayed. But the pain was excruciating.

She could see Benny and the severed head, see him holding it in his arms and laughing. She knew he didn't feel he had done a thing wrong. At least her Michael had not been that bad, had had some decency in him. And Michael had had a hard start in life whereas Benny had been given everything the telly and the newspapers told you a child needed to get on in this world. Yet he was still as mad as a March hare and she knew it was only a matter of time before he caused something even worse than the latest débâcle.

Yet she loved him, loved him with all her heart and soul. When he smiled at her or hugged her she felt like the luckiest woman alive. It was as if a wild animal had placed their trust in her, it felt extra-special. Benny had so little love to give that when he did give it, it was overwhelming because you knew you were one of a chosen few.

Sarah's heart was beating faster than ever now and she was sweating profusely. She forced her mind back to her prayers and hoped the night would end soon so she could get up and face another day. Whatever it brought with it she knew she would cope. God made the back to bear the burden, as her own mother used to say. Sarah had a broad back and a strong faith, and that was all that she really needed. She might go to eight o'clock Mass, take Communion. That always seemed to settle her when she was worried about anything.

Tony Dooley and Gerry Jackson surveyed the barn and surrounding area, now lit by arc lights. It looked spotless. There was nothing incriminating left, not a tyre mark or footprint to say any of them had ever been there. The whole place would not show a trace from a forensic point of view.

They sat inside the barn and smoked a joint together as they reminisced about the good old days. They had a feeling on them that disaster had been averted and they could go home in peace and tranquillity.

At least that's what they hoped, once the filth arrived. Then and only then could they all leave.

They were taking their fucking time.

Tony Dooley began to roll another joint.

'Man, I hate waiting about, don't you?'

Gerry nodded.

'Not a lot of choice, is there? But once we get them in position we can get it over with once and for all. You know, it's funny, Tony, but I always liked Vic. Me and Michael used to muck about with him years ago. It's the gear, ain't it? Sends them off their fucking trolleys.'

Tony nodded sagely.

'Seen it time and time again.' He licked the Rizla slowly and then said quietly, 'It's Roy I'm sorry for, you know?'

Gerry sighed.

'Tell me about it. If that was my boy I'd be in bits.'

'He's a fucking nutter all right, Ger, but then such is life, eh? He should have been sorted when he was a kid.'

Gerry agreed with his old friend and was so glad that none of his sons had ever shown a penchant for abnormal behaviour. They were lairy little fuckers admittedly but then, that had been used by them to good effect.

They leaned back and smoked the joint, sorry for Roy and his troubles but happy in each other's company. Both of them were dreading what was to come yet both knew it had to happen. In fact, they were amazed it had not happened before. Benjamin

Ryan had been an accident waiting to happen for the last couple of years.

Gerry took a deep toke on the joint and watched his handsome sons as they finished the job in hand. He was proud of them all, and glad that they were perfectly normal run-of-the-mill faces.

A car drove down the lane and they watched warily as Maura and Garry walked out to meet it. Both instinctively put their hands near their weapons. After all this wasn't over yet, not by a long chalk.

Carla was still awake and sitting on her bed, smoking a Silk Cut and feeling the deep fear that only an unplanned pregnancy can cause in a woman. She stared at the tester and once more the blue line was still evident. It had been there for the last five hours and yet such was her frame of mind she still hoped it was a mistake.

She was pregnant and it was Tommy's child.

She sipped the glass of water by her bed and lit yet another Silk Cut. This would cause murders. She wondered what the fuck she was going to do about it. Because the last thing she wanted at her age was a baby, another child.

Maura had been decent to her recently and that was going to go out of the window once she heard about this little lot. She picked up her mobile and rang Tommy's number once more.

It went straight on to voicemail and Carla left him

yet another message telling him to ring as soon as he picked this up because it was very important. She knew he wouldn't, but still hoped that he would come and take her away from all this trouble and look after her and the baby. If he didn't ring, then the child would have to be flushed away privately and with the minimum of fuss. That was all she could do because Maura would not want a reminder of Tommy Rifkind running around, that much she was sure of. Carla needed money – and the only way she would see any was to get back into the fold as soon as possible.

She glanced at the clock. It was gone three in the morning and she knew she was no nearer sleep now than she'd been five hours ago. She had been such a fool to fall for Tommy Rifkind, but he had been so sexy and so dangerous. He had also been hung like a horse. She smiled as she remembered some of his moves. Now she was in the club and not sure what she was going to do.

She wished she had never met him and that the madness that had overtaken her had never happened either. But it had and she had to deal with it.

What was it Joey called it? A reality check? Carla was getting the worst reality check she had ever experienced in her life.

Maura watched as Chief Inspector Billings turned the engine off and sat stiffly waiting for them to come to him. She could see the hatred in him and feel the futility of it because he was not man enough to do anything about the situation he was in.

Today he was earning his payoffs and nobody pretended it was going to be pleasant.

'Hello, Mr Billings. You were quicker than I thought.'

Maura's sarcasm wasn't lost on him or any of the spectators.

Garry opened the boot of the policeman's car and removed a large blanket-covered package. He weighed it in his hands and with a big smile on his face placed it on the floor and uncovered four automatic weapons made specifically for the use of police marksmen.

'They're clean?'

Billings nodded.

'Of course.'

Garry grinned.

'Good. Now you can fuck off.'

The three prisoners were aware that for them time had finally run out. Maura watched impassively as Vic and Abul were hustled out, kicking and protesting, even though they knew there was no way to avoid the inevitable. She'd told the others to leave her alone with Joe for a moment.

'I still don't get it,' she told him. 'I know Rebekka hated me and maybe she had cause, but you, Joe. We were mates once.'

He looked frail and hollow-eyed but his voice was surprisingly firm as he told her bitterly, 'Until you and Michael brought tragedy on my family.'

Maura was amazed.

'But you ain't got a family, Joe. You're the only eighty-year-old playboy I know.'

He sighed as he told her, 'Everyone has family. Everyone has roots. You Ryans aren't the only ones to value theirs. Sammy Goldbaum was my cousin.'

For a moment she couldn't meet his eye.

'I never knew that.'

'I never advertised the fact. He was a wastrel, a gambler – I'd have had people after me for his debts. But he was the son of my mother's favourite sister, the only one on that side of the family to reach England during the war. The rest of them died in Lodz. On my mother's deathbed I promised I would always look out for my Cousin Sammy, and when he died . . .'

Joe's voice faltered for the first time.

'Naturally I helped out his wife and the children. And Rebekka was such a bright little thing, the daughter I never had. A head on her for figures like you wouldn't believe. She trained as an accountant and came to work for me. Made me millions over the years, had a beautiful home, a son to be proud of. And still she couldn't forget the way her father died. She hated the Ryans for what they'd done and when she came up with this scheme and begged me to help her – well, what could I do? She was family. You know how it is.'

There was no need for her to reply. They both knew it was to safeguard her family's position as top dogs that he was going to his death. Before he went though he extracted a promise from her that the Ryans would not make any moves on his businesses which were to pass to his heir, Rebekka's son Sammy Kowolski.

No one dragged Joe from the barn. He walked out with head held high and climbed into the back of the car of his own accord.

Benny watched from a parked car as his friend since childhood was forced into the sterilised Range-Rover at gunpoint. He still wondered why Abul had tucked him up like he had but had lost the urge for revenge now. He knew he had to be on his best behaviour and not rock the boat in any way. He was chewing on his thumbnail, a sure sign of agitation, when he saw his Uncle Garry walking towards him. Benny put a smile on his face even though it hurt like fuck to do so and he wanted nothing more than to lie down and sleep.

When he realised he was actually going to be told to kill Abul, he was euphoric. He saw it as a fitting end to this whole sorry episode. This was his forgiveness, he knew it. It had to happen eventually but for it to be now and in this way pleased him no end.

He knew he had to make a good job of it and was determined to do just that. This was going to be his finest hour, he knew it. This would bring him back into the fold, the thing he wanted more than anything in the world.

Garry opened the car door and said to him gently, 'Come on, you. Time to sort the men from the boys.'

Everyone watched as Garry and Benny walked slowly towards the Range Rover.

Sarah finally got out of bed and sat on the large overstuffed chair by the window. The dawn chorus had started and she listened to it with half an ear. Her chest felt as if it was going to explode. She took more deep breaths and forced herself to stand up.

Her arm was still dead. She rubbed at it with her good hand, wondering if she had had a stroke even while she told herself she had felt like this before and each time it had been when one or other of her children had died.

She walked slowly and carefully out of the bedroom and made her way down the stairs. She would not sleep now. She knew she might as well make a nice cuppa and wait for her daughter to come home.

Her arm was hanging loosely by her side. She held it into her belly with her good arm as she stepped slowly down the staircase.

She was parched and she was frightened, but of what she had no idea.

* * *

Benny looked into Abul's face and smiled at him. He was handcuffed the same as the other two and there was no chance of escape.

'Get it fucking over with, Benny,' Abul said through a mouthful of broken teeth. He'd always been so proud of them, Benny thought. Handsome charming Abul, his best friend.

Vic started laughing.

'Shoot us, for fuck's sake, then we can all get some sleep!'

Vic looked almost diabolical in the dimness of the courtesy lights inside the Range Rover. Benny shot him in the chest and he slumped forward. Joe the Jew fainted and Benny took him out next using a different weapon. Then he stared at Abul. Garry and Maura watched intently, as did everyone else, as Benny was handed a third gun and slowly took aim.

Abul was staring at his one-time friend and all the arrogance had gone from his face. He too was remembering them both as kids. Remembering the japes they had got up to. Remembering the way he had always been a part of the Ryan family. He had wanted to be top dog, had wanted to be the main man, and this was what it had brought him to.

'I'm sorry, Benny.'

It was almost a whisper.

'So am I, mate.'

Benny felt his hands quivering with nerves. He had

never cared about violence before, never cared who he hurt, but he really didn't want to harm his friend. Didn't want to see Abul dead. Not now, not when he was in front of him looking at him like he used to when they were little kids and Benny had done something mean.

'Come on, Benny, we ain't got all fucking night.'

Garry's voice was low.

Benny looked at Abul one last time and then he slowly squeezed the trigger. This explosion sounded much louder in his ears than the other two. He felt the ringing start and dropped the rifle to his side as he stared at his friend.

He did not feel good about what he had done; did not feel good about it at all. The only person he had ever really cared about was gone. As Abul slumped forward across the passenger seat in the front of the Range Rover, Roy walked up behind his son and, turning him around gently, shot him in the heart.

Benny dropped to the ground, a look of surprise on his face.

Maura had turned away and Kenny had pulled her face into his chest to try and save her from seeing her nephew die.

'What the fuck was all that about?'

It was Garry's voice she could hear.

'You should have waited until he was in the fucking motor like we agreed!'

Roy was kneeling on the ground, staring at his

son's lifeless body. Maura pulled herself away from Kenny and went to him.

'Oh, Maura, what the fuck have I done, eh?'

She cuddled him to her as she cried. Benny looked so innocent lying there; he looked like Michael had looked while he slept and she and Marge would sneak into his room and pinch all his change to go up the sweet shop.

He looked so young and peaceful.

Garry sighed as Maura and Roy held each other and cried like babies. It had to be done, Roy knew. Benny was a nutter who would only have ended up banged away for the rest of his life, but what mayhem would he have caused before that happened to him? Maura had not needed to know about their plan for him until it was all over. She would see the sense of what they had done, he was sure of that. Her idea to put the others in the motor and leave them had been brilliant, but Roy had decided to place his son there with them and his brother had agreed it was the right thing to do.

Garry walked over to where Tony Dooley and Gerry Jackson were standing watching the spectacle and rolled his eyes heavenwards, tutting loudly. But then he saw the sadness on their faces and didn't say anything.

He glanced at the three dead men in the Range Rover. The police rifles would throw everyone, but as far as he was concerned it wasn't the first time the filth had executed known criminals, was it? It was getting to be almost a pastime with them. Then they just set up a few faces to take the flak and had their backs slapped for doing such a fine job in solving a terrible crime.

Well, let them work this one out without breaking into a sweat, that was his attitude. Fuck them, it was about time the filth tasted a bit of their own medicine.

Maura's desolate sobs were making even him feel upset now so he walked over to one of the vehicles and took a long gulp of Chivas Regal straight from the bottle. Then he strolled back and placed it in his brother's hands.

Roy took it gratefully and drank deeply. He stared into Benny's surprised face and kissed him one last time on the forehead.

Then, getting up, he said in a strong voice, 'Help me get him in the motor, Gal.'

Thirty minutes later the place was deserted except for the Range Rover and its grisly contents. There was nothing else to say anyone had been near or by the place in the last twenty-four hours. Not even any footprints around the vehicle. That was Garry's last laugh on the police and he smiled every time he thought of it.

The rifles were dumped nearby so a passer-by would find them, and the newspapers would be tipped off that they were actually police-issue guns that had never been reported stolen.

Benny and Abul were as united in death as they had been in life. Benny's body was slumped beside his old friend and they looked almost like they were holding hands.

Sarah suddenly felt much better inside herself. She stretched her arms and the pain was gone from her body. She smiled and put the kettle on. She stood at the kitchen window and looked out over Maura's extensive gardens. The sun was high now and the day was going to be glorious.

She would go to Mass, she decided. Give thanks for such a wonderful day and for the new lease of life she could feel pulsing through her old body. She heard Maura's car in the drive and put out another cup and saucer for her. She had a feeling on her that everything was going to be all right now.

# Epilogue

'Come on, Maura, get a move on, will you?'

She heard Kenny's voice coming up the stairs and took one last look at herself in the full-length mirror in her bedroom. She looked good, she knew she did, and it was important she looked good today of all days. She picked up a pale pink lipstick and ran it over her mouth. It finished off her toilette and she smiled at herself again.

Her gaze drifted to the photographs on the windowsill near her. Benny standing with Roy looked out at her with clear blue eyes. She and Michael laughing together in the club, both of them looking young and carefree. There was an old faded black and white of them all when they were kids and she remembered all her brothers, those still alive and those who were gone. Her father and mother looked so proud of their brood that Maura felt a sudden urge to cry.

She put a smile back on her face. Nothing was going to ruin today, she was determined on that.

'What you doing, Maws, you got another bloke up there?'

Maura ran down the stairs of her new house, laughing. In her arms was a large teddy bear dressed as a Scotsman, his sporran glittering and shiny.

'Where did you get that?'

'I saw it on Roman Road Market and had to have it. Where is she?'

'Where do you think? She's looking at the new baby.'

They walked through the house to the sunny morning room, smiling as they saw little Alicia petting Carla's new baby boy Michael.

'I love him, Maws. Look, he's smiling at me!'

Alicia was thrilled with the baby and adored being able to play with him.

'He loves you and all, Ali, look at that little face beaming at you.'

Carla looked on, smiling wanly. She was a different woman these days. Happier in some ways, or resigned to her lot anyway. It often took all Maura's will-power not to knock her to the ground with one fell swoop. But she knew she wouldn't, couldn't. Michael was Tommy Rifkind all over again and even that fact didn't stop her loving every bone in the child's body.

Kenny watched her closely. He knew it would be only a matter of time before Carla passed the baby over bag and baggage to her aunt, the way she had been passed over by her own mother. History repeating itself. Carla was already seeing a soot from Deptford, a nice geezer who would give her the earth, and in return Maura would see that he rose to the very top of his profession – though what that profession was no one had as yet established. But certainly if he could sell the skunk as fast as he could smoke it they would all be quids in.

None of them would ever forgive Carla, or Joey for that matter, but all the time Maura acted like she did her brothers had to swallow.

Who was it who once said: 'Keep your friends close, but keep your enemies closer still'? An astute man whoever he was, Kenny decided.

Maura looked down at the baby once more and he gripped her finger. He was a strong child, he would be a strong man, and of course he bore the Ryan name.

The thought made her smile.

'Is that for me?'

Alicia's little face was gazing up at Maura longingly.

'Of course he's yours. I'm too big for teddies, don't you think?'

She knelt down and the girl hugged her tightly. The feel of the pudgy little arms around her neck nearly brought tears back to Maura's eyes.

'Where's me mum?' Maura asked.

Carla grinned.

'Three guesses.'

'Not more tea surely!'

Even Kenny laughed.

'Tell her to get the champagne out, will you? They'll all be here in a minute.'

Maura picked up Alicia and the teddy bear and walked her out into the garden. 'You look lovely, you do.'

Alicia preened herself at the praise.

'Will you be my mummy after today?'

Her voice was full of hope as she asked the question. Kenny listened to them talking and felt as if his heart would explode with love and happiness.

'If you want me to be your mummy then that would make me very happy,' Maura replied.

He could see the love she bore his child shining in her eyes.

'I love you, Maura Ryan.'

She heard the emotion in his voice and laughed softly.

'I'll be Maura Smith soon.'

'I love you Maura Smith then.'

She grinned.

'Daddy is silly sometimes.'

Alicia said the words with all the worldly wisdom of a seven-year-old ancient.

'I know.'

'Can I go and show Nanny Sarah my teddy?'

''Course you can, sweetie.'

Alicia ran away clutching the teddy bear.

'Are you happy, Maws?'

She looked into Kenny's serious face. Kissing him gently on the lips, she said, 'Happier than I have ever been in my entire life.'

He smiled at her then, and she knew how lucky she was to have such a decent man at last. He might not be the handsomest in the world and, as they both joked, thank God little Alicia had taken her looks from her mother, but he had a rugged dependable quality about him and she was proud to be marrying him. She adored him and adored his Alicia.

'I love you, Kenny, more than you will ever know.'

He was the one for her and they both knew it.

Eileen Smith and Sarah Ryan were now bosom buddies and this made their children breathe a collective but heartfelt sigh of relief. Sarah loved Kenny because of his strength and dependability and Eileen loved Maura because she was not a nineteen-year-old idiot, the likes of which he used to bring home after Lana died.

'Now when we get back from the church, you and I will sort out the caterers, right?'

Eileen nodded in agreement and Frankie Barber, who was the chef in charge of the wedding breakfast, sighed heavily. It was only a small gathering but it was going to be perfect, he was determined on that. Despite what these two old bats might think. He kept that to himself, though, he wasn't stupid. After all, the same old bats were the mothers of enough villains to repopulate Chicago!

As Sarah watched her daughter and her soon-to-be son-in-law walking together in the rolling grounds of the new house in Essex she sighed with contentment.

At last her Maura was to be married. At fifty-one years of age she was finally shedding the name of Ryan, and Sarah knew in her heart that after all her trials and tribulations her daughter would finally find peace in the arms of Kenneth Smith.

Carla was watching her. She caught her grand-daughter's eye and smiled. 'You all right there, lovey?'

Sarah knew it would be hard on her today.

'They look good together, Mum, don't they?'

Garry's voice made them jump. Sarah turned to see her son and that little child he lived with standing in the doorway. Leonie was dressed in the finest Versace could offer and still looked like she should be charging men for her time, but Sarah swallowed down the thought and hugged the girl to her. She rather liked her really.

'You look gorgeous, child.'

'Thanks.'

Leonie being Leonie didn't think to return the compliment.

'Lee is outside with Sheila and the kids. Shall I send them through to the garden, Sarah, and we'll serve the champagne there?'

Sarah nodded at Frankie. She knew he was trying to get rid of her but he had another think coming if he thought she was going to let him rule the roost this day. Winking at Eileen, she carried out a tray of glasses and passed them to a subdued Joey who, smiling nervously, placed them on one of the trestle tables by the patio. He was still not forgiven and he knew it. Garry, Roy and Lee still blanked him and he knew it was going to take a long time to get back on an even keel with everyone.

Marge's loud voice could be heard reverberating all over the garden as she screamed with pleasure when she saw Maura in her white wedding suit.

'You look fucking handsome, girl.'

Maura hugged her hard and Dennis said loudly: 'You only take my Marge anywhere twice, the second time to apologise.'

Kenny laughed and Garry watched as the big man followed Maura's every move devotedly.

Roy came out holding his grandson in his arms. Walking over to Maura, he said gently, 'You are doing the right thing, Maws.'

She smiled happily.

'I know that, Roy.'

'I wonder what this little one will turn out like?'

He was gazing into his grandson's unreadable eyes.

'He'll be all right, Roy.'

He kissed the child's downy head and smiled.

'Maura Ryan getting married, eh? I never thought I would see the day.'

'Neither did I.' Then she said seriously, 'Do you think I'm too old for all this, Roy, honestly?'

She swept out her arm to encompass the garden and the house all decorated for what could be mistaken for a society wedding.

'No, I do not! You deserve this happiness, Maura. More than anyone else I have ever known in my life, you deserve to be happy. And you will be happy with Kenny, he loves you so much.'

Baby Michael started to cry, he was hungry, and Maura looked on as her brother walked back to the house where the baby would be fed and changed to make him happy again. Then she watched as the guests all started to arrive and saw her mother's deep happiness because her only daughter was finally going to be married, and she knew she had done the right thing.

Alicia ran to her with her arms outstretched. Maura picked the child up and hugged her tightly to her.

'Maura Smith. Daddy said that's his favourite name now, along with mine, of course.'

Maura grinned as she said honestly, 'Funnily enough, it's my favourite name now as well!' She kissed the little girl on one rounded cheek. 'Along with the name Alicia Smith, of course.'

They laughed as they walked back across the lawn together, holding hands, their faces radiant in the sunshine.

Kenny was waiting for them, and Maura knew he would always wait for her from now on and the knowledge made her feel good inside and out.

# Dangerous Lady

## Martina Cole

No one thinks a seventeen-year-old girl can take on the hard men of London's gangland, but it's a mistake to underestimate Maura Ryan: she's tough, clever and beautiful – and she's determined that nothing will stand in her way.

Together, she and her brother Michael are unbeatable: the Queen and King of organised crime. But notoriety has its price. The police are determined to put away Maura once and for all – and not everyone in the family thinks that's such a bad idea. When it comes to the crunch, Maura has to face the pain of lost love in her past – and the dangerous lady discovers her heart is not made entirely of stone.

Praise for Martina Cole's bestsellers:

'Intensely readable' *Guardian*

'Right from the start [Cole] has enjoyed unqualified approval for her distinctive and powerfully written fiction' *The Times*

'The slags and scum of Cole's fictional underworld are becoming the stuff of legend . . . It's vicious, nasty and utterly compelling' *Mirror*

'Martina Cole again explores the shady criminal underworld, a setting she is fast making her own' *Sunday Express*

0 7472 3932 0

headline

# Faceless

## Martina Cole

Eleven years ago Marie Carter was convicted of killing her two best friends. And she's paid the price. Now she's being released from prison. It's time to go home.

But life has moved on and Marie has nowhere left to go. Her parents have disowned her; her friends have abandoned her; even her children don't want to know.

But some people out there are watching her, following her every move – they know that Marie Carter wants retribution.

FACELESS is an explosive novel of East End violence and corruption from one of the most original voices in fiction today.

Praise for Martina Cole's bestsellers:

'Right from the start [Cole] has enjoyed unqualified approval for her distinctive and powerfully written fiction' *The Times*

'It's vicious, nasty . . . and utterly compelling' *Mirror*

'Martina Cole again explores the shady criminal underworld, a setting she is fast making her own' *Sunday Express*

'Set to be another winner' *Woman's Weekly*

0 7472 5542 3

headline

madaboutbooks.com